Praise for *The Girls with No Names*

"Burdick has spun a cautionary tale of struggle and survival, love and family—and above all, the strength of the heart, no matter how broken."

—*New York Times Book Review*

"Burdick reveals the perils of being a woman in 1913 and exposes the truths of their varying social circles. The first-person narratives place us into the minds of each woman, exposing her fears and hopes, and the strength needed to live through another day."

—*Chicago Tribune*

"Burdick's carefully researched narrative shines a light on the untold stories of countless real women, and fans of Joanna Goodman's *The Home for Unwanted Girls* will be consumed by the fast-paced plot and well-characterized, sympathetic girls at the novel's heart."

—*Booklist*

"The lives of women in early-twentieth-century New York spring to life through Burdick's deft sketching. A spellbinding thriller for fans of Gilded Age fiction."

—*Kirkus Reviews*

"I'm shocked I'd never heard of the House of Mercy, the asylum for fallen women at the center of Serena Burdick's beautiful novel. A mesmerizing tale of strength, subterfuge, and the unbreakable bond between sisters."

—**Whitney Scharer, author of *The Age of Light***

"Burdick weaves a stunning story of sisters, friendship, secrets, and ultimately survival. I fell in love with the courageous Effie and Mable and will not soon forget their stories."

—**Jillian Cantor, *USA TODAY* bestselling author of *In Another Time***

Also by Serena Burdick

The Girls with No Names
Girl in the Afternoon

FIND ME

in

HAVANA

SERENA BURDICK

PARK
ROW
BOOKS

PARK
ROW ™
BOOKS ™

Recycling programs
for this product may
not exist in your area.

ISBN-13: 978-0-7783-8936-1

Find Me in Havana

This edition published by arrangement with Harlequin Books S.A.

Park Row Books
22 Adelaide St. West, 40th Floor
Toronto, Ontario M5H 4E3, Canada
ParkRowBooks.com
BookClubbish.com

Printed in U.S.A.

For Nina

FIND ME
in
HAVANA

Chapter One

Cliffs

Mother,

In August, Big Sur crackles with drought. Grass dries to a crisp and turns gold as ember. Rattlers lay in wait. Fat insects purr, and banana slugs languish. The air is ripe with eucalyptus, their slender, green leaves blanketing the canyon paths. Poison oak claws the hillside. This is not the season of lemon trees or emerald hills or crisp sunshine. Summer on the coast is a season of bone-chilling fog.

Overlooking the Pacific, I stand on Nepenthe's stone patio, the restaurant's windows spilling light around me as I watch the gray mass of fog crawl and heave up the cliff. You would have liked it here, Mom, but we never drove up the coast together. We never had the chance. I close my eyes as the fog settles over me, damp and soft as a whisper. Below, the surf thunders against the rocks, and I feel the sway of the sea in my legs and picture myself stepping over the low stone wall and lifting my arms into the air. The ocean will catch me, release me, hollow out my body and wash it up on the shore like an empty shell.

I need a shell. Hard skin. A barrier against the world of missing you.

How is there no *you* left? No Mom. No Wife. No Movie Actress. No Singer. There are photographs, and moving pictures where you swing your hips and make funny faces, but I cannot touch or smell or feel or speak to this two-dimensional version.

I want an explanation.

Memories root and twist inside me, blossom, grow thorns, beautiful and gnarled, but the truth remains hidden, and I am left with the image of the bathroom floor and the weight of you in my arms.

I do not want this to be our last memory.

Opening my eyes, I take a deep breath, let the cool wetness lie over my tongue. Next to me, a fire crackles in the open hearth warming one side of my leg. I think how outdoor fires do this, warm only one side of you while the other side freezes. I wear a short skirt without pantyhose, white tennis shoes and a tight, knit sweater. The guests have all gone, the movie stars and bohemian artists, the former donning glitter and fur, the latter beads and loose-folding fabric, each hoping to authenticate themselves in originality. Each failing.

"Nina?" I jump at the sound of my manager's voice. He stands in the open patio doorway of the restaurant polishing a wineglass. "Your ride is here."

He looks at me kindly, unconcerned. He doesn't know anything about me. I feel the warmth of the fire on my backside and think how cold it will be in the hollowed-out redwood tree where I sleep.

"I'll just wipe down the tables," I say, stalling. I don't want to face my ride any more than I want to face the cold night on the forest floor with the insects.

My manager is a slender, vigorous man who looks as if he's

been breathing ocean air since birth. "It's late." He smiles. "You go on home now. I'll take care of the tables."

Walking away from the restaurant, the stone path slick with moisture, I dig my doll from the bottom of my bag and tuck her under one arm. She has a cloth body and a plastic head with blue eyes that open and close when you tilt her. Her plastic head is dotted with dark holes where her carefully arranged hair used to be. On her stomach is a scar—held together with a safety pin—from the time I cut her open and pulled out the stuffing.

Bret waits in his mint-green Volvo with the engine running. He is smoking a joint and doesn't open the door for me. I slide into the passenger seat and he leans over and gives me a sloppy kiss, his hand pressed to the back of my head as if this is something romantic. His tongue tastes of stale smoke and alcohol. "Hey, baby," he breathes into my face and passes me the joint. I take it, inhale and try to stifle a cough as Bret maneuvers the car onto the dark road.

We met five months ago when I first arrived in Big Sur. My friend Delia and I had eaten a handful of mushrooms and were dancing around a bonfire at a beach party when Bret slipped into the wavy, illuminated light of my vision. His embroidered shirt rippled over his chest and I thought he was something supernatural. The next morning when I woke up beside him on the beach, he'd turned solid. He was nothing more than a thin-chested man with a tangled beard and skinny legs sticking out from his cutoff jean shorts.

Bret hooks the car around a sharp bend, and the wheels kick up gravel that makes a sound like thunder under our feet.

"You're going too fast," I say, pressing my hand flat against the passenger window.

He grins and steps on the gas, a man who likes to challenge a woman. This is familiar to me. I watched men challenge you your whole life, each one of your four husbands, in their own way, pushing you to the edge. Despite your effort to understand them, to please them, it was, in the end, your unwillingness to be controlled or possessed that got you killed.

The car takes another corner, and the cliff drops to my right at a precarious angle where sumac and sagebrush cling to the edge. People love Highway 1 for its beauty. They think it cuts a benevolent path along the ocean cliff for our pleasure. What I see is a snake luring us with its curvaceous body, a thing of nature waiting for us to step on it so it can strike and fling us off.

I squish my doll's head in, making her face look like something in a distorting mirror. "I don't want to do this anymore," I say, watching the doll's features slowly inflate and pop back into place.

Bret's profile remains neutral, his eyes on the road as he reaches over and strokes my thigh. "Don't be like that, baby. This is good."

I've tried to break up with him before. I don't know why he won't let me go, or how he can feel anything for me when I feel nothing inside. After your death, they sedated me because I was angry and didn't behave properly. Now, I do what I can to sedate myself.

"I mean it. I'm done." I shove his hand away, and this makes him angry.

He puts both hands on the wheel, grips it with white knuckles, his eyes forward, his jaw clenched. "What the fuck, Nina?" he says.

The headlights strike the road. Yellow lines blink past like winking eyes.

His anger scares me. "I'm sorry," I say. I'm not good at this. Charming men. Giving them what they want. Doing what I watched you do, for the good ones and the bad. You appeased the good men, hoping they'd stay with you; placated the bad ones, hoping they wouldn't hurt you. With each husband you tried a little harder, stayed a little longer, so certain you'd get it right.

If Bret is any indication, I won't get it right, either. Looking at him, his hard profile reflected in the dashboard lights, his scruffy beard and long hair curling at the base of his neck, he reminds me of the rebel soldiers in Cuba.

This is not a memory I want. "Bret, I really can't do this. Please, pull over. I need to get out."

"You don't know what you need."

The arrogance in his voice disgusts me, the anger I'd been tamping down with drugs is now rising in my throat. For all his meditating and chanting and seeking enlightenment, Bret is a prick. I am twenty years old, you are dead, and there's no one to tell me what to do anymore. You are not here to laugh it away, or tell me to chin up, to silence me or put me in a mental institution or stick me in a boarding school. "Fuck you, Bret!" I shout. "Pull over. I want to get out."

"Fuck me?" He speeds up, swerves the car near the shoulder of the road, gravel and dirt hitting my window and ricocheting off the glass like buckshot.

I suck in my breath and grip the door handle. "Don't do that!"

"Do what? This?" He swerves again, and all I see, for a moment, is empty, black space.

What I should do is calm him down, convince him I'm sorry and that I won't break up with him. *Stop the car, and we'll talk about it*, I should say, but a part of me wants him to do something drastic. To pull the trigger for me.

We are crossing Bixby Bridge. The fog has receded, and I can see all the way down to the dark strip of beach where the waves crash and foam like a giant frothing at the mouth.

I know, in that split second right before Bret takes us over the edge, that he's going to do it. It's not the plunge into water I'd imagined on the patio at Nepenthe. I am not sailing peacefully off the cliff with my arms out but trapped in a metal box that jerks to the right so abruptly my head smacks the window. I expect free fall, silence, stillness, but the air is sharp and compact and splintered with glass.

And then you are in my arms, your face flushed, your dark hair limp on your wet forehead, vomit ringing the corners of your mouth. "Help me," I plead, even though you are the one dying. "Don't go," I cry. "I need you." But I have already hit bottom, and the world has gone quiet.

Chapter Two

Birth and Revolution

Daughter,

I am right here, Nina. I have not gone anywhere. I see you in the newness of your adulthood, and I will see you after, when you've come into the full force of yourself. I will watch you struggle to work the memory of my life into your own, to try and resolve our ending.

I did not set out to hurt you. When you were born, I gazed into the gray-blue of your infant eyes, touched your softly wrinkled forehead, your miniature nose and lips with a swell of longing. I wanted to wrap you back into myself, to protect you from any future that might harm your unworn heart.

It is June 14, 1946. I am eighteen years old. Newly married—hurriedly married. I have been in New York City for less than three years.

It was not the smell or noise or pace that stunned me when I first arrived here but the lack of color. New Yorkers, it seems, are too busy to paint their walls. They abandon brick and stone and cement to their natural pigment, fill their streets with black cars, their sidewalks with black coats, hats and umbrellas. They dress in gray and brown, and a drab arrangement of squares called plaid. I miss skirts that sweep up the blue of the sea and the yellow of the poui trees, fabric that holds the curve of a woman rather than boxing her in.

"Only turquoise and pink for you," I whisper, easing your arm from the tightly wrapped blanket and peeling your fist open. Your fingers latch around mine, quick as a crab, and from the foot of the bed your *abuela* smiles.

"*Mi hermosa nieta,*" Mamá says, moving closer and running a finger over your forehead. There is no hum or singsong to her voice, her tone and smile a practical one. You are not what Mamá wants, but now that you are here, she'll love you with the same efficiency she loves all of her family.

From the twelfth story of St. Joseph's Hospital, I can see the East River, a flat wash of gray running into a tower of metallic skyscrapers that shoot upward into a colorless sky. Puffs of black smoke rise from the ferryboats like bad omens. It is a city drawn of charcoal and pen. I want to dip a brush into the pink of your blanket and the gray-blue of your eyes and fill your world with the colors of Cuba, the colors of home. Because I cannot do that, I press you to my breast and sing:

Take me home to Cuba,
Cuba, where you'll sing to me
Cuba, where my heart lies free
And the handsome fellas, wait to tell us
Of their love
Where the sea shines blue.
And green.
Cuba where I'll stay

I am nine years old when I first sing in a Havana night-club to a room of satin dresses, shiny suits and slick pomaded hair where the effort of all that luster is dulled under a veil of smoke. Women prop their arms on round tables, the lamps tinting their white gloves orange, while men lean back in chairs as they sip iced drinks and suck cigars whose ends glow like click beetles. Last week, my sister Danita and I caught seventeen click beetles. Our jar was as bright as a lantern, and we marched around the house announcing our success at the top of our lungs, putting our eldest sister out of sorts as she was rocking our baby sister to sleep.

Tonight is the first time I am singing without Danita, but it will not be the last.

I cup the microphone with both hands and sway my hips from side to side with all the energy my small pelvic bones can muster. I wink and grin, the bemused adult faces laughing at a little girl pretending to be a woman. I play it up, jutting out a hip, cocking a shoulder and tilting my chin in mock seduction. There is a cheer and a whistle, and I raise my eyes to the back of the room where potted palms spread their wide green leaves against the wall. That's where Mamá stands watching, her arms crossed over the front of her brown polkadot dress. From her expression I can't tell whether she is pleased or annoyed.

Earlier that afternoon I watched her pull her dress from the back of her closet and shake it from its hanger. "After six babies this beauty still fits." She smiled, shimmying her hips, her silk slip rustling like paper around her knees. "Never let the babies go to your waist. Men won't look at you if there's not enough there, and they won't look at you if there's too much." She tucked an authoritative finger under my chin and lifted my face. Her dark eyes, deep set above her smooth cheeks, sober and resolute, as if it all came down to the size of my waist. "What do we say?"

"A perfect balance." I swung my hips. My starched white skirt did not rustle but moved as one unit. A doll on a pedestal.

Mamá kissed her fingertips, flinging the kiss into the air. *"Perfecto, mi hija."* Draping her dress over one arm, she tightened the purple ribbon holding up my ponytail. "Not too much swing. Not too much voice. Just enough to draw them in and make them want more." With a final yank to my hair, she shook out her dress and stepped into it, her movements labored, her arms maneuvering their way into the puffed sleeves, thick and round as the drainpipes sticking out of the dirt by the side of our house. Reaching around, she buttoned the back and secured the narrow belt around her well-proportioned waist.

Her solid body is beautiful to me.

I glanced at my reflection in the mirror over the dresser. Heat buzzed through the open window, and a cloud of gnats settled over the glass as I practiced my smile. Earlier that day, Mamá told me that if I sang well tonight she'd hang the mirror in my room, a room I share with my sisters, but the mirror would be all mine. It is large, rectangular, the frame intricately carved of a pale wood like the kind that washes up on the beach. We still have expensive furniture from the time before. A house filled with beautiful things despite the peeling exterior and shriveled gardens.

Before we lost everything, Mamá's plan was to send Danita and me to the Peyrellade Conservatory to study music. Now we can hardly afford the weekly lessons with Señorita Morales, a skinny woman with fallen cheeks and a chin that wobbles when she demonstrates our scales. Danita and I marvel that a voice so beautiful can come from a woman so ugly.

It's hard to tell if I'll turn out beautiful. Mamá is pretty, but I don't look or move like her. I am small for my age and skinny as a twig. Mamá says this will change when I become a woman, which is a relief.

On stage in the nightclub, I try to imagine myself as full-bodied and sturdy as Mamá. The brass instruments of the band vibrate in my belly, and the drums pulse under my feet where new shoes pinch my toes. My sisters didn't get new shoes. Neither did Mamá. I should feel badly about this, but I don't. They are the loveliest shoes I've ever owned: white patent leather with brass buckles and tiny heels that tip me forward when I walk.

I finish the song, holding my final note in the air like a dazzling object as the instruments halt, and silence fills the room. There is a moment of unbearable stillness before the audience erupts into applause. Dizzy with excitement, I curtsy and smile, the thrill of attention hot and satisfying.

The applause quickly fades, and I disappear into the tumult of voices, clinking glassware and large bodies that rise up around me. A hand lands on my shoulder, and the cigarette pinched between its fingers sends smoke spiraling into my nostrils. I try not to cough. "Look at you, kid. Boy, can you sing." A man grins down at me from a mouth filled with shiny, white teeth. I recognize him as one of the drummers. He wears a starched shirt as white as his teeth with billowing sleeves and gold cuff links shaped like cigars. His dark hair is swept up off his forehead, and a line of sweat glistens along his hairline. Even at nine years old, I understand he is wonderful to look at.

Mamá appears in a rustle of fabric and a scent of jasmine, her perfume momentarily overpowering the cigarette smoke. She latches her arm around my shoulder, pulls me from under the man's hand and clamps me to her side, my cheek bumping her breast. Held there, I feel small and ridiculous.

The man flourishes a bow. "Señorita, your daughter is a gem. A pure gem! That voice!" He winks at me, and my cheeks grow hot. "Has she done any recordings?"

"Not yet." Mamá's voice sounds curt, defensive.

The man's grin only widens. "What are you waiting for? You can't hide talent like that. I have a band in Miami. She should come and record with us in America."

Squashed against my mother, I feel her intake of air sucked into her lungs and the slight expanse of her chest. *America* is all she needs to hear.

"Desi Arnaz." The man proffers a hand, and my mom takes it, releasing me. The heat and strength of her body moves away from me as the wealthy woman she once was returns to her shoulders.

"Juana Maria Antonia Santurio y Canto Rodriguez." She smiles a rare, flirtatious smile. "But, you may call me Señorita Rodriguez."

"It is an honor to meet you, Señorita Rodriguez." He holds her hand, a playful glint under the rapt, seductive look in his eye. A cat with a mouse. It is the same look I saw Miguel Santo give Yolanda Farrar in *El veneno de un beso*, the only film I've ever seen. "What do you say?" Mr. Arnaz says this to Mamá but winks at me as if we are in on something together. "You want to bring this little gal to Miami, make her a star?"

I expect an immediate refusal, but Mamá remains silent, her wide cheeks flushed. The air becomes electric with possibility. *Am I to go to America?* I curl my toes against the tight leather of my shoes and pitch forward, excitement and fear pressing into my throat.

"She's too young," Mamá says, regretfully, as if my age is a sorry fact of life utterly out of her control.

Mr. Arnaz shrugs. "She'll grow."

Mamá squeezes my shoulder so hard it hurts. "And when she does, we will consider your offer."

Mr. Arnaz clicks his tongue and cocks his hand at me like a gun, saying casually, as if I am refusing him a dance instead of my future, "Well, then, we'll be seeing you, kid."

He turns, claps his arm around a man in a shirt with wide, ruffled sleeves and bellows to the bartender for a rum on ice with extra mint and two limes, the *two* punctuated in the air with two fingers.

The din of the room, the sharp smell I have already learned to recognize as alcohol and the choke of cigar smoke make me light-headed as I watch my luck slip away on the back of that white shirt drifting into the crowd.

Mamá tugs me through the throng of bodies and out onto the cobblestone street. It is late, and the street is steamy and smells of gasoline. Boisterous voices spill from open doorways that illuminate the pavement like patchwork.

"You're a sweet-looking one," a woman whistles from an open patio, swaying slightly, her arm latched around another woman's shoulder. They wear dresses that are much too small, and I am sorry to think they've grown out of them and can't afford new ones.

Mamá pulls me along so fast the backs of my stiff shoes begin rubbing the skin off my heels.

"Why didn't Papa come?" I ask. He might have let me go to America. We need money. Danita and I could make money in America. Everyone in America is rich, at least that's what I've heard Mamá say. If we don't go soon, I'll end up in a too-small dress with my knees exposed, like those poor women on the patio. "Why, Mamá?" I press.

"He's a busy man," she answers sharply, and since we've hardly seen Papa after losing our land nearly three years ago, I think this must be true.

★ ★ ★

It changed overnight. One day Papa was living at home overseeing the plantation, the cutting and transporting of our fields of henequen to the mill to be crushed and made into rope, and the next day the peasants took over and Papa moved to Havana.

I woke that morning with Danita standing over my bed, shaking my shoulder. "Hurry, get up, something's happening." Danita is only a year older than me but bosses me as if she were as big as our sister Oneila, who is eighteen years old and has a right to boss me.

I hear shouting through the open window.

"Come on." Danita grabs my hand, and we hurry down to the kitchen where normally glasses of guanabana juice and great slices of warm cassava bread are waiting for us. This morning there is nothing. The air has a burned smell, but there is no fire in the stove. Not even the coffee is brewing. Mamá stands with her back against the counter as Mercedes clings to her full, bright skirt.

When she sees us Mamá gives a nervous laugh and says, "I don't know how to cook," looking at the stove as if it is a great, black beast ready to attack.

"Where's Aayla?" Danita asks. Aayla is our cook.

Mamá shakes her head. "She's gone. They are all gone." Mercedes starts to cry. Mamá does not shush her or lift her onto her hip. She stands perfectly still, moving her eyes around the room as if everything familiar has suddenly become foreign.

Secretly, I am glad Aayla is gone. I hate her. Mamá says *hate* is too strong a word, but that's exactly how I feel. Aayla is tall and bony, with arms wound tight as cording, her hand springing out and slapping me whenever she feels like it, especially if I try to take a slice of cake before my brother Bebo, who is her favorite.

"Farah's not gone," I say, matter-of-fact. Farah is our Haitian nanny who loves me. She is the exact opposite of Aayla, and she'd never leave. She is plump and warm with the darkest skin I've ever seen. When she hugs me, her flesh is so consuming I am sure she has no bones at all. Every night she and I sing Haitian lullabies together after everyone is asleep. She is the one who taught me the mambo and the rhumba.

"Farah is gone, too." Mamá makes no attempt to soften the blow, and tears spring to my eyes. What will I do without Farah? I fly to the open window, wondering if she is out there whooping and shouting with the others, but the mist is so thick all I can see is a gray-green soup of clouds.

"Get away from there." Mamá yanks me back, pulls in the shutters and latches them with big, angry movements. Just then the outer kitchen door swings open, and Papa stomps in, his face grim. My two brothers are right behind him, shoving each other to see who will get through the door first. Bebo wins. He is smaller and quicker and beats Manuel at most things.

"Where is my father?" Mamá asks, her voice high.

Papa tosses his straw hat on the counter. Papa is thin and muscular with a wiry energy that makes me nervous even when things aren't out of control. "He left for Havana early this morning."

"Is Mamá okay?"

"She's fine. She said she'll stay put until your father comes back."

Despite the pandemonium, Papa doesn't look at all out of sorts. His black hair is slicked back, his mustache neatly brushed. Standing at the counter, he taps the jar of coffee beans grimacing as if the absence of coffee is the most disturbing prospect ahead of us. Resigned to this difficulty, he sits mugless at the head of the long wooden table fisting his hands in front of him. "Sit, all of you," he orders.

My brothers sit on either side of him, my father's parallel shadows. I realize Oneila has been sitting silently at the table all along. Her white blouse is pressed, her black hair parted and pulled away from her face so tightly I can see the white line of her scalp. How did everyone else have time to put themselves together? Danita and I are still in our cotton nightgowns.

Despite this indiscretion, we scurry to our seats. If not for the loss of Farah, I would find this all very exciting. It's the same feeling I get before a storm, when the warm wind picks up as the sky turns wild and tints everything a shocking orange.

Mamá sits at the opposite end of the table from Papa, and Mercedes climbs into the chair next to her, sucking on her fist. All we need now is something to eat, I think, pressing my hand into my stomach to quiet the grumbling, wishing tragedy had struck *after* breakfast.

Glancing around the table Papa meets our eyes with deliberate soberness, speaking as if he is broadcasting the news over the wireless. "There has been an uprising. The student-run Directorio has taken over."

I give Danita a *what does that mean?* look. She shrugs. Outside there are pops like fireworks and a clanging as if spoons are being banged against pots. I feel like I am missing a party.

Oneila, generally timid, startles us all by saying, "We're entitled to know what our family has done to deserve this," as if three-year-old Mercedes, Danita, my brothers Bebo and twelve-year-old Manuel and I are entitled to anything.

I stare at Oneila leaning forward in her chair trying on a new expectant expression. She said *we* but means *I.* If her questioning is a test of maturity, she passes it in a single leap. Instead of scolding her for being insolent, Mamá looks her directly in the eye and says, "Nothing, Oneila. Our family has done absolutely nothing to deserve this."

Papa, ignorant of the momentous exchange taking place between mother and daughter, says, "That is not true, Maria."

Mamá starts. "What does that mean?"

"That we're not innocent."

"What have we done?"

"Exactly what they accuse us of."

"Whose side are you on?"

"I don't know. I haven't made up my mind yet. These are our people. They have a right to fair wages, fair labor, education, a modern university."

"They are Negroes. Haitian. Jamaican. They are not Spanish."

"We are all Cuban!" Papa bangs the table, charged with an energy that springs off of him in quick bursts. "This—" he waves his hand in huge circles over his head, conjuring a storm "—is your world. Your father's land. Your father's money. Did you know—" Papa's eyes flash around the table, the *you* now directed at all of us "—that your mother's people and mine all come from Asturias, from the exact same region in Spain? Our backgrounds are identical, our people no different. But *here*, here in Cuba we are different, and do you know why?"

We quickly shake our heads, *no*.

"No, of course you don't. My father gave his life so that you would not know. Before the Cuban War of Independence, the only difference between your mother's people and mine is that her father was born in Spain and mine was born in Cuba. This made my father a creole. It made *me* a creole." His voice dips down right before he spits out, "We were nothing.

Dirt!" He then falls silent, letting the unjustness of it sink in as he eyes each of us in turn.

Before this, we'd heard very little of Papa's people or the war. His parents died before any of us were born. His two brothers and one sister seem no different than Mamá's brothers and sisters. It doesn't appear that anyone thinks Papa is dirt. Grandpa lets him run the plantation, and Grandma kisses his cheek when she greets him.

The vigor returns to Papa's voice. "My father was an heir to Spanish greatness. Born of dignity, fortitude, courage, pride. When I was a boy, a Spanish general rode up to our front door. General Weyler Valeriano. The Butcher, they called him."

"Manuel," Mamá says, in a warning tone, but Papa silences her with a raised hand. She sighs and pulls Mercedes onto her lap. He is going to tell us what he is going to tell us. Discreetly, I press my fingers in my ears and pretend his nose is the dial on the wireless that I can turn up or down with my eyes. He speaks so loudly, however, I cannot turn him off.

"It was February 24, 1897, the height of the rebellion. Valeriano had been sent over from Spain to suppress the insurgency. I was standing in my front yard dissecting a frog under our algaroba tree when he rode up to our house." Papa's voice drops a notch, serious as death. "The horse startled me, but when I looked up, I wasn't frightened. The general had a mustache that curled down all the way to his chin, and he wore a white jacket with silver buttons that flashed in the sunlight. I thought he looked very fine and noble and that my mother would be pleased to have such a visitor. When he asked where my father was, I pointed to the door of the house. I didn't know to lie. When my father stepped out and saw me pointing, there was fear in his eyes, and this froze me where I stood. I'd never seen my father afraid. At first, I thought he was afraid for himself, but after, I understood that he was afraid for me, too." Papa pauses, clears his throat and continues. "The man slid from his horse and shoved my father to his knees. 'Hail to the king of Spain!' he ordered. My father said nothing. 'Hail to the king of Spain,' the general ordered again, and this time he drew his sword. It was long and thin with a marble handle and a blade as shiny as the bright green underbelly of the dead frog I still clutched in my hand. The sword looked heavy. Too heavy for me to lift or wrestle away from him. I didn't look at my father's face, which was cowardly of me. Instead, I stared at the puddle he knelt in. Mamá was washing clothes down at the river, and I worried she'd have to make a second trip to wash the mud from his pants. I didn't know how much harder blood was to get out. You think this is bad?" I jump in my seat as Papa flings an arm toward the window, drawing our attention from the story to the ruckus outside. I don't understand what is going on out there any more than I understand why he is telling us this story.

As if suddenly regretting the retelling of this moment, Papa abruptly ends with a single sentence. "I was five years old when I saw my father quartered in front of me for not hailing to the king of Spain."

The room is silent. *Quartered?* You quarter an avocado or a coconut. How do you quarter a human? With a sword, it would seem.

I am no longer hungry. The house feels eerie and still without the servants. Under the table, I reach for Danita's hand. Her palm is as sweaty as mine. Bebo starts to whimper. No one comforts him. Even a story of our grandfather being hacked to pieces is no excuse for a boy to cry. Glancing at our terrified faces, Mamá says soothingly, "Nothing like that is going to happen here. That was a different time and a different war."

Papa, intent on holding our terror, presses his knuckles into the table and stands. "This is no different. It's the oppressed fighting back just as they did with Spain. Machado changed the constitution so he could maintain power. *Por amor de Cristo*, he ran for reelection against himself!"

"Manuel!" Mamá cries. No amount of injustice is worth taking the Lord's name in vain.

Papa ignores her. "Machado's closed the high schools as well as the university. Students and professors have been beaten and arrested. They're left with no choice but to fight back. Armed action is the only thing that's ever proved successful at ridding this country of corrupt power."

Mamá shakes her head vigorously. "The Directorio is not an army or a government. It's a reckless, irresponsible, student-organized rebellion." I picture kids in military jackets swinging swords on a playground. "They demand economic and political reform and then go and use the same violence and corruption as Machado's regime to get it. It's hypocritical. Politics in this country has always been about ascendency. There's no heroics in it. No national unity, no purpose. It's just men vying for power."

I understand none of these big words, but Mamá's confidence is reassuring. No one is going to chop us up with a sword, I tell myself.

"The Directorio is not really in charge, Maria." Papa sounds patronizing, as if Mamá has simply misunderstood the situation. Didn't *he* tell us the Directorio had taken over? "Fulgencio Batista's low-level army is rising to power. They'll be the ones in charge soon. Batista is a powerful man, from what I hear, and an admirable one. A laborer who rose up out of nothing. A man who will no longer be forced to the bottom of the pile, and I say *hurrah* for him."

Mamá stands up so fast Mercedes tumbles to the floor with

a wail. "I know perfectly well who Batista is. I will not have you revere this man in front of our children!"

"I'll revere whoever I like." Papa sounds churlish and smug. Nothing like I imagine his noble, proud father sounded.

Trembling, Mamá walks over to him. "How dare you," she says, and Papa's hand springs out and strikes her across the face. The force sends her to her knees.

It is a slap to put her in her place, just like how she slaps us. We've seen Papa hit her before, but this time it's different. Something irreparable is happening, a tear in the seam of our family, a moment that will lead to Mamá getting on a plane with me nine years later, my parents' prideful, stubborn beliefs destroying an already-fragile marriage.

After being struck, Mamá stays bent over on our Persian rug. Mercedes stops wailing and shoves her fingers in her mouth, snot running over her hand. Bebo begins to sob, and Manuel kicks him under the table. I feel numb with confusion. Across from me Oneila hangs her head. *This is all her fault*, I think. *She should never have asked that stupid question in the first place.*

I slip from my chair and go to Mamá, pressing my hand into her fleshy thigh. The touch rouses her, and she stands up, snapping her skirt into place and swinging a pointed finger between us. "You remember this day," she says. "You remember this day when your papa betrayed us."

"Maria," Papa says in an exasperated voice that he might use on one of us. She is being a silly girl, his tone says, an unreasonable woman.

Mamá ignores him. Since I am the nearest, she snatches my hand and says, "Come," and I mimic her prideful stride into the kitchen where she picks up a plantain, lays it on the cutting board and chops the top off with one swift blow of the knife, like she's beheading it. "I've seen Aayla fry these. It

can't be too hard. From now on this will be breakfast. Peel,"
she snaps, handing me the plantain.

Not long after, Papa moved to Havana. In the beginning,
he came home every weekend, then every other weekend.
Mamá doesn't speak of it, but we all know he's gone to work
for Batista. His brown military jacket gives him away. He
makes a performance of removing it, hanging it on a hanger,
front facing forward so the pressed lapels and polished buttons decorating the shoulders can be seen. He brushes it down
with the flat of his hand, adjusts it just so and then hooks it
on the wall by the door like a painting to be admired. It is a
putrid brown and in no way goes with our blue-and-white
tiled entryway. Neither do his boots, which he places under
his jacket, the laces looped and tucked into the tops, the brown
leather hard and shiny, boots and coat waiting at attention.

I figure, now that Papa is working, we'll have our servants
back, at the very least Farah, but nothing changes other than
Mamá telling us over dinner one night that she is going to
work as a seamstress for the rich ladies in town. "As a wealthy
young girl, I was at least taught to sew, if not cook." She
forces a smile.

We would all prefer the latter. Since Oneila has taken up
the cooking, every meal consists of beans, picadillo and boiled
yucca. I am sorry I hated Aayla so much. I'd take a hand-
slapping from her any day for a slice of her coconut cake.

I don't like Mamá going to work. It's bad enough losing my
soft-footed, gentle Farah and having to be bossed by Oneila—
the authority on all things since her newfound adultness—but
Mamá's absence makes me ache with missing. Every morning I stand on the front step and watch her stride away in her
best dress, hips swaying, her wide-brimmed hat tilted at a
daring angle. When I ask why she wears her finest clothes to

work she says, "To show these women I know what fashion is," but I know she's too proud to dress in anything less. How they are still rich and we are poor I will never understand.

Home is torture without her. Oneila makes us sit at the table until midday doing arithmetic and grammar. Even worse is the afternoon when she releases my brothers to the outdoors and lets them romp under a canopy of leafy trees, while Danita and I are forced to embroider and crochet in the dark kitchen. Whenever Oneila is out of the room, I sneak under the table and play paper dolls with Mercedes. Danita threatens to tell, but she never does. My brothers come to supper bright-eyed, with scratches on their arms and red soil under their fingernails. Danita and I only have neat stitches to show for our time, and there is never a speck under our nails; Oneila makes sure of that.

All day I wait for Mamá, pouncing on her the moment she walks through the door and dragging her to the wireless where *Rita de Cuba* comes on at six o'clock sharp. Danita and I press our hands to our hearts and shimmy around the room singing "El Manisero" at the top of our lungs. Mamá gives us her full attention, sitting on the edge of her seat with her head tilted in concentration. Oneila's bland dinner, the boys' impatient appetites, Mercedes's whining…all wait while we sing.

Now, three years after the rebellion, I've had my first public appearance in a nightclub, and next week I will sing on Radio Havana Cuba.

Holding tight to Mamá's hand as we hurry through the streets, my shoes grating away at my heels, I ask, "Why didn't Danita sing with me tonight?"

"You both auditioned, and they chose you." Mamá pulls me down a narrow street where a sky-blue car waits to take us home.

"Will she sing with me at the radio station?"

"No."

I am sorry about this but not very sorry. "When do I get to go to America?"

"What makes you think you get to go to America?"

"You said when I grew."

"I said I would consider it." Mamá nods to the driver as he opens the door for us. *"Gracias, Señor."* She climbs into the back and adjusts her skirt over her knees.

I slide in next to her. My skirt bunches beneath me, and the leather seat sticks to the backs of my legs, but I am too tired to adjust anything. I lay my head on Mamá's shoulder. She slips the ribbon from my hair and shakes out my ponytail, running her fingers over the sore spot on my scalp where the hair has been pulled tight. The car bumps down the road, the engine like the steady moan of a large animal. Slowly the city lights fade, and a fat moon appears over the dense, lush fields.

I sleep all thirty-six miles from Havana to Guanajay. Mamá shakes me awake as the car stops in front of our house, leaning over to open the door and scooting me out with her hip. I stand sleepily in the dirt street as she pays the driver. The air is rich with the scent of night-blooming jasmine.

The driver pulls away, and Mamá snaps the remainder of her money back into her purse. "What little money you made tonight isn't enough to cover half the ride. You are a lucky girl. Don't forget that."

I don't feel lucky. Mosquitoes bite my arms, and my heels hurt so much I want to throw my pretty new shoes into the road.

"Let's get you to bed." Mamá guides me toward the house. The front balcony sags like an overstuffed belly, and the blue trim crumbles around the tall, narrow windows. The windows are all dark. Oneila has put everyone to bed. I hope Danita isn't too sorry I went without her.

"When, Mamá?" I ask.

She shakes her head, turning the key in the lock. "You are a spoiled child," she sighs. "Fifteen. We will go to America when you are fifteen."

In her voice, I hear that she decided this long ago.

Chapter Three

Boxed Up

Mother,

For most of my childhood, I know little of your life in Cuba. It belongs to a time of siblings, a father, war and poverty. You and I are of a different time.

I am as American as towheaded, pasty-faced Sandy Plummer who lives next door. I eat hamburgers from Whistle 'n' Pig, watch *The Ed Sullivan Show* and wear Mary Janes with white bibbed plaid dresses. You wear chiffon and lipstick, are on your third husband and sing and dance on Hollywood's big screen. There are no siblings or father for me, just Grandmother Maria who bosses us both and your new husband who I don't like and will never call Dad.

In August there is a drought. The ground beneath our feet cracks and splits with thirst. The wind blows hot and tumbleweeds roll. Dirt crumbles down the Hollywood Hills, turning roads and once-shiny cars the color of sand. Convertible tops remain closed, and windshield wipers battle dust instead of rain.

Sucked dry, the city holds its breath.

I hold mine, too, but for different reasons. Winter rain and boarding school are a package deal. I'd take the heat and dry air in Los Angeles forever if it meant summer wouldn't end and I didn't have to go back to Villa Cabrini Academy.

At twelve years old, my anger is already taking root. Angry girls are not good girls—this much I have been taught—which makes me certain that I am to blame for what happens.

It is midmorning on Saturday when the telephone rings. I am in the kitchen stirring ice cubes into my lemonade when you scurry from the living room to snatch it up. Our home is a one-story bungalow with a living room you step down into from the kitchen. An open doorway separates the two spaces, which means anything said in one room is heard in the other.

You cradle the lime-green receiver against your shoulder as you squirt lotion from a Jergens bottle that sits on the counter and rub it vigorously up your forearms. You are still wearing your pink silk bathrobe and feathered slippers which you stay in until noon on your days off. "Oh, you're a doll. Of course we'll be there," you say, and I feel a flurry of excitement. You promised we'd spend the evening watching *Maverick* and eating orange sherbet, but I'd easily give up both for a night out. The last time you took me out we went to a charity ball at the Palladium, and I got to meet Lucille Ball.

I am picturing what glittering event you are taking me to when you hang up. "That was Uncle Duke inviting Alfonso and me to a cocktail party. I'm sorry, sweetheart, but I simply couldn't turn him down."

Under my palm, the perspiring glass feels slick and wet, the ice cubes already melted to slivers. The slightest motion would send it sailing off the counter, drown our feet in shattered glass and sweet lemonade. I look at you, meet your eyes.

"Why do you still call him *Uncle Duke*? He's not my uncle," I say, hoping this will sting more than broken glass.

John Wayne became my uncle after you married his best friend, Grant. Now that you are married to Alfonso, a *gorgeous*, dark-haired juggler—*gorgeous* being your word, not mine— you have no right calling John my uncle or dining at his house with your new husband, for that matter.

Unfazed by my comment, you smile and wrap an arm around my shoulder. "He'll always be your uncle, dearest. Now, don't be glum. I promise to make it up to you tomorrow. We'll stay up until midnight watching television and eating buckets of sherbet, just the two of us."

I sink against you, melting under the scent of the orange-blossom skin cream you slathered over your arms. For the briefest moment, I let my head rest on the bridge of your shoulder before pushing you away. It isn't fair that you can soften my anger when you are the cause of it. "Turn Mr. Wayne down. Tell him you already have plans."

You cross your arms, looking sorry but unwavering. No one tells you what to do, other than Grandmother Maria. "That would be rude, now wouldn't it, Nina?"

Catching hold of the tassel on the tie of your robe, I give it a childish tug, "He'd understand, and besides, he wouldn't want you leaving me all alone."

"Don't be silly. You're old enough to stay home alone, and even if you weren't, your *abuela* is here."

"She doesn't count!"

From the next room Grandmother Maria shouts back, "Oh, I don't, do I?"

"Nina," you scold, "don't hurt your *abuela*'s feelings."

"She doesn't have any!" I cry, my anger finding a target with my grandmother. Grandmother Maria is the ruler of the house and the cause of many bad things, namely boarding school, which she enforces. I know you'd never send me away to school if it wasn't for her.

"Stop it, Nina. You're being childish. Sometimes things come up that can't be helped."

"Why do you want to see Uncle Duke, anyway? He was Grant's best friend, not Alfonso's. He doesn't even like Alfonso. He hasn't come to see us once since you married him."

Grant's name strikes where I want. Your eyes slide away from mine, your smooth cheeks twitching as you press your lips together in an effort to keep whatever you'd like to say to yourself.

"Sorry, I didn't mean it," I say quickly, but you just shake your head and leave the kitchen, looking disappointed in me.

I would have felt genuinely sorry about bringing up Grant if it had changed your mind, but it doesn't.

By the time dusk arrives, the sinking sun making everything glow hotter, I am waiting on the sofa for you to emerge in your shimmering evening attire and forgive me. The ceiling fan sends little hairs tickling across my forehead, and the mohair cushion prickles the backs of my bare calves. I should be wearing stockings with my skirt, but they're too sweaty. I stare at the enormous painting over the stone fireplace— colorful geometric shapes floating on a white canvas—and imagine myself boxed up, a girl configured of precise angles and neat points. Fixed. Perfectly contained.

I think of Grant. The orange chair he died in is still here, pushed up to the floor-length window that looks out onto our teardrop swimming pool. The last time I saw him he was slumped in that chair with a bottle of alcohol between his knees, his eyes red and swollen. Grant was handsome once, in films and photographs, but by the time he married you he was old and puffy.

I should have known something was wrong that day. Despite the drinking, he always noticed me, even when I felt invisible, which made me love him. No matter how drunk he was, he always managed a smile or a wink, never failing to ask how I was faring with the wretched nuns at boarding school. "If I had my way," he'd say, "you'd go to school down the street and be home for dinner. Between Grandmother Maria and that mother of yours—" an elbow nudge to my side "—don't try and change those gals' minds about anything. You know what I mean, darling?"

The day he died, he had no words for me. When I walked into the living room, he glanced up, but there was a flat, vacant look in his eyes, their clear blue turned watery as if he was fading from the inside. "Hi, Grant," I said, but he didn't answer, just dropped his gaze back into his lap. I remember how the light from the window poured over him, uncomfortably bright as I walked past him to my room, waiting for you to return with Christmas packages. Eventually, I heard your car pull up, the front door open and then a scream. I flew into the hallway only to be met by Grandmother Maria who was rushing toward me with her hands raised in the air. She pushed me back into my room crying, "Do not come out," and slammed the door behind her. Terrified, I dropped to my stomach and pressed my face to the crack under the door. There was sobbing and hurrying feet, and then after what felt like a lifetime, a distant police siren that grew louder, roaring to a halt in front of our house. I ran to the window. People spilled from their doorways and gathered in the street, our quiet, Sherman Oaks neighborhood coming to life.

Not until two white-coated men appeared carrying a stretcher with a lumpy body covered in a sheet did I understand that someone was dead. I went sick with dread until I saw you walking down the path, Grandmother's arm tight around your waist. I banged the glass. I wanted you to look up, to tell me what was going on. But you only clung to the side of the stretcher and climbed into the back of the ambulance without a backward glance.

It was Grandmother Maria who took me to a diner and told me over a bottle of Coca-Cola and a pastrami sandwich that Grant had died of a heart attack. I knew she was lying. Grant's silence, the emptiness in his eyes, made sense to me now. You and Grandmother Maria like to believe the nuns keep me innocent, but the Catholic girls at my school know all about suicide. Last year, a girl hung herself in her dorm room. She was a sophomore, so I didn't know her, but rumor had it she wasn't fully dead when they found her and she died later in the hospital.

On the couch in the living room, I peel my calves off the prickly upholstery, and tuck my feet underneath me. I cross my eyes so the geometric shapes on the canvas double and swim into each other. More boxes. More angles. How does one get to be a perfectly formed configuration of shapes? You are. A woman beautiful in her skin, utterly sure of herself. I know where all of your angles start and stop.

Or at least, I thought I did.

There is a slap to my knee, and I jump as Alfonso breaks into my reveries. He drops next to me stinking of spicy cologne, a tumbler in one hand. "What are you looking at?" He tilts his head, staring at the painting with mock concentration.

"Nothing." One side of his blue gabardine pants presses into my foot, and I move to get up, but he puts a hand on my bare leg.

"Where are you going? Your mom will be out any minute. She asked me to keep you company."

Alfonso is charming, black hair swept up Elvis-style, perpetually tan skin and brown eyes that do, actually, twinkle. He always looks as if he is just about to compliment you. I'm not sure why I don't like him: he's nice enough, just annoyingly glossy and confident. A stage guy, an entertainer. Maybe it's because Grandmother Maria told me one night—when she was in a *mood*—that he married you for your money, which I suppose is true since he bought himself a shiny, yellow Cadillac with white leather seats and hasn't booked a juggling gig in the two years since.

Looking at him now, I think I hate him just because he took Grant's place.

"Cat got your tongue?" Alfonso shakes the last of his drink into his mouth, crunching ice between his teeth. He drinks the same stinky, dark stuff Grant used to, only he is never sloppy or sad.

I scoot to the other side of the couch. "That's a stupid question. How can a cat get my tongue?"

He knocks the glass against my bare knee, cold and wet. "It's a saying from the English navy ships. They had whips called the cat-o'-nine-tails. Used to whip the sailors to keep them in line. Hurt so much the poor boys couldn't speak. *Cat got your tongue*, they'd say."

"Fine, whatever," I grumble. Alfonso has an answer for everything.

Just then you appear, twirling in front of us and landing with one hand on your hip, the other bent at the wrist above your head, your profile angled in a dramatic pose. "What do you think?" you say, holding perfectly still.

Green silk dips over your chest, hugs you to your knees and flares out at the bottom like petals opening at your feet. Your dark brows are penciled high into your forehead and your lips are a lustrous red. You look stunning. "Oh no!" you cry, tipping dramatically to one side, pretending your hand is stuck to your hip. "Who put the glue in my nail polish?" You dance around the room, yanking yourself along with a tortured expression. It is hard to stay mad when you make a joke out of everything. I smile.

"Help me! Peel it off." You bump my knees with yours. "Just rip it quick like a bandage. I won't scream, I promise."

I reach for your hand, pretending to pull as you release it from your hip and go tumbling onto the couch with a screech. "That was a close call." You laugh, wrapping me in your arms and kissing my cheek before standing to shake the wrinkles from your dress.

Alfonso smiles up at you. "You are a rare one."

You beam back at him, looking as if he holds something precious you'd do anything to get your hands on. I want you to look at me that way.

"Ready, darling?" You reach for Alfonso, and he stands, wrapping an arm around your cinched waist and kissing you in a way that disgusts me. I slouch down into the couch and cross my arms tightly over my chest.

You push him away laughing. "You're smudging my lipstick."

Alfonso drops his empty drink on the coffee table, missing the coaster, and jingles his keys in the air with an eye roll in my direction. "I'll be in the car." He walks out leaving the front door open.

You give me a hurried look. "Promise you won't sit here sulking, please? It's still light out. Why not pop next door and see what Sandy is up to? Maybe her mom will let her come over and watch *Maverick* with you?" You lean into the mirror hanging by the door and nestle a black hat onto your head, little points capping your forehead like an acorn. "You know how your *abuela* likes to go to bed early, so don't wake her if you stay up. There's food in the kitchen. I ordered you steak and pecan pie from The Apple Pan, your favorite. Love you."

You step out, hooking your purse over one arm. I jump up

and trail after you down the path. Alfonso is already behind the steering wheel of his butter-colored Cadillac. If only it would melt in the sun. He leans an elbow out the window. "Hurry up, doll. I don't want to insult the legendary John Wayne before I meet the fella."

"I'm coming." You round the car and pull open the passenger door.

Switching tactics from earlier, I plead, "Can't I go with you? Uncle Duke wouldn't mind. Please, he adores me."

You smile at me over the top of the car, your fat, pin curls lacquered around your face. "He does adore you, but it's too late for you to be out, and besides you'd be bored silly. There won't be any other children there."

"I'm twelve. That's hardly a child."

"Well, it's hardly a woman yet, either." You pat the roof with your white-gloved hand. "Don't worry, you'll have all my womanly problems soon enough. Now, go on next door and see if Sandy wants to play."

You're always trying to get me to play with Sandy, telling me I need friends my own age, hoping I'll need you less.

Blowing a kiss, you climb in beside Alfonso, and I watch your handsome portraits recede out of the driveway.

I follow the car into the street, standing on the scorching pavement as the silver tailpipe glints and disappears around the corner. *I could run away*, I think, picturing a tiny figure of myself disappearing into the glimmering haze up ahead.

Just then Sandy Plummer bursts from her front door, jump roping over to me with wide, nimble leaps. "Want to race?" she pants, her Mary Janes clicking on the pavement, her face already a vivid red.

"My jump rope broke," I lie.

Sandy can jump rope faster than any girl in the neighborhood, attends public school, has a perfect, slender nose and a mom who wears aprons and makes heart-shaped Jell-O. She is enviably normal, which is why I can't stand her. That, and she's sneaky, a girl who wins adults over with her smile and sticks her tongue out at their backs.

"You just don't want me to beat you," she sneers.

"Maybe I just don't want to die of heatstroke."

"At least I don't stand in the street staring out like an idiot," she calls, jump roping past me, her shoes click-clacking away as she makes her way down the street, heading to the park where other girls will be clustered around the drinking fountain or sailing high on swings, their socks falling around their ankles, shiny calves catching the sunlight.

I have no interest in them. I'd rather be by myself.

It is uncomfortably hot, but I don't want to go inside yet. I stand for a long time watching the heat waver off the pavement like shimmery, blue liquid wishing something dreadful and exciting would happen. If only there were a spell to turn my grandmother into a soft-eyed old lady who didn't care about boarding schools. If only dry grass could swoop off the lawns and turn my stepfather into the Scarecrow like from *The Wizard of Oz*, turn him stupid and lifeless. Something dreadful is necessary, I think, so you and I can be together.

Only, once the dreadful, unknown thing takes shape, it is out of the scope of my twelve-year-old imagination.

Chapter Four

Rio Bravo

Daughter,

I admit that I did not think about you that night at Duke's party. Or if I did, it was only to wonder if Sandy had come over, or if you'd eaten all of your dinner and not upset your *abuela*. I was instead absorbed in the rumors that Republic Pictures was shutting down and I'd be losing my contract.

As the iron gates of Duke's estate slide shut behind our car, suppressed memories rise up. Grant and I were here just three days before he died. He was in an unpleasant mood and hadn't wanted to go out that night. His drinking had gotten worse, and war memories haunted him. We spoke of divorce and fought over the most insignificant things, things that became huge and meaningful to me after his death, like fighting over going out when we could easily have stayed home. Why did I insist? Maybe all Grant needed was for me to pay more attention to him, to have listened.

I look over at Alfonso as he parks the car behind a black Buick. I am someone who moves forward, onward and upward, keeps at it. Alfonso was my keeping at it. We met in the bar at Radio City Music Hall. He and his brother were jugglers. They could juggle sticks of fire and knives while riding unicycles in circles around the stage. We'd seen each other perform, and our attraction was instant.

Alfonso turns off the engine and leans over, kissing my shoulder, and I want to slither down into the seat under the sweet smell of his skin. Instead I kiss the top of his head and wriggle away before he lays a hand on my breast.

"Not here," I scold and haul open the heavy car door.

Duke's walled-in property is lush and lively, the hillside watered green, the burned earth a crusty outline behind the sweeping ranch house. Music and chatter drift from the patio, car doors slam, and people shout in greeting.

I loop my arm through Alfonso's, focusing on the distinct scent of his vetiver cologne and the muscular feel of his arm as we make our way down the flagstone steps to the pool house. If I hold him tight, stay enchanted, I can ward off the memories.

Pilar Wayne greets us at the door, drawing me away from Alfonso before I can protest, all smiles as she places a martini in my hand and drops me on Duke's arm. "I expect you two to get right down to it," she says with a wink before gliding back to her post, her dress a red flame behind her.

Duke smiles down at me, the skin around his eyes crinkling. "Glad to see you, sweetheart."

The sound of his gravelly voice, his woody scent and the smell of tequila swimming in his glass flood me with memories spent drunk under the sunshine beside the pool, Grant's hands on my bare thighs, his mouth over mine. The nights we didn't make it home, Pilar and Duke retiring to the ranch house, the pool house all ours. The things Grant and I did on this marble floor, I think, as shame and pleasure pulse through me.

Taking a huge sip of my martini, I fold my grief into a tight square and shove it into the pit of my stomach, glancing around the large, open space for cheerful distraction. There's a bar at one end, a black lava-rock wall at the other. The white leather couches, rattan chairs and marble floor do their best to absorb the heat beating at the windows. In a few hours, the sun will set and the place will cool to a soft blue. I miss the cooling hour. At home, I am always hot.

Through the floor-to-ceiling windows, I spot Maureen O'Hara on the patio wrapped in pink chiffon, cheeks rouged, hair aflame, pool water shimmering behind her. The other preened men and women look dull in her presence, and I am glad to be inside.

"That new fella of yours treating you right?" Duke nods at Alfonso, who has settled onto the sofa next to a blonde in a short, boxy dress.

"He treats me like a queen." I smile, all girlish charm as I tilt my head back to catch Duke's eye.

"As he should." Duke plants a kiss on my forehead, endearing and fatherlike. I don't mind. I will never be a Maureen O'Hara. Carmen Miranda is the biggest Latina star Hollywood has, and she's still known as the lady in the tutti-frutti hat. If Hollywood had its way, all its women would be white and blonde, the more ambiguously blonde the better.

I learned this early on, sitting on a bale of straw on the set of *Cuban Fireball*. My director must have assumed I'd gone to lunch with the others or else he didn't care if I overheard. He leaned against the porch railing of our make-believe saloon and boasted to a cameraman about casting Grace Kelly in *High Noon*. "I'm after the drawing-room type. The real lady who becomes a whore once she's in the bedroom. Poor Marilyn Monroe has bedroom written all over her face, and Grace Kelly isn't very subtle, either."

What's the difference? I thought. *One way or another, all men want is to sleep with us.*

Which makes me appreciate the fatherliness of Uncle Duke. I'll take a man who pats the top of my head instead of my bottom any day.

"Come, I want to introduce you to someone," Duke says now, and I follow him onto the patio where he waves over a woman dressed in white with copper hair falling in shoulder-length waves around her dewy complexion.

"Estelita Rodriguez, meet Angie Dickinson, soon to be the brightest star in Hollywood."

"That's flattering but ridiculous." Angie's voice is thick and husky, her attitude bold and deeply sexy. She yanks up her glove, smoothing it over her elbow, and I have no doubt Duke is right. She has an open-faced purity and seductive brown eyes that could easily command a room.

"And you, my little lady—" Duke hugs me to his side, my martini splashing over the delicate rim of the glass "—will be working alongside us both. How do you like the sound of that?"

"I like it very much." I beam and press my arm into my side so the tops of my breasts rise ever so slightly. This is why I have come. A Warner Brothers' movie, a Western, with just the right dark heroine for me to play.

"What's this movie called that I've heard so much about, and how are you going to get me in it?" I slide out from under Duke's arm and pluck the onion from my martini. I hate onions—and martinis, for that matter. I prefer gin and tonic, but nobody asked.

"Rio Bravo," Angie answers. "And if Duke here wants you, you're in."

She gives me a conspiratorial wink before sauntering away as Duke leads me to the opposite side of the pool where a bar is set up under an awning. The bartender, a dreamboat with crystal-blue eyes, fills a glass with ice, pours tequila over it and hands it to Duke before he's even asked. Duke tips the drink in a salute of thanks, while I drain the rest of my martini, drop the onion into the empty glass and set it on the bar. "She's right, you know." He cocks a finger at Angie who waves from across the pool. "I told Warner Brothers you were the perfect Consuela. We've got Ricky Nelson and Dean Martin. It's going to be a bang-up picture."

The alcohol spreads through me, and I feel elated. I've never done a picture this big. Onward and upward.

From behind, Pilar wraps her arms around my waist. "*Mi belleza*, we have missed you."

I adore Pilar, a dark beauty like myself, Peruvian, although she jokes about how everyone assumes she's Mexican. "With our accent and dark hair, it doesn't matter where we come from…Cuba, Spain, Peru…it's all just *México* to them."

"I gave up correcting people that I'm Cuban long ago," I told her once, as we commiserated the ache of betraying our heritage with a shrug and a laugh.

Now, I kiss Pilar and say, "I've missed you, too."

Releasing me, she waves to the bartender. "Two mojitos," she orders, and I love her even more as she hands me the clear, icy drink, mint leaves floating at the top.

The smell of rum brings me back to the Gran Teatro de La Habana where I sang every weekend during my last year in Cuba. I'd be singing there now if it weren't for Monte Proser, the Copacabana nightclub owner who saw me perform and brought me to New York City. I miss New York—not the weather or the drab buildings but the grit of the people, the realness. Here in LA, success is cladding yourself in false sincerity, making sure you're liked, above all else.

But I am good at that. I glance around at the sunlit guests, peachy light spilling over the hillside, and wonder where I'd be if Mamá hadn't convinced me to sign that ten-picture deal with Republic Pictures. The commitment had scared me. What if I was no good on-screen? I was only familiar with a live audience at the time.

"Estelita." Mamá had swatted at the contract Herbert Yates placed in my hands. "This is what every girl dreams! Don't be so arrogant to think you'll go on singing at the Copa forever. They'll tire of your act, replace you, and by then it'll be too late for a debut in Hollywood. You will be old. No one will want you."

She was right, I remind myself. Even now, at thirty, I am already what they call Hollywood old.

I watch Pilar move to her husband's side, her small frame dwarfed under his arm. She reminds me of Mamá, straight-forward and uncompromising, determined to have things play out exactly as she's orchestrated. She nods at the pool house. "You didn't tell me your new husband was such a catch. Now I see why you've kept him away. The ladies can't get enough."

Past the mingling of bodies, I see Alfonso through the window seated on the couch. The blonde who sat with him earlier has inched her way closer, and a woman with bobbed brown hair has joined on the other side. The blonde throws her head back in laughter, and I look away, wondering if he is trying to make me jealous. It's an easy thing to do.

"He's harmless," I say, hopping up on a bar stool and giving Duke a provocative, pouty expression. "More importantly, how are you going to get me out of my contract with Republic Pictures?"

Pilar slaps him lightly on the belly. "Yes, dearest, how are you going to do that?"

Duke offers his slow, slanted smile. "They've already agreed to loan you out."

Like a prop, I think, jumping up to kiss him on the cheek. "You're too good to me. What would I do without you two?" Warner Brothers can put a basket of fruit on my head and call me Brazilian or Mexican or whatever they want if they make me a star like Carmen Miranda.

"We'd all survive without Duke, but luckily we don't have to," Pilar says, Duke shaking his head lovingly at her. "Now, go lure your husband away from those devilish women, and tell him the good news."

When I enter the pool house, Alfonso doesn't move to get up. Instead, he folds his arms across his chest and sinks deeper into the couch with a sulky expression. The two women look at me as if I've interrupted some secretive tête-à-tête, and I flush with embarrassment. I'm always upsetting Alfonso in ways I don't understand. He's the one flirting, not me. In that moment, I have no patience for it. I whirl around, linking arms around Kitty Taylor, the wife of a photographer I met the first year I moved here. She is not an actress, which is a relief, and she hugs me and begins a stream of chatter about her three children.

It is dark by the time Alfonso finds me sitting on a pool chair with a shrimp cocktail in my hand. I have kept a sideways glance at him all night. We've both had too much to drink.

He drops into the chair beside me, his hair slicked back from running his hands through it, a gesture indicative of nerves. Even after two years of marriage, the sight of him sends the same burning sensation through me as when we first met.

I am thinking about coaxing him into one of the bedrooms in the pool house when he ruins it by saying, "So, you're too embarrassed to introduce me?"

"What?" I drop the tail of my shrimp back into the cock-tail cup.

"You're embarrassed by me."

"That's ridiculous. Why would you say that?"

"You dropped me the moment we arrived, gliding away on *Duke*'s arm to hobnob with all your movie-star friends with-out even introducing me." He says Duke's name with disgust, and it angers me. I notice the sweat along his brow and the knotty mole on his chin. Annoyingly, even his mole is sexy.

"You're the one flirting the moment we came through the door. If anyone should be insulted, it's me."

"You walked away first."

"Pilar dragged me away."

"Then, tell me why we haven't been here before tonight? We've been invited, but you've always found an excuse not to come."

He knows I came tonight because of the possibility of a new movie role, but he wants to hear me say it. I don't feel like placating him. Instead, I stand up and take his hand, tug-ging gently. "Let's not fight. Dance with me."

A string band plays beside a wooden dance floor laid over the grass. Couples glide under strung yellow blubs shaped like sunlit tears. I want to join them, but Alfonso doesn't budge. He likes this power play, his childish, pouting act. Usually, I give in, pacify, apologize, giggle and smile and lure him into the bedroom reminding him of all the things I love about him.

Tonight, I have no desire to expend the energy he needs to feel good about himself.

I pick up my drink, finish it off and say, "Fine, I'll find someone else to dance with."

I do. There are plenty of dance partners, the blue-eyed bar-tender, for one, and I have no idea Alfonso has left without me until I stumble up to the driveway hours later and see that his Cadillac is gone. I shiver, suddenly aware of how cool it's gotten and how drunk I am.

Pilar, who has walked up the stone steps with me, puts an arm around my shoulder. "Don't worry about it, honey. You can stay here."

For the first time all night, I think of you, daughter. "No, thank you." I shake my head. "I'll call a taxi. I need to get home to Nina."

Only, I am too late.

Chapter Five

Hide and Crawl Away

Mother,

I am watching *Gunsmoke* when Alfonso stumbles into the living room, knocking into the side table and making such a racket that I miss the final question. I glare at him as he pours a drink from the bar cart. Grandmother Maria went to bed hours ago, her door closed against the sound of our television drifting down the hall.

"Where's Mom?" I ask, glancing toward the front door, which he forgot to close all the way.

He shrugs and sits sullenly in the orange chair. For a moment, I consider telling him that your last husband killed himself in that chair but decide against it. "I'm going to bed," I say, standing up. "Do you want the television on?"

He nods, and I leave him staring at a Campbell's Soup can dancing across the screen with little arms and legs waving out from it.

I put on my nightgown, a kitten print that I still love, and crawl into bed without brushing my teeth. I am tired, and I ate too much pie. My stomach has a distended, bloated feeling, and I roll onto my side and drift into an uncomfortable sleep. I don't know what time it is when I feel the weight of a body climbing into my bed, Alfonso's acrid mix of cologne and sweat and alcohol pulling me out of a dark dreamlessness. His hand is in my hair, his fingers tugging through the strands, and I can't understand why he's doing that, or why, when I open my eyes, I see him lying under my blanket. He moves his hand from my hair to my shoulder, and I go cold as his fingers trace my collarbone, stopping to rest in the divot below my neck. He presses slightly, and I wonder if he means to choke me. I want to scream, but I am paralyzed, my mouth frozen shut. Then I feel his penis through his pants, hard against my thigh. I don't know how I even know what it is, but I do. I want to throw up. I want to cry out for you, for my grandmother. Only, I can't. My twelve-year-old mind has nowhere to put this dreadful, unknowable thing. I squeeze my eyes shut, little pops of light bursting behind my lids, all of my neatly constructed boxes, my precise angles, flying apart.

Alfonso's breath is warm and wet against my neck, his fingers working their way to the bottom of my nightgown that he begins to edge up my leg. I should shove him away, tell him to stop, but I can barely gulp air into my lungs. My heart races, and my stomach seizes as he presses his hand between my legs.

And then, "Nina?"

My eyes shoot open as the light clicks on, the ceiling a blinding white above me. There is a throaty scream, your scream, and I struggle to sit up as Alfonso scrambles from the bed. You are standing in the doorway, your eyes startled wide. Your expression makes me think I have done something terrible and you will hate me for it.

Everything moves very quickly, the room nauseatingly bright. Alfonso is barely on his feet when Grandmother Maria's bulk shoves past you so quickly I can't imagine how she got out of bed that fast. She pulls me to my feet with a look I've never seen before. I feel skeletal and laid bare.

"Dios mio," she cries. "What have you done?" I think she is angry with me, but she shakes her fist at Alfonso, who pulls back, confused.

"What?" he says. "She cried out, and I was comforting her."

"You a sick, sick man!" Grandmother Maria spits at his feet. *"Fuera de aca, fuera!"*

She begins wailing, and Alfonso moves to the doorway where you stand with your hand clamped over your mouth. He reaches out as if to touch you, but your hand flies from your face and smacks his away. I want you to spit in his eye like Grandmother spat at his feet, but you just turn your head, and he slinks past into the hallway.

Grandmother Maria sits me on the edge of the bed, her cries trailing off to small groans, and you hurry over, sitting next to me and smoothing my hair out of my face.

"Did he hurt you?" you say, your voice weak as a thread.

I look into my hands, not knowing which kind of hurt you mean.

Reaching behind me, Grandmother Maria yanks back the covers and says, "There is no blood. Is your underwear still on?"

My face flames with embarrassment, and I don't answer, wishing Grandmother Maria would go away and let you handle this.

A silent exchange passes between the two of you, something fierce and personal. I don't know what it means, or who is angry with whom.

Your fingers are cool as ice as you take my hand and ease me back into bed. You don't make a joke or smile or try to sing the sadness away. That is how I know what has happened is catastrophic.

"Can you sleep?" you say. Such simple words.

I whisper "I think so," and you wince as though I've pinched you.

Grandmother Maria watches from the doorway, her shoulders pulled back as if trying to hold us all up with them.

You kiss my forehead, and Grandmother Maria clicks off the light. The room fills with shadows and shapes and a ringing silence. I want to hold on to you, but you slide your arm away and slip out the door into the dark hallway. I wonder if you are going to comfort Alfonso, and I think about shutting my door and pushing my chair under it in case he tries to come back. I wish you'd stayed and lain next to me singing songs into the darkness like you used to.

After a while I drift into a thin sleep, waking to the soft whisper of Grandmother Maria, her breath pungent in my face. "Come." She guides me to my feet, her hands gentler than when she'd pulled me from bed earlier.

Out the window, a pale strip of dawn leaks through the dark sky. I take the skirt and blouse my grandmother holds out, the stockings and shoes, and put them on without question. I am too tired to ask what we are doing. Grandmother Maria leads me out the front door, and we climb into the car. It isn't until I see my teal luggage in the back seat—*Nina Martinez* embossed above the Samsonite label—that I worry. "Where are we going?"

My grandmother is already backing out of the driveway. "School." She yanks the gear crank toward the steering wheel and takes off down the road with a screech of the tires. She always drives too fast.

"I'm not supposed to go back for another week," I protest but half-heartedly. School suddenly seems promising, an escape. I never want to see Alfonso again, and I am afraid to face you in the light of day, afraid of what you will think of me.

A breeze whistles through the cracked open window, and I lean my head against the glass and let the air caress my forehead. You want to be rid of me. That was the look that passed between you and Grandmother.

I would want to be rid of me, too.

Grandmother Maria doesn't like the freeway so we drive through Studio City and Toluca Lake on flat, wide roads lined with low buildings and large billboards where mustached men advertise Wilson cigarettes. In thirty minutes we are in Burbank, racing down the long driveway to Villa Cabrini Academy. The car circles the drive, and our brakes slam as we halt in front of the stone steps leading to the three arched doorways of the shaded portico.

Above the twisted columns, Jesus stands with his arms outstretched in welcome. But he is not the statue I pray to. On the hot, dusty lawn, flanked by stubby palms that look like overgrown pineapples, stands a ten-foot-tall statue of Mother Cabrini, a stone mantle frozen over her head. I do not believe in God, or Jesus, but I believe in that statue.

She was the first thing I saw from the back seat of the car when I arrived at Cabrini Academy as a little girl, squished next to Grandmother Maria who had strategically positioned herself between us, her fat thigh pinning me to the window. The sun beat off the stone figure, and the glare stung my eyes, but there was life in Mother Cabrini. I could see breath unfurling from her mouth like moisture in cold air. I decided right then and there that I would pray only to her, this larger-than-life statue of Mother Cabrini, and at night she'd kneel at my window, tall enough to see right in, and sing me to sleep like you used to.

Only today, in the shadow of a morning that doesn't feel

real, she looks lifeless. I stare into her huge, vacant eyes, wanting to make them shift and blink as I used to, but they don't move. She is just stone. There is nothing to pray to. No Mother.

My grandmother and I climb out of the car, dust and gravel embracing us as we make our way up the wide steps. Old Sister Katherine is at the door, circling her arms around my grandmother, her chin leaking from under her habit like soft rubber. Grandmother Maria must have called her the moment the gong sounded at 4:00 a.m. Humiliated to think that Sister Katherine knows what happened, I drop my eyes to the floor as we move inside where Sister Caroline—a woman I suspect is quite pretty beneath her shrouds—hugs my grandmother with the same, sorry look on her face as Sister Katherine. She gives me a sickly sweet smile. "Come. Let's get you settled in."

Upstairs, the dorm room smells of bleach so strong it smarts my eyes. It is strange being the only one here. The twin beds are stripped bare, the desk is a clean slate of wood, the hangers are empty in the closet. It reminds me of a deserted ghost town I once saw in a book, shells of houses with missing walls and neatly arranged, abandoned furniture.

Sister Caroline pats my shoulder, her eyes a delicate brown. "Your suitcases are being brought up, and you can unpack before breakfast. You'll get to eat with us in the dining room until the other girls arrive. Won't that be fun? I assure you—" she leans in with a hand propped on each knee as if speaking to a small child "—the coffee cake is worth the boredom of Sister Mary detailing every ailment she's ever had, but don't say I said so." She puts a conspiratorial finger to her lips, smiles and leaves Grandmother Maria and me to our goodbyes.

This is not the first time I've been left by my grandmother—when you were on set or singing in Palm Springs or at Radio City Music Hall—and yet the look on her face says that everything is different.

She plants a firm hand on each shoulder, holding me at arm's length and looking me sharply in the eye. "Last night had nothing to do with you. Do you understand?" It had everything to do with me, but I nod in agreement. "It's not your fault. There are wicked men in the world. Sometimes we stumble into their path, and there's nothing we can do but hurry on out of it. I'm going to fix this, I promise you that." She embraces me with strong arms. Her fleshy bosom and the smell of talc fill me with complicated sadness.

She doesn't let go until I do.

Chapter Six

Perimeters

Daughter,

When I wake I am covered in sweat and hot sunlight and my head is pounding. I have fallen asleep in my slip, and it sticks like tape to the inside of my legs. There is a sick feeling in my stomach, as if something awful has happened, but I don't remember what that is until I sit up.

I barely make it to the bathroom before I vomit over the toilet, strands of hair falling into my face. My stomach lurches over and over as if my body thinks it can purge the image of Alfonso in your bed. It can't. When I am emptied, I kneel on the bathroom floor, the tiles cool under my calves, my heart pounding, my hair sticky with bile. The house is silent, and I wonder where everyone is. I know I should find you straightaway, but I don't want you to see me like this so I pull myself to my feet and start the shower, stepping into scalding water and letting it pound over my face. I shampoo, condition, brush my teeth, towel dry my hair and lotion my face with the illusion that if I hold on to normalcy, I can defuse the severity of the situation.

I do not yet know that our lives have changed completely, and I will never be able to set things right.

Mamá's hushed and hurried voice drifts down the hall as I make my way to the kitchen still zipping the back of my dress. I think she is talking to you until I step into the room and see that she is on the telephone. Sunlight peppers the red speckled Formica tabletop and the backs of the empty chairs. You are nowhere in sight. The clock on the wall says ten fifteen. You never sleep this late, and I am about to go to your room when I hear muffled Spanish through the line. I take a step toward Mamá, but she turns her back, cupping the receiver to her mouth and hunching over as if I mean to grab the phone from her.

"*Si, si, adios,*" she says quickly and hangs up.

The only people Mamá speaks Spanish to other than me are in Cuba: Papa, who she calls on the first of each month, and my sisters, who she calls every Sunday.

It is not the first of the month or Sunday.

"Who was that? Where is Nina?"

The collected, steady look on Mamá's face worries me. I prop my arm against the counter, pour a glass of water, rinse and spit the lingering taste of vomit from my mouth into the sink. I see your face from last night, washed white under the shock of the overhead light, Alfonso scrambling from your bed, guilt writ large on his arresting face. I remember the strangled scream that escaped my throat, my body realizing that it had come upon a crisis even as I tried to convince myself it was a mistake and I had the wrong idea.

"Where is Nina?" I ask again, certain now that you are not here and neither is Alfonso.

Mamá faces me, legs apart, hands clasped, and I think of the time after the revolution when she handed me that plantain and told me to chop. She is ready to defend whatever it is she's done. *"Donde esta Nina?"* I repeat, my voice rising with frustration.

"At school."

"School? When did you take her?"

"Early this morning. I arranged it with Sister Katherine."

"Why didn't you tell me?"

"You were asleep."

"You could have woken me."

"I thought it best not to."

I refill my glass with tap water, drink it down, the cool expanding through my chest. I'm sorry I didn't have a chance to say goodbye but relieved that you are gone. I have no idea how to face this humiliation. I think of the blonde at Duke's party in her short, colorful dress and wish he'd gone home with her, cheated on me like a regular man, returning hangdog in the accusing light of day. Then I could have kicked him out properly. Told neighbors and friends he was unfaithful, and everyone would understand. What do I say now? He likes little girls. Children. My child. It sickens me to think of it.

Out the window over the sink, I watch a crow land on the fence post, screeching hideously. We will never talk about last night, I decide. No one can know. It will harm you, and me, more than it will harm him.

"Where is Alfonso?" I say, keeping my back to Mamá.

"In Hell, God willing."

I don't argue. "You haven't seen him this morning?"

"He was asleep on the couch when I left and gone when I got back."

"Who was on the phone?"

"Chu Chu."

I whirl around, the glass teetering on the edge of the

counter. "What? Why would you call Chu Chu? What did you tell him?"

"The truth."

"Why would you do that?"

This is what she's prepared to defend. She has called your father and my ex-husband, a man who made me choose either my career or him. I am trembling, the water I just drank sloshing around in my hollow stomach. The thought of your father knowing what kind of a man I brought into my house, into your life, drowns me in shame. No matter how small a role he has played in our lives over the years, his opinion still holds power over me. Mamá, sanctimonious and determined, moves from the window and sits at the table. I am reminded of the revolution, how my parents sat across from each other, stoic and calm in the face of tragedy. This is my tragedy, now, and I feel totally out of control.

"Why did you call Chu Chu?" I say, steadying my voice. "What can he possibly do?"

"He will kick Alfonso out of this house. His daughter's safety is in jeopardy, and if you are too pigheaded to see that, Chu Chu will make you."

I tingle with anger. "I can kick him out myself!"

"You haven't yet."

"It's barely morning! I just woke up!"

Mamá locks eyes with me, her voice low. "You should have kicked him out immediately."

"Thrown him into the street in the middle of the night?"

"Exactly."

"He slept on the couch."

"Not good enough."

A rage hits me, then turns on Mamá for being so rational, for being *right*, and then back at myself for being naive, but mostly the rage flies straight at Alfonso. I want to rip his hair out, claw his eyes. It amazes me to think how attracted to him I was last night, how envious I was of that girl he had his eye on. Now the thought of his flushed, drunken face rising from my daughter's bed revolts every part of me.

I storm from the kitchen and into our bedroom. I pull his clothes from the drawers and closet and smash them into a suitcase. I dump his toothbrush and shaving kit in, slam the top down. The suitcase bulges as I lean in to latch it. I curse as I do this, out loud, in Spanish, spitting and swearing as I drag the suitcase down the hall, through the kitchen, past Mamá—who sits exactly as I left her—and out the front door. I kick the heavy luggage down the stone path, hard, bruising my toe and wincing in pain. I kick it again. I don't care who sees. I'll tell the neighbors he slept with another woman, anyway. When Alfonso shows up, I'll scream the lie for everyone to hear. Damn him to hell.

Back inside, I slam and lock the door, catching a glimpse of my scrubbed-clean face in the mirror, my pale lips and showered hair that is drying into a frizzy puff. I take a deep breath, calming myself as I take a barrette from the hall table and secure my hair into a knot behind my head. I smile into the mirror, distorted, fake and then stick my tongue out at my reflection.

In the kitchen, I make coffee and ask Mamá if she would like a cup. *"Sí, por favor,"* she says and I take two cups from the cabinet.

I am rung out, exhausted and hungover.

The practical task of scooping coffee from the tin into boiled water, the smell and warmth of the cup in my hand, grounds me. I think of the role Duke has promised me, Consuela, the success filling me with a bloated excitement that allows me to push the events of last night to the dark edge of my mind.

There it will become an outline, a perimeter, thin as a pencil mark, erasable with time, and we will never speak of it. I will call you tonight, tell you that Alfonso is gone and that I love you, and that will be that.

Chapter Seven

Chu Chu

Mother,

Except, that night stays between us, sharp and tender as if carved into me with the point of a knife. And when you call, you forget to tell me that it wasn't my fault, that I did nothing wrong and that you forgive me.

What I think, when you hang up, is that I have ruined your marriage and that you will marry again, and this time you will make sure I am never around.

Behind the front desk, Sister Katherine takes the buzzing receiver from my hand, looking uncomfortable as she drops it back into its cradle. She shifts her eyes so they don't meet mine and asks if there's anything I need.

So many things, I think but say, "I'm fine, thank you." I make my way upstairs to the bathroom, the empty hallways echoing and ghostly, the vacant rooms with their wide-open doors: frightful, dead spaces. It is creepy being here by myself. I'd take Sister Katherine's company over the emptiness, but she does not have personal relationships with the girls.

It is one thing to talk over our heads at assembly or lecture us in front of a classroom, another to face a single, damaged girl head-on.

I brush my teeth, splash my face with cold water and return to my room, leaving the door open. One of the sisters has made up the bed while I was at dinner, and I slide under the starched sheet and pull the blanket over my head. My room still smells of bleach and cleaning detergent, but my window is open, and the air is finally cool. In the distance, I hear a steady swish of cars and wonder what it would feel like to run away. It is satisfying to imagine how much you would miss me, how sorry you'd be.

On the phone, you told me you kicked Alfonso out, and I want to believe you, but I am sure Grandmother Maria made you do it. This should make me love my grandmother more, but it doesn't; it makes me angrier, proves that you'll do whatever she says. I hate that you don't know how to protect me without her.

Pulling up my knees, I roll onto my side and squeeze myself into a tight ball thinking I may never sleep again as I try to forget the wet warmth of Alfonso's breath in my face, his fingers on my neck and his stiff, gross penis against my thigh. Instead, I focus on the feel of Grandmother Maria's firm hands on my shoulders, her deep-set eyes on mine, the even tone in which she said she'd take care of it, and within minutes my thoughts break apart, and I drop into a heavy sleep.

The nuns don't wake me. When I finally drag myself from bed the next morning, my room is bright and the city noisy with traffic. Not being woken at the crack of dawn is one advantage of being the only girl at school. That and the fact that I don't have to wear my uniform. I put on the checkered skirt and blouse I wore yesterday and go downstairs to the large, industrial kitchen where a cook wearing a cap shaped like a paper boat is wiping down the metal countertop. She is old, the hair sticking out around her neck lavender white.

"That's for you." She nods at a plate of eggs and toast. "Rinse the plate in the sink when you're done," she says, tossing her rag in the sink and leaving me to eat alone. I had hoped she would stay. The disadvantage of being the only girl here is how lonely it is.

I decide not to eat in the cold, chrome kitchen. I hate eggs, anyway so I scrape them into the garbage bin, rinse the plate and leave with a slice of buttered wheat toast clutched in each hand.

The library is where I spend the next three days. The chairs are stiff and uncomfortable, but I prefer the colossal ceilings and wood-paneled walls to the bright white box of my dorm room.

It is midmorning on Wednesday, while I sit reading *Jane Eyre* at a table slick with fresh polish, when the loudspeaker crackles my name, calling me to the front desk. I shut my book and slide back my chair, the legs scraping the floor and echoing against the vaulted ceiling. It seems ridiculous to be called over the loudspeaker when I'm the only student in the building, but I suppose the nuns don't know where to find me. My only interaction with them has been at dinnertime and morning prayer, where they treat me delicately, clearly confused how to handle a girl who's been *molested*—a word I will learn years later, not from you or Grandmother Maria but from my psychology professor in a class on post-traumatic stress disorder.

For now, I think what happened is singular and freakish, something that has only ever happened to me and that I did something wicked to bring it on myself.

As I approach the front desk, I see a man leaning against it, impeccably dressed in a white suit jacket and pants, a white fedora with black ribbon trim tilted forward on his head. Behind him stands Sister Katherine, smiling widely, her mouth all teeth.

The man turns, and I stop as if I've run smack into something, my mind scrambling to make sense of why my father is standing in the entryway of Villa Cabrini Academy. My father has never stepped foot in my school before, or shown up anywhere in my life unannounced, and the only thing I can come up with is that something terrible has happened. There's been an accident. *You are dead*, I think, and my heart accelerates with irrational fear. Only, my father is smiling, walking toward me with his arms raised as if he means to embrace me. Chu Chu—I have never called him Dad—is as handsome as you are beautiful. His skin gleams as if he's had a recent facial, and his eyes blink rapidly like someone caught in a lie.

"Nina!" He embraces me, and I fall stiffly against his chest, my arms pinned to my sides, my nose pressed into the lapel of a coat that smells of cigars and something faintly sweet, like honeysuckle.

My father and I do not have a hugging relationship, and when he releases me, I am more certain than ever that the worst has happened. "What is it? What's wrong? Where's Mom?"

Chu Chu pulls back, surprised. "Something has to be wrong for me to visit my daughter?"

"No," I mumble, dropping my gaze to the tops of his white pants with their perfectly ironed crease down the middle.

He gives my shoulder a gentle shake that irritates me. "Is this any way to greet your father? I thought a surprise visit would delight you."

"It does. It's fine."

"Well, all right, then." He yanks the bottom of his coat into place. "I'm taking you to lunch."

He turns on his heels, his movements crisp, sharp and deliberate. He walks past Sister Katherine, who gives us a little wave. "Have a lovely time."

None of this makes sense, but I hurry to follow him, knowing that if my father is here to take me to lunch, he'll do exactly that. Chu Chu Martinez is a man of few words and zero explanations, a famous singer in Mexico who visits me once a year when it coincides with his US tour. He was just here two months ago, in June. He brought me packages from Mexico, stuffed with gaudy dresses I'd never wear and took me to lunch at a restaurant with chandeliers and waiters in white jackets who laid a napkin in my lap and refilled my water the moment I took a sip. *Snobby*, you said and laughed when I described it to you later. We prefer diners with greasy fries and apple pie à la mode. But Chu Chu has no idea what we prefer.

Once he must have known what you liked, but you never speak about him, and when he visits, you are nowhere around. This is either because you still love him and it hurts, or because you hate him and it hurts. I've never asked which. Once I found a photograph of the three of us: you and Chu Chu kneeling in front of a Christmas tree with plump baby me on your lap. Chu Chu's arm was around you, and you were smiling. But people always smile for photos, so this doesn't mean much.

I follow my father into the portico and down the stairs to a car that waits with the engine running. A driver in a black cap leans against the bumper, righting himself as we approach. He opens the back door, and I slide onto the cool leather seat and lean my elbow out the window. The sky is white hot, the sun ablaze.

We pull away, and I keep my eye on Mother Cabrini, that boneless mass of stone. I wonder if I love her more not being real; she looks immutable and dependable and indestructible.

All the things you, Mom, and I are not.

Chapter Eight

Gone

Daughter,

From the porch I hear the telephone ringing while I fumble with my keys. It is getting dark. The porch light is off, and I can't see a thing. The phone was ringing when I got out of the car, then it stopped, and now it's started up again. The lock finally gives way, and I hurry into the kitchen and snatch it up. "Hello?" I gasp. "Hello?" but I am too late and there is only static.

I hang up, my purse sliding from my arm to the floor. There's something nerve-racking about someone hanging up right when you pick up. I'm later than I intended, and it's unusual for Mamá not to be home. Clicking on the light, I pick up my purse and pull out the signed contract for *Rio Bravo*, with *Warner Bros Pictures* stamped in gold at the top. I am supposed to meet Dean Martin, Duke and Angie Dickinson at Romanoff's in an hour to celebrate. I was hoping to have a glass of champagne with Mamá beforehand. Where is she?

I prop the contract against the crystal vase on the table, picturing Mamá's face when she sees it. A part of me wishes this was old hat and I didn't feel so gaga over the new role, but Mamá and I are banking everything on this picture. Duke told me about the emergency meetings last week at Republic Studios. Things aren't looking good. If the studio goes under, my contract with them is bunk. I'll have to return to singing full-time, which wouldn't be too bad but a step backward nonetheless. *Rio Bravo*, on the other hand, is a gigantic leap forward.

The phone rings again, startling me, and I pick it up. "Hello?" I stretch the cord over the kitchen table and reach for the bag of bread on the counter. "Hello?" There is no answer, and I wonder if Alfonso is harassing me. I haven't seen him since the day I kicked him out. He came home that afternoon—sheepish but unapologetic—took one look at the stuffed suitcase in the driveway and told me I was acting crazy. He insisted he'd done absolutely nothing wrong and that if I was going to kick him out, he'd take me for all I've got. "Go ahead and try," I'd spat at him.

Through the receiver I finally hear, "Is this Mrs. Rodriguez?"

"Yes."

"It's Sister Katherine."

"Oh, hello, Sister." I pull a slice of bread from the bag and take a bite, chewing discreetly. "Is everything all right? I hope Nina isn't in trouble." I've been worried that you might act out but hoped you'd at least wait until the other girls arrived.

"No, no, she's not in trouble, exactly. It's just that..." her voice trails off. I've never liked Sister Katherine. She is grim and vague and has never had anything good to say about you.

"I'm so sorry, but what exactly can I help you with? I don't have much time. I have a dinner reservation."

Sister Katherine clears her voice. "I'm sure there's nothing to worry about, it's just that her father hasn't brought her back yet, and it is getting late."

I choke on my bread and sputter. "Her father? What do you mean her father?"

"Chu Chu Martinez." Sister Katherine sounds confused. "He was here this morning. Mr. Martinez said he'd just seen you, and he was making a last stop to take Nina to lunch before heading home."

This lie sends a cold slice of fear down my spine. Why say he's seen me when he hasn't? I drop the remainder of my bread on the counter, following the swirls of gray-and-white tile with my eyes. "What time did he take her?"

"A little after eleven this morning."

"Did he say where they were going?"

"No."

"You didn't ask?"

"Well, no." Sister Katherine takes on her best schoolteacher voice. "He's her father."

"Has her father ever shown up at school to take her to lunch before?" I shout, not letting her answer before saying, "Call me the instant he brings her back." I move back across the kitchen to slam the phone down, look at the clock and do some quick math. What could you and Chu Chu possibly be doing for nine hours? The telephone book sticks in the drawer as I yank it out, tearing the front cover. Thumbing through it, I find a number for the Chateau Marmont, but when I call, they say there's no reservation under Chu Chu Martinez, and he hasn't stayed there since June.

I close my eyes, praying Mamá has something to do with this.

When she returns, it is after nine o'clock. I've canceled dinner and spent the last hour calling every LA restaurant where Chu Chu has ever dined. I've called his booking agent and everyone else I could think of.

"Where have you been?" I rush at Mamá as she comes through the door.

"Goodness, what's wrong with you?" She takes a step back, pulling off her gloves and tucking them into her purse. "I was at the movies."

I tell her what's happened, my hands moving rapidly, spit flying from my mouth. "Have you spoken to Chu Chu? Did he tell you anything?"

Mamá stands very still. Her eyes are on me, and I don't like the look in them. "This is not good," she says quietly, taking a deep breath, her chest bulging against her jacket as she walks past me into the living room. She drops onto the narrow arm of the couch in a compromised, awkward position.

"Why? What do you know?" I follow her, hovering, hoping for some impossible good news.

She shakes her head. "All I know is that Chu Chu is a calculating man. If he hasn't returned her, I'm not sure he means to."

A strangling sensation pinches my rib cage. "What do we do?" I cry, needing Mamá to snap to her feet and put everything back together.

Only, she sinks farther forward, her knees oddly bent, her eyes on the floor. "We wait. Either he will bring her back, or he won't."

No, no, no, I want to scream. This is not a solution. I wonder if my mother is weakening because she believes this is her fault. *It is,* I think bitterly. She should never have called him.

I move to the window hoping by some miracle that you and Chu Chu will step out of the darkness. Under the patio lights, the bushes around the pool shudder and bend in the wind. Pool water ripples, and dust blows across the stones, but no one steps from the shadows. I drive my fingers through my hair, scraping my nails against my scalp as I tell myself Chu Chu is doing this to teach me a lesson, to frighten me, but that he wouldn't dare keep you out all night.

Chapter Nine

Faults

Mother,

The car picks up speed and the statue of Mother Cabrini disappears from sight as we race down Cohasset Street. It feels indulgent and devious to be whisked away from the boring old nuns by my enigmatic father. His attention, however lacking, has always made me feel important, and since he's never taken me out of school before, it makes all of this especially exciting. Grandmother Maria grumbles about his neglect, and you complain that he could show a *little* more interest, but I'll take what I can get.

There was a brief time when I thought I missed Chu Chu, when I wished he'd visit more often. When I was little and he showed up, I wanted to cling to him and make him stay. I was certain he had something to offer. But over the years, I realized it was the idea of a father that I missed. A father you depended on. This man who came once a year had nothing to offer besides gifts and candy, and after he left I stopped feeling sad. I never knew this father well enough to miss him, or long for him. Over the years, our annual luncheons became a nice holiday with an indulgent relative, a day to look forward to, like a birthday, which makes today like a fortuitous gift.

I pull my head in from the window, glancing at my father as he gazes out the opposite one.

"Roll it up. The air-conditioning is on," he says, not looking at me.

I crank the window closed and feel a leaky bit of cool air coming from the front. Not enough to warrant shutting us in.

"Where are we going for lunch?" I bounce a little in my springy seat.

Chu Chu removes his hat to his knees, his eyes fixed out the window. "What are you in the mood for?"

"A hamburger."

"I know just the place." His voice is cold, and I think I've displeased him.

"Or whatever you want," I say quickly.

"No." He shakes his head. "A hamburger is perfect."

After that we are silent as the car weaves through the city streets. We pass numerous restaurants but don't stop at any of them. By the time we are headed south on 101, I think Chu Chu must know of a special hamburger place near Santa Monica. I like the idea of eating with a view of the ocean, maybe even out on a pier.

Traffic is slow, and we drive for an hour before getting off on Sepulveda Boulevard. The car is stuffy, and I am grateful when it pulls to a stop. The driver lets us out onto a crowded curb, handing Chu Chu a leather traveling bag. I look around at the people unloading suitcases and trunks, confused as I realize that we are at the airport. I have only been here once before, when you took me to New York City for winter break.

"Where are we going?" I ask, following Chu Chu through a set of double glass doors.

The airport lobby is crowded, and Chu Chu pushes past a

man with a plaid suitbag thrown over one shoulder. "Excuse me," the man says rudely, but my father doesn't give him a backward glance as he makes his way to the front of the line and slaps a large, folded bill on the counter. I miss what he says to the brightly smiling woman behind the counter, because a woman at the front of the line says loudly, "Who do you think you are?" as she cuts her eyes at me and ticks a finger at Chu Chu's back.

My father shoots her a hard look that makes her snap her pink mouth shut and look away.

Behind the counter, the woman's smile changes to a sly, disapproving one. "Next time, wait your turn," she says with a flirty wink, taking my father's money and handing him two strips of white paper with black lettering.

At this point, Chu Chu circles his hand around my upper arm, firmly, and I am pulled alongside him as we make our way deeper into the airport. I glance back at the line of people blocking my view of the doors, feeling claustrophobic and panicky.

"I need to make a phone call," I say quickly, and my father releases my arm as suddenly as he took hold of it.

"Certainly, let's just have a bite to eat first. I'm starving."

My breath settles as I see that we are in front of a restaurant with square tables abutting large windows that look out onto the tarmac.

Chu Chu smiles. "Not the most glamorous dining, but since you wanted a hamburger and I need to make an early flight, thought this would serve us both."

Feeling foolish, I follow him to a table and sit down. For a moment, I thought he meant to drag me onto an airplane with him. Out the huge windows, brilliant flashes of light glint off the metal wings of a plane with a massive red W painted on the side. A line of people in clean-cut suits and tailored dresses make their way cautiously down the steps, holding the side rails as if maneuvering down a mountainside.

I'm starving, and the restaurant smells temptingly of baked cookies. A hefty waitress in a starched yellow apron pours my father a cup of coffee and scratches my order on a pad of paper. My father doesn't eat, just drinks his coffee while watching me consume a hamburger and french fries and suck down a watery chocolate milk, which is not as good as the ones I usually get. He says nothing, and I wonder why he's bothered to take me out at all. Maybe he's counting this as next summer's obligatory visit, getting it over with early. I think of the long drive back to school and wonder if I can trick the driver into taking me home instead. If Alfonso is really gone, it will be like the year after Grant died, when it was just you, me and Grandmother Maria.

Thinking of Alfonso suddenly makes me wonder if my father's visit has anything to do with what happened. I drop my straw into my glass, my stomach somersaulting at the idea. There's no way you told him. Why would you? Chu Chu has never had anything to do with what goes on in our lives.

Chu Chu glances at his wristwatch. "Don't want to miss my flight." He tosses money on the table, swigs the rest of his coffee and rises, pulling out my chair for me. "My lady," he smiles, and we leave the restaurant and head through another set of glass doors into a blast of heat that sucks the breath out of me, the air full of fumes.

"Walk me to my seat," he says. It is not a question.

"Is your driver still waiting for me?"

"Of course."

I walk hesitantly in his shadow, across the sweltering tarmac and up the narrow stairs, the metal railing hot under my palm. Through the clamshell door, the cabin is warm and dimly lit. Each seat has a curtained window that's been drawn shut and gives the cabin a reddish glow.

"Try it out." Chu Chu nods at a cushy window seat, and I plop down, pulling the curtain aside as a high-pitched whirring sound fills the air, and I see a plane hurtle down the runway and lift into the air.

My father drops into the seat next to me as a stewardess in a blue skirt suit with a matching pillbox hat asks if he'd like something to drink.

"Tequila," he orders. "On the rocks."

"And you, my dear?" She turns her head toward me.

"Nothing, thank you. I'm not staying."

She laughs as if I've said something charming, and my father says, "She'll have a pineapple juice."

I don't want pineapple juice. The plane is filling with people, and I begin to feel uneasy. "I'm in someone's seat." I move to get up, but my father clamps his hand on my thigh, his fingers hard as steel. I immediately think of Alfonso's hand, softer, but just as frightening.

"You are not going anywhere," he says under his breath, his hard, dark eyes on mine.

Panic leaps inside me, and I claw the back of his hand.

"Jesus!" my father hisses, pulling his hand away. I have scratched a line of blood into his skin.

"I am not going anywhere with you," I say, loudly. "I'll scream. I'll tell them you're kidnapping me."

He scoots forward, angling his body to block my view of the aisle. "Nina." There is quiet terror in the way he says my name. "I am your father. There is nothing anyone can do about that."

"Well, you don't own me. You've never even cared about me." At that moment, there is a grinding and rumbling so loud I can hardly hear myself speak. "Why are you doing this?

I don't want to go with you." My heart thunders against my ribs, and my breath comes so fast I feel light-headed. *I can't go up in this plane*, I think madly.

Over the commotion of the engine, my father leans closer and says, "It's what your mother wants. She asked me to take you."

I jerk back against the seat as if he's slapped me, this blow of betrayal vibrating through my whole body as the plane moves slowly forward. We pick up speed, and the pressure flattens me to the seat as if the air has weight to it. The airplane lifts, and my stomach drops, the engine roar deafening. I grip the armrests and close my eyes, wanting to be furious at you for sending me away but feeling only terrified that I will never see you again. I don't want to go to Mexico. I have never been my father's daughter. I have only ever been yours. I don't know how to be anyone else's.

Chapter Ten

Mexico City

Daughter,

It is still dark when I step out the front door, easing the latch down so it doesn't make a sound. I run my tongue along the roof of my mouth as I lug my suitcase down the steps and drag it half a block to where a cab waits with the engine running. A sick taste lingers in my mouth, a taste that has accompanied everything since you disappeared. The cab pulls away from the curb, and despite the darkness, I slide sunglasses out of my purse and over my eyes, dimming the streetlights to faded orbs and buildings into amorphous shadows.

My whole life I've woken most mornings with a sense of anticipation, forward motion, momentum. With each success, I've imagined there is a bigger one waiting for me, the lure of possibility driving me determinedly from one undertaking to the next. I feel that now. Even though I've hardly slept or eaten in the one month, three days and nine hours since the police told me Chu Chu Martinez took you on an airplane to Mexico, your kidnapping has filled me with the same sense of determination and fight.

The police gave me no choice but to take matters into my own hands. From the outset they were uncooperative. In maddeningly efficient, businesslike tones, they informed me that, because Mr. Martinez was legally your father and you were now out of their jurisdiction, there was nothing they could do.

I spent weeks dialing Chu Chu's number, standing in our Los Angeles kitchen with the telephone pressed to my ear, picturing the rooms where the endless ringing was echoing on the other end of the line, rooms I once lived in, though it feels like a lifetime ago. No matter how hard I tried, I couldn't picture you there, and no one ever picked up.

Then, three days ago, the call went through to an operator. "Sorry, ma'am. The number has been disconnected." I screamed at the poor girl and slammed the phone down.

My taxi pulls to a stop, and the driver helps me out, leaving my bag on the curb as I pay him. Waving over a skycap, I have him carry my luggage into the busy lobby, my eyes still secured behind my sunglasses. I do not remove them at the counter, or at the restaurant overlooking the runway while I drink a black coffee, or even after I've settled into my airplane seat where the stewardess serves me a Bloody Mary from a silver tray, the olive and celery stick stabbed through with a toothpick sharp enough to draw blood.

Not until I step from the cabin into the fierce sunlight at Central Aeropuerto do my sunglasses serve their intended purpose. I am tipsy from the cocktail, and I lean against the top rail of the stairway wishing I'd eaten more than a tin of peanuts. The last time I walked across this tarmac you were eighteen months old, balanced on my hip, the smell of sour milk and baby powder coming from your soft toddler head, your tiny hands and feet latched to my side. You reminded me of the Cuban tree frogs that Danita and I used to watch suction their way up palm fronds in our backyard. I always wondered at babies who sat limp and trusting on their mothers' hips. Not you. From the start you put your whole, small body into the act of being hoisted into the air, tensing every muscle, latching on for dear life. An unexpected sob rises in my throat. Why did you do that? I would never have dropped you.

I stand paralyzed as people maneuver around me and down the stairs. My plan feels ridiculous now that I've arrived. The only person who knows I'm in Mexico City is Edward Adelman, my short, bald, fiercely Jewish manager. He was the one who taught me, at nineteen, that his job was to be as tough as a pit bull, while mine was to be sweet as cream pie, and that no matter what happened on the set, in his office or anywhere else, my job was to smile while his was to bite.

Marching into his office two days ago, my hair a mess and not a stitch of makeup on my face, I told him—not smiling—that this cream pie had had enough. "There's no way in goddamn blazing hell I'm going off to shoot *Rio Bravo* with my daughter kidnapped!" I was certain he wasn't going to help me, like everyone else. Friends kept saying how sorry they are, with no urgency behind their concern. Underneath their empathy I could see they all thought I was being histrionic. *He is your daughter's father*, they would emphasize, as if this somehow gave Chu Chu a right to take you from me when the man has never played a serious role in your life until now.

As I expected, Ed felt the same, remaining infuriatingly calm while he told me not to get so worked up. "Look at it from all sides," he'd said, "Mr. Martinez taking Nina for a while might be to our benefit. He is her father, so it's not exactly kidnapping," at which point I turned into the pit bull, calling him presumptive and arrogant and inhuman, knuckling my hands into his desk, ready to swat his sweaty, bald head if he said one more word. I told him I was going after you and that he was to wait for my call and send help the moment it came or there'd be no picture contract. I also said that when my mother called, which she would, he was to tell her that I was sorry, but I wasn't going to have her talking me out of this, either. Ed sighed deeply and shook his head at me but agreed to do what he could to help.

I feel badly I didn't tell your *abuela* my plan, but we both know how she can talk me in, or out, of anything. She loves you as I do, but she's too rational for this. While I wasted the past month calling a number no one ever intended picking up, she was on the phone with lawyers. She said it might take longer than we wanted, but the legal route would get you back. I didn't have the nerve to tell her it wouldn't, that I'd royally screwed up eleven years ago when I signed the divorce papers and agreed to fifty-fifty custody. How was I to know Chu Chu would suddenly want you at twelve years old? When I signed those papers, your father was in Mexico, single again and happy not to be raising a child. He'd gotten over my running off on him as soon as the first new woman walked into his life. His yearly visits suited all of us, until now.

"Señorita?" I jump as an older gentleman takes my elbow. He is lean and tan with a stylish panama hat pulled low over his forehead. "May I? These steps are tricky." The other passengers have left the plane, and I let him guide me down the steep, narrow stairs and across the paved tarmac, his firm hold making me suddenly miss my father, a prideful, controlling man, but one who protected us at all costs.

Inside the terminal the air is stale and smells of damp rugs. The man lets go of my arm, and I thank him, watching him move into the crowd where a woman in a wide, purple skirt greets him with a hug. I feel hopelessly lost here, on my own. I'm not used to being without a man. As I watch passengers swept into arms, kissed on the cheek and ushered by loved ones down the corridor where the skycaps place luggage on a long counter, I think of Alfonso, how stupidly I loved him, how quickly and shockingly he disappeared from my life. Guilt churns my stomach as I think how much I miss him.

Retrieving my suitcase, I tip the skycap and climb into a white-topped, orange-colored taxi, urging the driver to the Gran Hotel Ciudad de Mexico, the only hotel I can remember from living here so long ago.

There is little traffic, and my driver is in no hurry, waiting patiently behind slow-moving buses, amiably letting pedestrians cross while he leans out the window to shout at a fellow taxi driver. His Spanish dialect is hard to understand, and I only catch fragments of what he says.

I haven't slept much in days, but I am alert with fear and anticipation running electric-hot under my skin as I watch the low-slung buildings and open-air markets give way to pillared civic buildings and baroque-style cathedrals, the city grittier but still more beautiful than Los Angeles. Not until we drive lazily past the Metropolitan Cathedral—stretched out like a dragon showing off its scales, its stone facade and intricate portals glinting in the sunlight—do memories burst to the surface.

I am eighteen years old, riding in a cab just like this one with Chu Chu's arm around my shoulder. At six weeks old, you are curled like a snail against my chest. I cup a hand over your head, your fuzz of black hair soft as kitten fur, and I'm struck with awe at my love for you, for my husband and for this vibrant, alive city. It's the same awe I felt entering the Copacabana at fifteen as a headlining singer with a bizarre sense that all of it was natural, expected, anticipated and yet totally surreal.

As a young mother and bride, I arrive at a wide street lined with jacaranda and enter a three-story building with high windows and glass doors opening onto large balconies. The house is pleasantly cool, filled with breeze and light and color, the smell of chili and cinnamon drifting from an unseen kitchen. There is a maid, Rosa, who wears a frilly-topped apron and takes you gently from my arms. She leads us upstairs to a nursery decorated in yellow, where a rocking horse and dollhouse wait under their respective windows. You are so tiny and immobile it is hard for me to imagine that you will ever play with these toys. Rosa places you in a cradle, and Chu Chu draws me into the adjoining room with pastel walls and a honey-colored bed.

Holding me with one arm, he shuts and locks the door, then peels my clothes off, slow and deliberate, as if introducing himself to me for the first time, his eyes taking in the full measure of my new vulnerability. We make love as evening sunlight melts around us, and I melt with it, into your father, into this life of his.

I loved your father. That is the truth of it. I first set eyes on him at the Copacabana. He was on stage crooning "Solamente una vez" into the microphone with puckered lips, his eyelids at a sultry droop. I'd been singing at the Copa for five months and had never heard anything so beautiful. Sometimes I wonder which I fell in love with: the song or the man? That night, he pulled the crowd into a standing ovation and two encores. When I spotted him in the lobby later, surrounded with admirers, I gave him an audacious wink. In an instant he'd crossed the room, drawn me around the side of a fake palm and was kissing me, urgently, my back pressed up against the scales of the cardboard tree trunk. Every inch of me tightened and quivered. Heat pulsed in my chest, part terror, part aching desire. I was sixteen and had never been kissed.

After that, I'd wait for Chu Chu backstage, slipping past the Copacabana girls with their plumed hats and slit, satin gowns, their pedestal legs visible all the way to their thighs. Chu Chu would sing his last number, throw a kiss to the crowd and come find me in the dressing room, where I'd pretend to be checking my costume for the next night or looking for a missing lipstick. He'd come up from behind with a rose he'd plucked from another singer's vase and press it against my chest, the flower tickling my chin, his hand between my breasts. When he first locked the door and pulled me onto the dressing room sofa, the sensation of his body pressed against mine sucked every thought from my head. Sex was like being devoured, swallowed whole and then brought back gasping for air and tingling with new life.

Mamá warned me, "Whatever you do, don't fall in love. Love's the worst thing that can happen to a woman who wants something more than babies."

No amount of warning would have mattered.

My memories dissolve as the cab lurches to a stop, startling me into the present.

"We're here, Señorita." The driver slides into Neutral and throws his arm over the back of the seat, turning to me.

The hotel is a massive corner building, more French in style than Spanish, with wrought iron balconies and miniature pillars flanked by arched windows. People move through the revolving glass door looking elegant and busy and important, and it occurs to me that I can't possibly stay here. Chu Chu is sure to have the whole city watching for me, and if you want to be invisible, the Gran Hotel Ciudad de Mexico is not a discreet place to stay.

"Can you recommend something smaller? Off the beaten track?" I ask, sorry to lose what I am sure is a heavenly soft bed.

"Not your style, Señorita?"

"No." I smile, and he smiles back.

"Mine, either."

A short ride later we pull up in front of a modest, stucco building in a residential section of the city where I have never been. Three barefoot children sit on the curb kicking glass bottles into the gutter, and a man, lingering in the open doorway of a small grocery store, watches them with a wistful smile as if remembering his bottle-kicking days.

"Is this it?" There's no sign of a hotel.

"You said 'off the beaten track.'" My driver is already out of the car and placing my suitcase on the sidewalk.

I climb out after him. "Is it safe?"

"Maybe safer, for you, than the Gran Hotel?" He raises his eyebrows, and I pay him quickly, paranoid in my exhaustion that Chu Chu has every taxi driver in the city on the lookout for me. I don't know what Chu Chu will do if he finds out I am in Mexico City. Hide you, my girl, in a place where I'll never find you? He may have done that already.

I watch the taxi merge into the traffic before dragging my suitcase through the front door of the building that does, once inside, look like a shabby motel. Keys dangle from a nail behind a low counter and I can see a small, open kitchen in the back where a very pregnant woman with hard lines around her mouth presses tortillas, a cracker-thin stack beside her, creamy yellow and steaming. I ring the bell on the counter, and the woman looks up, her hands balling dough, her face unreadable. She turns back to her work as a man enters through a door behind her.

He looks me up and down. *"Hola, Señorita."* His dark face is wide and round, his black hair cut short to his head. "Are you looking for a room?"

I press my sunglasses hard against the bridge of my nose. "Yes."

"How many nights?"

A simple question, and it stupefies me. The realization that I have no idea collides with my exhaustion. I lean against the counter staring at the man in silence.

He glances at my suitcase. "You want to pay for one night now, more if you need later?"

"No, no, I'll pay for seven," I decide and snap open my purse.

Tiny creases appear at the corners of the man's eyes. His grin is delightful. "If you say so, Señorita. Three hundred and fifty pesos."

I count out an exact amount, relieved I had the wherewithal to exchange my money back in LA. I also brought my checkbook, but that won't do me any good here. The man folds the bills into his pants pocket, takes a key from the wall and comes around the counter. He is only a foot taller than I am, with a broad chest, sturdy arms and large hands, one of which he extends. "Miguel Espino."

"Estelita Rodriguez."

His wide palm consumes mine, and I remove my sunglasses as he gives a gentle squeeze that sends a tingle up my legs. I feel disoriented and annoyingly attracted to this stranger. Mamá accuses me of being attracted to the first man I meet the moment I am without one. She might be right, I think, watching Miguel throw my suitcase up onto one shoulder, the arm he latches over it a ridge of muscle. If there was ever a time not to be thinking about a man, this would be it.

Not bothering to divert my eyes, I follow him outside and around the building to an open courtyard set with metal tables and chairs. The circular edges of the tables are rusted with chipped red paint. Off the courtyard, Miguel wiggles a key into a door that falls open and hits the opposite wall with a thud. The room is stiflingly hot and smells as if it's been shut up for an age, but it's clean. The speckled tile floor is polished, and there is a brightly embroidered coverlet tucked around a double bed. Nightstand, lamp and dresser appear dust free, and the single window where the curtains have been drawn against the sunlight look freshly washed. A fan rotates from the ceiling with a slow, clacking noise as it pushes the hot air around.

Miguel sets my suitcase at the foot of the bed. "Is there anything else you need, Señorita Rodriguez? My sister opens the restaurant at four, but I'm sure she'd make you something now if you're hungry."

"No, thank you, I'm all right." I should eat, but all I want is to lie down and sleep for an eternity.

When Miguel leaves, I kick off my shoes and stand on the bed, teetering to keep my balance as I pull at the cord to stop the fan. I'll take heat over that sound. The fan moves slower and slower as I collapse on the thin, hard mattress, its *clack, clack, clack* quieting as I think about how Miguel said *sister* not *wife*, chiding myself immediately. I need to put him out of my head. I am not going to let myself get distracted by a man.

Regardless, I fall asleep thinking about kissing the tiny creases around his eyes.

When I wake, I am still heavy with exhaustion, as if I've only slept for a tantalizing few minutes. My neck perspires against the pillow, and moisture has collected under the seams of my tight girdle, sweat stains seeping into my dress. The curtain flutters, and a breeze shifts the hairs on my arm. It is strangely quiet, and I wonder if you feel this same breeze, if your room is as silent in this city as mine.

I picture you in the yellow nursery with the rocking horse and dollhouse set under each window as if Chu Chu has been waiting all this time to snatch you back. At first, I convinced myself that your father kidnapped you out of impulsive anger, that he had no intention of keeping you for good. Now, I worry that for good is exactly what he intends.

Doubt and fear wash over me, and I struggle out of bed and over to the window for a breath of air. What if I can't find you? I pull back the fabric of the curtain and stare into the courtyard. In the dark, the tables look like hunched men about to spring off of skinny legs. Chu Chu is a rich man, which makes him a powerful one. He will have the airports guarded, the bus stations, every corner of this city.

Even if I find you, how will I ever get you out?

Chapter Eleven

The Taste of Tequila

Mother,

My room is a creepy baby's room frozen in time. The walls
are pale yellow, and everything looks aged and smells faintly
of rose water. Past the faded orange curtains there is a park
filled with trees and pathways where people walk and bike
and stroll with baby carriages. I am not locked in; I just don't
want to go outside.

When I'm not in school, I sit on my floor peeling thin strips
of paint from the walls, snaking white veins through my solid,
lemon-yellow room. I like that it doesn't come off in whole
chunks but in ribbons that I pile under my bed like Christmas wrapping. If things get bad enough, I can eat it and it
will make me sick, and then you will have to bring me home.

The night we arrived here, Chu Chu stood in the doorway
of this room with his too-tight hand on my shoulder and told
me that, other than the twin bed, the room looks exactly as
it did when I was a baby and you and I lived here with him.
You never told me I lived in Mexico City. This makes me
wonder what else you haven't told me.

It's a stupid room for a twelve-year-old. There are no books, just a chest of dolls, a rocking horse and a dollhouse, mementos clearly not saved on account of me. Chu Chu has two other children with a woman who is no longer his wife but demands his attention more than his current, childless wife. His current wife is named Florinia, and she wears wide dresses with cinched waists and big hats. She is beautiful, with brown hair that waves over her shoulders and eyes slit at a sharp angle. Her voice is faint, her laughter fierce. She pretends to be coy and childish, but she's mean. I can see it in her eyes, even though she mostly ignores me.

She and Chu Chu are almost never home. They have another house somewhere near the ocean that they prefer over this one and have never taken me to. They're only here on the weekends when the beaches are busy and Chu Chu has nightclub performances in the city.

Chu Chu says I will meet his other children, one day, when he sees fit. *One day* makes it sound like I will be here forever. I have thought about running away, but how does one run away from a foreign country? I don't have money for a plane ticket or cab fare. And even if I did, I'd have nowhere to go. I have gone through all of the scenarios of why you would send me away, and the only thing that makes sense is that you lied about leaving Alfonso. It was him or me, and you chose him. At other times, I am certain it was Grandmother's idea to send me to live with Chu Chu. *There are wicked men in the world*, she'd said. *Sometimes we stumble into their path, and there's nothing we can do but hurry on out of it.*

Maybe she was the one who hurried me on out of it.

When I first came, the phone rang over and over, and I was sure you were calling to check on me. But there is only one phone in the house, and Señorita Lucinia Perron, my *niñera*, stands guard over it, and I don't dare cross her. She's a thick-chested, dark-eyed woman with legs like a squat bulldog who fires guttural Spanish at me. When I asked Chu Chu why I wasn't allowed to talk with you, he said long-distance phone calls were too expensive.

"I'll send a telex, then."

"Still expensive," he said. "But you can write a letter."

I've tried, but all that comes out is *Why*?

Eventually the phone stopped ringing. Now, I try not to think about you, or why I am here, or what is going to happen to me. Whenever despair tightens its fingers around my throat, I think about the painting above the fireplace back home and picture myself separated into sharp angles, each body part in its own box, my heart and brain disconnected, beating and thinking in isolation.

This calms me only a little. Most of the time I feel as if I'm on a ledge about to be pushed from behind with no ground in front of me.

The house is big, filled with high windows and brightly colored tile floors. There's a woman named Chara who comes in the mornings to cook and clean and do laundry. She reminds me of you, petite and attractive with dark hair and little hands. She moves about the house like a swift bird. She doesn't say much, glancing at the clock, working as if she always has somewhere urgent to be, or maybe she's just anxious to get away, like me.

I wish Chara lived here instead of Señorita Perron, whose only job, it seems, is to watch over me. She sleeps in the room next to mine and keeps the adjoining door open so I can hear her snoring all night. Once, when she was down in the kitchen, I snuck into her room, a bare, white space that stank of body odor. There were empty hooks on the walls, a single bed with a fringed, embroidered blanket, and a bare-

topped bureau. The only decoration was an altar displaying a
statue of the Virgin Mary surrounded by candles and rosaries.

Sneaking open her drawers, I hoped to discover something fun, like a bottle of perfume or a fashion magazine,
but there were only thick bras, cotton underwear and skirts
in varying shades of brown. I was reminded of a day last year
when you'd stayed home with me playing checkers and eating
salted crackers with peanut butter, and how when we'd gotten bored of checkers, we'd snuck into Grandmother Maria's
room looking for the *Cosmopolitan* magazine with Marilyn
Monroe on the cover she'd confiscated for herself. Only, we
couldn't find the magazine in any of those drawers, and you'd
gotten to your knees, your pedal pushers tight around your
calves, your hair tied up in a scarf, and triumphantly slid the
sultry actress out from under the bed.

Thinking of this in Señorita Perron's room, I dropped to
my stomach and looked under her bed. There was no fashion
magazine, but I discovered a blue bottle of tequila with *Don
Julio* written on the label. It was the exact bottle I'd seen in
the dining-room cabinet. Thievery, at least, made her more
interesting. This also explained the stink on her breath.

I pulled the bottle out, large and heavy, and yanked out
the cork, taking a swig that burned, making me sputter and
cough half of it into my lap. Hurriedly, I recorked it, shoved
it under the bed and retreated to my room where I removed
my alcohol-soaked skirt and buried it at the bottom of my
laundry basket.

After, I stood at the window missing you and Grandmother
Maria and wondering how long it would be until I got to go
home for a visit, or at least call you. Watching the cars slide
by, I pictured Marilyn's smile on the cover of that magazine,
a smile people said was sexy but which always made me sad.
I thought about sitting on the couch flipping through *Cosmo*'s

glossy pages, sipping ice-cold Coca-Colas with you, and how you'd said, "I thought your grandmother was smarter than to hide something under the bed. Shame on her; she should have been sneakier!"

You are the sneaky one. You arranged for me to leave your life without my suspecting anything at all. I'd like to be sneaky, but I'm probably more like my grandmother, unable to find a good hiding spot or think up a good lie.

I wait for my father to discover the missing tequila and punish Señorita Perron, but he doesn't. The bottle hasn't been replaced, and there's no way he can't miss it, which means he doesn't care one bit about leaving a drunk liar to take care of me.

This thought angers and emboldens me.

That Friday night, sitting at the dining-room table with Chu Chu and Florinia, eating chicken drowned in a spicy, brown sauce, I look up at my father and ask, "Why do you want me here? I know my mother asked, but why did you agree?"

He washes a bite of food down with a swig of wine and shrugs, as if my question is of little importance. "Because you are my daughter."

At the opposite end of the table, Florinia has finished eating. She leans back in her chair watching me. Tonight, she has thickened her lashes into clumps, painted her lips maroon and curled her hair into waves alongside her face. Chu Chu looks impeccable in his starched, light blue shirt, greased hair and shiny complexion. On your nights off, Mom, you've been known to come to dinner in a bathrobe and hair curlers with a mask of cold cream on your face, dismissing Grandmother Maria's disapproving look with the remark that your face deserves a night off, too. I imagine Florinia and Chu Chu sleep faceup so their pillows don't crease any lines onto their smooth, shiny skin.

I set my fork down, push my shoulders back in my chair and narrow my eyes at my father. "I've been your daughter for twelve years. Why didn't you want me before now?"

He looks dully at me over the rim of his glass. "It wasn't the right time."

My attempt to rile him isn't working. I want him angry. I need someone to push against, someone to give me a reason to feel something other than sad. Gratitude? Anger? Hate? Love? I have no idea what I'm supposed to feel toward this man.

"I want to go to one of your shows," I demand, daring him to take me into his world and declare me his daughter.

"Sure," he says, and I feel something close to pride at how easily he agrees.

Then I notice him glance across the table at Florinia, who has a smirk on her dark mouth. Chu Chu grins back at her.

"What?" I ask, sure I've been left out of a secret.

"Nothing, dear." Florinia's breathy voice sails out at me, her *dear* infuriatingly sweet.

"Okay, then, when will you take me?" I persist to my father.

"I'll have to check my schedule." Chu Chu's tone is sardonic, mocking, his eyes locked in a seductive look at his wife.

I can't understand what they're playing at or why I'm being made fun of. Anger twists in my gut, and I switch tactics. "Why was now the right time?"

"What?" Chu Chu pulls his eyes away from Florinia, looking at me as if I've finally become a nuisance.

"Why was *this* the right time to bring me here? Why not when I was five or seven? Is it because Mom asked? Why did you say yes? Why hasn't she ever asked before, and why can't I talk to her?"

My father straightens, sucking his teeth and looking at me crossly. Now I've gotten his attention. He sets his wineglass down. "Your mother's recent choice of a husband has not proven to be a good one. I won't have my child turned into a Lolita. After what she let happen, your mother's phone calls are no longer welcome in this house."

The air leaves my lungs: he knows about Alfonso. You told him, and then you sent me away because you wanted me here, watched over by a wicked old Mexican lady so I wouldn't become some kind of temptress, getting in the way of your marriage. How could you choose Alfonso over me? How can you love him more?

I keep my eyes on my plate and don't ask any more questions. I finish my dinner in silence and retreat to my room where I peel a long piece of paint from the wall and curl it through my fingernails before sliding it into my mouth. It tastes metallic, like biting down on a spoon. I chew it and swallow and decide I will never forgive you.

Now, I am no longer scared of Señorita Perron or of my father or of being here. I'm angry—fistfighting, spitting angry. But only in the daytime. At night, when I close my eyes and the city noises sound exactly like the city noises back home, a deep, weighty sorrow takes over. It's different from the sadness when I first came here, or when you first left me at school, or when Grant died. It's a darker wretchedness, one that rests over my insides and weighs me down like a water-soaked towel. I've tried squeezing it into nothing, but it just gets heavier and more compact and harder to fish out.

Surprisingly, my one comfort is school. For the first time in my life I almost like it. At Villa Cabrini Academy I was not considered smart or athletic or artistic or good at anything at all. Here the teachers marvel at my English, and since I grew up speaking Spanish at home, I understand the lessons perfectly. Señorita Casas smiles at me when I enter the classroom, calls me Señorita and brings me to the front of the class to read from English books, praising my skill.

You, of course, wouldn't know what it's like to not be good at anything. You've been praised your whole life for your singing and acting, your petite hands and feet, your figure and complexion. I can't hum a tune, and I have none of your beauty. I am thin-lipped and small-nosed and wide-eyed. My skin is paler than Chu Chu's but darker than yours. I have none of your beauty and none of your ambition. At least, that's what Grandmother Maria used to tell me every time she found me sitting in front of the television. "What is this?" she'd cry. "You may not have your *madre*'s beauty, but you have a mind, no? Where is your ambition, *nieta*?"

What does *ambition* even mean? Wanting something badly?

I want lots of things. Maybe I just don't want them badly enough.

Chapter Twelve

Unexpected Allies

Daughter,

The next morning, I sit at the rusty, red table on the outdoor patio while Miguel Espino's sister, Dominica, serves
me scrambled eggs with tortillas, black beans and tomatoes.
"More, Señorita?" She holds the enamel coffee pot in the air,
her heavy eyelids puffed from sleep, her bowling ball stomach
rising under her dress. So far, I have seen no sign of a husband.

I nod and thank her, trying not to scratch at the wig itching
my hairline. I have abandoned my sunglasses for round spec-
tacles, my traveling dress for a heavy, floral skirt and shawl—
the old-lady disguise I stole from Republic Studio's costume
department before I left California. It's a stiflingly hot getup,
and I am grateful for the early-morning clouds in the sky.

The coffee is divine with a hint of cinnamon, the eggs
light, the tomatoes tangy with lime. I eat all of it, feeling full
and grounded for the first time in weeks. I am the only cus-
tomer, and when Miguel steps from the restaurant doorway,
moving to brush off a tabletop with his hand, he takes no notice of me. Not until I rise, unhook my purse from the back

of my chair and take a shaky step over the stone slabs does he looks over. "Señorita, do you need assistance?"

"Thank you kindly." He offers an arm, and I lean heavily on it.

"Where are you headed? Do you need help to the bus stop?"

"I'm staying here." I make my voice gravelly, keeping a hold of him as I push my purse under my arm and against my skirt. It's the only item I'm carrying from yesterday that he might recognize. Despite everything, I am finding this charade ridiculously fun and a good test of my disguise.

"Staying here?" Gently, Miguel slides his arm from under mine, keeping a cautious hand out in case I topple.

I nod at my empty plate. "Will you have the kind woman add it to my room charge?"

"Yes, of course. Which room are you in?"

"Number three."

Miguel looks confused, and then he leans in, a slow grin spreading across his face. "Estelita?" I pull off my wig, and he claps as I give a dramatic curtsy.

"Did I fool you?"

"Did you ever!"

Just then the restaurant door bangs open, and Dominica strides over, scanning me up and down, her eyes dark slits. "Whatever *this* is—" she makes a wide circle with her hand "—I want none of it here. I don't need trouble. If someone's looking for you, they'll have to find you elsewhere."

Miguel touches Dominica's forearm. "She doesn't look too criminal to me. Maybe we let her explain?"

I am nervous, jazzed up with eagerness, and not until this moment have I realized how much I need to confide in someone. The story comes out in a rush, everything from the night at Duke's—I omit Alfonso from the narrative—to your father taking you, my stealing this costume and getting on a plane.

By the time I finish, the three of us are seated around the table. The hard lines of Dominica's mouth have softened, but her expression is grave. She pats my hand and says, "You need a drink," heaving herself from her chair and disappearing into the restaurant. It's seven o'clock in the morning, but I don't argue.

Miguel rests his chin on his fist. "Chu Chu Martinez." He whistles. "Do you know where he's taken your girl?"

"His family home is on Yautepec in La Condesa. I'm hoping she's there. I can't imagine he'd take her anywhere else. It's a starting place, anyway."

"Starting place for what?" Miguel moves his arm into his lap as Dominica returns, setting two mugs in front of us. "You plan to steal her back dressed like an old woman?"

"What else can I do?" I wrap my hands around the mug and take a sip. The drink is strong and sweet, *café con leche* mixed with alcohol and chocolate and cinnamon. I'd prefer to sit here all morning with this drink and Miguel, but I think of you and glance at my wristwatch, convincing myself that the heat in my belly is the drink warming me and not Miguel's eyes on me. It is six minutes past seven.

Miguel gives his sister a satisfied smile. "Dominica makes the best *pajarete*. Puts the hair on." He slaps his chest, and Dominica rolls her eyes.

"Not that you need any more." She sits heavily, her swollen stomach pressed up against the table. "It's a shame. I love Chu Chu Martinez. Now, if he comes on the radio—" she snaps her fingers "—I will shut it off! What is your plan? You steal your daughter back, and then what? How do you get out of the city? Where do you go? How does he not take her again?"

All things I have considered, none I have answers to. I

throw up my hands in a helpless gesture, and Dominica slumps back, picking at a piece of thread on her skirt, her face scrunched up. "We will think of something. First thing is, you find her. Then we'll make a plan."

Miguel lifts the wig from the table and says, "Come, I will get you a taxi."

I spend the thirty-minute drive to La Condesa holding onto my wig so it doesn't blow off from the open windows. When we finally slow along the wide, tree-lined street, I drop my hands into my lap and slink down, scanning the sidewalk for any sign of you or Chu Chu. Not that I imagine for one minute that your father would walk you to school. I just don't know who else to look for. Chu Chu's parents passed away a few years ago, and his only sister lives in New York. I know he has two other children and is married to a third wife, but I've never seen a photograph of any of them.

The taxi crawls past elegant buildings with their crisp blue, orange and red facades abutting each other like tropical birds on a wire. There is an earthy smell to the air, of grasses and cosmos lining the walkways. It crosses my mind that you might be happy here with Chu Chu's new family, and for a moment I wonder what our lives would have looked like if I'd stayed, given you a father, siblings, a beautiful house in a beautiful neighborhood.

"Here," I cry out, thumping the back of the driver's seat. "This is it. Pull over."

Chu Chu's house is one of the few colorless, stone exteriors on the street. Below the high, second-story windows and wrought iron balconies, a row of *casahuates* shield the first-floor windows from view, their white flowers parading over the branches like mini, upside-down wedding dresses. The house looks exactly as I remember, and I begin to sweat under my wig, my glasses slipping down the bridge of my nose. I push them up and peer at the upper windows for any sign of life. A curtain flutters, and I quickly tell the driver to park at the end of the street. He obeys wordlessly. This man is less interested in me than the last driver. When I ask him if we can sit here for a while he nods, takes out a newspaper and spreads it over the steering wheel.

The longer we wait, the hotter and more impatient I become. Eventually I peel off my shawl and then my stockings and shoes, my calves itching like crazy. And then, looking up, I suddenly see you, the sight of your dark hair parted down the middle, your thin lips pressed together and your concentrated steady gaze sends a piercing ache through my whole body. It's all I can do to not jump from the car and pull you into my arms. But I stay still, flatting against the seat with an elbow propped on the door handle to shield my face as you walk past with an intimidating-looking woman. Her middle is a solid block of flesh, and she appears to have no neck at all. Her shoulders are hunched and wide, but her arms are bizarrely scrawny, sticking out from her body like twigs. It's a wonder anyone that size could have such skinny arms, I think, wondering if I could wrestle you from them if I had to.

You look miniature beside her, wearing an absurd outfit for a girl your age: a belted, white dress, pleated and starched to a crisp, ballooning out from your waist like an umbrella. You have on high white socks and white patent leather boots that remind me of the shoes Mamá bought for me the first night I performed in Havana. I wonder if your boots are pinching your feet as much as those shoes pinched mine.

You round the corner out of sight, and my heart seizes. "Go!" I slam a fist into the door as if this might move us forward. "*Por favor*, follow those two, but slowly, at a distance."

My driver carefully folds his newspaper and lays it on the seat next to him before pulling into the street at a crawl. I don't breathe until you are in sight again. Your back is to me, and I can't see your face. Is it a happy one? Your body looks weary, one shoulder hunched under the weight of a leather bag that keeps sliding down your arm. I worry that your cumbersome chaperone will hear the low, growling engine and look behind her. Thankfully she doesn't, and we follow you down another street where you disappear inside the iron gates of a school building, engulfed by a crowd of girls in identical white-pinafore dresses.

I stare after you wondering how I am going to get inside as we slowly pass the troll-woman who stands tipped back on her heels with her hands latched behind her, watching you enter the schoolyard. Who is she? A nanny? There's no way she's Chu Chu's newest wife.

Just then she turns, sharply, and for one horrible moment our eyes meet.

Chapter Thirteen

Caught

Mother,

A light rain falls as I walk home from school, my eyes on the sidewalk trying not to *step on a crack and break my mother's back*. I hear someone walk up behind me and turn as a hand slides over mine, sweaty and rough, and I nearly cry out, but the man hurries past before I have a chance to make a sound, and I realize he's slipped something into my palm. My hand squeezes around what feels like a hard-edged piece of paper. The man, short and wide as a tree trunk, retreats around a corner, and I glance up at Señorita Perron who walks slightly ahead of me, oblivious in her hurry to get out of the drizzle.

When we arrive home, I dash up to my room, shut my door and slide down it, sitting on the floor as I uncurl my palm. In it is a piece of paper folded into the size of a quarter. It peels open like a tiny book, and hot tears spring to my eyes as I see your neat, looping cursive. In my anger, I imagined if you ever contacted me I'd tell you I had a father now and I didn't need you anymore. But I am crying so hard I can't read the words you've written.

Blinking my tears away, I finally read that you are here, in Mexico City, and you are going to take me home. I am to tell no one. *Tomorrow,* you write, *when you leave for school, a taxi will be parked outside the house. You are to get in fast. Can you do this?*

My chest heaves with confusion and excitement and relief. None of this makes sense, but I don't care. I want you this instant. Nothing matters anymore but being with you. I'd do anything, even if that meant sleeping under the same roof as Alfonso. Why do I have to wait for tomorrow? Why don't you come right now? The thought of escaping Señorita Perron's smelly breath and heavy footsteps, dinners with Florinia and my distant father—who has not mentioned taking me to see him perform since I brought it up—and this peeling paint and the creepy dollhouse makes me want to run screaming into the street after you.

I fold the note back into its tiny square, tuck it into the waistband of my underwear and close my eyes, bringing back the memory of your orange-blossom scent, the slick feel of your fingers through my hair and your tumbling laughter. Tomorrow is Friday. With glorious satisfaction, I picture Chu Chu and Señorita Florinia Martinez arriving for dinner, a seaside tan on their skin. They call up the stairs for me, and Señorita Perron descends slowly, alone, ashamed to admit she's failed at her only job as she tells them with sniveling sobs that I have disappeared.

I'd like to imagine my father's face as devastated, but it's hard to believe he'll care one bit. After all the trouble he went to he'll probably just be mad that you changed your mind. Why have you changed your mind? Why not just tell Chu Chu to send me home?

I get up and watch out the window as the cars pass, wondering if you are in any of them. The drizzle has turned to a heavy rain. The window was left open, and I run my fin-

gers through the puddles on the sill, keeping my eyes on the
street, slick and wet and shiny as tin. The steady splash under
the car wheels reminds me of the swishing sound our washing
machine made back home. I miss the sound of that machine.
I miss loading the wet sheets into my arms, then standing in
the dry heat of the sun with Grandmother Maria, pinning
them on the line. I miss watching you stretch out on a pool
chair in your big sunglasses, telling Grandmother that the
cleaning lady can do that and how she'd shake her head at
you and say, "How will Nina get anywhere in this world if
she can't hang a sheet on a line or make her own breakfast?"
I never imagined missing my grandmother's sharp tone and
cutting eyes, her deep authority. But now, I think about her
hands on my shoulders when she left me at school, how she
said, "I'm going to fix this," and then Alfonso steps into my
memory, walking out onto the patio in his tight swim shorts,
slinging a towel over his shoulders as he leans down to kiss
you. In a flash my anger is back, full-blown. I slam the window shut and turn to my aging, yellow room.

Maybe I won't sleep under the same roof as him after all.
Maybe I will refuse to get into the car with you tomorrow.
Why should I? Why should I keep doing exactly what you
want me to do? I'm sick of being left at school, left in hotel
rooms when you've dragged me on location or left behind
with Grandmother Maria when you haven't. You think you
can send me off with my father and snatch me back whenever you want?

I bite the inside of my palm, tiptoe to Señorita Perron's
door and press my ear to the wood. It's quiet so I ease the door
open, prowling like a cat over the creaky floor. Sipping her tequila has become an after-school ritual. Just one swig, enough
to feel the floaty sensation that leaves an empty, cool space in
my head so the pinpricking thoughts in my brain slip away.

Only this time, I am on my knees pulling the cork from the bottle when the door to the hallway opens. Before I can scramble to my feet, Señorita Perron's fist hits the back of my head hard enough that the cork flies across the room, bouncing over the floor.

"You like this?" Señorita Perron grabs the bottle from me and sits heavily on the bed, the mattress sagging under her fat bottom, her thick ankles brushing the tops of my knees. She plants her wide, flat palm on my shoulder, shaking the bottle in my face. "Go ahead, drink up." I stare at her, disbelieving, until she presses the bottle against my lips, tilting it so that a huge gulp burns down my throat and sputters out the sides of my mouth. Señorita Perron smiles a neat, yellow row of teeth at me. She takes her own swig, hands it back. For once, she doesn't speak in rapid-fire Spanish, but slow and clear. "We drink together, yes?"

I feel hot and queasy, and I don't want any more. I press my lips closed and slit my eyes in defiance when she grabs my hair and yanks my head back. "You like it so much, you will drink it." My anger surges as her words spray a fine mist in my face. I think of biting her wrist that is near my face as she holds my head back. I want to pin her to the bed and dump the tequila down *her* throat, scream at her that I will be gone tomorrow, *my mother is coming for me!* Only by now the tequila and her heavy hand are weighing me down. When Señorita Perron tilts the bottle to my mouth again, I don't fight her. My eyes smart and water, and my throat goes numb as I gulp it down, this time without coughing.

By the time the bottle is empty, I am soaring so far outside my body I wonder if I even have one. From this strange height, I see Señorita Perron fling the bottle on the floor and flop backward onto the bed, her voice slack and drawling. "Go to your room."

I steady myself against the wall, trailing my hand through our adjoining door to the yellow skin of my walls, tearing a piece as I go by. My bed looks far away, and when I step forward the room tilts away from me, and I drop to my knees and roll onto my back watching the ceiling circle around me. My throat begins to burn like a hot poker's being stuck down it, and I'm vomiting into my hair, my stomach heaving and retching until the room spins black.

I wake up in the dark, curled on my side in a tight ball on the floor. Rain sputters against the window, and every now and then I hear the swish of a passing car. A thin, sour liquid rises from somewhere deep in my stomach as I pull myself onto my knees. I spit onto the rug, pull my vomit-stained dress over my head and crawl to my bed in my underwear, collapsing onto the covers with my boots hanging off the edge.

The next time when I wake, the dismal gray light of dawn floats through my window. I sit up, but a blinding pain shoots through my temples and pushes me back down. I keep very still. Gingerly, I reach into my underwear waistband for your note, but it's gone. I pull myself out of bed with my ears ringing as blood pounds through my head. I search the floor, but there is only the rug over wooden planks with cracks too small for a note to slide in undetected. Holding one cool hand to my temple, I creep to Señorita Perron's door. She is snoring open-mouthed, her feet on the floor, knees bent, back flat on the mattress. Stealing in, I drop down on my knees and search her floor until I see a little, white square winking under the bed. I reach for it and stand unsteadily. Holding it tight against my chest, I tiptoe back to my room.

Even though I don't have a clock, the light through the window convinces me it is too early for you to come yet. I'm dying to lie back down and stop this throbbing, but I am afraid if I oversleep I'll miss you. I force myself into a clean pair of underwear, socks and a freshly ironed school dress. I have to at least look like I'm going to school.

In the bathroom, I wash the vomit from my hair in the sink, brush out the wet strands and secure them at the back of my pounding head with a barrette, every movement slow and painful. Señorita Perron's snores come in steady grunts as I pass her door and make my silent way to the kitchen. At first, I think the two plates of cold tortillas and beans on the counter have been left from last night. They can't be breakfast. Why would Chara have come so early? She's never here before seven. I look at the clock. 10:12. I stare at it, my mind slowing like a machine running down its gears, the heavy gray sky a deceiver of time.

My legs are rubbery and weak as I rush to the living room window. No taxi waits outside. I don't cry or scream, just slide to the floor and bow my head to my knees. My stomach twists, and my raw throat burns. I have lost you. Lost my chance to leave. Thick wedges of sadness slam into me, the weight so devastating I cannot imagine rising off the floor ever again. I regret thinking for one moment I wouldn't go with you. "I'm sorry," I whisper into the empty room. If only I hadn't gotten mad and gone into Señorita Perron's room. If only I wasn't so stubborn. "I'm sorry," I whisper again, but you are gone, and there is no one to hear me.

Chapter Fourteen

Disguised

Daughter,

Dominica thought it would be best to warn you, but it was Miguel who slipped you the note. Until this moment, I had thought it was a good idea, but now it's eight thirty in the morning, and you are nowhere in sight. I stare at Chu Chu's house, the windows like the watchful eyes of a great beast holding you in its belly. I want to break every one of them. Why haven't you come out?

Minutes tick by. I hardly slept all night, and now I'm jittery from too much coffee. I glance at the back of the taxi driver's head, a smooth, bald circle stamped amidst tufts of black hair. He taps his hands on the wheel, the engine running, the windshield wipers making a smacking noise every time they hit bottom. I feel as if I am about to hit bottom. I was certain of getting you out of here, but with every minute lost my confidence slips. Maybe you don't want to come home? Your father is generous when he wants to be and good at giving people what they want as long as it suits him. Maybe he has given you exactly what you want?

What do you want, Nina? Why don't I know your desires and dreams? I look at the immovable front door, the wood carved in deep, swirling grooves, and contemplate barging in and screaming down that cold-tiled hall for you. If Chu Chu found the note, why doesn't he come out to meet me? He could have one of his bully friends haul me back to the airport and force me on a plane without you. I press my hands to my hot cheeks. Why is he doing this? To get back at me for running away all those years ago? I want to tell him he's won, he's done it, he's punished me, now give me back my daughter!

The day I left him rushes back at me, a day very much like this with indecisive weather, rain coming and going in bursts. I didn't plan on leaving that day. Something snapped when I stood at the front door watching Chu Chu cuff his sleeves and pull on his coat. It was early morning, just like now, and we'd had our papaya and coffee, and he was headed off to the recording studio, leaving me to my boredom. I hadn't been on stage since I told Monte Proser I was pregnant. He'd congratulated me and said he was sorry to lose the act, but that I'd make a wonderful mother.

Mother, not singer. At the time, it never occurred to me I would have to choose.

For the longest time, I thought Chu Chu was letting me settle in, get my bearings, but the night he came home after a sold-out performance, radiant and boastful, it occurred to me that he might not have any intention of letting me sing again.

He tried to embrace me where I stood by the bed, sliding down the strap of my nightgown, but I pushed him away and threw my hands on my hips. "When will you book me a gig?"

"Book you a gig?" He stepped back, a look of surprise on his face.

"Did you forget...I am a singer?" I rapped my chest, and

Chu Chu smiled and reached for me, his hands running over my fleshy bottom.

"Of course not, my little nightingale. You will sing for me and Nina."

I shoved him away again. "Is that what you think? You get to sing for the world, and I sing for you? I have been singing since I was child, on the radio, on stage. I will not give that up for you or Nina."

The air changed. Chu Chu looked offended and arrogant. "Estelita, you will not sing outside of the home. You are married now, with a child to look after." His tone was reasonable, as if this was the most obvious thing in the world.

"That means my career is over? I can't sing because I am a mother and wife? That is ridiculous! We never discussed this. You said I would sing here."

"That was before we were married."

I stomped my foot, my anger ignited. "You want me stuck at home having babies so I don't outshine you!" I shouted into his face. I expected him to hit me, put me in my place like my father did with my mother. I almost wanted him to. After five months of pacing the house in a restless stupor, I was looking for any excuse to leave. If you cried, the nurse tended you. If we were hungry, the cook made dinner. What was I supposed to do? "Chu Chu, you promised I would sing. You promised!"

Chu Chu did not get angry. He turned his back on me and calmly headed toward the bathroom. "Things are different now. A wife does not parade herself on stage for other men to gawk at. There is nothing more to discuss."

In that moment, whatever love I had for him slithered away so fast it made me wonder how true it could have been. I would not be my mother. I would not stay home birthing babies and lose the very thing that defined me: my voice.

It was a year before I found the courage to leave. By the time Chu Chu leaned in that January morning with his full, charming mouth over mine, I couldn't breathe. He had sucked the air out of me. I was suffocating. When the door shut behind him, I stared at the back of the door thinking I might never inhale again. When I did, the gasp propelled me up the stairs where I grabbed a wad of money I kept in my underwear drawer—Chu Chu was generous with money—shoved it into my purse and stormed into your nursery. I plucked you from the floor where you sat playing with a stack of brightly colored blocks. I told Rosita, who was folding baby clothes into your drawers, that I was taking you for a walk.

"You will need a sweater for her, Señorita," she said, handing me the green knit sweater of yours I still have. I went straight to the bus stop, lifted you out of the stroller and stepped onto the bus leaving the empty, black-topped baby carriage on the sidewalk looking like a small, abandoned hearse. Not until the plane tickets were bought and we were taxiing down the runway did I take a full breath.

In the end, it was quite easy. Chu Chu never tried to get you back. Three months after we settled in LA with your Grandmother Maria, he sent divorce papers.

So, why now, Chu Chu?

By nine thirty you have not come out of the house, and I am crawling out of my skin. I have no idea what to do. I tell the driver to go. He asks where, and I say anywhere, just drive around. I can't bear the idea of heading back to the motel, and I've already paid him a ridiculous amount of money to drive us to Real de Catorce. Money I am sure he won't give back just because my plans have changed.

We drive down a side street, past thick-walled residential houses and a tiny grocery store advertising dried beans, corn and rice by the kilo handwritten on a cardboard sign. I crack open the window and let the rainwater splash onto my arm. Watching the drops pearl over my bare skin reminds me of standing in my yard in Cuba with Danita, our heads tilted to the sky, our mouths open to catch the rain on our tongues.

I miss my sister. We write to each other monthly, discussing our children and husbands, but none of it is real. Envy makes us exaggerate the best aspects of our lives and gloss over the bad. This year we started sending telexes, they're faster than telegrams but still expensive so we limit them. Lately, hers have contained references to the local uprisings and mass demonstrations against President Batista, student protests and the University of Havana shutting down. She's careful not to take any political viewpoint and keeps the messages informal and breezy.

Last week, I had every intention of telling her that Chu Chu kidnapped you, but I ended up telling her about the new movie contract with Duke, adding that you were doing well in school and Alfonso had booked a juggling gig in Palm Springs where we'd be spending Christmas. I thought about taking back my lie even as the ticker tape spit it out but didn't. Not that it matters. My sister and I stopped confiding in each other a long time ago. It crushed her when Monte Proser asked me to sing at the Copa all those years ago and not her. I don't think she's forgiven Mamá and me for leaving her behind, despite the fact that she has a husband she loves, children and her own career singing at Teatro Nacional de Cuba. How can I admit to her that my success has landed me three failed marriages and now the kidnapping of my child? Singing and acting might be the only thing I can do right.

I feel a dull ache in my chest where the memory of my sister lives, the child she used to be, my best friend. I miss her in the way that I miss the familiar little girl you used to be, Nina. I don't know how to mother you with your budding breasts and lengthening limbs, with your opinions and judgmental looks. I don't even know if you've started menstruating yet. I never spoke to my mother about those sorts of things. I learned from my sisters, but I didn't give you any sisters to learn from. I wonder what challenges you've met alone, without asking anything of me.

"Señorita? You still want me to drive?" The driver looks at me through the rearview mirror, his eyes separate from his body in that reflective rectangle. His questioning look annoys me. This whole goddamn city annoys me. I am not going back to that motel, and I am not leaving here without you.

"Take me back to Yautepec Street."

I adjust my wig, push up my glasses and check my watch. It's almost ten thirty. I am envisioning breaking a window and climbing through to find you when we turn down the street and there you are, walking with your schoolbag hanging down your arm.

"Slow down," I order, rolling down my window as rain pelts my fake glasses, which are already so scratched I can hardly see out of them. We take the corner, and you are only a few feet away, the back of your head invisible under the black umbrella you hold in one hand. "Stop." The car halts with brakes squealing. Your burly, unshakable chaperone is beside you, but I don't care. I fling open the door and scream your name as you and the woman turn, your faces startled. I have forgotten about my disguise, and when you don't move I panic that you don't want to come with me until there is a shift of recognition in your face and you spring forward, your bag sliding from your arm to the ground. The woman makes a clumsy attempt to grab you, but you fling your umbrella and she trips over it as you reach the curb and leap into the car. I stretch across you, slamming the door shut as I shout at the driver *"Ándale!"* and we swerve into the street. Twisting around, I watch from the rear window as the woman steps into the street with a raised fist, the umbrella blowing away behind her.

"Nina." I reach for you, tears springing to my eyes, but you flatten against the door like a caged animal, bewildered and frightened. I imagined us laughing and crying and holding onto each other, and I wonder if it's the disguise that has frightened you, which is stupid, you are not a child, and yet I yank off the wig and glasses. But you just curl away from me, sobbing with your head pressed up against the door.

I probably should fight your resistance, hold you even if you don't want me to, but your rejection burns, and I slide to the other side of the seat and fix my gaze out the window. The taxi driver turns up the radio—a folk ensemble playing *ranchera*—and speeds through the streets. I wriggle out of my costume to the tight-fitting navy dress I wear underneath. Bunching up the skirt and blouse, I shove them under my seat with the wig and glasses and sit back as you suddenly reach over and wrap your fingers around mine, turning to bury your weeping face in my lap.

"Oh, Nina, my sweet girl." I brush the hair off your neck and stroke your back, sorry I didn't hold you first. "It's going to be all right, now." I watch as the traffic slows down and worry about how fast that woman will get word to Chu Chu.

Fast, it turns out.

Before we are anywhere near the city border, the music on the radio is interrupted by an announcer in a resonant, dramatic tone saying that the famous singer Chu Chu Martinez's daughter, Nina, nine years old, has been kidnapped by an old woman in a taxi cab. Anyone with information is to go directly to the police.

You bolt up, looking at me with frightened, red-rimmed eyes, and I cup your chin in my hand. "Well, they got that wrong, didn't they? You are certainly not nine, and I'm no old woman."

At that moment, the car lurches to a stop, and my shoulder slams into the back of the driver's seat.

"Out." The driver's voice is low, serious.

I don't move. "I paid you good money to drive us out of the city."

The man doesn't look at me. All I can see is the back of his head as he white-knuckles the steering wheel. "Chu Chu Martinez is a rich man, and rich men are connected with powerful men, and powerful men are dangerous men. You never said anything about kidnapping. You are lucky I don't drive straight to the police."

"It's not kidnapping. She's my daughter, and I'm taking her home. I need you to get us out of the city. If it's money you want, I'll wire you more as soon as we get back to Los Angeles."

The man glances out his window, a nervous twitch in his neck. "You are no match for these men. Why would I risk my life? For money? And that is if you get home? No. Out."

He reaches over the seat for the back door handle and swings the door open. "Go. I want no trouble."

We climb out, and I slam the door as the car jumps forward and leaves us standing in the street. You are speechless, your face ghastly white as if you might be sick. A car honks at us, and I take your hand and move onto the sidewalk. It is thick with people. The drizzle has stopped, but the sky is still over-cast, and the smells of trash and spiced foods and body odor swell in my nostrils. I don't bother telling you that we'll be all right. I don't know that we will be. I don't have enough pesos for another taxi. A bus would be cheap, but all I see are trams, and they won't get us out of the city.

I hurry you along looking for a bus stop, the street pulsing with heat. Bodies gather like flies around a pushcart selling tacos and enchiladas, the smell mouthwatering. All I want is to sit with you under a palm tree and eat a decent meal, I think, painfully aware that you haven't spoken a word to me. I weave around a woman who bats away her clinging child, making the boy drop his taco. He wails so loud it drowns out the mariachi music blasting from a cantina's open door. I clasp a hand over one ear just as I spot a policeman coming toward us, his movements slow and deliberate, his eyes scanning each person he passes. Ducking behind the woman, I tug you across the street and stand stock-still in front of a perfumery pretending to gaze at the etched-glass bottles, the atomizers like tiny balloons. Your hand is sweaty in mine. When I look at you, you don't turn your head but keep your eyes on the crystal bottles. I want so much to know what you are thinking, but more than that I want to get us out of here. Slanting my eyes over my left shoulder, I see the policeman moving away down the opposite street at the same time as I spot a cab coming toward us. To hell with the money, I think, moving into the street and hailing it with a wild arm gesture.

I help you into the back and situate myself up front with an easy smile at the driver who is a young man with long limbs and fingers that curl like tentacles around the steering wheel.

"Where to?" he asks.

"Tula, *gracias, Señor.*" It's the only town outside of the city I remember. Chu Chu took me there to see the *Tollán* ruins when we first moved here.

"That's a long way. It'll cost you. Much cheaper to take a bus."

I don't tell him we really need to get to Real de Catorce, which is over three hundred miles away and will cost far more than Tula. "I'm here on vacation with my daughter from Los Angeles and buses don't suit us. Money is no object."

At this, I draw a tube of lipstick from my purse and lean out the window, using the side mirror to paint my mouth red. My hands are shaking, but I manage to get the lipstick on evenly and pull my hair into a twist at the base of my neck before securing a small black hat—also taken from my purse—on my head. It's cloudy, but I slide sunglasses over my eyes and rest an elbow out the window. A movie actress on vacation with her daughter.

I can't believe my silly, old-woman costume trick worked, but it's not a stretch for Chu Chu to think I sent someone in my place to get you back. Over the years, our brief phone conversations consisted of him accusing me of abandoning you to boarding school because I'd rather flaunt myself on stage than raise you. It's not an entirely untrue statement. I would rather be on stage or in front of a camera than anywhere else, but it doesn't mean I don't love you. Chu Chu is too narrow-minded to see that a mother's heart can manage it all, and he's too full of himself to believe I'd come here myself to bring you home.

He is, however, smart enough to have the roads north of the city blocked.

Chapter Fifteen

By Bus or By Foot

Mother,

From the back seat, I watch you hide your eyes and balance your elbow out the window, wondering if my silence is why you worry the lipstick off your lips with your teeth, nervously biting top to bottom. I want to talk, ask why you're here and why we're running and why Chu Chu would put out a search for me instead of just letting you have me back, but the blue-bottled tequila from last night has stripped me dumb, left me raw and wordless. I am afraid if I open my mouth I will throw up again, and so I let you believe my silence is a kind of punishment for sending me away.

Not until the car slows and I see two policemen up ahead does a gut-wrenching fear hit me. They are stiff and uni-formed, holding rifles easily in their hands as they question the driver of the car in front of us. You snap your head around and say in English, "Nina, we have a long ride ahead and it would be best if you try and take a nap." The sharp way you say *nap* makes me drop to the seat and squeeze my eyes shut. Adrenaline has replaced my exhaustion, and my lids tremble and threaten to pop open. I roll over and press my face into the scratchy wool upholstery. There's a fusty smell to it that makes me want to gag. I feel the car inch forward, and the driver mutters something about the inconvenience of the roadblock.

There's a thump as if someone has banged a hand on the roof, and I hear, "Where are you headed?" The voice is a man's, throaty, deep. And then, in your fluid Spanish, "Señor, we're going to see the ruins in Tula. Our driver has agreed to take us all that way. My daughter wasn't feeling well so I'm letting her sleep. Have you been to the ruins? Are they much to see? We're from New York City. Dilapidated buildings are the only ruins we're privy to there!" You give a burst of bubbly laughter, and I think you should stop talking, it's too much: they'll be suspicious.

But your vulnerable charm does the trick, and the man whistles. "The ruins are something. New York City, huh? You on vacation? Your girl's not in school this time of year?"

"She had a week off, and her father was on a business trip, so we thought we'd take a little trip of our own."

"Where are you staying?"

"The Gran Hotel."

Another long, low whistle. "Never been there myself, but I've heard it's something."

"It's quite lovely."

A new voice, the driver's, silent during this exchange jumps in. "Why are you stopping people?"

A fourth voice, closer, as if this man is leaning into the back-seat window just above my head. "Chu Chu Martinez's little girl's been kidnapped. It's all over the news. We're patrolling the airport and train stations and every road out of this city. Some old lady nabbed her. I'm sure we'll get them before too long. How far can an old lady with a small child get, anyway?"

There is an oily smell to the man hovering above me, and the last thing I want to do is see his face, and yet it takes all of my willpower to keep my eyes shut. What is it about knowing I can't peek that makes me so desperate to do it?

I hear you gasp. "What a shame! Poor man, losing his child. I can't imagine."

There's another rap on the roof that echoes through the car like gunshot, then the throaty voice. "You have a nice trip, now, and you," speaking to the driver, "get this lovely señorita safely where she needs to go."

The engine revs gently, and there's a slow kick of gravel under the tires as we ease forward. I roll over and open my eyes, my body unclenching, my limbs melting over the edge of the seat. You glance back at me and wink, a slight smile on your face. Your shoulders have relaxed, and you no longer bite your lips. The car picks up speed, and the oily man's smell is replaced with the scent of dry earth and a warm wind that blows the hair around my face. The last thing I hear before falling asleep is the driver saying, "New York? I thought you were from Los Angeles?"

I sleep and wake in spurts, the bumps in the road making my head bounce against the seat, my stomach seizing at every jolt. After a while, I shake off my grogginess and sit up, rolling the window all the way down and sticking my head out. I am desperately thirsty, but the wind helps the nausea, and I stay pressed up against the car door watching the landscape fly past, red hills and brown earth, spiky leaves shooting out from thick-stemmed, silvery-blue yucca. No one talks, which feels strange, even though the wind in my ears and the roaring engine would make conversation difficult. Hours go by, and I wonder how far away Tula is. Every now and then, you reach a hand over the seat and give whatever part of my body it lands on—knee, forearm, finger—a squeeze. I want to hold on to you, but you keep pulling your hand back into your lap. I keep your profile in view, your curved cheekbone, thin nose and rounded lips. It's not that I think you will actually vanish, but one can never be sure.

The driver fiddles with the radio knob, switching stations, music and chatter bursting in and out of static. I strain to hear any more announcements about my disappearance, but no more come. It's shocking to think that my father could get a message over the radio so fast, but deliciously satisfying thinking of Señorita Perron, hungover and puffy-eyed, running to report it to him. Hopefully punished. At the very least fired.

When the car finally stops, it is late afternoon, and we are in a small town, the dirt road lined with flat-roofed adobe homes with dark, cavernous windows. An old woman, her face so shriveled I can hardly make out her features, sits in a purple shawl next to an open doorway watching us. I don't ask where the ruins are.

"I can make a phone call here?" you ask the driver, and he nods and points to a building that says *Cabrito al pastor* and *Buñuelos* in red neon paint on a cardboard sign. "And the bus?" He points down the street where two girls stroll arm in arm. They wear flowy dresses that shift around their full bodies. They look cool and comfortable and make me overly conscious of my starched, belted dress squeezing my waist and the sweat trickling between my thighs.

We climb from the car and you walk around to the driver's side and rest your hands on the edge of the open window. I notice now that the only thing you are carrying is a small, alligator purse. The driver looks at you with squinty eyes, his mustache twitching as he extends his hand, his fingers long and delicate and strangely manicured. Your hand disappears inside his and you lean forward and plant a kiss on his cheek. Clearly, I missed something while asleep.

You pull your hand to your side. "I will send the money to the address you gave me, I promise. Thank you for your kindness and bravery. I will not forget this."

The man slaps the side of his car, points a finger at me and says, "You look out for *tu madre, si*?" and pulls away.

"Now, let's find a telephone," you say cheerfully.

We cross the street toward the restaurant, and I watch a layer of dust settle over your shiny, blue pumps wondering why you haven't asked me a single question or even tried to get me to speak. I have so many questions, but I am still too hazy to figure out how to ask them.

Inside, the restaurant is empty except for a single man sloppily eating a taco over his plate. A woman with a stained apron and open-toed sandals comes from the kitchen to ask if she can help us. A thick braid runs down her back with a ribbon woven through it, shiny red fabric winking between sections of black hair. She lets you use the telephone in the kitchen while I perch on a stool at the counter gulping down a lukewarm Mexican cola she's given me in a skinny glass without ice.

The kitchen is separated by a half wall, and I can see a man with a pair of tongs dropping dough into a vat of smoking oil. The dough is twisted like rope, and it bobs, golden brown, to the surface, spitting and crinkling. You stand on the opposite side of the room next to a phone that is attached to the wall talking with animated facial movements, the hand piece held in both hands as if you're afraid you'll drop it. When you hang up, I can't tell if you are relieved or troubled as you take my half-drunk soda from the counter and move us to a table near the window.

We sit silent, your arms folded over your chest as the

woman serves me a plate of tamales wrapped in cornhusks. I pick one up, peel the husk back and bite into it, the cheese oozing hot into my mouth. At home, you make me eat tamales with a knife and fork. Now, you don't even notice, and I wonder what else I can get away with. I set the tamale down and pinch an edge of it as a string of oily cheese leaks onto the plate.

"Don't play with your food, Nina. Your hands are filthy," you say, and all at once everything is weirdly normal. Suddenly, I don't want to get away with anything. All I want is to go home. I think of sitting in the airport restaurant with Chu Chu months ago, how he didn't order food either, just sat watching me eat like you are now.

You lean over and sip my soda, pull off a small piece of my tamale and place it in your mouth. I'm not particularly hungry, but the tamale is delicious, and a few bites takes the nausea away and clears my head.

As if you knew all along that food was all I needed, you say, "All right, it's time for you to speak, young lady. I know you haven't gone mute on me. I know you've been through a lot, but I'm here now, and we're getting you out of here come hell or high water. I've put a call in to my manager, and his personal assistant is meeting us in Laredo. All we have to do is get over the border." You slap the side of your purse secured between your lap and the table. "If the directions I've been given are correct, we'll be back in the United States the day after tomorrow. Funniest thing, did you know Laredo's near the real Texas town of Rio Bravo? Isn't that a coincidence? Uncle Duke will get a hoot out of that once we tell him about this little adventure."

"Where are we?" I ask, my first question.

You glance around with a light laugh. "In a restaurant, in a town I've never been to and don't even know the name of."

"I thought we were going to Tula."

"That wasn't far enough away. Our cabdriver said that from here we can take a bus to Real de Catorce."

"Why couldn't we fly home? And why are we running away?"

"Because your father would like to stop us."

"Why? He doesn't even want me. I hardly saw him. He was just doing you a favor."

A curious look crosses your face. You scoot my soda glass aside and lean forward with your elbows on the table. "What do you mean he was doing me a favor? What did your father tell you?"

"He said you asked him to take me."

"Bastard," you hiss, dropping back against your chair, arms folded over your chest.

"You didn't ask him to?"

"Good God, child, no! Why would I do that? For what earthly reason would I suddenly ask your father to take you? A man who has never cared one bit for you?"

This new thought is like a sharp-toothed crane, lifting the sadness but still pinching. "Then, why did he take me?" It is clear to me now, but I want you to say it.

You blanch for a brief moment before recovering with a quick reply. "I have no idea."

I look down at the table. Have you forgotten about Alfonso? Have you choked and strangled and buried this truth? I want to tell you that my father does care about me. In his own twisted way, Chu Chu was trying to protect me, which is more than you did. I look up, prepared to ask you if Alfonso has come back, if you ever sent him away in the first place, but I can't. I can't say his name out loud. I don't even want to think it.

We look at each other for a long, uncomfortable moment,

and I know you understand what I'm trying to ask, what I really need to say, but your face is closed off, your expression begging me not to bring it up. If we speak it, we give it life. Only, you don't seem to understand that strangling something into silence doesn't make it go away. It just shuts it up for a while.

"You going to finish that?" You reach over for my tamale and say, "Your father's a snake," because this is easier said than the other.

You finish my food and drink the rest of my soda before paying our bill and heading us into the street. There are so many things I want to tell you: how relieved I am knowing you didn't send me away; how bold and brave and clever you are; how shocking it is that you are here on your own; and how important this makes me feel. But I don't know how to express these emotions any more than the sad ones, so I say nothing. Instead, I pretend great interest in the women who kneel in front of many-colored blankets, their wares spread out before them: pottery, folded shawls, turquoise jewelry, carved wooden bowls and tiny animals polished to a rich brown. The women gesture and smile, asking us in gentle, pleading tones what we'd like. You smile back, sympathetic and polite, but you don't buy anything until we are at the last blanket where you stop and pick up a carved wooden spoon. *"Cuanto?"*

The woman holds up two fingers, and you hand her two pesos, turning to me and placing the spoon in my palm. It is tiny, like a baby spoon, the wood almost black and smooth as silk. You are beaming at me. "It's for your coffee, when you learn to drink it," you say, and I know this is your way of apologizing for what you cannot say. "You are going to grow into a beautiful woman, Nina."

Embarrassed, I slide the spoon into my skirt pocket and mumble a thank-you, but I keep my hand wrapped around this memento and imagine sitting with you when I am a grown woman, sipping coffee stirred by this tiny spoon. I will not be beautiful, but I will not need to be. Even in old age, you will be beautiful enough for both of us, I think.

At the end of the street the buildings and sidewalk drop off into a bumpy dirt road with the desert stretching away to an empty, blue sky. A white bus is parked on the side of the road. On the roof, a man crouches behind a metal rail tying down duffel bags. He eyes you as we approach, his hands continuing to loop the rope in big swirling motions, and I realize how out of place we look, me in my starched, white school uniform and you in a fitted, dark blue dress that hugs your rump. The bus door opens, and we climb aboard. You push your hair off your sweaty forehead and smile. "How much to Real de Catorce?"

The driver barely glances at us, his eyes searching the empty road ahead as he puts out a hand. "Three pesos."

You retrieve the money from your purse and drop it into his palm. "And how far?"

He shrugs. "Four hours, if we're lucky."

What does that mean, *if we're lucky*? We turn down the aisle. Women in colored blouses with children on their laps and men in rough, brown shirts watch us from under straw hats and pulled back hairdos. You nudge me into the nearest window seat, squeezing next to me with your knees pressed tightly together. I'd rather sit in the back where we're not so noticeable, but I imagine you've chosen to be near the door for a hasty exit if necessary. The stillness is nerve-racking, and it's strangely quiet. Even the baby on the woman's lap across the aisle doesn't make a sound, looking at me with curious, wide eyes.

A young girl climbs aboard holding the hand of a smaller child. Their mother appears, nudging them from behind.

The driver starts up the engine, and we move forward, the bus picking up speed, swerving around ruts in the road, the landscape slipping past with a steady motion that eventually rocks me to sleep with my head against your shoulder.

I wake up to a loud bang and a jolt, which nearly sends me flying off my seat. It is dark, and through the blue light of the moon, your face is a mask of terror. The bus sways, and I am thrown toward the window where I can see a fat moon shifting in and out of mountain peaks. We are climbing upward, tipping precariously on the narrow road toward a sheer drop into blackness. You have one hand pinned to the seat in front of you, the other planted firmly to my chest as if that small extremity will save me from a drop off the side of the cliff. I curl my hands around the edge of the seat, holding on as the moon and mountains suddenly disappear with a loud whooshing nose.

You gasp, and from across the aisle the woman with the baby on her lap—asleep, his arms and legs hanging every which way—leans over and pats your leg. "It's just the tunnel, love. It's a mile and a half long, so don't hold your breath for it. This road used to be where the mining train went right through the mountain. No other way in or out."

I don't like the idea of being inside a mountain, and from the look on your face you don't, either. I think of stories I've heard about mines collapsing and blowing up, and it feels like an eternity before we come out on the other side, rock formations emerging under moonlight like ancient artifacts.

Before long the bus screeches to a halt, the door bangs open and people shuffle quickly to their feet. I step out in clear, cool air. The bus has dropped us at the foot of a town made of stone structures that look, in the dark, as if they are carved from the hillside. People spill around us, gathering luggage tossed from the roof, their footsteps and hushed voices disap-

pearing quickly into the dark, narrow streets. The driver cuts
the engine, and the bus sighs and sinks down for the night.
He snaps off the lights, climbs down the stairs, secures his
hat on his head, his bag over one shoulder, and tramps off,
his footsteps pattering away into the night.

Alone, we make our slow way up the street, tripping over
uneven cobblestones, your pumps a ridiculous thing, my white
boots at least flat and easier to manage. There is no sidewalk,
and the doors of the houses open right into a road that is so
steep I have to prop my hands on my knees to push myself up
it. Through tiny windows, lamplight flickers behind closed
curtains.

"This is a rather fun adventure, isn't it? I bet this town's
a flutter of tourists," you say jokingly, breathless, panting as
you turn to look at me, your face exhausted, despite how hard
you're playing at being alert.

We reach the last house before the mountain takes over,
and you stop and stare at it, biting your lips. From a fence
post, a burro watches, stolid and unblinking.

"Pretty sure this is it." You don't look or sound sure.

"What's it?" I ask.

"Miguel, that man who slipped you the note? Supposedly
his aunt and uncle live here. He told me theirs was the last
house on the left. Only..." you hesitate, looking back down
the street "... I don't know which end of the street he meant.
I wish it wasn't so late."

I hang back, watching you step up to the front door and
give it a gentle knock. The door opens, and an older woman
appears in a pool of light wearing heavy trousers and a button-
down shirt with the sleeves rolled past her elbows. Her dark
hair is pulled into a bun, and the white streaks along her temples look like brushstrokes of paint. You say something, and

the grooves around her mouth shift into a smile as she opens the door wide and beckons for us to come in.

We have no luggage, toothbrushes, pajamas or change of clothes. We step empty-handed into a house with stucco walls hung with paintings of fish and seashells and eat a dinner of rice and beans with avocado and mango rolled into soft tortillas. The man and woman are Fede and Rubenia. They are old, their faces filled with lines, and yet they insist we take their bed and fold themselves into a blanket on the wooden floor. It is the first time I ever remember sleeping beside you. The bed is soft, and I curl against the flat of your back and press my feet against yours and listen to night insects buzz like an electric hum until everything sinks and settles into silence.

Sunlight through the open door wakes me up. A beam stretches to the table where you stand next to Rubenia as she pours a glass of water from a ceramic pitcher. Your city dress is gone. Today you wear a heavy white cotton blouse with wide sleeves and a matching skirt, embroidered with large yellow flowers. The old woman hands the glass to you, and the water catches the light and casts prisms of color up your arm. My heart clenches as if you are a dream and will disappear in a puff of smoke.

Turning, a smile spreads across your face, and the prisms on your arm disappear as you step toward me. "Good morning, darling."

I rise out of bed feeling rested and sturdy. "Morning," I say in English, catching myself in time to say *"Buenos dias"* to Rubenia.

"Buenos dias," she says with a soft smile.

Yesterday it seemed I'd be nauseous and shaky-legged forever. This morning, I am hungry. I eat two helpings of black beans and politely decline the eggs. Fede is gone, but Rubenia sits at the table nodding encouragement with each bite.

She offers me a third helping, but I shake my head and thank her, feeling as if I'm going to burst. You have stepped outside. Through the open doorway I see you speaking to a man wearing wire-rimmed glasses and a checkered shirt.

When I join you, you introduce him as Jesus, Miguel and Dominica's brother. I shake his calloused hand as Rubenia comes out with a burlap bag, opening it to show us a stack of soft tortillas and cheese wrapped in thin cloth and a jug filled with water.

"You are the dearest," you say, throwing your arms around her.

Rubenia pulls away, nodding shyly and giving me a wet kiss on the cheek, her lips velvety soft. I can't think of anyone back home who would take in strangers, clothe them and feed them and kiss them when they leave.

Jesus drives a faded, pink truck that he says used to be bright red. "Twenty years ago," he laughs. The truck rattles at every bump as if it's going to fall open around us. I sit squeezed in between you two, keeping an eye out for ruts in the road so I can hold on to the dashboard instead of bouncing up and hitting the ceiling. The gearshift is pressed against my leg, and Jesus apologizes every time he takes hold of it, the engine roaring with each shifting gear. The narrow road, tunnel and steep cliffs are just as terrifying in daylight as they were last night, and I close my eyes every time the truck lurches toward the edge.

It's a relief when we finally drop onto flat desert, no trees in sight, just pointy cacti and lumps of rock and sage. The sky is a bundle of white clouds, the hills crusty and dry, the road empty, save for the occasional truck loaded down with crates that Jesus steers around without slowing down. We pass a man on horseback as he herds a group of skinny cows, a dog yapping them into order. Strange things begin appearing out of nowhere: piles of abandoned cabbages and chickens that scatter as we roar past. How chickens or cabbages came to be here, all alone, I can't imagine. You laugh at these oddities, looking from the window to me, squeezing my hand and smiling as if we're tourists in this barren land instead of escapees. Your hair is tied back with a scarf that crests the top of your head, and your face is scrubbed clean, no lipstick or mascara, which makes you look young, your loose-fitting skirt and blouse—a gift from Rubenia—folksy and modest. I like you this way.

By early afternoon, we are in the town of El Brasil. Jesus parks on the street, takes the money you offer for the ride, wishes us luck and walks off waving his hand over his head. You drop your purse into the burlap bag Rubenia gave you and shift the fat strap onto your shoulder. This town is bigger than the last one, full of gray-plaster buildings and washed-out adobe huts with faded tapestries hanging behind open, carved-out doorways. Soda bottles roll in the gutters, and scraps of newspapers flutter across our path.

I glance at you, wondering if you have a plan, not daring to ask how we're getting home or what will happen if Chu Chu stops us or if we'll run out of money. The concerned expression on your face makes me even more nervous, but you perk up when you see a store with a faceless mannequin in the window wearing a red, flowered dress. You eye my dress, socks and boots—none of which are white any longer—and say "First thing is to get you out of that ridiculous outfit."

Inside the small store, we crouch behind racks and try on clothes that are nothing like what we'd buy in a department store in LA. I think of you back home needing matching bags and hats and lipstick colors. Nothing matches here. The blouses are made of thick cotton with square necks and wide sleeves, and everything is embroidered or printed in diverse, colorful patterns. There are no children's clothes, but we eventually find a small blue dress sprinkled with white birds, and it fits well enough. The cotton is light and breathable and a relief after my belted, buttoned school uniform.

"Your boots will have to do. But these pumps of mine will never make the journey." You bend over and unbuckle the top strap of your shoes. "We don't have far to go to the border now."

"How are we getting there?"

"Walking."

"Walking? Why can't we take a taxi or a bus?"

"I don't have enough money for a taxi, and if Chu Chu is as thorough as I know him to be, he'll have the bus drivers around here looking out for us."

This seems unlikely, but clearly you're taking no chances. "I thought he was looking for an old woman?"

"He might be, or he might be looking for me by now."

"How far is it to the border?"

"Jesus said it was about twenty miles."

"Twenty miles! I've never walked more than a few blocks in my whole life."

"We'll be fine." You slide your feet into a pair of leather sandals and wiggle your toes with their pink-painted nails. "So long as we don't have to do it in heels."

We wear our dress and shoes out of the store, leaving our discarded things with the woman behind the counter, who you've bargained a trade with. Standing under a crude awning strung between two buildings, you pull a crumpled map from the bag that Jesus drew for you before we left Real de Catorce, lines shooting off from each other, and street names scribbled in pencil. You turn the paper sideways, peering at it.

"What if we get lost?" I ask.

"We'll stop and ask someone."

"But what if they're on the lookout for us?"

"Nina, you're going to have to trust me."

Despite how dependent you always seemed back home, needing Grandmother Maria's advice on everything, you seem bizarrely sure of yourself in this foreign place.

On the street, we buy straw hats to protect our faces from the blazing sun, two bottles of *Jarritos*, bananas and warm tortillas we get from a street-food stall to add to Rubenia's store before heading out of town.

It's too hot to talk, and the silence becomes oddly peaceful as the road lengthens and stretches away to low hills, the land bare and brittle, beaten down by sun and wind. The only things alive are thick-trunked, pale green cacti lining the road like prickly armed beggars and the occasionally stunted mesquite we rest in the shade of, sipping soda gone flat and munching tortillas, before moving on.

As we walk, a stillness settles inside me. I don't even mind the weariness in my legs or the blaze of white sky overhead. I sink into the pleasure of Itime with just the two of us. No school or husbands or Grandmother Maria or film sets to compete with. For hours, we don't see a single car or truck, just the straight, hard-packed road disappearing into ripples of heat. I wonder if it is only in moments of crisis that I will have you to myself or if things will change when we go home. Maybe the fear of losing me will make you more devoted, I think, walking closer to you, the heat like breath between our bodies.

When the sun sinks low in the sky, we picnic in an empty church, washing down our mushy, bruised bananas with clean water from Rubenia's jug. The church walls are white stucco, the benches dark wood. You ask about my time at Chu Chu's, and I tell you everything, except the part about the tequila. My impression of Señorita Perron makes you laugh, and you snort with disgust as I mimic Florinia's accent. I tell you she's not half as pretty as you, and you smile your stage smile, and we fall silent.

The church is so quiet it's like our own world.

"We should pray," you whisper, and we clasp our hands and hang our heads. I pray for selfish things: that Alfonso is gone and I never have to go back to boarding school; that Grandmother Maria moves out and you never marry again; that we spend every Saturday night eating orange sherbet and watching television.

Afterwards, as you stand in the half darkness singing to me, I wonder what you prayed for. Your voice is achingly beautiful, the notes rising and falling in a way that makes my chest hurt with a pleasurable sadness, like a good cry.

I want you to always sing and to always be with me.

We fall asleep curled on the floor behind the altar, watched over by a statue of Juan Diego set into an alcove above our head. He kneels at the feet of the Virgin of Guadalupe, white stone carved into white stone. I press my back closer to you, into your soft, full chest, your arm around my shoulder. Body carved into body.

Chapter Sixteen

Border Crossing

Daughter,

The truth, dear one, is that I pray we make it to LA in time for my screen test for *Rio Bravo*. I should pray that we make it safely over the border, but as I sit with you in the quiet and warmth and safety of the church, I have a resounding feeling things will work out. So I pray for something that feels more useful.

But when I wake up the next morning with you curled under my arm, stiff and sore from that hard church floor, I am filled with doubt. I think about that night with Alfonso, how I should have come home earlier, kept him enticed, been a better wife. I'm sure I could have prevented it. And your father, I should never have let Mamá tell Chu Chu what happened, never let her pack you off to school. If you'd been home, Chu Chu wouldn't have taken you so easily. Now we are in his country, under laws I don't understand, headed toward one of the largest, most popular border towns with police and border patrol looking for us. I keep imagining you being dragged into a car with that oafish woman or, worse, handed over to Chu Chu and his young, beautiful new wife who I picture smiling at me as she shoves you into the back of their car.

Keeping an arm around you, I twist my cramped neck and look up at the high beams thick as railroad ties leading to blunted dead ends. I think about the time I left Cuba for New York with Mamá when I was fifteen, how clear-eyed and confident she'd been getting on an airplane for the first time, heading to a strange country, how sure of it all. Even after I married Chu Chu and went to Mexico City, Mamá stayed in that foreign city of New York and waited for me. I was angry with her for not returning to Cuba, for being so sure of my failed marriage. "Men you cannot control," she'd said, "but your talent is yours. If you fail at that, you have only yourself to blame."

Not entirely true, I think now. My talent is dependent on men and greed and a film industry I have no control over, even as I've learned to love it. And I do love it, the attention, the allure, how men look at me, how I know exactly what to do to direct their eyes where I want them to go. All eyes on me. I need that.

I slide my numb arm out from under you, watching you sleep and knowing that even if I can get you out of this country, I have failed you. If I had been shooting *Rio Bravo* when all of this happened, I would have convinced myself to finish the movie before coming for you. You have never been my first priority, no matter how much I want you to be or how much I love you. It is an obvious and unsettling fact I now fully understand about myself.

"Nina?" I gently shake you awake, your confused eyes adjusting as you rise up on one elbow and take in the soft light through the stained-glass windows. "Look," I whisper, pointing to a yellow-breasted bird perched on the back of a

pew. It tilts its head, searching us curiously before fluttering
up to the rafters.

You get to your feet, watching the bird dart around the
high ceiling. "How will it get out?"

"Through the open door, if it's smart enough." I stand and
stretch, reaching my arms up and then touching my toes, easing the stiffness from my lower back before sliding my feet
into my sandals. I check to make sure my alligator purse is
still nestled safely at the bottom of the burlap bag, then take
stock of our water supply. The jug is only a quarter full. We'll
have to be sparing, but Nuevo Laredo is not too far, maybe
nine miles. I sling the bag over my shoulder. "We should get
going while it's still cool. Maybe we'll find a ride today. I
don't fancy another night in a church. You?"

"I didn't mind it."

"Well, my bones are not as young as yours." I hand you
your hat, secure mine on my head and walk to the church
door, pulling the heavy handle to open it.

There is only a faint, orange glow at the edge of the horizon, but the day is already warm, the sky a hard blue over
the pale, red hills. You stand in the doorway, your back to
me, still watching the bird.

"Come, Nina."

"What if it doesn't know how to get out? It will die in
there."

"It can sing, can't it?"

"Yes."

"And what have I taught you about song?"

"That songs transport us."

"That's right. If it has its voice, it is not trapped."

You follow slowly, looking back, waiting for the bird to
escape. I look back, too, even though I know it's more likely

the bird will bang into a window than find a way out that door. Either way, I fear it's a bad omen.

I pull your attention to the road, pointing to the horizon and telling you to watch for dust up ahead. "That's the sign of a car coming," I say, handing you a tortilla rolled into a tube which you nibble like you would crust from toast. I take a sip of water from the jug and return it to the bag where it bangs heavily against my side. The ground slopes upward as we walk, sagebrush and thistle edging onto the road.

Hours go by, and we don't see a soul, not even a scraggly cow or donkey. We are out of water, and when a large crate appears in the distance I hope for abandoned fruit or vegetables, even cabbage would do, but as we approach a rifled soldier steps into the road. It's a sentry box, not fruit. He holds his gun easily in both hands, and the sight makes my heart hammer in my chest. A large sign with the words *Alto/Stop* is jammed into the dirt next to him. When he sees us, he gives a tight nod, and I ask him, sweetly, how much farther to Nuevo Laredo.

"A little over a mile," he replies, and all I can think about is fresh, cold water to drink when we get there.

"Thank you," I say with a smile and start to proceed past when he puts a hand up.

"You're not from here?"

"No," I say, honestly, wondering if my Cuban accent tipped him off.

"Where are you from?"

"The United States."

He raises an eyebrow. "Where are you from originally?"

"Cuba."

"No belongings? You came empty-handed to Mexico?"

My burlap sack must not be enough for him.

I tell him we were visiting friends in El Brasil. "The girls loved our dresses so much we left them behind." I give my skirt a seductive twirl. "And we loved theirs."

The man's face doesn't move, his bristly cheeks as fixed and rugged as the landscape. "That is a long way. Why not take a bus?"

I kick myself for not preparing answers to questions like these. If not this soldier, border patrol will certainly ask. "We were robbed," I blurt out, knowing how ridiculous I sound and grateful I stuffed the last of my pesos in my garter belt before falling asleep last night. If he searches my bag, hopefully he won't search me.

"Why walk past and not report this to me?" His tone is accusing, as if missing this blatant practicality offends his authority.

My mind races trying to think up something when you step forward and say, "It happened while we slept so we think our friends robbed us, but Mamá didn't want to report them." It's impressive, and slightly disturbing, how quickly and cleverly you lie.

The soldier frowns and retreats a step, wiping the back of his hand across one cheek. "I see," he says, clearly unconcerned about tracking anyone down who has robbed us. "Well, take better care, and get yourself safely to Nuevo Laredo." He steps off the road, resuming his post, body rigid as the cactus at his feet.

When we are out of earshot, I say, "Well done, you," and you give me a triumphant look, the child curled under my arms this morning vanishing with your aura of confidence. I notice the maturing shape of your body, and how your face, in just a few months, has lengthened and eased out of its baby fat. "If you're not careful, one of these young soldiers will scoop you up, and I'll have to rescue you all over again." I nudge my elbow into your arm, but you step abruptly away looking as if I've hurt you. "I'm just teasing," I add quickly, but it's too late. You snap back into your shell like a poked crab, direct your gaze to the horizon and walk slightly ahead of me, the crack of misunderstanding widening between us.

You think I don't get it, but I do. What happened with Alfonso makes you feel vulgar and disgusted with those budding breasts, as if your body is to blame. You think all men are like this. They aren't, Nina. It's not that there are good ones or bad ones: it's not that simple. It's more a matter of which ones are damaged and which are not. Watching you stride ahead, your arms swinging, I wonder how I can keep you from making the same mistakes I made, but you can't know a mistake before you make it.

Within the hour, Nuevo Laredo rises up in the distance, and we leave the vast desert and drop into a city that makes me feel claustrophobic, everything tight together and old and dilapidated. I thought I'd be relieved to be around people again, but the parched, windy desert was more hospitable than the lopsided buildings packing us in, the sun edging through in paper-thin slats. A snot-nosed boy runs up with a tray of cigarettes and shoves them toward me with a desperate plea, as if he's selling emergency medical supplies. I shake my head, push past him with my eyes down, ignoring the street vendors hawking toys and clothes and food, their voices loud and urgent. I am disgruntled at the people sitting on benches with their feet stuck out on the sidewalk, at the children racing around throwing balls that whiz by our heads, at the nauseating smells of exhaust and sweat and oily food. As soon as I see the Rio Grande bridge, I grab your hand and hurry across the street, almost careering into a boy who jumps onto the running board of a slow-moving car, waving his goods through the window at the passengers.

Light-headed, I lean up against a cool clapboard building and pull off my hat, fanning my face with it.

"Are you okay, Mamá?" You put your clammy hands on my cheeks, and it's all I can do not to burst into tears.

I drop my hat to my side, cupping a hand over yours. "I must look a sight."

"You look sunburned," you say.

"I'm sure I am." I right myself, smooth my hair and put my hat back on.

"What's going to happen? What if they take me?" Your face is open with fear, and I try hard not to show mine. I brush the front of your dress with the flat of my hand and tuck a piece of your hair under your hat. "No one is taking you. We are walking home across that bridge. Do you hear me? Shoulders back, head high."

"What if we can't? What if they take me back to Chu Chu and throw you in jail?" Your voice is slightly hysterical.

"Shush," I say, harshly. "Do you think I'd get us this far and not make it through? We're crossing that bridge. That's all there is to it." I draw my shoulders back, push out my breasts and beam a smile. "You have an American accent, use it. If you are asked any questions, speak English. Tell them you don't know Spanish. They'll never believe Chu Chu Martinez's daughter can't speak Spanish." You frown at this, and I continue. "You may not be the actress in this family, but you'd better put on a better face than that. I don't know about you, but I'd do just about anything for some orange sherbet right about now. If I have to eat one more tortilla I'm going to roll myself up like one and die a slow death." I give your chin a shake and a reluctant smile creeps across your face. "That's more like it. Now, let's go take in a view of that mucky river."

The customs building is a barrack of rough stone that sits directly on the water at the bridge's entrance. No cars can

FIND ME IN HAVANA

cross without stopping to claim whatever goods they're bringing into the country. Even on foot, with nothing to claim,
we have to make it past the Mexican officials to US customs
on the other side of the river.

As we approach, I see two customs inspectors pulling valises
from the trunk of a car and opening them on the sidewalk. A
square case holding a typewriter seems to be of great interest.
One man pokes the keys and speaks in a quick, low voice to
the other before snapping the case closed, lifting the handle
and carrying it into the building as the driver, an elderly man
with tufts of white hair circling the ears of his otherwise bald
head, is escorted in after him.

Walking steadily, I take your hand, and I fix my eyes on
the line of cars moving slowly across the bridge. Ahead of us
people are strolling down the sidewalk as if getting from one
end to the other is the simplest thing in the world. For one
glorious moment, I think it might be that easy. Then, a man
steps from the shadow of the building into our path. He's
dressed in the same brown uniform as the others but stands a
foot taller than any man I've seen in this country. He's skeletal, with narrow hips and birdlike eyes, sharp and searching. I cringe as he slides them down my dress. "Your bag,"
he orders, and I hand it over, reaching up like a small child.

"Where are you headed?" He sticks his hand inside the bag,
moving items around while keeping his hawk eyes on me.

"Laredo, Texas," I say in crystal clear English.

He switches as well, his accent heavy. "You are US citizens?"

"Yes."

"How long have you been in Mexico?"

"Just for the day." I keep my voice light and casual, but my
words stick in my throat.

"Your reason for visiting Mexico?"

"Friends."

"Their names?"

"Fede and Rubenia Espino."

He pulls my alligator purse from the bag, snaps it open and draws out my diner's club card, driver's license, checkbook—which, thankfully, means nothing to him—three pesos I seem to have missed when tucking money into my garter belt, and a tube of lipstick. He tosses everything back in except the money, which he slides into his pocket, and my driver's license that he holds out, glancing from my face to the photo.

"Estelita Rodriguez from California." His eyes slide from my face to yours. Impressively, you gaze out over the river with a look of perfect boredom. "Is this your mother?" he asks you, and you nod and bite your lip, keeping your eyes on the moving water. "How old are you?"

"Twelve."

"What's your name?"

Worried you'll give your father's surname, I blurt out, "Nina Rodriguez."

The man nods, slowly, a corner of his lip curling upward with a look of subtle satisfaction. "Come with me." His voice is as slippery as his eyes, the tone falsely inviting. He moves toward the building, holding the door wide open as we pass through.

Inside it is cool and damp. Bare bulbs hang from the ceiling. Typewriters click. There's the whisk of paper pulled from carriage returns, the ring of a telephone. Behind the counter a clerk wearing thick-framed glasses leans over and whispers something into another clerk's ear. Down the hall, I see the man whose valises were being searched sitting in a lone chair filling out a pink card. He looks fed up, as if he's been through this before. The inspector leads us into a small office with no windows, and all I can think of is a jail-cell door clanging shut behind us. The room is stark, the overhead bulb flickering as if at any moment it's going to leave us in total darkness. I find it hard to swallow. My bag is dropped onto an empty desk, and the man sits, propping his elbows on the scarred wood and webbing his fingers together.

His eyes are on you. "Why is your mother lying?"

I squeeze you to the side of my body, hip on hip. You are almost as tall as I am. "She will not answer that."

"Okay, you answer it."

I glare at him, keeping my mouth shut. Can one be jailed for silence? I've already been caught lying, although how do they know I didn't give you my maiden name at birth?

Again, to you: "You are Chu Chu Martinez's daughter, Nina Martinez, yes?"

"She's my daughter, goddamn you." My voice climbs up my ragged throat. "She lives with me in California, and I am taking her home. We are US citizens, and you have no right to keep us here."

It's infuriating how calmly he looks at me, his watchful eyes barely glancing away as he picks up the phone. "Rosita, put me through to Salvador... Hello? Yes, she's here, and the girl."

Your body goes taut, your fingers digging into my waist. "I won't go with him," you cry. "Can he make me?"

"No, baby. I won't let him take you anywhere." This is not a promise I know how to keep.

The dingy light bulb keeps flickering, and the air turns thick with the scent of this man's sweat as he hangs up the phone and leans back in his chair rolling a cigarette. He taps down the tobacco, twists and tucks, licks the edge of the paper with the tip of his pink tongue. I think of Mamá, her hard eyes and deliberate tone, how she holds her ground when she's angry, her shoulders tense and hunched forward like a cheetah ready to pounce. Everyone backs off. Even my father used to ease himself away when she looked like that. I've spent my life practicing a smile this man could care less about. The doorknob turns, and I suck air through my teeth, preparing to face Chu Chu with every fighting bone in my body when Edward Adelman steps through the door.

"Sweet Jesus!" He claps a hand on my shoulder. His bulbous nose and swollen, pasty face never looked so wonderful.

"Ed!" I throw my arms around him, his hard belly bulging between us. I've never hugged my manager in my life.

"There, there. None of the mushy stuff." He gives me a quick pat on the back and pulls out of my embrace, straightening the front of his gabardine jacket and looking pompously out of place with his slicked back, pomaded hair, scrubbed pink skin and manicured nails, rings flashing from every finger.

I kiss his white, baby-smooth cheek. "You're here."

"Don't get sentimental. This is all business, and not any business I was willing to leave to some incompetent assistant. Young lady." He tips an imaginary hat at you as you bite your lip and drop your eyes to the floor, looking like it's taking everything you have not to cry.

"Nina, say hello to Mr. Adelman."

"Hello," you mumble.

The inspector rises, smug and self-satisfied, coming around to the front of his desk and half-sitting on the edge of it with his unlit cigarette in one hand.

"You all right?" Ed tips back on his heels giving me a once-over. "You still look like a million bucks. How do you pull that off?"

"I'm exhausted."

"Well, you don't look it, thank God. Although you could use a little makeup, but this whole situation is going to be good for us. Publicity. I've already lined up a reporter. You've staged a real-life drama, Estelita Rodriguez."

"This is real life, Ed. I haven't staged anything."

"You know what I mean. This is the stuff of Hollywood. Come on, let's get you gals out of here. We good?" He looks at the inspector, who strikes a match with his thumb and lights his cigarette. Ed raises his hand, open-palmed. "We have an agreement, yes?"

The inspector exhales a cloud of smoke, looking as if Ed is the most ridiculous man he's ever dealt with. "We do."

Ed's hand drops to his thigh with a smack, and he grunts, giving the man an incredulous look as he opens the door. "Bastard drove a hard bargain," he whispers as I pass. "You're worth a lot to some folks."

"Not you?" I manage to say, and he shakes his head at me and grins.

Everything seems so easy after that, getting into Ed's rented car and driving over the bridge as if we'd never hidden out like criminals, walked for miles or slept in an abandoned church. The US inspectors wave us through without a glance, and I twist around, looking at you as Nuevo Laredo falls away in the distance. "It's over, love. We're going home," I say, and a trembling breath rolls through you, relief or sadness, and you press your lips together. A tear rolls down your cheek, and I reach over and wipe it away with my thumb. "It's all right. We'll never be separated again."

A ridiculous thing to say, but you perk up. "Promise," you whisper holding your pinky in the air. I hook mine around it, your tiny nail bed reminding me when you were a baby and I'd have to bite your soft fingernails so you wouldn't scratch your cheeks.

"I promise," I say.

It is a promise no parent should ever make.

Chapter Seventeen

Brown Bellies

Mother,

My fear does not go away so easily, even as we move farther from the border. I was sure they would take me away from you. Now, I shiver even in the heat through the open car windows, terrified someone will stop us.

I wonder if love is a thing you grow into and out of, like shoes. If I'd stayed, maybe I would have grown into my love for my father. But I didn't want to stay. Besides, you wanting me enough to risk everything to come get me means more to me than any father ever could.

Watching the brown water swirl and surge under the bridge, I think if someone jumped in, they wouldn't be in any country at all. Not Mexico, not the US. No one could claim you in water. No parent could tell you which side you belonged to or who got to have you in which country.

At the US customs station, we slow down as a man in a stiff jacket, with a flashing silver pin stuck below his lapel, waves us through. Mr. Adelman shoots a hand out the window to salute his thanks and steps on the gas.

I never liked Mr. Adelman, and he's never liked me, either. On the rare occasion when you'd take me to his office, I'd spend the whole visit slouched in his overstuffed leather chair glaring at him. He'd glare right back. Kids getting in the way of business negotiations annoy him, and grumpy old men who tell me to stop talking annoy me, so we're clear with each other.

Even now, he's as dislikable as ever: loud, arrogant and demanding; ordering us into the car, telling me not to put my shoes on the runner and muck it up with dirt. The car, like everything else about him, is annoyingly white and shiny. My shoes have already left dirt marks on the rug, and he's already grimaced at me.

And yet, technically, he's our hero.

The bridge drops from view, the road in front of us as narrow and torn up as the one we left behind, curving through the same brown, sandy soil that devours the landscape. I had this idea that when we crossed into the United States, I'd feel the divide as distinctly as one moves their finger over the line on a map, but as Mexico falls away in the distance, nothing looks or feels different.

The shift, I realize, is not in our surroundings, but in you, Mom.

When you look back at me, the determination in your face is gone. Your eyes have that too-bright, LA quality, and you smile your abashed smile. "It's over, love, we're going home," you say, and I feel overwhelmed at the thought of things going back to how they were. A tear escapes, and you reach over and brush the soft edge of your thumb across my cheek. Wherever we are, you assure me, we will be together. Then you slide your suntanned arm back over the seat, and you rest a hand on Mr. Adelman's shoulder, your alluring, charming character intact. "How did you do it, Ed?"

He pats your knee. "Money, darling. Those brown bellies are easily paid off."

I have never heard the term *brown bellies*, but from the way your smile tightens along the edges, I'm sure it is an insult. You've told me how men assume they're right about everything and how it's a waste of time trying to convince them otherwise. "Smile to their face, and laugh about their stupidity later," you coached me.

This must be one of those times, I decide, hearing you say lightly, "Well, then, money really can buy anything."

"Good ol' capital knows no borders. Paperwork and lawyers don't mean a damn thing down here. But money...that always closes a deal."

"Didn't know I was worth that much to you, Ed."

"You're not." He grins, slanting his eyes at you and then back onto the road. "But you have friends in high places, little lady. One cowboy, to be precise."

"Duke did this?"

"He sure did. Told me I was to get my big behind down here and get you and your girl out any way I could, at whatever cost."

Of course, he did, I think. Uncle Duke is a proper hero. Ed's just following Duke's orders and trying to steal his thunder.

"How much?" You tilt your chin with a playful look, but I can tell you really want to know what you're worth to these men.

"Let's just say it's more than a plane ticket and less than a movie contract. Considering how little the peso is worth, I'd say we got a bargain."

You don't press for a dollar amount. "I'm surprised Chu Chu didn't outbid you."

Ed shrugs. "I didn't deal with Chu Chu. Doubt the man

even knew I was there. It's the inspectors I had to pay off. They were the ones keeping an eye out for you, and they'll keep their mouths shut if they want to keep what's in their pockets. Your ex-husband will think you vanished into thin air."

Until my father knows we haven't, I think, watching the horizon, that flimsy, narrow divide between earth and sky.

"How you holding up, honey? You need something to eat?" Mr. Adelman glances at me through the rearview mirror.

I am hungry, and my legs ache from walking, but I say, "I'm okay, thank you." He's never called me *honey*. Looking at the side of his sweaty face, his eyes glancing earnestly from the mirror to you, eager to please, I feel sorry for him. He could have sent his assistant to get us, but he came himself. Maybe he's lonely. Maybe saving his client and her daughter is the most exciting thing that's ever happened to him.

"There's not much to choose from in Laredo, but the restaurant at the hotel has decent food," he says.

"If it's good enough for you, it's good enough for us. We've just spent the night on the floor of an abandoned church for goodness' sake." You turn to me. "We're lucky to have Ed, aren't we? We'll be sure to put that in the news reports. *Manager goes all out for his client.*" You lean over and kiss Mr. Adelman's sweaty cheek, and for one horrible moment I wonder if you'll make him your new husband.

New husband. I still don't know if you have an old husband.

I lean out the window and let the hot wind whip my hair back. I don't want to think about Alfonso or home. I want our night in the church—our mushy, sweet bananas, silent prayers and your voice climbing in song to the rafters—to make our relationship into something new. But already that cherished time alone with you is dissipating into memory, breaking apart like clouds vanishing into wisps of nothing, no meaning at all.

I need our time inside this adventure to have meaning, for you to see that I can't go back to the way things were.

Chapter Eighteen

More Than We Bargained For

Daughter,

How can I keep my promise to you, Nina? I have to work. I *want* to work. I know you don't like Ed, but he's the one who gets me that work, and we need him. He's a decent man. He means well, and despite your dislike for him, I find myself relaxing under his big presence, his take-charge authority. It's a relief to have someone else navigate the streets, find our hotel, lead us into the hotel restaurant and then order for me: steak and potatoes, peas and rolls with pads of melting butter. Plus, I am high from our success, our escape. We did it, and it will make a damn good publicity story.

Ed talks while I half listen. He's always been a talker, but tonight he seems to speed through his stories at a faster clip than usual, grunting, laughing, shaking his head, amusing himself. You have gone totally silent. I worry Ed will think you're rude or ungrateful, but he's tolerant for a man who has no children and chides me with, "The girl's been through enough," when I insist you respond. "No need to make her suffer through another one of my stories." Yet he tells another, not asking what we've been through or how we made it to the border.

Halfway into my buttermilk pie, I'm finally able to ask after Mamá, at which point Ed goes completely silent.

"Ed?" I push my pie away. "What are you not telling me?"

"Well, now…"

There is a smudge of whip cream at the corner of his mouth, which he doesn't wipe away, and I find it annoying. "Ed!"

He chews, swallows, sighs. "Your mother's gone to Cuba."

"Cuba? She hasn't been to Cuba in twelve years. Did she tell you why? Was it because I left?"

"She didn't go into the details but said something about your father. I guess he's unwell? Or missing, or something?"

"Unwell or missing! How do you not know which?"

"Hell, I don't know. Your mother was in a state. You should have seen the look on her face when she heard I knew you were coming to Mexico and didn't stop you. She started spitting Spanish at me, which I didn't know the half of. Not too many women intimidate me, but she sure as hell does." He points his fork accusingly at me. "You always send her in when we've got contracts to negotiate. Which is precisely why I make it a rule to not get involved in my clients' family affairs. You put me in this position." The fork smashes into the top of his pie, beating the crust flat. "There was some emergency telegram about your father. That's all I could gather. There's a lot of shenanigans going on down there in Cuba right now. Political unrest and what have you."

Mamá in a state, throwing Spanish words at Ed, worries me more than what's going on in Cuba. Political unrest we've lived through. Mamá losing her cool we haven't. Ed may feel she's intimidating, but she's never been anything but clear-headed and professional in his office.

I glance at you, hunched over your plate with your eyes down. Our conversation hasn't hampered the steady pace of your pie eating, and if I didn't know better, I'd think you were pleased with the news.

I stand, quickly. "I'll be right back."

The restaurant proprietor is a stiff-backed, white-haired man who takes his job very seriously. Once I assure him that Mr. Adelman will take care of the long-distance telex charge, he slides the phone across the desk, hovering in listening proximity as I dial the operator, trying to remember Papa's address in Havana. When the telex office comes on the line, I give them Danita's address, which I know off the top of my head because it's the house I grew up in. I give a brief message: *What's happened? Are Mamá and Papa all right? If I don't have a return telex by morning, Nina and I will be on an airplane to Havana tomorrow.* I give the hotel address and room number for a return telex, press my finger over the telephone hook, and try to think of who else to contact. I haven't memorized my other siblings' addresses, and without Mamá I have no way to access the address book I stow in my desk drawer.

I release my finger from the telephone hook, hear the click and buzz of a dial tone going through, and then the switchboard operator's calm voice asking, "Would you like to be put through to anyone else?"

"No, thank you." I hang up the phone and bury my head in my arms. I barely made it out of Mexico with you, and now Mamá is gone?

"Are you all right, ma'am?" I look up at the proprietor who slides the phone back under the counter as I shade my eyes from the harshly lit chandelier in the lobby.

"I'm fine, thank you."

Back at the table, you've finished your pie and are slouched down in your seat glaring at Ed. I have never hit you in my life, but I have the urge to slap the back of your head for being so rude and ungrateful. Of course, I don't. I don't even tell you to sit up straight as I sink into my seat. My, I think, how quickly we've slipped back into our old selves.

I had imagined that some part of our relationship would stay fitted together, as we were on the church floor this morning, that our brave escape would bond us, but you've gone sour and distant, and I am irritated with you. This pretentious restaurant with its white-jacketed waiters and American businessmen make me feel as if Mexico—the church, the dusty road and hot sun, even the fear and anxiety over getting across—were from another time, another world.

"Everything peachy?" Ed slides money into the billfold and waves it at the waiter.

"I just needed the powder room."

Our waiter hurries over, and Ed tells him to keep the change. To me he says, "What you need is to rest up and keep the puff down around those gorgeous brown eyes of yours. We'll get you back to LA and find out where your mother is, no problem. I'll make some calls. *Rio Bravo* is scheduled to shoot in three weeks, and you're expected on set for costume tests in two. Duke said to tell you he'll get his lawyers to look into sole custody of this one." He jabs a thumb at you. "To make sure this doesn't happen again." To you he says, "Just don't go getting into any cars with strange men, little lady, and we'll be all right."

"My dad is not a strange man," you say, with a clean, hard look, and I cringe, worried you've offended Ed, but he just barks a laugh.

"You're right about that. Well, you know what to expect now, so don't get into a car with the old man, either. Come on." He heaves himself from the table, his stomach like a perfectly round melon under his slick shirt. "I got us a flight out

at noon tomorrow. Thought we could all use some morning shut-eye."

In our room, I pace, unable to sleep. I told the proprietor
to call me at any hour if a telex comes in, but it's three o'clock
in the morning and still no word. I keep remembering the
letter Mamá showed me months ago from Papa. At the time
I'd found the confident tone of his words reassuring. *Why
are you worrying, Maria? We've been here before. The youth are no
match for Batista. They'll settle down soon enough. You're not here,
so you can't possibly understand what is really going on.*

Mamá was outraged, slicing the letter through the air, as if
that would shake some sense into the man who'd written it.
"I damn well do know what's going on over there! Has your
father forgotten all about President Machado? He fell quick
enough, and your father jumped to the other side with Fulgencio Batista because he claimed Batista would be different.
This man understood the people, poverty and suffering, but
none of that mattered once Batista was in power, did it? What
has he done for the people? Allied with the US, profited off
the sugar plantations, taken away political liberties of the people he claims to have come from. The people were bound to
fight back. How can your father not think he is in danger?"

"Batista is a powerful man backed by a powerful country,"
I'd said, more concerned about the length of my dress for that
evening's affair than I was the political unrest in Cuba.

Mamá, for once totally uninterested in my affairs, continued waving the letter about, exclaiming. "That's never made
any difference before. Everyone appears to be underestimat-
ing the passion of depraved youth. They have strength and
anger on their side. A lot is accomplished with pure, passion-
ate hate. Your father is too hotheaded and stubborn to see that
he's putting himself and your brothers in danger. Loyalty be

damned! I won't have my boys killed because of his idiocy. They all need to get out of Cuba while they still can."

But only my brothers had.

Out the hotel window, the streets of Laredo are empty, the night hot and still. I haven't showered in days, and my scalp itches. I am sure if I scratched my nails down my arm I'd have a layer of grim under them. It's still eighty degrees here in Texas, where the mosquitoes hang on, surviving into winter. I think of the year-round mosquitoes in Cuba, of our screenless windows and the netting over our beds. I imagine Mamá sitting on the porch in her polkadot dress and her wide-brimmed hat sipping cane juice. Other than my brief time with Chu Chu in Mexico, I have never lived without her.

I move quickly then, shower, wash my hair, tying it up in a handkerchief to dry as I squeeze back into my girdle and shake out my skirt and blouse before putting them back on. My clothes from Mexico will do nicely in Cuba.

The blue streetlights flood the room as I nudge you out of sleep. "Nina, wake up. I know this sounds crazy, but we have to catch a flight to Havana and quickly." You blink at me from your pillow, half-asleep: none of this is registering. "Come, get up. We have to get going before Ed makes a fuss."

I toss the covers off you, flick on the light. You're still wearing your wrinkled, cotton dress, little white birds sailing across your chest.

"We're going to Cuba?" You slide your legs over the edge of the bed rubbing a fist into your eye.

"Yes." I give a crazed laugh. "I know, it's madness."

"Why?"

"To see your *abuelos*."

"I see my grandmother all the time, and I don't even know my grandfather," you say. Then, stubbornly, "I don't want to go."

"My papa is still your *abuelo* whether you've met him or not. *La famila es familia.* You go when there's trouble. Now, go use the ladies' room while I call the front desk and have them bring a cab around."

You drag yourself to your feet and say, "Does this mean I don't have to go back to school?"

"Is that all you can think of?" I pick up the phone. "And no, this doesn't mean you don't have to go back to school. It just means another week off. I have to be on set in two weeks, so we can't stay long. Now *vamos*, shoo! Use the washroom and sprinkle water on your dress to get the wrinkles out."

With the cab ordered, we slip quietly out of our room leaving unmade beds and wet towels for the maid. My only belongings are in Rubenia's burlap bag that I hoist onto my shoulder as I slip a note under Ed's door, which will infuriate him when he wakes. But by that time—thanks to the checkbook I've carried around—we're on an airplane from San Antonio to Fort Lauderdale where we have a six-hour layover. And by the time he's boarding his plane to LA, we're seated on Pan American Airlines with fruity drinks in our hands winging our way to Havana, a flurry of anticipation and utter exhaustion running through me. I've been up for over twenty-four hours.

This drink should knock me out, I think, lifting the fluorescent cherry from the ice and plucking it from its stem with my teeth as I look past you out the window to a layer of white clouds spread under us like perfectly peaked meringue.

"It's beautiful," I say, but you're not looking out the window.

"Why haven't we gone to Cuba before?" you ask, your dark eyes fixed intently on me.

I shrug. "I don't know. We never found the time."

"Why haven't I ever met my grandfather or your siblings? Why haven't they ever visited us?"

"You met my youngest sister, Mercedes, in New York once. Don't you remember? She came to one of my shows."

"I don't remember." You take a sip of your drink, twirling the pack of Chiclets the stewardess gave you on your tray. "How can Grandmother Maria still be married to Grandfather Manuel if she hasn't seen him since before I was born?" Your cardboard packet whizzes in circles, and I'm tempted to slap a hand out and to make you sit still.

Why this barrage of questions when I'm so tired! "You can stay married even if you don't live with someone."

You squint at me, trying to work something out. "That doesn't make any sense. Grandmother Maria and Grandfather Manuel don't even know each other anymore."

"Of course they do. You don't un-know someone just because you haven't seen them in a long time. They have an understanding. It was a different time when they were married."

You lean over the armrest, your face very close to mine as the Chiclets slow to a stop. "Why does Grandmother Maria live with you and not her other children?"

"There's no need. They're all grown with children of their own now."

"So are you."

"That's different."

"Why?"

"Because I do need her."

"Because of me?" Your voice is breathy, almost a whisper.

"No." I sigh, smoothing a finger over your forehead, the pressure of the question scrunching your lovely face up. "Because of my career. You heard Ed: your *abuela* is an intimidating woman. She gets things done. You know, I had very little growing up. The only reason I became a singer and actress is because of your *abuela*. She managed everything when I was a girl, booked me shows in Havana, worked so that I could have new shoes and proper dresses. I was too young to go to New York on my own, so she came with me."

"Well, now it's all managed, and we don't need her anymore."

"Nina, that is a mean thing to say."

You grimace and slump into your seat, twirling that damn box of gum again. "I didn't say I don't love her, just that we don't need her to live with us. She's bossy, and she's the only reason you send me away to boarding school."

You bite down on your thumbnail, and I reach over and pull your hand from your mouth. "That's not true, and don't bite your nails. It's a dirty habit." I can't understand why you want your *abuela* gone. She's never been anything but good to us. I wonder if giving you so much has spoiled you. If you knew what it was to just survive, maybe you'd be more appreciative. "What about when I have to go away? When I'm on location? I can't pull you out of school. And what about my weekend bookings in Las Vegas?"

"I could go with you on the weekends. Or maybe you don't have to sing. You could just do movies. Isn't that better, anyway?" I am too tired to hear what you are really asking. All I hear, in the moment, is the whine in your voice, the neediness.

"I love singing, Nina, and those Vegas hotels are no place for a young girl." I take a sip of my drink, sweet and thick and so cold it hurts my teeth. "Drink up, and stop talking nonsense."

My fingers tingle around the icy glass, and I look around for the stewardess to hand it back to, but she's down the aisle laughing with a young man in a blue suit. You rip open the packet of Chiclets and pop three white squares of gum into your mouth, pressing your body up against the window.

I take hold of your chin and force you to look at me. "Nina, all I want is what is best for you. Your grandmother and I both do."

You sink toward me, your chin growing heavier in my hand. "You said we wouldn't be separated. You promised," you say, and I think how utterly confusing motherhood is. One moment you are pushing me away, and the next you are as dependent as a small child.

"You have to go to school, love."

"But maybe not boarding school?"

I drop my hand, exasperated, but loving you. "Drink your punch before the ice melts, and let me get some sleep. We only have a few hours before we land."

You turn your head to the window and mutter "I have gum in my mouth," as if refusing punch is a form of defiance.

I am too tired to keep arguing with you, and I drop my drink on the stewardess's tray as she passes and lean back, closing my eyes. I drift into sleep envisioning the blue exterior of my childhood home, Mamá in the window. She is young, looking out at me and my siblings playing a game of follow-the-leader. We each hold a hand on the other's shoulder as we walk single file around the house, the tallest, Oneila, at the front followed by Manuel and Danita, then Bebo between me and Mercedes. I don't know if this is an accurate memory or if it ever even happened, but I see each of their faces, the curve of Bebo's puckered mouth, the mole on Oneila's cheek, the shade of Manuel's brown eyes that are the exact color of my own, the enviable height of Danita's cheekbones and Mercedes's double, toddler chin lifted in soldierly obedience.

None of them are like this now.

When we arrive in Cuba, Mamá will be old, my sisters will be grown and my brothers will be gone, exiled to Miami with their wives. You and your cousins will be the children marching around the yard, but even that will not last long.

I have no way of knowing that it is in Cuba where our family will crack and divide and never find a way back, that the face I just held in my palm will change forever, a whole new form of pain and betrayal stamped across it. No way of foreseeing the violence that will hobble us at the knees and cripple us into silence.

Chapter Nineteen

Cuba

Mother,

The plane wheels hit the runway and jolt me out of a deep sleep. There's a violent whir and rumble as we slow, my sleepy body jostling from side to side. The cabin is silent, people gripping armrests and holding their breath until the plane finally stops and everyone springs to life. Compartments are banged open, bags retrieved. You still carry the burlap sack from Mexico that you slide over your arm as you nudge me down the aisle. I feel disoriented and groggy, my eyes struggling to adjust to the light and commotion. In front of me there's a woman in a pillbox hat and plaid jacket who's wrestling with her carrying case. Angling the case to get it out from under her seat, she apologizes and takes a step forward, stopped by the back of a wide-shouldered man.

The woman leans around the man to see. "What is the holdup?"

"That." The man points out one of the narrow, oval windows where a dark green jeep is parked under the shadow of the plane's wing. Armed men spill from the back of it like ants. They move quickly, forming a semicircle around the plane, backs erect, feet wide, long-barreled rifles held across their chests. You latch a hand onto my shoulder, and I think that these men don't look like the armed men in Mexico. The Mexican police were intimidating but had at least looked official, crisp and clean-cut and appeared slightly bored like the policemen back home. These men out the window look excited, and something about this frightens me. They have scruffy beards and dirty faces and wear wrinkled fatigues with scraggly hair sticking out around berets pushed up high on their foreheads. They look like a pack of scrappy teenagers playing soldier, their expressions tense and alert, the guns shifting in their hands like toys just taken from their boxes.

"What's going on?" you ask, and the man who drew our attention outside says with resigned annoyance, "Any number of things, these days."

Your face is pale, and your lashes flutter as if a speck of something has landed in your eyes. Slowly, the line moves forward, the woman in the pillbox hat huffing audibly as she leans from side to side to see down the aisle. Cookie-cutter stewardesses in matching blue uniforms stand on either side of the cabin door waving white-gloved hands, looking glamorously cheerful with their perky hats and toothy smiles as they send us off into our postcard vacation, utterly unconcerned about the men with guns at the bottom of the stairs.

Outside, the sun sets in a purple sky. The air is thick with fumes and brine, sea mist caught in a current of gasoline. When we reach the tarmac, Pillbox-hat Lady is asked for her identification by a squat man with dirt-stained hands, the butt of his rifle brushing the sleeve of her coat. Flustered, she drops her papers as she pulls them from her purse, and the man chortles and picks them up. "Do you have something to be nervous about, Señorita?"

She shakes her head, her left cheek twitching uncontrollably. The man looks at her papers and waves her through,
the woman scurrying away like a mouse let loose. When it
is our turn, you step around me and block my view as you
dig into your bag. It feels like the border crossing all over
again, only this man does not ask any questions. He glances
at your California license, jerks his head up and snaps his
fingers at another man who steps forward and takes hold of
your elbow. This man does not have a gun, but the handle of
a large knife secured into a leather sheath at his belt is somehow more terrifying.

You have told me nothing about what is going on here in
Cuba. And as we are ushered forward, then made to climb
into the back of an open jeep, I am convinced that Chu Chu
has somehow managed to track us down.

Two men swing into the front seat. Doors slam. The engine kicks to life. A third man—more a boy who hardly looks
older than me, with a shadow of new whiskers and an easy
smile—jumps into the back, perching on the doorframe with
his feet on the seat, a portion of my skirt pinned beneath the
worn, leather toe of his boot. He wears a red-and-black arm-
band that says *M-26*, and he has no gun in his hand. When I
glance at his waist, I only see a thin belt holding up his pants.
It's a relief he does not have a visible weapon. The jeep backs
out from under the shadow of the plane, the boy holding onto
the doorframe with both hands as the low, bright sun slants
into my eyes. Now, no one is checking IDs on the tarmac,
and the remaining passengers walk freely toward the building, heads down, eyes diverted, as if looking at us will make
the soldiers come after them, too.

We rattle down a narrow road past shacks of tin and cardboard, the homes held together with laundry lines like beads
on a string. Buildings rise in the distance. A tall sign reads

Casino with letters stacked top to bottom. The streets are cracked as eggshell, pavement splintering out, dirt and sticks collecting along the edges. There are people everywhere, men in bright white collared shirts and women in solid-colored dresses, barefoot children and elderly who sit on overturned buckets with their elbows on their knees. Heads turn as we pass, some nod. One man tips his hat, and our driver waves. In LA, I always imagined the poor were just temporarily down on their luck. No one could actually live on the sidewalk or eat out of a tin can forever. I remember a time when Grant refused a man change and I'd felt badly for him, but Grant told me that in the United States everyone had the opportunity to work. It was just a matter of will. Grandmother Maria told me that was a bunch of rubbish, poor was poor, and rarely did a person have a choice.

These people don't have a choice, I think, and yet they don't seem sad to have houses made of tin with fabric for a door and a bucket for a seat. I like the idea that you can make a home out of nothing. If everything falls apart, I might also be able to make something out of nothing.

We leave the slums behind, picking up speed on a bumpy road with green fields stretching on either side. Despite your effort to remain cheerful, your eyes are uneasy, and I wonder why we are going with these soldiers so willingly, not even demanding an explanation.

To my left, the lush, tropical vegetation is burning. Not huge flames, just a smoldering that crawls along, eating the leafy fronds and spiraling black smoke into the air. It makes me think that whatever is going on here in Cuba is bigger than us.

The boy perched on the jeep's doorframe slides down, pinning me between your elbow and his. He might look young, but he's as tall as any man. He tilts his head out of the wind and cups his hand around a cigarette he's pulled from a pocket, attempting to light it with a match he strikes against his shoe. He goes through four matches before the tip finally glows red-hot, at which point he leans back exhaling a cloud of smoke that whisks across my face. He extends the cigarette out to you, his arm stretched across me. It looks nothing like the filtered cigarettes you smoke back home, but you pinch the rolled paper between thumb and index finger, the end wet from the boy's spit, and slide it into your mouth.

After a good puff, you hand the cigarette back, pulling a strand of hair away from your lips that the wind whips right back.

The man smiles. "Riel."

"Estelita."

"Yes. Rodriguez. A picture star." His Spanish is familiar to me, the rolls and lilts exactly the same as yours.

Modestly, you say, "Only an actress. Movie stars are another thing entirely."

He holds a hand out as if I'm supposed to shake it. "Movie star's daughter?"

"Nina." I stick my hand out, and he pumps it up and down a few times, his fingers thin and delicate for a soldier.

"Nina, nice to meet you." He lets go of my hand and leans back in the seat, smoking steadily.

We drive past rows of huts with palm-leaf roofs, shirtless children and diapered babies playing in mud-filled front yards. Here, women with weary, hardened faces tend contained fires, cooking food over them. The gutters along the road are filled with a stench worse than the smoke, and I pinch my nose closed as we cross a narrow bridge over a thin strip of water, the paved road crumbling under us. We drive into a town with single-story, cement buildings, the windows and doors gaping black holes in their facades.

"Guanajay." Your pinched lips relax into a smile. "My home."

We drive past the town square where, you tell me, on hot days you and your siblings sat on the steps under the pillared gazebo sucking lemons soaked in sugar cane. "There—" you point at a stucco church with black mold crawling up the side like moss "—is where your grandmother took us every Sunday morning, and that theater," across the street stands a boarded-up building that looks as though it used to be quite grand, "is the Vincent Mora Theater where I saw *El romance del palmar*, starring Rita Montaner. Danita and I waited for months for that movie to arrive. We spent hours staring at the poster on the wall of the only hotel in town. Rita was the most beautiful woman we'd ever seen. We practiced her smile in front of the mirror and tried to tie up our hair in perfect bows like she wore hers. Once, we snuck Oneila's mascara and painted our lashes so thick we couldn't blink. Oh, and Rita's gorgeously thin, arched brows!" You wiggle yours at me. "I've been trying to perfect those brows ever since."

So, Rita is why you pluck your brows as thin as wire, I think, finding it hard to picture this childlike version of you pretending to be the thing you've become.

We drive a little way out of town, and the jeep stops in front of a house surrounded by fields filled with wide leaves that release a pungent scent into the air. Tobacco, I will later learn. The house looks like a Spanish version of the mansion in *Gone with the Wind*. Only this house seems split between two different eras. It's as if the sky is eating it from the top down. On the second story, shutters and trim crumble around graying walls and cracked windowpanes. Black mold creeps along the edges of the flat roof, and the stone balcony sags as if it's about to collapse over the front porch, which, weirdly, looks brand-new. The downstairs pillars and steps are painted a warm blue with crisp white trim around clean glass windows. There's a decorative white grill over the front door, and a well-groomed cat sits primly watching our arrival.

A trio of children explode out the front door, and the cat leaps off the porch. A woman rushes after them, her hair falling from a loose bun as she charges toward the jeep. You yank open the jeep door and spill into her arms with a cry of joy. I slide out behind you, the two of you hugging and weeping as the men climb from the jeep, training their eyes off into the horizon. The children, two little boys and a girl who looks about eight or nine, watch us with their hands shoved into their pockets.

There is a shadow in the doorway, and Grandmother Maria's commanding figure steps out. All eyes, even the soldiers', turn to her. Her silver hair is wound on top of her head, each strand coiled and shining like metal as she comes toward me, hips swaying, arms out. Her solid body folds around me, pliable as clay, and I bury my head into her shoulder.

"Mi hermosa nieta," she croons, rubbing the flat of her hand in small circles over my back, and something inside me melts. Everything that's happened over the last few months rises up in gulping sobs. Snot and tears wet the upper sleeve of my grandmother's blouse, her soft neck against my nose. The familiar smell of vanilla on her skin makes me feel as if I am going to crack and splinter off in a million directions.

When I finally raise my head, I see that everyone has moved away from us. You stand in the yard with your arm around another woman I don't know, the three children gathered around you, the woman you'd hugged by the jeep clutching your hand. On the porch are now two teenage girls and a girl who looks about my age. The soldiers have scattered. Two by the road, one near the porch steps. Riel is the only one who still leans against the jeep shuffling his boot in the dirt, arms crossed, eyes on the ground.

"Come," Grandmother's voice is commanding as she nudges me forward, and I am reminded how bossy she is. "Meet your family."

It is my cousin Josepha who untangles herself from the crowd, stepping up with a keen smile. She has a high forehead, wide nose and inquisitive large brown eyes. Without hesitating she pulls me into an embrace and says, "I've been waiting for you!"

And in that moment, I know I will love her.

Chapter Twenty

They Took Him in the Night

Daughter,

This is not a homecoming: it is a pulverization of memory. My sisters have become women I don't recognize; they are now mothers with solid identities and rooted habits. When I left Guanajay, Mercedes was a scrawny twelve-year-old who still played with paper dolls, Danita sixteen and self-conscious and angry, Oneila a woman of twenty-two who had not yet fallen in love. Now, the gap in their ages has closed into comfortable comradery. They are full of opinionated ideas and loud laughter, full of contentment with each other.

I do not belong to them or to this house anymore, modernized under the hands of Danita and her husband Sergio. Whole walls have been removed, floors stripped, our great-grandparents' dark, intricately carved furniture replaced with teak and chrome. Bulbous light fixtures dangle overhead, and shag rugs decorate the floor. It is LA incarnated in Cuba, and the only remaining part I remember is the crumbling, second-story exterior.

Danita, however, is proud of her home. In her immaculate, frilly apron, she leads me from room to room, a manic quality to her movements as she points out each new addition, Eames chairs and Nelson lamps. She desperately wants to impress me, but something weighty is wrought beneath the sheen of her smile. This tour is her crowning glory, and she's determined to carry it out, never mind the growing restlessness of rebel soldiers armed outside.

By the time we make it to the living room, where we used to sing along to the radio, I am tired of pretending to like the ostentatious home she's created. The room is swank and cold, and nothing looks comfortable to sit on. Boxy throw pillows are propped in the arms of white tufted chairs, and the sofa, upholstered in pale pink leather, sits off-center from the oval coffee table as if they, too, are distant relatives. Out the window, the ficus tree is the only thing calling to me from the past, its aerial roots still hanging like thickly braided hair from its massive branches.

I watch you, Nina, with Josepha, my sister's daughter, huddled beneath that same ficus that sheltered my sister and me so long ago. You whisper close as if you've known each other your whole lives. From the porch, Mercedes's and Mamá's low voices drift in, and I see Oneila walk past under the window to join them.

Danita moves around the room, straightening pillows and brushing down the arms of the chairs with the flat of her hand. Of all my siblings, we are the most alike. Her narrow nose, full lips and wide brown eyes mirror my own. It was just luck that landed me on-screen and not her. This show of domesticity from her feels desperate, her strained movements fearful.

"Danita, what is going on? Why were we escorted home by soldiers?"

She looks up, her eyes hard and glassy. "Escorted? Oh, no,

dear sister, you've been arrested." She waves a frantic hand around the room. "House arrest. I responded to your telex, but it must have been too late to stop you from coming. Did you think they were the Rural Guard?" She laughs, the sound as hard as her eyes.

She means to say *You've been gone so long, little sister, you've forgotten what our side looks like*, and the insult throws me. "I know who they are." My voice is petulant. "I just thought Castro's rebels were still in the Sierra Maestra, that Batista had things under control."

"The rebels have been flooding out of the hills since August. They've lit the country on fire, stopped train lines, drained gas tanks, intercepted telephone calls and telegrams. Bombings and executions are a daily occurrence. Batista has nothing under control." Danita grinds the heel of her bright red pump into the rug.

"And Papa?"

"Papa is gone."

"Where?"

"We don't know. They took him in the night."

"They? Who's they? Castro's men?"

"Yes."

"Where did they take him?"

Danita throws up her hands. "God only knows."

I do not understand how these scrawny young men, lounging in our front yard with stubbly facial hair, are defeating anyone. President Batista is powerful, the Rural Guard a force to reckon with. His chief of police, my father, is a fighting man. Manuel Rodriguez's ferocity and loyalty date all the way back to the day he slapped Mamá in Batista's defense. Since then my father's years of service as a military officer, his alliance with Batista during his elected presidency, and after during the overthrow of President Prio, have all earned him the title he carries today.

"What's happened with Bebo and Manuel?" Even as grown men, our brothers still follow Papa in all things, their loyalty as officers to Batista unwavering.

"They left three weeks ago for Miami. Papa insisted. He arranged it but refused to go with them. I didn't know what else to do besides send for Mamá. She's the only one who could have convinced him and Sergio to leave."

"Sergio wouldn't go, either?"

"I begged him, but he's as stubborn as our father."

"What of Mercedes's and Oneila's husbands?" Through Papa, all of my sisters' husbands are connected to Batista.

"They were smart enough to leave with Bebo and Manuel."

"Why didn't all of you go with them?"

"It's not easy to uproot a life." Danita holds two fingers to her temple and makes the motion of a gun going off. "They'll shoot our husbands and brothers in the head or string them up and gut them like pigs, but they're not going to kill us. Haven't you heard? Fidel and his brother Raul are decent men. They don't go around killing women and children. They want what is best for the people." She spits out the words, and it strikes me how bitter she's become.

"And where is Sergio now?"

"They took him with Papa." Her tone is cold, unemotional, as if she's frozen this unimaginable reality for her husband into a tight corner of her heart. Outside, the light dims, and shadows dance across her face.

"Oh, Danita, I'm so sorry." I take a step toward her, but she raises her hand to stop me.

"Papa never believed it would come to this. He told me that when Batista defeated Castro we'd all go to Miami and

bring the boys home. He said that if Sergio insisted on staying, he'd keep him safe. He promised."

"Do you think they're all right?"

"No, I do not."

"They might be. Maybe they're negotiating? Don't coun-
tries trade prisoners in war? Batista is still in charge. He can
do something."

Danita gives a twisted smile, throwing her arms out and
shimmying her hips as she whistles. "Estelita, always looking on the bright side of things. Shall we sing and dance to a
wartime romance? Or maybe we can seduce those men outside into giving away their secrets, like a good Hollywood
story, yes?"

Stress always made my sister mean. She sashays over to
me, her smile collapsing as her arms drop to her sides. Her
apron has shifted out of place, and there's something about
the crooked frill across her chest that makes her appear to be
completely unraveling. "I don't go through husbands like you
do," she says. "For me, it has only ever been Sergio."

This hurts, but I am not going to fight with her the first
hour I arrive home, so I say simply, "Sergio is a good man,"
and take her hand despite her resistance. "I can help, Danita.
I'll get word to my manager. Or Uncle Duke. I know people
who can help us. We'll find him."

My sister softens a little, her shoulders sagging, and I think
she might say something kind when Mamá strides into the
room, Mercedes and Oneila right behind her. They perch on
the sofa like birds on a wire, alert, focused. The rebel soldiers
are right behind them, stomping their boots over the rug. One
of the soldiers settles into a chair; the other two drop to the
floor and sit cross-legged as if they're boys around a campfire.

"Is it that time already?" Danita asks perky and sarcastic,
striding over to the shell-pink, Westinghouse radio on the

bookshelf and clicking it on. Static crackles into the room. Danita fiddles with the dial until there is a moment of silent, dead air before a smooth, male voice booms out, *"Aqui Radio Rebelde,* the voice of the Sierra Maestra, transmitting for all Cuba on the twenty-meter band at 5:00 and 9:00 p.m. daily. I'm Station Director Captain Luis Orlando Rodríguez."

This Rodriguez is not related to us. I glance from the soldiers to my sisters, the men lounging, the women tense. Danita folds her arms, her heavily rouged face held in strait-laced obedience. Mercedes rests plump hands over her knees, her teeth clenched around a half smile, and Oneila tilts her head as if the rebel news is of great interest. Mamá's face is placid, her chest stilled as if she is holding her breath.

I listen, standing at the far end of the room wishing I could lie down. My legs are weak, and I am terribly thirsty. The last thing I had to drink was the fruity cocktail on the plane, but I don't dare excuse myself for a glass of water. The dark-pitted eyes of the soldier who took my papers and drove the jeep are on me. His hair sticks out from under his beret, curling thick around his ears, shiny and brushed, his mustache trimmed down to a thin beard that circles the bottom of his chin. He stares at me with intrigue as the station director reports a successful attack on the Bureau for the Repression of Communist Activities carried out by rebel leaders and the rural underground movement. The man nods, smoothing his lips together as we are given a detailed description of the gunning down of three of Batista's secret police and the capturing of a fourth before the announcer's satisfied voice snaps off, and a female singer begins an upbeat song about love under a coconut tree.

I glance out the window to the ficus, its roots like a hundred snakes slithering to the ground. Under them it is dark with shadow, and I can no longer see you.

★ ★ ★

That night I lie with you pinned under my arm. Mamá sleeps in the bed next to us, Oneila and Danita are in a second room, and Mercedes with her three small children—the youngest of which, I am told by Oneila, wakes screaming with night terrors—in a third bedroom. You begged me to let you sleep in the room where Josepha and Oneila's two teenage daughters sleep, but I said, *No. I want eyes on you.*

Despite how little sleep I've had, I am wide-awake. It was a mistake to come. A horrible miscalculation. If I miss the costume screen test *for Rio Bravo*, they'll recast my role. I can fix this, I think, rolling over to face the breeze from the window. I will get word to Ed or Duke. I will get us out of here. All of us. I can't let Mamá face this alone, or my sisters. Besides, I have missed the company of women, these women, my sisters. Even Danita's anger is a comfort. We always fought, and I like that she still treats me as a sister and not a friend. I have enough friends; family is different. There is spit and fight and love between us. There is loyalty.

Outside the wind picks up. The palms slap their leaves together, and the air through the window smells of rain. It is typhoon season. As a child I loved typhoon season. With the doors bolted and windows latched, I would watch the wind tear up the earth and the rain slam it back down. I always knew I was safe, the house around me still and quiet and solid as rock.

I do not feel that way now. The walls have become porous, the armored men who have bolted us behind our own doors mightier than the wind.

You stir in your sleep, and I roll back over and rest a hand on your forehead remembering my nanny Farah, how she danced at the foot of my bed, how much I loved her. I never saw her again after the day the fields burned. For years I'd look for her on walks into town or when we'd drive to Havana, search the dark faces of women washing clothes in the river or bent over outdoor fires. When she'd worked for Mamá, she was a young woman with no children. Where is she now? Fighting with the rebels or fighting at home to protect her family?

Low, male voices float through the window, and I wonder if they are directly under it keeping watch. I can't hear what they are saying. How stupid I've been. News in the United States reported Fidel Castro as an uncontrollable dissident hiding in the hills with underfed men and makeshift weapons. How did we not know what was really going on? I had watched the black-and-white clips, miniature soldiers marching across the television screen to thematic music, the announcer's voice declaring that, after President Batista deployed ten thousand soldiers to get rid of three hundred rebels, the US now saw Batista as a corrupt and brutal dictator and would no longer back him. Mamá had slammed a fist into the arm of the sofa. "Disgusting, suspending assistance to a country they have reaped the financial benefits of for years."

Cuba will always be my homeland, but I have been a US citizen since I married Grant, and even if I've not been very politically minded, I'm a fan of Eisenhower. I figured the US president knew what he was doing. Batista's strength in numbers spoke for itself. But now that I am here, I feel betrayed by the US. They are supposedly an ally and neighbor to Cuba. How could they let it go this far?

The soldiers keep us locked in, stationing guards outside the house. Within a week, I have lost hope of getting word to anyone in Los Angeles. By the time this ends, my film career will be long forgotten.

I sing to stay hopeful. We all do. There's music with breakfast and lunch and dinner and most hours in between. If I'm not singing, then one of my sisters or nieces is. Even Mamá joins in, and Josepha has taught you that singing isn't all about skill. The two of you stand arm in arm belting out notes that fold into the sounds of the instruments, guitars strummed by Oneila's older daughters, pots banged by Mercedes's little ones. While we cook and clean, before bed and while falling asleep, our voices soar and hum and harmonize. It keeps us partly sane. More than anything, it is the stagnation of the ceaseless days that makes me feel crazed. With no forward motion, there's nothing to anticipate. With nothing to anticipate, life pales into a ghost of itself. And I am becoming a ghost of myself.

At least the soldiers don't sleep here. They come for dinner, listen to *Radio Rebelde* and then head across the street to their barracks in the stone building Mamá's father, *Abuelo* Gonzalo, built to house the slaves before slavery was abolished in 1886, at which point it housed Black people. I remember asking my *abuelo* what the difference was. He'd looked at me over his reading glasses and said they were paid, that was the difference, and that they could leave anytime they liked. He had Mamá's eyes, rich and brown and reassuring, a thin, old man with great wrinkles down his neck and a white beard trimmed long and pointy over his chin.

"Where would they go?" I asked, thinking of the Blacks I'd seen washing their clothes in the river and cooking over open fires.

"Anywhere they damn well please."

It seemed far nicer to me to live by a river than across our dusty road in a building like a small fortress. "Then, why don't they go? Why don't your workers sleep and eat in huts with their families like the rest of the *guajiro*?"

"If the Blacks eat and sleep in one place, they'll be united and work with each other instead of against each other," he said. "So if they want to work for me, then they live across the street."

After they united and worked together to burn down the henequen and sugarcane fields and oust Machado, I wondered if my *abuelo* ever felt guilty that he'd been so right.

After the 1933 revolution, I never saw my *abuelo* again. He moved to Santiago with *Abuela* Osita and didn't visit. Papa turned against him by siding with Batista, and Mamá turned against Papa by siding with her father. Thinking back, my parents were as young and stubborn and sure of themselves as these rebel soldiers who now sit—nightly, demanding food— at the same table we all sat at the morning our servants disappeared.

Even though none of the women in our family are good cooks, my sisters do their best to feed these new rebels. Oneila at least knows how to boil yucca, fry plantains and cook horse-meat into stew. We have little food to work with. The rebels bring whatever food supplies they have and don't seem concerned about what we set in front of them.

Riel, I learn, is only fifteen years old. The man who led me to the jeep by my elbow, Riel's elder brother Alipio, is all of seventeen. The third man, the one whose eyes track me when I move in and out of the kitchen with plates of poorly cooked food, is an Argentinian by the name of Ernesto Guevara, but everyone calls him Che.

Danita tells me he is Fidel Castro's second-in-command. And I wonder why we Rodriguezes are so important to him.

I have known different versions of men like Che. Not ones who have killed, but ones who find pleasure solely in power. Whatever version—fat, red-nosed producers in gabardine suits, alluringly handsome directors in white jackets and bow ties, or angry young men in armbands and berets—

they all have the same simmering look in their eyes. Drunk on ego, they believe that their power is a drug we all feed on, that we obey them not out of fear but because we desire to please them.

I wonder if they know, or care, how much hatred pours into our hearts as we smile, serve them plates of warm food and pretend we don't notice their hands violating our thighs, the curve of our rumps and the tender skin at the small of our backs.

Chapter Twenty-One

Dirty Secrets

Mother,

I never knew it was possible to know so many secrets about one person. Josepha said that, even though she has eighteen other cousins, she's never had one she could trust before.

"I knew the moment I saw you that you were trustworthy and we were going to be best friends. I've never had a best friend. Have you?" she says, her intense eyes probing mine.

"No."

We sit in the grass eating the figs we've plucked from the branches of the ficus, warm and swollen and thickly sweet. The ground is littered with them, the air sticky with the scent of overripe fruit. Here, I speak nothing but Spanish, which reminds me of the time before Villa Cabrini Academy when I was little and we spoke only Spanish at home. When you left me at boarding school, the nuns were horrified that I couldn't speak English. I remember the humiliation on your face when Sister Katherine scolded you for not raising me as a proper American.

After that, you and Grandmother spoke only English to me.

I bite the nubby end off of my fig and spit it into the grass. The sky is tense with low clouds and a sharp warm wind. A storm wind, Josepha says, brewing since we arrived a week ago.

"Do you think your papa will come back?" I ask, wondering how long our house arrest can last. The soldiers keep the front of the house locked and guarded, but it's easy enough to climb out the back windows. They've seen us in the yard and don't seem to care. When we first met, Josepha told me rebel soldiers took her father in the night, marched him and our grandfather from their bedrooms in their bathrobes, put them in a jeep and drove away.

Josepha brightens at the question, sucking her fig like a lollipop. Unlike me, she wears her emotions on the outside, flitting from sorrow to delight in seconds. "Of course he'll come back. Fulgencio Batista would never let anything happen to him. My papa's a hero, you know. He killed two men and wounded three in the attack on the Mancado barracks. Mamá says Batista should never have let Fidel and his brother out of jail and that the rebels have as good as won, but I don't believe her. If that was true, we'd be in Miami already. Aunt Oneila says we're here because my mamá refuses to leave without my papa, and they refused to leave her. All but your mamá. But that was different: she left a long time ago. Mamá says sisters are the best thing a woman can have, even the ones who leave you." Josepha tosses her fig aside and leans close to me, hugging her knees. "What is it like, to live in Hollywood and have a movie star for a mother?"

I finger the wooden spoon you gave me in my pocket. I carry it everywhere. "It's boring. I go to boarding school."

"No!" Josepha cries.

"I am not the movie star."

"I suppose not. You're too ugly, which I can say without

being mean because you're still prettier than I am." Josepha
bulges her eyes, making me laugh as she wiggles her eyebrows,
which are as thick as caterpillars. "Our wicked mamás didn't
give us any of their beauty. I suppose it's for the best. If one
of us was beautiful, the other would be jealous. My mamá
would never admit it, but she's wildly jealous of Aunt Estelita.
Who wouldn't be? Your mamá is grand. Mine said the rebels
keep your mamá here for political advantage: an expatriot,
an American citizen *and* a Hollywood actress!" She leans in
and whispers, "Really, they just want to sleep with her. Either
way, she's a valuable catch for the Castro brothers."

"Then, what am I?" I ask, partly in jest and partly fearful. I imagine the soldiers trading my mother like a ring in
a pawnshop.

"Useless. We both are without breasts for them to fondle."
Josepha reaches into her shirt and cups her hand around the
very small rise of a beginning breast. "Wouldn't fill a teacup.
Let me feel yours." She reaches under my shirt, her hand hot
against my nipple. "Nothing."

We burst out laughing. My eyes water, and I snort, the
laughter like soda bubbles coming out my nose, which makes
us laugh harder. I don't even know why I'm laughing, but it
feels intoxicating, like a sensation I've been reaching for my
whole life.

On our backs, not looking at each other, we finally catch
our breath. Heavy clouds press overhead, but I am light as
sunshine. "I don't want breasts," I say. "I don't want any boy
ever looking at me."

"Not even Riel? I've seen him looking at you. Maybe he
likes flat-chested women. Lita says there are men who prefer women with small breasts." Lita and Enricua are Oneila's eldest daughters, glorious teenagers maturing before our
eyes. "Riel is only fifteen." Josepha props up on one elbow,

meeting my eyes. "I heard our aunts talking about him in the kitchen. 'A baby! No one that age should be holding a gun!' I'd kiss him. His brother is ugly, and Señor Guevara is old, although if I were old I'd probably think he was cute. Lita and Enricua say he is."

I have never thought about men in this way. "Riel is not looking at me. I'm not even thirteen."

"Kings used to take brides at twelve. Have you started your period?"

"Yes."

"Then, you're a woman."

"Have you?"

"Barely. I've only gotten it once. I'm hoping that's why my breasts haven't grown yet."

Josepha drops back down, and we stare at the sky in silence, small stones prickling our backs. I want to tell her about Alfonso, about what happened and how sickening his hand felt between my legs. The first day we met, she said we had to tell each other our darkest secret. "That's the only way we'll ever really trust each other," she said, squeezing my hand as if trying to wring blood from it. She told me she's learned to rub her finger between her legs until there is a bursting feeling that makes her whole body shiver.

"Now, I do it every night, but I'm sure it's a sin. I also stole my cousin Maria's gold-leaf barrette out of her suitcase when she was packing for Miami. She's Uncle Bebo's daughter, two years younger than me and full of herself. I know I should feel badly about the barrette, but I don't. Okay, what's your darkest secret?"

I told her my darkest secret was sneaking Señorita Perron's tequila. Now, lying in the heavy air with the imprint of her hand on my breast, I wish I hadn't lied. I want to tell her my darkest secret. I just don't know how.

The wind picks up, the branches of the ficus so heavy they barely shift under the force.

"Storm's almost here," Josepha says. "I hope it's a big one."

It is a big one. Whole branches are torn from trees, and the rain slams down sideways, hitting the windows like pebbles. The road becomes a river, fat frogs and snakes careering down it on palm leaves, the yard swirled up with mud and sticks and leaves like a witch's brew. From the window, you, Mom, sit with Josepha and me watching little green frogs twirl away in the current. You swear the roof won't rip off, but Josepha and I are not so sure. The wind sounds like bones cracking against the tiles. The roof has seen worse, you reassure us.

Tucking your feet under you on the sofa, you tell us about a storm that landed a tree on the house and another when you and Aunt Danita snuck out at fourteen to meet two boys in town, but the boys never showed.

"My Sergio was one of them." Aunt Danita leans against the doorframe on her way to the kitchen. "Imagine your father scared of a little wind! I tease him about it to this day. And you, Estelita, you never looked twice at that other boy. Too proud to date a coward, you said."

"Not true," you argue. "That boy had horse teeth and pimples, and I never liked him in the first place!"

Danita swats her hand at you. "Liar," she says laughing and continues down the hall.

So much about you makes sense to me here: your big laughter, your over-the-top energy. Your sisters might not be movie stars, but they match you in this, laughing and fighting, dancing and singing and crying, all four of you boisterous and dramatic. Your sisters' stories of you, your stories of them, of your brothers, the ones given privileges you all envied, all becomes a rich and colorful past I envy. My life back home pales beside all this grand aliveness.

For days we are not allowed outside, and the house is chaotic. Mercedes's boys, Tabo and Victor, cherubic little devils, toddle around stabbing sticks into the furniture and throwing fantastic tantrums. Mercedes's daughter, Marta, follows Josepha and me like a puppy, begging to be included in whatever secret plan we're devising. She's only seven and, in the hierarchy of cousins, still a baby. Josepha tells her to shove off. "We are too old to play silly games," she says with an upward tilt of her chin.

Not true. While the sky boils overhead and the earth is chewed into a pulp, we nestle in our dark closet with a tapered candle playing truth or dare by a single flickering flame. Truths we exaggerate into lies, dares we play on poor, unsuspecting Marta. Smashed banana on the sofa or an upturned chair is blamed on Tabo or Victor. But our most calculated dares we play on Lita and Enricua, writing fabricated love letters from Riel and Alipio and slipping these under their doors, or sprinkling ash from the fireplace into their pot of rouge.

They find none of this funny. The storm has made them irritable. Because of the torrent, the soldiers have not crossed the road, and our teenage cousins are bored without the distraction. I don't know why they aren't frightened of these sharp-eyed, jumpy young men carrying guns. Maybe it is because the rebels keep their eyes on our mothers and take little notice of them.

When the men trail in at six to listen to *Radio Rebelde*, we are sequestered in our rooms. Half an hour later, when the soldiers make the journey from the living room to the dining room for dinner, Lita and Enricua sneak to the top of the stairs to watch them. They return sighing and whispering to each other, drawing Josepha and me down on their beds and making us choose which rebel we'd have. Once, Oneila came into the room as we were deciding and her face went shell-white. She dragged her daughters up by their arms, scolding them in the voice of a lioness. She is the quiet aunt, but when she roars it is mighty.

After that, Lita and Enricua no longer included us in their daring discussions.

Day four of the storm, Josepha and I huddle in the closet in flickering candlelight, the wind moaning in the background as Josepha reads aloud from an anthology of Cuban poetry she took from our Grandfather Manuel's room. Josepha told me he moved in with her and her parents a year ago. "It's terrible having him around. He's the strictest. Never speaks to me unless he's scolding."

"I've had to live with Grandmother Maria my whole life," I say, and Josepha says she'd take living with her any day over our grandfather.

Grandfather Manuel's things are in the room where Mercedes sleeps with her children: a shaving kit, history books on the Cuban War of Independence and a military jacket that hangs on the back of the door. No one ever touches these things, and I wonder if we'll get in trouble for taking his book of poetry.

From the closet, we hear a door bang shut. The soldiers are back.

We blow out the candle, slip into the upstairs hall and peer between the stair railing as Señor Guevara wipes his boots on the mat, politely, like a visitor, his hair falling damp and curly around his face. He is handsome, but so was Alfonso. I wonder if handsome men might be the worst kind. Alipio is right behind him with two more rebels I've never seen before.

They are older, one slightly taller than the other, full beards on their faces and lines wedged deep around their squinty eyes. I don't see Riel, which gives me a funny, worried feeling until the door swings open again and he steps in, slapping his wet hat against his thigh. He doesn't look up. None of them do as they pass below us heading for the living room. Oneila steps out of the kitchen brandishing a dish towel. She, on the other hand, darts a look right at us, and we scurry back, but not before I see you through the living room doorway standing in lamplight, your hair down, your face clear and open.

Your beauty does not serve you here, I think, slipping back into the closet with Josepha. Here it is dangerous.

Chapter Twenty-Two

Men

Daughter,

Tonight, I want you to stay shut in that closet. I want your eyes and ears closed.

The men gather like wolves in a pack, circling, eyeing, assessing, the oil lamp sending ankle-deep shadows dancing across their legs. The radio is battery-operated so not affected by the loss of power from the storm, but tonight they are here for more than rebel news.

Che settles into a chair watching his comrades with the ease of one who knows his orders will be obeyed without question. He looks pleased with himself and with these new soldiers he's brought. These men don't have the youthful, soft eyes of Riel and Alipio. They are seasoned and arrogant.

We never learn their names. It doesn't matter. Best not to put names to their faces.

Mercedes and Mamá are seated on the couch. I stand at the other end of the room with my hand pressed flat against my stomach. Riel and Alipio take their positions on the rug, legs crossed, boys at the feet of men. The older of the two new men steps up to me, his cigar breath nauseating, his greedy eyes searching me like a mangy, hungry dog. A small, white scar runs through one eyebrow, and there are pits in his cheeks like inverted gravel. He reaches out and strokes the side of my neck with a single, rough-tipped finger, running it over my collarbone to my blouse where he places his whole sweaty-hot hand over my breast. Humiliation shoots through me, and it is all I can do not to spit in his face.

"Not her" I hear and look over at Che who watches, non-chalant, as if his friend is choosing a side dish. The hand falls, and the man moves to the couch and plants himself next to Mercedes, who has gone stiff and white as sun-bleached driftwood. Her hands fold and unfold in her lap. I think of how she used to play with paper dolls under the low, wide branches of our manchineel tree, how she'd spend hours cutting them out, little pieces of paper trailing everywhere she went. Mercedes, now twenty-seven. Mother of three. Mercedes the Gatherer. Mercedes the Cheerful.

The man says, "We are missing the news," his voice silkier and more cultured than I would have expected, given his coarse exterior.

The other man—slightly younger, openly hostile—goes to the radio and clicks it on as Danita appears in the doorway, fists balled at her sides. I give her a quick, warning look. *Go back. Retreat. Hide.* But her eyes fall on the couch where Mercedes's small, plump hand has been placed on the man's wide thigh.

"What's going on?" Her voice bristles as she steps into the room. Mamá rises quickly and puts a hand on her arm, but Danita shakes it off, her eyes flint-hard, steadily moving from one rebel soldier to the next. The man at the radio straightens and turns. He has not found the station, and static buzzes into the room like a swarm of bees.

"Señorita," he says with a smile, his teeth crooked, "we were going to listen to the news, but the station isn't coming in." His words are genial, everyday, like a husband home for the evening. "What should we do now?"

It is not a question. A gust of wind drives the rain against the window. The man on the sofa draws Mercedes up by her arm as the other man strides over to Danita, swift and agile as a lynx. Her body stiffens in his grip, her face stone. He leads her from the room, the other man yanking Mercedes in front of him and kicking the door shut with the heel of his boot.

Static continues to crackle in the air like the end of a movie reel going around and around. Mamá and I look at each other, our fear twisting expressionless inside us. "Don't let them see your fear," Mamá had said to me that first night we arrived.

"They haven't touched us," Oneila had reassured me then.

"Doesn't mean they won't," Danita had answered.

"They would have already. Don't scare Estelita," said Mercedes the Cheerful, squeezing my arm.

Fear crawls over every inch of me now, and I wonder where you, Nina, and Josepha are. At least us and not our daughters, I think.

Riel and Alipio scramble to their feet as Che directs a firm, fatherly tone at them. "You two, go wait in the dining room for dinner."

Riel glances at me, his face flushed with embarrassment, while Alipio looks thoughtful, as if he's considering his options for the future: dinner, or a woman first?

When they have gone, Che says to Mamá, "You go on and finish the cooking."

Mamá doesn't move. She stands looking at him with cold pride, and for a moment they are equals, matched in authority, him over his men, and she over her daughters, but that is where their equality ends. He is a man, and she is a woman, and she will do what he says.

"What do your men prefer tonight?" she stalls, knowing there is little choice other than a pot of beans and cassava bread.

"Roast pig." Che gives a sardonic smile, and Mamá returns it with a genial, pleasant one.

"Wouldn't that be nice? Pork is my favorite. John Wayne served a whole roasted pig at his last gathering, didn't he, Estelita? The look on Jayne Mansfield's face when it was set on the table, head and all with an apple in its mouth. Does Señor Castro like roast pig on a spit?" She is reminding him who I am, and who he is, a man below Fidel Castro who should watch his step if he doesn't want bad publicity with the Americans.

This amuses Che. "Señor Castro prefers vegetable soup," he says, draping an arm over the side of his chair, legs apart, looking as if there was nowhere else he'd rather be.

"I'm sorry he's not here, then. Vegetables are more plentiful than meat, these days." Mamá turns abruptly to me. "Estelita, there are two decks of cards in the cupboard. Why don't you and Señor Guevara play a game of canasta while I get dinner on the table?" She faces Che. "Estelita is excellent at canasta. She beats me every time. You do play, don't you?" Her brows rise questioningly, a skilled hostess directing her guest exactly where she intends for him to go.

Che leans forward, a man who likes a game. "We need four players."

"It's the same as four-handed canasta, only each player plays for himself." Mamá glances at me as if to say *Let him win, every time.* "Estelita will show you."

Not believing for one second that this man will be distracted by cards, I bring them from the cupboard, Mamá giving me a last, hard look before leaving the room. Che scoots his chair to the edge of the coffee table and rubs his hands together. "You shuffle and deal."

I sit on the sofa, my stomach pulsing. The house is too quiet. I try not to picture what is happening upstairs as I shuffle and deal, terrified you and Josepha will hear or see something you should not.

Che fans his cards in one hand, concentrating as he rearranges them. "You go first."

I pinch my mouth into a smile, thinking cards might be all he wants after all as I place three queens faceup and discard a three of clubs. Che snatches up my discarded club and sets down seven cards of the same rank. "This is going to be fun." He grins like a schoolboy. "Every time I make a meld, you'll remove a piece of clothing. Go on, then. One meld, one article of dress."

Revulsion rises in me at the look in Che's aggressive eyes, at his slimy, self-assured smirk, and I think of all the things men have told me to do, where to stand and what to wear and how to smile. "No." I bite the word off.

"No?" he repeats dumbly, my disobedience momentarily disarming him.

"Rip them off if you choose, but I am not playing this stupid game with you." I toss my cards down, my defiance a taste like metal in my mouth.

Che's anger is instantaneous. He springs to his feet, his face frightening as he grabs my arm and in one swift motion drags me off the couch. I knock into the coffee table, cards scattering, his hand ripping at my blouse. The fabric tears easily, the edges hanging ragged, my brassiere exposed. A vein pulses in my neck so hard I think it's going to burst through my skin. Che's lips are close to mine, but he doesn't kiss me, just breathes hot in my face, his jaw set as he grabs my breast with one hand and tries to yank down the side zipper on my skirt with the other. It sticks halfway, and he shoves me backward into the couch, reaching up under my skirt while unzipping his pants.

I want to fight. Kick and spit and bite, but for some reason I go completely limp, squeezing my eyes closed as if this will somehow make it stop. His damp, clumsy hand is between my legs, and I wait for him to rip my underwear off, for the pressure of his detestable body against mine, his stink and wet. But it doesn't come. The hand slides away, and when I open my eyes Che is standing in front of me with his pants around his ankles, his hand moving up and down the shaft of his penis, the tip bobbing in the air, bulbous and red and grotesque as the swollen nose of a drunkard. There's a twisted look of ecstasy on his face that repulses me. Acid burns in my throat. He's at that point where a man's mind goes wildly blank. A point of weakness.

Holding my tattered blouse closed, I say, "Don't trip over your pants," and get up, leaving him grunting.

I drag myself to the kitchen, not wanting to face anyone, but not daring to go upstairs. I pray you and Josepha are distracted in the closet, that you have seen and heard nothing.

Oneila is spooning black beans into bowls. "Dear God, your blouse," she says, and Mamá turns, cutlery clutched in her hand.

"This wire contraption stopped him." I snap my bra strap and give a sharp, fake laugh.

Mamá drops the silverware on the counter, takes a cardigan from a hook by the boarded-up kitchen door and tosses it at me. "Cover yourself, and help me set the table." Her voice is angry, her look reminding me of the time I confessed my pregnancy, how disappointed she was at my lack of self-control. Does she think this is my fault? She arranged an innocent card game, and I went and exposed myself?

Oneila diverts her eyes, ladling soup with deep concentration, and I remember a night when I was a child and Oneila came home with blood on her lip, my almost-grown sister, crying in the hallway. It was the Diazes' eldest son, she said. He shoved her into a bush, ripped her underwear off and ran away with them. Mamá had looked at her just like she's looking at me now, as if Oneila was at fault. She told her to wash up, go to bed and not say a word to Papa. The incident was never mentioned again, and when the Diazes' boy came over for dinner, Mamá served him a second helping of coconut cake.

I pull the cardigan on, jabbing the buttons of the sweater closed over my ripped blouse, furious at all of them. These men, my family. None of this should be allowed to happen. None of us should even be here. Mamá should never have come. My sisters and Papa should have left when they had the chance. Now I have to lose everything for them? If the rebels win this war, what's to stop them from dragging us out back, shooting us and burying our bodies in a ditch? What's stopping them now?

Unable to look at my sister or Mamá, I pick up two bowls of steaming soup and march them into the dining room where Riel and Alipio wait to be served, just like that Diaz boy.

When the rebels leave, the house settles like a thing smashed.

Mercedes and Danita don't come out of their rooms, and you and Josepha don't come out of the closet. Oneila's daughters put Mercedes's children to sleep in their own beds, singing them to sleep and hoping they won't remember the sounds that came from their mamá's bedroom earlier. After this, those girls make themselves as ugly as possible, leaving their hair tangled and mouths pale, free of lipstick.

When I go to bed, I find Danita in the bedroom lying in her underwear on top of the covers, her breasts defiantly exposed, her hands resting on her stomach. White stretch marks curve like commas over the soft skin of her belly. I sit carefully next to her. She doesn't turn to me. I sense that she is not shocked or wounded into submission but rippling with bitterness. Active bitterness. Her hand slides from her stomach, and she finds mine, squeezing it hard.

"Are you all right?" I whisper.

"Of course I am all right." Her breath is fire.

"Was it awful?"

"He was a limp rag. Could barely push his way in." Somehow, I know she is lying. "Che didn't touch you, did he?"

"No," I say. "Not really."

Danita pulls herself up, drawing her knees in to her chest, but not before I catch a glimpse of the bruises inside her wrists. She sits, balled naked and tight on the bed. "Fidel Castro has ordered them not to touch you," she says, and it is without resentment.

"How do you know?" I think of the frenzied look in Che's eye, how he pleasured himself, anyway. Does that not count?

"My new lover told me. Did you not see him on the way out?" Scorn saturates her sarcasm. "You are our only hope, Estelita Rodriguez. Fidel loves his publicity. He seeks allies where Batista loses them. Fidel started scheming the moment your telex alerted them of your arrival. You are a bargaining chip. Which means you will be the one to get us out of here."

"How?" I haven't been able to use a telephone or send a letter since I arrived. Ed knows I'm in Cuba, but he doesn't know what's going on here. Even if he did, this will require more than bribery at a border crossing. Edward Adelman

would be squashed like a bug under the boot of a man like
Fidel Castro.

"We wait." Danita's resolve is rock-hard, her arms iron-
tight around her bare knees. "He'll trade you for something.
All you have to do is make sure he trades all of us. I'm not
leaving here without Sergio and Papa." Unclasping her arms,
she stands up, opens a dresser drawer and pulls out her husband's nightshirt, buttoning it over her low-hanging breasts.
"I don't blame you," she says, and I don't know if she means
for my special treatment now, or if she's finally forgiven me
for leaving when I was fifteen.

"Danita." I slide off the bed and move toward her, but she
backs away, arms raised.

"No sympathy. That's all we need to say on the subject."
She looks like Mamá, her face closed off to the pain. "We'll
talk of the future. What does an American future look like?
Do you think you could get me a job at the Copa?" She smiles,
and it is genuine.

"I'll do you one better and get you a job in Las Vegas. The
weather is much nicer."

"Oh, yeah? How are you going to do that?"

I plump the bottom of my hair with one hand and make
one of my spectacularly funny faces. If nothing else, I can
make Danita laugh.

She does, slightly, and I pucker my lips and dip my chin
over my shoulder like we used to when we were pretending we were Rita de Cuba. "The mayor of Palm Springs is
in love with me. He's even named a street after me. He said
all I have to do is say the word and he'll get me a headlining show in Las Vegas. I'll tell him it's a two-act, *Estelita and
Danita, the Rodriguez Sisters.*" I swoop out a hand, drawing
our names in the air. "It's all I can hope for, now that my
picture career is over."

"I'm sure you're exaggerating, as always. A Hollywood actress imprisoned under rebel rule will draw plenty of fans."

"It won't get me a job. *Rio Bravo* is shooting as we speak. I have no doubt I was easily replaced. For every role, there's a younger, prettier, more committed girl waiting to snatch it from you. Hopefully, Castro doesn't know I'm not worth much anymore."

"Come on." Danita turns me to face the mirror. It's the same rectangular mirror Mamá hung in my room, as she promised, after my first show in Havana. It strikes me that Danita didn't replace it like she had with so many of our childhood furnishings.

"How do we look?" she says, and I suddenly remember standing with her in this very spot after coming home from seeing *El romance del palmar*. We had clasped hands and looked at each other's reflections, and I'd said, "Let's promise we'll never be tiresome or strict or boring like Oneila. We'll be spirited and interesting and beautiful until we die."

"I promise!" Danita had cried with conviction.

In the glass, now, we look pale and puffy-eyed and older than I want to admit. "Not so good," I say with a laugh.

Danita scrunches up her face. "Then, we'd better sound amazing." She raises her hand, inhales and begins to sing "Besame Mucho," the low notes soft and husky. The sound is like the beginning of a thought, growing richer with each breath until the whole grand idea of our escape echoes around us, sweet and sorrowful.

I think of watching Rita Montaner on-screen with my sister, how it poured that night, flooding the first three rows of the theater. How the speakers crackled, distorting Rita's magnificent voice, and the screen went black every time they changed the reel. How none of it mattered, and we sat, transfixed, our feet in a cold puddle, our eyes glued to the screen until the last white flickers of film danced at the end of the reel and the houselights surged on. Even then, we sat, immobile, not wanting it to end.

My sister is as good as Rita, I think, without jealousy, believing that all we have imagined is truly possible.

Chapter Twenty-Three

Grandfather's Gun

Mother,

After the storm, you and your sisters are different. You are less argumentative, less loud. You turn cold, distrustful eyes on the soldiers, bristling and guarding each other like tigers. If two of you are in the kitchen, the other two are setting the table; if one has gone to do laundry, another follows to help hang it on the line. Auntie Oneila takes her place as the eldest, directing and ordering everyone around. If Tabo and Victor need scolding, she steps in for Auntie Mercedes who has gone soft as butter, her familiar belly laughs silenced. Between you and my Auntie Danita, there's an intimacy, something firmed up, an acceptance and understanding. Neither one of you leaves the other alone.

When the soldiers stomp home after dinner to their cement-walled bedrooms, we gather in the living room where you and Auntie Danita sing, determined to keep at it, wrapping us in the sweetness and beauty of your voices where we can suspend all thought, all fear, all worry. Sometimes the songs are funny, comic bits where you make goofy faces and wiggle your bums at each other. This sets us all into fits of laughter. We squeal until it hurts. Laughing as if laughter is the last thing in our control.

Josepha and I plot great things together: how she's coming to America with us, and we'll go to boarding school together. Villa Cabrini Academy would be tolerable, possibly even enjoyable, if Josepha were with me. She has a way of making me see all sides of a thing. When I told her how much I hated school, she sat down with a sheet of paper and made me list everything bad on one side and everything I could do about it on the other. In the end, school didn't look so hopeless. We did the same thing with our talents and our looks. Josepha says there are positives about not being attractive.

"For one thing people take you more seriously. We could be scientists or astronauts. No one cares what you look like if you're an astronaut. Smart girls are expected to be ugly."

"I'm not smart, either," I say.

"You're twelve. How do you know what you are?" She sounds motherly, but I don't mind. She always makes me feel better about myself.

The kindness between the aunts trickles down to the cousins. Josepha and I start including Marta in our games, and Lita and Enricua let us use the makeup they abandoned and teach us to tie up our hair at night so it falls out in curls in the morning, with the cautionary warning that we are never to wear it that way around the soldiers. The little boys aren't always a nuisance, and at bedtime we take turns telling them stories.

I believe this is normal, that this is what comes from living with people you've learned to love. But I am unfamiliar with big families and do not know that kindness made of guilt melts as fast as ice under hot sun.

★ ★ ★

Christmas is humid, ninety degrees and sunny. The soldiers have left us alone. It doesn't seem possible those men have families to go home to and holidays to celebrate, but the barracks have been empty for a week. There is no Christmas tree or presents, but we have letters from our uncles in Miami brought by a man named Marco, a friend of Oneila's husband, who also brings food: rice, beans, plantains and a precious rum cake.

We are in the kitchen, Oneila and Mercedes huddled together reading their letters, while Grandmother Maria directs the rest of us to light the stove and get out pots to boil water. Our waterlines have been cut off, so we collect rainwater in buckets outside. Tabo and Victor keep sticking their fingers in the rum cake, and Marta slaps their hands away, pretending she's in charge. Mercedes tells her to take the boys outside, and Enricua goes with her, leaving Lita to the annoying task of sifting through the dry beans for tiny stones so no one breaks a tooth.

Marco takes a bag of sugar from the pile of food and hands it to Grandmother Maria. "For rice pudding." He smiles, briefly, his white teeth shining in his dark face before his expression falls.

"I don't know how to make rice pudding," Grandmother Maria says in a tone that seems to have nothing to do with rice pudding.

Marco takes her hand. "All these years and you still can't cook?"

I watch them, wondering how my grandmother and this man know each other and why they are talking in code.

"Thank your mother for the cake, otherwise we'd have no dessert at all." She places a hand on Marco's cheek and says softly, "Tell me."

He has a strong face, smooth and unlined and dark as chocolate. He sighs. "There is word of Manuel."

The room stops, pots in hand freeze in midair, drawers are
held open as we all look at Grandmother Maria, dressed in red
for Christmas with a white scarf tied around her silver hair.
A few loose strands brush the back of her neck. She lets go of
Marco, takes a breath, steps back. "What news?"

"He is alive, but not well. He's in the hospital."

"Where?"

"Havana."

"Will he live?"

"I don't know."

Her gaze is forward, her jaw working this information over
like food. She drops her voice, but not low enough. "What
did they do to him?" Josepha and I look at each other. It
doesn't matter what we hear now. That night in the closet,
peeking out the closet door, we saw the man drag Mercedes
by her arm, watched her feet slow as he pulled her into the
bedroom, heard her pleading for him to stop. We didn't see
or hear Auntie Danita because, by that time, we'd shut the
closet door and stopped up our ears. We learned about it later
from Lita and Enricua, but Josepha told them to shut up. It
wasn't true, and they weren't to talk about her mom like that.

Marco looks helpless at Grandmother, not wanting to tell
her. He holds out the bag of sugar as if this will make up for
his lack of words. She nods in understanding and takes his
sugar offering without any more questions. Auntie Danita sets
down the pot she's holding with a bang on the stove. Water
sloshes over the side and hisses into the flame.

"What of Sergio?" Her voice trembles.

Marco raises his eyes, but it's my cousin Josepha he looks
at. She stands with her hand in the cutlery drawer. She looks
at her mother, and there is a flash of understanding between

them, something so thick it's like coiled rope in the air, the ends held unrelentingly in the hands of mother and daughter.

There is a silent pulse to the room, heads raised, eyes on Marco. He sets the sugar on the counter and collapses onto a stool. "I didn't want to tell you on Christmas. Mamá just sent me to deliver food."

Auntie Danita's mouth twitches. "I don't give a damn what day it is. Tell me."

Marco holds her eyes like he held Grandmother's. "They shot him."

A sound between a gasp and a whimper comes from my cousin, and I want to rush to her but her mother gets there first, Josepha collapsing into her arms with great sobs. Auntie Danita holds her, looking up at us with eyes like small, wet stones, but she does not cry. Only once have I seen you cry, at Grant's funeral, an open weeping that made me uncomfortable, but not nearly as uncomfortable as Auntie Danita's tearless, glinting eyes.

You hand me a pitcher of cane juice and tell me, sharply, "Nina, set this on the table," and the rest of us—aunts, cousins, sisters and mother—spring to life, trying to avoid the inevitable plunge, as if movement, apologies, hard, quick hugs and food preparation will keep us from sliding under the grief.

Beans cook slowly, and we do not eat for hours. By that time, Josepha and I have spent half the day lying under the ficus tree talking revenge, her emotions raw-edged and exposed.

"I'll slit their throats in their sleep." Her hands are propped under her head, elbows bent at an angle, heat heavy as a blanket over us.

"Shooting them would be easier." This is only practical.

"True. I could get more of them at one time. How could we get a gun?"

"Maybe they left one behind?"

I don't mean for us to actually check, but Josepha bolts to her feet. "You're right. They might have. Let's look." This is a terrible idea, but I follow her across the road toward the barracks, the dirt hard-packed and sun-warmed under my bare feet. Josepha walks with a slow cat stalk, her skirt swinging steadily below her knees. I can see the imprint of grass stamped into her bare calves and the rough edges of her heels.

She hesitates at the door, a block of wood as formidable as the cement walls on either side. "You're not really going in there?" I whisper.

"It was your idea."

"I didn't say we should go in."

"It's fine. I'll protect you."

She's no bigger or stronger than I am, but for some reason I believe she can protect me. The door opens with a groan, swinging heavily into a dark hallway, the walls skeletal, holding dead air. I picture Mercedes being dragged by that man, his hard, bristled face and glassy eyes. I tug Josepha backward. "What if they left a soldier behind to guard the place?"

She twists out of my grasp. "That's stupid. If they were here, it would be to watch us not hide in this building. I'm going in."

She steps through the door, her small back disappearing into shadow, and I rush in after her, cold air slipping over my skin as if I've walked into a refrigerator. "Why is it so cold?"

"Shhh." She puts a finger to her lips, her face full of ordinary annoyance.

It is a single-story building, wide and flat, with small square rooms that we peek into. The walls are cool to the touch, the stone floor gritty underfoot. It smells of wet towels and rotting fruit and something sour and sweaty, a smell I will forever after associate with men. There are beds on the floor made from sugar sacks, wool blankets and hard, flat pillows with no pillowcases. Hurricane lamps sit next to the beds, and in the kitchen, we find small plates with candle nubs stuck into melted wax at their centers. There's a battery-operated radio, which surprises us, and a stove. Apparently, news and hot food are not the reason they invade our house every night.

We scan the surfaces for a gun, wounded countertops and a rotting wood table, but touch nothing. When a creature scurries in the corner of the kitchen, we jump and run down the hall and out the front door so fast we forget to close it behind us. Under the ficus tree we double over, breathless, red-faced and gasping with fear.

When Josepha looks up, her eyes are brilliant and teary. "That's the most terrifying thing I've ever done."

"Me, too." My heart thunders in my ears.

"You're the bravest friend in the world. I will love you forever." She hugs me, her arms thin as twigs, her skin damp and tangy with sweat. It strikes me how small she is, how skinny her limbs and narrow her hips. I will think of this in the years to come, how easy it is to snap a body, make it do what you want no matter how thick-spirited a person is inside.

It is Josepha's idea to go into our Grandfather Manuel's room. "He had a gun," she whispers as we slip unnoticed past the bustle of dinner prep. "I never thought about it before, but when the rebels took him from the house, he was in his bedroom slippers and bathrobe. He couldn't have taken it with him, which means it has to be here somewhere."

In his bedroom, we pause, glancing at the bed and then back at each other. This is where the man took Mercedes, and I think we are both expecting some evidence of violence, but the embroidered coverlet is pulled neatly into place, the pillows fluffed, the boys' small stuffed bears sitting upright, watching us with shiny button eyes. *We witnessed nothing*, they say.

Josepha goes to the closet and eases open the door. It creaks on its hinges. Our grandfather's shirts and pants hang in a neat, ironed row. I think of the grandfather I've never met lying in a hospital bed, how I might never meet him now because he might not live. If he dies, it will be Grandmother Maria who will pull these clothes from their hangers and fold them into bags like she did with Grant's clothes after he died. You left for Palm Springs because it was too painful for you. I didn't want to touch Grant's things, and so I did not offer to help my grandmother. I think of Josepha's father, Sergio, and wonder if my grandmother will clear his things from his closet, too. Grandmother Maria, the Protector of Life and Death. The Guardian of Past and Future. In time, I will come to fully understand the scope of my grandmother's endurance, but it is in Cuba where I first recognize her strength.

It is a strength neither Josepha nor I have yet.

Josepha stares at the clothes, her eyes red-rimmed. She is thinking of her papa.

"My stepfather committed suicide," I say, knowing this isn't the same but wanting to offer her something.

She nods, and a single tear tips over her bottom lid and rests on top of her cheek, a lone bead of sadness. "How?"

"Pills, I think. No one told me. They said he had a heart attack, but I saw him right before he died and knew they were lying."

"Did he look sad?" Josepha's face is earnest and perplexed, trying to work all of this out.

I nod, remembering Grant's empty, blue eyes that day. Water-colored eyes. He drowned in himself, I think.

"I miss my dad." Josepha's voice quivers. "They took him

a month ago, but it already feels like forever. I'm afraid I'll forget everything about him."

"You won't." I put my arm around her hoping this is true. There's so much about Grant I don't remember, but he wasn't my real dad. If he was in my blood, I'm certain I would remember more of him. "At least you have a dad to love in your memory. My dad's alive, but he means nothing to me."

Sometimes, I wonder if I'd stayed in Mexico whether Chu Chu would have taken me to hear him sing after all, if he would have introduced me to his other family. I might have had siblings, siblings as nice as Josepha. Now, I'll never know.

"I hate them!" Josepha suddenly cries, giving a little jump. "These bastard soldiers. I'm going to find that gun and shoot every one of them in the head."

I know this is ridiculous. We are too young. We are girls. We will shoot no one. But I play the game. This is truth and dare rolled into one.

"You check the floor, and I'll check the shelf." Josepha pulls the desk chair over to the closet and climbs onto the seat, standing on tiptoe and sliding her hand along the shelf above the clothes. Dust scatters like pollen, sifting overhead as I drop to my knees and feel around under a pile of socks. Grandfather Manuel does not seem the sort of man to pile socks on his closet floor. Most likely Mercedes tossed them in here to make room in the dresser, which would make the chance of finding a gun under them slim. I search, anyway, uncovering balls of dust thick as pillow batting but no weapons. In the other corner I discover a shoebox, which is hopeful, but find only letters inside, each one slid neatly back into its open envelope. They are from Grandmother Maria, the date stamped into the corner going as far back as January 7, 1945.

"Anything?" Josepha looks under her armpit at me, her hand still rummaging.

"No." I put the top back on and slide the box in its corner next to a pair of chestnut-colored leather boots.

Josepha climbs off the chair, kicks it away with one foot and starts going through suit-jacket pockets. None of them bulges with a gun.

"This one looks promising." I pull out a brown military jacket with a row of bronze buttons down the front and two tiny, silver stars pinned into the collar. Above the left pocket is a pin of the Cuban flag with a round, gold medal hanging beneath. Josepha pats the coat down, shakes her head, and I hang it back up.

"Where would he hide a gun?" she mutters, going to the bureau and looking through each drawer.

I don't want to look anymore. The smell of food coming from downstairs makes me hungry, and the idea of spending Christmas searching for a gun now seems silly and impractical. Game over. I quit. "I'm hungry. Let's go downstairs."

Josepha ignores me. "Come on. Don't just stand there. Help me look."

"What would you do with a gun, anyway? You aren't actually going to shoot a soldier."

"Yes, I am." She's moved on to the mattress. Her hands are jammed under it, and I can just see the tip of her pink nose and her wide eyes over the top of the bed. There's a manic look to them, her cheeks flushed red. She looks as if she really means to shoot someone.

A prickle of fear goes up my neck. This is a game, right? Thinking what you, Mom, might do, how you would make it playful, I take Grandfather Manuel's military jacket from the closet and pull it on, buttoning it up to my throat. The jacket hangs past my knees, and the sleeves flop over my hands, but I raise my arm and point a finger gun at Josepha. "Freeze,"

I say, furrowing my brow into a hard scowl like the men in Western movies.

Josepha pulls her hands from under the mattress and stands up. She smiles, amused, and I think I've succeeded in pulling her back into a world of make-believe. "Put on his boots," she orders.

I pull the heavy boots from the closet, the rich leather soft under my hands, the laces dragging. When I slide them on, my foot hits something cold and hard.

Josepha comes over, securing the last button on the jacket like a mother sending me off to school. I flatten my toes over the metal object, and Josepha gives me a suspicious look. "What?"

"Nothing."

"You're keeping a secret."

"No, I'm not."

The lie burns in my belly. Lies have always been easy for me, small ones directed at nuns (*Of course I said my prayers*) or at Grandmother (*Yes, I ate all my dinner, and Mom said I'm allowed a second bowl of ice cream*). Lying to Josepha is different, a breach of loyalty.

"Kill me an enemy," she demands, and I cock my finger and pretend to shoot the bedpost. "Your technique is sloppy." She flaps her hand at me. "We'll work on it after dinner. I'm starved. Do you think the beans are ready by now? Our mothers are going to skin us for not helping."

I haul my feet out of the boots, slide them back into the closet, unbutton the coat and hang it up, meekly enduring my guilty knowledge.

At the door, Josepha says, "I dare you to wear that outfit when the rebels come. Can you imagine their faces?" I think she's joking, but she stops me with a hand on my chest. "I'm serious. It's a dare. Or do you want truth?"

She knows I lied. She is insulted and determined to find out my secret. She's going to ask me what was in that boot. "Dare," I say quickly.

"All right, then." She drops her hand, looking at me with the thrill a dare brings on. Maybe I miscalculated. Maybe she doesn't suspect anything. I hope she'll drop it, but she presses me. "Next time the rebels come, I dare you to wear that coat around the house as if it's any old thing."

"I'll get in trouble."

"If you do it, I'll give you the gold-leaf barrette I stole, and it will be worth it." She links her arm through mine as we head downstairs to the smell of roast garlic and fried oil and the prospect of rum cake.

After, I will try and remember every detail of that night, the sunlight sliding from the window, the smell of wood smoke and the low crackle in the hearth, flames dancing like finger puppets on the walls. I will think of the Christmas carols you and Auntie Danita sang in English, my aunt's lips trembling around the words of "O Come, All Ye Faithful." How, when she started to cry, Josepha leaped up and put an arm around her mother and sang with her, the notes so tender and graceful they hurt. I will remember how you stood on the other side of your sister with your arm around her, too, and that I was jealous. I wanted to have a beautiful voice, to stand beside you and sing and be held.

Most vividly, I will recall sitting next to my grandmother, how that powerful matriarch laid her hand over mine, her finger pads soft and wrinkled as boot leather.

I will blame the boots. For years they will walk through my dreams without anyone in them. Empty. Soulless. And I will blame my grandmother. I will hate her for protecting me.

I will try, unsuccessfully, to erase the sound of skull against wood, the sight of bright red blood and a face turned white and empty as paper.

Chapter Twenty-Four

The Sins of Our Husbands

Daughter,

On January 1, 1959, I gather with my sisters and Mamá around the wireless in Guanajay as a boisterous voice announces that Che Guevara blew up an armored train in Santa Clara and took the city. Batista has fled. Castro's rebel army has won.

The voice on the radio continues, but I stop listening. Out the window, the sky is silky black, the stars sequins. The air is pleasant and cool, and I can see you and your cousins running around in light sweaters playing a game of hide-and-seek.

"What does this mean?" Mercedes looks frantically from one blank face to the next. Since that night with the soldier, she carries a slight tremor.

Mamá gets up, clicks off the wireless. "It means the rebels did not empty the barracks for Christmas but were gathering to march to victory while Batista ate roast duck with his family."

"Will they come back? Are we still prisoners of war? Will

they execute us?" Mercedes's rising hysteria echoes my own fears, and I sit bewildered and silent.

"Calm down," Danita snaps at her. She has been subdued since news of her husband's death but still willful. She has a daughter to protect. "They don't execute women. We pose no threat. We're their candy."

"Estelita and Nina are American citizens," Mamá says. "Castro will need good relations with the United States, which means nothing will happen to us."

"Do you mean to all of us? We're not American citizens." Oneila, derisive, waves her hand in a wide circle in front of her sisters as she sits on the couch between Mercedes and Danita, old resentments rising. I sit alone in a cool, leather chair that Danita took such care to purchase for her modern home, Mamá standing behind me, the configuration of our bodies summing up our family history.

For once, I have nothing to say.

Mamá clips over to the window, throws open the screen, and shouts for everyone to get inside and help set the table for dinner. When she turns, her daughters are all looking at her, the three on the couch a solid body of accusation, but no one risks voicing the bewildering questions. No one asks Mamá to explain why she left Oneila to raise Mercedes, why Danita was left behind even though her voice is as beautiful as mine. They don't ask Mamá why she never came back for their weddings or when their children were born, why I was more important than all the rest of them combined.

Instead, our formidable, clamorous, enduring family sits in uncomfortable silence watching the cracks between us widen.

The next day a jeep comes for Mamá. It is early morning, the sky grayed over. I am heating *pan tostado* for breakfast when I hear the distant grind of the engine. Mercedes and Danita don't notice. They sit at the table drinking coffee and discussing what it will be like when they get to Miami. Danita assures Mercedes that she'll stay long enough to see her settled before heading to California.

"You can come to California, too," I say, and Mercedes nods, the reality of leaving Cuba still unimaginable.

Oil spits in the pan, and the engine outside grows louder as I see a jeep grind to a stop outside the window.

"Who is that?" Mercedes leaps to her feet, coffee splashing over the rim of her cup.

"Rebel soldiers." I keep a steady tone, my stomach tightening as I watch them climb from the jeep and walk toward the house in an easy manner, no guns drawn.

There is a knock, and Mercedes jumps, spilling her entire cup, a dark stream running off the side of the table. "The rebels don't knock," she cries, frantically trying to wipe up the coffee with the palm of her hand.

"Este, toss me a towel," Danita says, and I throw her a towel which she hands to our baby sister. "Stay here."

Mercedes nods, sopping up the coffee, her fear of the soldiers written all over her face. The dark circles under her eyes are carved so deep into the tops of her cheeks I wonder if she sleeps at all. Danita squeezes her arm. "It's all right. Estelita and I will take care of it."

I am not sure what we will take care of, but I follow Danita out of the kitchen.

The soldier who raped Danita has returned many times. It doesn't look like rape anymore. When he's done eating our food, Danita walks up the stairs ahead of him with mock complicity. Danita the Mighty. Danita the Merciless. She made a deal, she told me, but I'm not to say a word to our sisters or Mamá. "It's just sex, and he's promised me he'll keep the others off Oneila's girls. They're too young. They'd never recover. At least he's not violent. He pretends he cares, and I pretend he doesn't repulse me."

A practical arrangement, and she has still never told me his name.

I think of Che, his raptured eyes and quick breath, how instantly an act of sex can turn vile. He has only been here a few times in the last month, but when he comes my gut clenches to a fist. I pretend indifference, but the carelessness with which he runs his hand under my skirt, the pompous, prideful smirk on his face fills me with hot shame and astounding meekness. Knowing he has been ordered not to drag me down under him does not mean he won't.

At the door, Danita hesitates and looks at me. "We're in this together," she says. "No matter what, we keep them away from Mercedes."

There are two of them. They wear M-26 armbands and fatigues and are unnervingly polite, clean-shaven with hair trimmed around their ears. One steps up, removes his hat and asks after Mamá, which startles us.

"She's sleeping," Danita answers quickly.

"If you'd be so kind as to wake her." Never mind his courtesy, it's an order.

Danita heads slowly up the stairs, leaving me waiting in the doorway. The men move to the edge of the porch and lean against the rail with their backs to me, their eyes on the road. Mamá wasn't really sleeping, and within a few minutes she is descending the stairs, Danita a step behind her.

She walks to the threshold, polite, alert, dressed in a clean, lavender skirt and white blouse. "How may I help you?"

The men turn, and one extends his hand. "Señorita Juana Maria Antonia Santurio y Canto Rodriguez?"

Danita and I look at each other, impressed. No one uses Mamá's full name.

Mamá is not so charmed. She raises her chin with a look of condescension. "Yes?"

"You are to come with us."

There is a dry buzz in the air, wasps or mosquitoes, a windless moment, the tree branches motionless. It is the man's gentle tone that frightens me. Up until now we've been demeaned and rough-handled, but he is courteous, tactful.

"What is this concerning?" Mamá asks, reasonable, but sounding tired, as if she knows it doesn't matter how they answer.

"I am afraid I cannot say."

Danita shoves her way between the man and Mamá. "If you can't say, then she's not going anywhere with you."

"It's all right, Danita." Mamá steps around her, and my mind scrambles to think what leverage I have as the two men lead her to the jeep and help my mother into the back. I am struck by how frail she looks, how old. The engine kicks to a start, and she reaches out and holds the side of the door as the vehicle lurches forward, hard sunlight reflecting off the green metal like shiny armor. She does not look back, and I watch until the plume of dust and gravel settle onto the empty road.

It is an interminable day. Heat lies still, insects smack against the screens, and ants soldier across the floor. The boys throw tantrums, and Mercedes retreats to her room. Oneila and her daughters keep to the kitchen, while you and Josepha escape outside. I talk a blue streak to Danita, who listens patiently. I will get us out of here. I will get word to my manager, to John Wayne and Herbert Yates. I prowl back and forth over the living room rug, grasping for solutions. "I'll write a letter directly to Fidel Castro. I will tell him I am friends with Desi Arnaz. Maybe I can contact Monte Poser."

"Estelita, stop." Danita's voice slices through mine with singular clarity.

I stop. Silence, then. We sit and wait…for what we do not know and cannot imagine.

That night, I can't sleep. Danita is restless beside me and Mamá's empty bed taunts me in the dark. Where did they take her? Why? Three times I get up and check on you in the next room. You are curled beside Josepha, your limbs entwined with each other as if you both belong to a single body.

Eventually, I put on a robe and slippers and go out to the porch, the building across the street a lump of black against the stars. There is no moon, and I search the dark road for a beam of light, listen for the sound of a jeep, but there is only the croaking of frogs and the buzz of insects.

Watching the click beetles come out, sparking across the lawn, I think of the night when Mamá took Danita and me to El Jardin for milkshakes after a concert. I was fifteen years old and had just signed a contract with the Copacabana.

Danita and I had been in a fight all day over who got to wear the dress with the taffeta rose. In the end, she got to because she was older, and I drank my frozen treat in grumpy silence, glaring at her the whole time.

Later, in our beds, she had said, "Do you know how selfish you are?"

"Me? You got to wear the dress."

"You never keep promises."

"Like what?"

"You never gave me your white shoes. You said you'd give them to me, and then you didn't."

"Geez, Danita, I was nine years old. And Mamá bought you your own pair."

"No, Estelita, she did not." Danita sat up. "That's exactly what I mean. You only notice the things you have, never what anyone else has. That dress—" she pointed to the mound of petal-pink organza I'd left on the floor "—I told Mamá I wanted that fabric, and do you know what she said? She said it was a better color on you."

"You can have the stupid dress. I don't even like it. I wanted the one with the rose, and you got to wear it."

"Oh, you don't get it." Danita flopped back down and rolled over with her back to me.

It was a stupid fight, but we were not fighting about dresses or forgotten shoes. I looked at the unflinching wall of my sister's haloed back in the heavy moonlight and knew that she was right: I was selfish.

I still am, I think, watching the beetles blink across the lawn. I want things that are bigger than my family, bigger than you or Mamá or my sisters.

Despite our fight that night, I still convinced Danita to sneak out and collect beetles with me, our full-moon tradition, each beetle offering one wish. We could use some wishes now, I think, tempted to wake my sister so we can gather them together again.

I don't. Instead, I gather them myself—Estelita the Dream Collector—in a dusty jar I find under the kitchen sink, taking the beetles upstairs to show my sister.

"Danita." I shake her awake.

"What?"

I hold the jar up like a prize. "Click beetles."

"Estelita, it's the middle of the night."

"We have to make a wish."

"Don't be ridiculous." She rolls over with an arm over her head. No nostalgia, just annoyance.

I set the jar on the bedside table and climb into bed.

I am restless and wake early. Already, the sun boils the room. Sections of green paint pucker and swell like fat limes on the walls. Danita is still asleep beside me, and when I roll over, I see that the beetles are dead at the bottom of the glass.

I get up quietly and go downstairs to dump them outside, their weightless husks fluttering to the ground. In the kitchen, I make coffee, packing the Moka pot with grinds as dark as earth. I pour the brew thick and hot over a spoonful of brown sugar, thinking I will never go back to Folgers. The one thing Americans do not know how to do is drink coffee. I take a sip, the nutty, rich flavor such a simple, human pleasure. I wish all pleasures were so simple.

I have only slept a few hours. Exhaustion makes what comes later feel like a watery dream, impossible things floating in a disproportionate reality.

No one else is awake to hear the jeep coming down the road. I am on the porch watching a pale disk of sunlight rise over the hills and wondering if Marco sent the telex to Ed, as I'd asked, when I see Mamá in the back of the jeep. I rush forward, down the stairs and across the yard. I struggle to open her door, my coffee still clutched in one hand, my robe slipping down my shoulder. The driver gets out, the same man who took her yesterday. "Señorita." He opens the door and holds out an arm, and Mamá leans against him as she climbs down. I reach for Mamá who brushes me away as if I am a nuisance, which makes me smile. She thanks the soldier, who tips his hat at her like an old-fashioned beau bringing her home late from a dance.

The man climbs back into the jeep and drives away, and Mamá looks at the coffee in my hand and says, "May I? I've had very little sleep." I nod, hand it to her. She takes a small sip. "It's cold."

"I'll get you a hot cup."

She sits on the porch while I make another cup and bring it out to her steaming hot. We sit in silence, rays of soft, morning sunlight falling at our feet. The skin under Mamá's eyes is swollen smooth, her lids heavy, lines deep as trenches stretching across her forehead. She wraps both hands around the mug and lifts the steam to her chin. "They took me to see your father."

With slow, careful breaths, she explains how she sat with him all night in a hospital with white walls and small windows. How a nurse offered her cold water but no food while my father lay unconscious in a twin bed with a thin blanket and no pillow. They had beaten him but left him to die on his own time. His face was bruised on one side, and his eyes were swollen shut. A woman in tan pants and a button-down shirt came to check his pulse and told Mamá he had asked for her yesterday and that it was a kindness of Señor Castro's to allow her to say goodbye.

"A kindness." Mamá spits a stream of saliva at her feet, her disgust glistening in sunshine. "Batista is a coward. He did not lift a finger to save your father, or this country. I distrusted him from the start for good reason." She pauses, takes a slow sip of coffee and then, "He killed men. Your papa. I watched the news and didn't speak of it because I knew what my husband was doing. Batista had men shot in the head at gunpoint. He strung rebels up from lampposts and left them as an example to others. He is a horrible man, and your papa was part of it. We are all complicit, as far as I'm concerned."

I picture Papa on the porch the day Mamá and I left fifteen years ago, watching us climb into a cab, thin and strong and proud, his hands in his pockets, his chin up. I wonder if he's gone bald, or if his dark hair has grayed, if he wears a beard or still has sandpaper cheeks dotted red from razor burn. It's impossible to picture the man I knew as old or silent or beaten. It is easy to picture him in a firing squad. He was a father who related to his children by dominating them. I knew only to fear him, to wait in a cold sweat for either punishment or approval. I have no idea what it would have been like to know him as an adult.

"Is he dead?" I ask quietly.

"He wasn't when I left, but he will be soon." From her face I cannot tell how deep her sadness runs, just that the pain is fresh. It doesn't matter how little she approved of what he did or how their views differed, a part of her still loves him.

"Why did you leave Cuba?" I ask.

Mamá's gaze is straight ahead. "For you, and for myself. I didn't want to be a part of what was going on here. I didn't want to be the wife of a man who shot people in the streets. If I stayed away, I could forget what I was."

I reach for her hand. "You are not to blame for your husband's actions."

"Neither are you," she says, a small token, but one I take as forgiveness. I didn't think she understood my guilt over what Alfonso did to you.

We keep our eyes on the horizon, fingers entwined on my knee, coffee cooling in our cups. The sky stretches endlessly in front of us, clear blue and cloudless. But the air is smothering with humidity. I miss the dry heat of Los Angeles, the weightlessness of it. A flock of birds rise with a flutter of beating wings from the flamboyant tree that grows so close to the house that fern leaves fan the siding, and the long, brown tree pods litter the porch floor. I haven't seen a flamboyant tree in bloom since I was a child, red petals lucent as fire. Danita and I used to make crowns from the petals, and when the pods dried out we used them as musical shakers. I kick a pod that lies at my feet, and it slides to the edge of the porch with a tinkle of sound. I will collect some for you and Josepha, I think, show you how to move your hips to the rhythm.

When the house wakes, Mamá is covered in children, big and little. Despite her Herculean reputation, we were all afraid she wasn't coming back. There are hugs and wet kisses and questions she gives no-nonsense answers to, repeating her story, leaving out the description of their *abuelo*'s face. She doesn't go to bed, but in the late afternoon, before the soldiers arrive, I find her asleep in the chair on the porch. The sun has shifted behind the house, and she sits in shadow, her head rolled to the side, the skin under her neck bunched up. She does not look peaceful. Her eyes flutter, and her lips contort. I think of waking her but don't want to startle her.

The rebels do that for me. The jeeps arrive fast and loud, all three of them, engines revving. Brakes screech, doors slam and Mamá's eyes fly open.

Chapter Twenty-Five

Viva Batista!

Mother,

In the afternoon silence, before the jeeps arrive, I find you sitting on the bed you share with Danita, wearing your sister's borrowed clothes, a cap-sleeved blouse and shorts, your untamed hair brushed out over the hollows of your neck. You have been crying. When you see me, you open an arm, and I crawl under it and lay my head against your shoulder, burrowing into your hair as the frizzy wisps tickle my face. You smell different, like the blue-flaking soap in the bathroom, like sea air and boiled beans. I touch the mole on the inside of your arm, a tiny polka dot on your cream-colored skin.

"Are you sad because your papa died?" I ask.

You squeeze me. "A little. I don't know why. I hadn't seen him in fifteen years, and he wasn't a very nice man."

I think how my dad is not a nice man either, but I'll probably be a little sad one day when he dies, too.

"When are we going home?" I ask.

"I don't know."

"Are we ever going home?" A part of me doesn't want to, another part does.

"Of course. Soon, I hope."

"All of us?" I look up at you through a curtain of hair.

A smile fills your face. "All of us, *mi hija*. I've sent a telex to Ed, and your grandmother spoke to the man who drove her to the hospital. I guess he's someone important to Fidel Castro. He said he would speak to him about getting us home and reuniting your aunts with their husbands in Miami."

"Will Josepha and Auntie Danita come with us to LA, since she has no husband in Miami?"

"Maybe. I don't know."

I tuck my chin and drop my head to your shoulder wanting to lick your salty skin and push my fingers into the softness of your belly like I did when I was little and those things were acceptable. I want you to always be like this, simple, with messy hair and time to sit with me and do nothing.

Hours later, the jeeps roll up. I am in the closet with the door open waiting for Josepha, who went downstairs for a candle. The electricity is back on, but candles are more suitable lighting for confessing secret desires. I sit on the floor watching a fat, black ant march with unwavering certainty around my big toe and out the closet door. It'd be nice to feel that certain about anything, I think, the sound of screeching brakes sending me leaping to my feet. I hear doors slam and men's voices and think of the gun in the boot. I haven't been back into Grandfather Manuel's closet to check if it's real, but I can still feel the cool, hard shape against the bottom of my foot.

Below me, I hear the front door open and heavy boots clomp down the hall. I creep to the top of the stairs and peer down. Lita looks out of her bedroom door, a scarf tied into a knot at the top of her head.

Her eyes flit past me to the stairs. "They're back?"

I nod, and she pulls her head in, closes and locks the door. She and Enricua have been told to lock themselves in whenever the rebels come, and they have no desire to disobey.

Pots clatter in the kitchen, and radio static comes from the living room. The front door has been left wide-open, and I see you walk through, alone, your face sapped of good intentions. And then I see a man leaning against the wall in the hallway. His back is to me, but I know it is Che from the curl of his hair and the easy manner with which he steps in front of you.

Your face stiffens, and he laughs. "Not excited to see me?" In a swift motion, he pushes you against the wall, his hands on your hips, his mouth over yours. There is confidence in him, victory. He is a hero. You jerk your head to the side, and when he comes at you again you send a glob of spit flying into his face. He flinches. I'm afraid he is going to hit you or force his mouth on yours again, but all he does is lean toward you running the back of his hand slowly down the side of your face, the touch tender, like one might caress a tiny kitten or something very dear to them.

You've gone rigid as a plank, flattening into the wall as if hoping it will swallow you. All you have to do is look up and you'd see me, but you keep your eyes angled to the floor. I think of Alfonso's hand running up the inside of my thigh with a feeling of powerlessness. Why do they get away with it? Why do we do nothing? I slink backward, slowly, so the floor doesn't creak, back into Grandfather Manuel's room and head straight for the closet.

I pull the gun from the boot. It's heavier than I expect, solid black and terrifyingly real. I wonder where Josepha is and why she hasn't come back with a candle. If she comes in now anything could happen. Or, I could make something happen on my own. I curl the edge of my finger over the trigger, the metal slippery. Uncle Duke would know how to shoot this thing. In his gunslinging movies he made it look easy. He never missed. The idea of not missing sends a shiver through me. I slide the gun back into the boot and pull Grandfather Manuel's jacket from the closet. I put it on, button it up and adjust the bottom that hangs above my knees. It smells of stale cigarette smoke. I am tempted to take the gun out again but don't.

Downstairs the hallway is empty, the living room door wide-open. A song plays on the radio, ukuleles and maracas and a droning female voice. Male voices talk over the singer. From the kitchen I hear running water and can smell yucca croquettes frying in oil. I take a deep breath, my heart firing in my chest. I think of Josepha and the dare, of Che's hand on your cheek, of Alfonso, and my father, and Señorita Perron, and the nuns, all of the ones in power over me. I want that kind of power.

With a cry of *"Viva Batista!"* I charge into the room. I don't see you or Auntie Danita or the rebels, I only see Josepha standing near the door staring with wide, startled eyes. I am pumped with adrenaline, reckless and out of control. I shout, *"Viva Batista! Viva Batista! Viva Batista!"* until a hand clamps over my mouth. My vision clouds with dust stirred up in sunlight. Through it, Che's face looms, his eyes black kernels of rage, his ease and carelessness turned ruthless. There is a moment of stillness, as if he doesn't know what to do with me. He has dealt with ferocious men and submissive women. I am neither. His nostrils flare, and I think he means to pull his hand away when I bite him, his fleshy palm salty on my tongue.

My head cracks against the wood floor so hard my jaw

rattles, and for a split second my vision goes black. Rough fingers are on me, ripping the jacket off, pulling up my skirt and drawing down my underwear. I try and clamp my knees together, but they are yanked open like springs. My scream is cut off as a hand slams over my mouth again, the fingers smelling of rubber. This time it means to suffocate.

"*Por favor, por favor, Señor!* God have mercy, she is a child." My grandmother kneels beside me, her hands in prayer. She rocks and begs, her voice shrill and contorted, and the frenzied hands suddenly stop.

Che pulls away, snapped out of something, but not far enough. He stays kneeling over me, his hair falling into his face, his beard like a sharp tool pointed at the end of his chin. A man who knows how to use a sharp object. With calculated brutality, he wraps his fingers around my throat and squeezes. Our eyes meet. His are empty. Impersonal. Black holes in a body. He keeps his hand there long enough for panic to set in. Bright spots float in front of my eyes. Someone screams for him to stop, either you or my grandmother, and he lets go, the air choking back into my lungs. Behind the floating spots, I see him stand with the disgust and satisfied proficiency of someone who has kicked a disobedient dog.

He is finished with me.

Powerful arms pull me up and into a lap: Grandmother Maria's, her chest heaving as if she is the one whose breath was cut short. You drop to the floor beside both of us shaking and crying, your hands on my neck, my face, my shoulders. My throat stings like the rope burns we used to give each other at Villa Cabrini Academy, twisting the skin on each other's arms until the person begged for mercy, red welts marking the spot for days.

The room stills, and collectively we see Che reach for Josepha, a last attempt to assert his power, make up for his act of generosity with me. Or, perhaps, just pure, male brutality. A cry rises and dies in my throat. Auntie Danita cries out instead, a scream to split walls, and Che barks an order at Alipio, who wraps an arm around her as she lunges, her limbs grabbing air, her guttural howls like hot oil burning scars into our ears.

Against the bulk of Che, Josepha is weak as dust. She tries to fight back, but he stops her with a single blow, her cheek splitting open, wide and red as a calendula bloom. Blood runs from her nose over her stunned, open mouth. Grandmother shoves me off her lap, but Che is in no mood for more pleading. He is scrupulous, but not fair. He drags Josepha from the room without a backward glance at the old woman crawling across the floor. The door slams, and Riel steps in front of it, his sunken cheeks unsmiling, his body stiff as any soldier's despite his shocked and apologetic face. Grandmother begs on her knees for him to step aside, but he tilts his head in silence, his eyes fixed on the opposite wall. They have trained him well.

I stay on the floor watching as the room fractures into prisms of inexplicable realities. Auntie Danita's arms flap like a trapped bird's wings in Alipio's unshakable grasp. Grandmother drags herself up and goes toward her daughter, but Auntie Danita screams and claws at her. Your arms are around me, pushing too hard, and I want to shove you off, to scream and claw, too. What is he doing to her? Are his hands around her neck? Will he kill her? Grandfather Manuel's coat lies torn on the ground. A fat ant crawls over it, undeterred, straight-pathed and confident. I slide from your grasp and press my throbbing forehead into the cool floor. Red dots float behind my eyes, my vision bloodied. I feel Che pressing my legs open and see the alarm in Josepha's face, her split cheek and red, gaping mouth.

I don't know how it ends, just that the living room is empty, and I am curled on my side on the rug wondering if it is possible to sleep without remembering sleeping. I stand, and my legs buckle under me, weak as dry grass. My grandfather's coat is no longer on the floor. I go to the window and watch the last shard of sun slide into the horizon, a feeling of fire sinking in my gut. Cigar smoke and sour sweat hangs in the air as if the men have just stepped out. Rape and a cigar, and they're off to dinner. Sick men. Damaged men. Men I should have let Josepha shoot in the head.

I stay where I am. The evening sky rots to purple and black. There are no stars, just a fat, curdled moon. After a while I worry that no one has come to find me. It's too quiet for a house full of people. I expect Oneila and her girls to be in the kitchen cleaning up, but there is only a pan of burned yucca croquettes rolling around in oil. I turn off the flame and scrape the burned bottom with a spoon. Plates and cups and cutlery are stacked unused on the counter. No one has eaten dinner. Not even Mercedes's boys are making a sound, and I have the terrifying thought that everyone's been taken by the rebels.

I rush upstairs, my bare feet slapping the wooden steps, the noise sending Enricua charging out of her room after me. She catches me by the arm and pulls me into the bedroom, shutting the door with a finger pressed to her lips to shush me. The boys are asleep in bed. Lita pulls the covers up to their chins and gives me a warning look. Marta is there, too, sitting on the edge of the bed next to her brother with her arms folded crossly.

"Where's Josepha?" I ask. "Where's my mom?"

Lita gives a sharp shake of her head and jerks her chin at Marta, indicating we shouldn't speak about it in front of her.

Marta narrows her eyes. "I'm not a baby. I know something bad happened. I heard it, too."

Enricua has not let go of my arm, and her small eyes are filled with stark fear. Blameless eyes, I think, wondering if she can see guilt in mine.

"What happened?" she whispers. Marta's ears are perked and listening. "We heard the commotion, and then my mom came with the little ones and locked us in. She told us we were to stay in here no matter what."

Marta kicks the wooden bed frame with an angry foot. "I don't want to be in here. I'm hungry."

"Stop it," Lita scolds. She is wearing a dark navy dress buttoned to the neck, which makes her look older than her sister, who has taken to wearing untucked men's shirts over baggy pants.

Lita comes around to Marta's side of the bed and pulls back the covers. "How about a story? If you climb in I'll tell you about the witch Cayetana and how she defeated the great crocodile of Las Tumbas."

Marta stays put, arms crossed. "Was he going to eat her?"

"Maybe. Or devour her children. I'll tell you if you lie down."

"Fine." Marta flops over and pulls the covers up. "But I'm not going to sleep."

"Fine. Scoot over." Lita crawls in next to her, four to the bed, the boys' small faces pressed together on one pillow, their dark hair tousled like fur standing on end.

Enricua shields the side of her mouth with her hand and whispers, "Is everyone all right? I heard someone being dragged upstairs. Why isn't Josepha with you?"

I shake my head, my mouth chalk. A single lamp glows on the nightstand, and Lita's voice, gentle and soothing, begins a story of a witch with sea-green hair and emerald eyes who comes from the sea to warn the town of a hungry crocodile.

With a hand on my shoulder, Enricua says, "Mamá didn't tell you to stay in here. Go find Josepha. She should sleep with us tonight."

I obey because I still think Josepha is a whole person who will want to sleep with us tonight.

I slip out of the room as the crocodile bites a fisherman's boat in two and Marta says she's glad: fishermen deserve to be eaten for killing innocent sea creatures.

The wooden floor creaks underfoot as I walk toward the open door of Grandfather Manuel's room. I stand in front of it, rooted in shadow, too afraid to enter. Auntie Mercedes sits on the floor with her back against the bed, her legs sticking straight out from under her skirt. I can see a tear in her stocking running like a widening river up her plump, colorless calf. I wish she'd changed out of them or at least tried to mend them. But there are some things that can't be darned or mended, and you have to throw them away and start over.

I don't see you or Grandmother. Auntie Oneila sits in a chair next to the bed with her elbows propped on her knees. She's taken her hair down, and it falls at odd angles over her shoulder. I watch her reach out and take ahold of Auntie Danita's hand. My aunt stands with her back to me, her body the exact height and size of yours. She faces her daughter who lies on the bed staring out at me. From the doorway, I can see flat, vacant eyes that don't look like Josepha's. Her cheek is held closed with strips of tape pulled over a wad of tissue that is soaked with blood. It occurs to me that I have not seen any Band-Aids or gauze or antiseptic here. Under Josepha's taped cheek, her lips are swollen fat. She blinks, expressionless, and I think she must not see me so I step into the doorway. I will make it up to her. I will tell her about the gun. We will plot our revenge. We will find Che and kill him ourselves. We will be our own heroes.

All three of my aunts turn and look at me. There is no sympathy in their eyes, only pity and fear and caution, as if I am a rabid, unpredictable animal.

Auntie Danita comes at me, her face distorted. "Out!" she orders. I think she will shove me backward, but her hands on my shoulders are gentle as she eases me into the hallway and shuts the door in my face. I can't move. I stand staring at the dark, hardwood floor, the skin around my throat burning where Che clutched it. Surely one of my aunt's will open the door and come out and say everything is going to be okay. *You can see Josepha tomorrow,* Auntie Mercedes will say with her motherly kindness. *She needs to rest. We understand it wasn't your fault.* Auntie Oneila, Protector of Daughters and Keeper of Family, will say, *Your Auntie Danita just needs time. She'll forgive you soon enough.*

But no one comes out. Behind the closed door the room is silent.

I find you and Grandmother in the bedroom that you share with Auntie Danita. From now on, just the three of us will sleep in here.

"Nina." You have been crying. You embrace me, kiss the top of my head. Over your shoulder, Grandmother looks at me and says nothing. One granddaughter sacrificed for the other.

I will never know what this does to her. We will never speak of it. In my head, it will become The Cuba Incident, tucked tightly next to The Alfonso Incident. *Incident* as in *resulting from.* Not *accident.* There is a difference. Cause and effect. In time, I will learn to believe I am the cause, and this will eat away at me in the same way our silence eats away at you and Grandmother, shrinking us into ourselves.

★ ★ ★

The rebels don't return, and your sisters don't speak to us. It's me they should blame, and Grandmother, but there are old jealousies ripe with time and injury. You are your mother's favorite, the root of it all, some might say.

I don't know what Lita and Enricua have been told, but there are no more questions. Even Tabo and Victor are subdued and keep to their mother's side. Marta asks me to play, but I ignore her out of respect for Josepha. Auntie Danita does not treat me unkindly, she simply acts as if I don't exist. She has an incredible ability to shift her eyes past me, not once letting her gaze slip. She leaves a room if I enter it, won't eat meals with us and spends her time by Josepha's bed. Auntie Mercedes and Auntie Oneila don't outright ignore me. They will speak to me briefly but only if absolutely necessary. They don't look angry, just beaten down and terribly sad.

Everywhere I look I see the empty black holes of Che's eyes. I wonder if Josepha sees them, too. I can't ask because she won't speak, and she doesn't come out of her room. Only once do I sneak in, but she stares at me, unresponsive, and when I ask her if she's all right, she rolls away and faces the wall.

It is then that I take the wooden spoon from my pocket and lay it on the bed next to her, giving away your apology gift. It's mine to give, I think, looking at the sleek dark wood I have worn my fingers over a million times. Reaching out, I put it in Josepha's limp hand and wrap her fingers around it.

"It's for when you grow up," I say. "To stir your coffee, because you will grow up, Josepha, and you will want to drink coffee like our mothers, and by then none of this will feel so bad."

And then I leave her.

After a while, my days become endless and identical. Since the soldiers bring no more food, I'm given the task of walking to town for groceries. There's a bodega with limited supplies rationed to each family. The man who runs it, Iago, gives me rice, salt, sugar, oil and coffee. There is no meat or beans, but there are matches, which I use to light the candle in the closet. Out loud, I read Grandfather Manuel's book of poetry pretending that Josepha is listening. Or I spend silent hours of the day flat on my back under the ficus tree, thinking about the gun, and waiting for Josepha to come back to life.

She never does, at least not when I am there to see it.

A man comes for us early on a Monday morning. I used to dread Mondays when the school week was just beginning. It's funny to think how the days hold no meaning for me here. I only know it's Monday because the radio is on and the man says, "It is Monday, January 26th, 1959, and we're listening to Olga Guillot," at the same moment that I see a red car, with a shiny white top, pull to a stop in front of the house.

A man in a black suit gets out, and I jump up and hurry into the hall as Mercedes opens the front door. The man removes his hat and wipes his damp brow. He looks uncomfortably hot, his face blotchy and flushed, his pale, red hair flattened sweaty around his ears.

"Hello there," the man says in English, putting out a hand, salesmanlike, and Mercedes hesitates but gives it a quick shake. "Robert Stikes. Pleasure to meet you." The distinct Southern twang in his voice makes him seem wildly out of place.

Mercedes doesn't offer her name, and the man clears his throat and pats his breast pocket, glancing self-consciously behind him. "Well, um, sorry to bother you, ma'am, but is this the home of Estelita Rodiguez?"

Mercedes, unsmiling, turns to me and says, "Get your mother."

I holler into the kitchen, and you step into the hallway

wiping your hands on your apron. "Jiminy Cricket, Nina, you don't have to shout so loud."

"There's a man asking after you."

"Oh?"

You head to the front door, and Mercedes steps aside, keeping her eyes on Mr. Stikes.

"Señorita Rodriguez?"

"Yes?"

"Oh, thank goodness," he says, clearly relieved. "It's an honor to meet you." He does a funny little bow, and you laugh.

"I'm not the queen of England."

"Well, no." Mr. Stikes smiles, embarrassed. "But I am a fan, and it's a privilege."

Reaching inside his breast pocket, he pulls out a red leaflet with white lettering and hands it to you. I wonder if he's a salesman after all. You open the leaflet, and I peer over your shoulder to see a washed-out picture of a smiling woman in a square hat pointing to the words *Welcome Aboard! This is your TWA passenger ticket and baggage check.* Under it are two more tickets.

There is a feverish intake of air over your teeth. "Who arranged this?"

"Warner Brothers, ma'am. I was sent to personally escort you to the airport."

The airport? I register this with cautious excitement.

You do not even smile. "Why only three tickets? What about the others? I specifically told them I wouldn't go unless they got us all out."

The man pulls a second, thicker packet from his pocket. "Your plane leaves this afternoon. They wanted you back as soon as possible to begin shooting. The others were given a week to get their things in order."

Mercedes, hovering, says, "We're going? Where? Miami?"

You say, "Shooting? What do you mean shooting?"

"*Rio Bravo.* They told me you were needed back pronto."

"That was supposed to shoot months ago."

Mr. Stikes runs a hand through his hair like he's thinking hard on this. "Well, I don't know the original production schedule, but they've not shot anything yet. I'm just a film loader."

"A film loader?" You laugh, giddy, your face ablaze with the news. "What are you doing here?"

"I know—" he puts his hands in the air "—not the most likely fella to fetch a gal such as yourself home, but I was the first person they thought of who could speak Spanish, so here I am. I am friends with Jack Warner's assistant, so I've got a good reference."

"You are the perfect fella to fetch me home," you cry and throw your arms around Mr. Stikes, whose ears turn bright red.

Upstairs, we change back into the clothes we escaped Mexico in, leaving borrowed dresses, skirts and button-up sweaters folded on the bed. Grandmother Maria packs the modest bag she came with: girdle, two bras, three pairs of stockings, skirt, blouse and two dresses. She takes nothing of Grandfather Manuel's. Not a single letter from the box in the closet, not a shirt or sock or book or bottle of hair oil. I wonder if his torn jacket is back in the closet or if someone destroyed it. We move around each other with half smiles and diverted eyes. This is what we've waited for, and none of us seem sure we want it. There was supposed to be enough time to reconcile.

We pass Auntie Danita's closed door without a word.

She and Josepha are the only ones who don't see us off. The rest of our family stand in a disorderly arrangement trying not to get their feet wet in the muddy front yard. The sky is overcast, and it looks as if it will rain again. Mr. Stikes has reassured them that the tickets are official, but Oneila just mutters "We'll see." Clear where her family loyalties lie, she shoves her hands into her skirt pockets and says her goodbye with a cool nod. Mercedes, crying, is genuinely sorry to see us go. Lita squeezes me hard and says we're sure to see each other again, while Enricua gives a stiff-armed hug, glancing at her mother for approval. You tell your nieces you hope to see them in California one day. "I'll give you a tour of Paramount Studios," you say, to which they can't help smiling.

I tell Marta that I'm sorry I didn't play with her more and that I left the book of poetry in the closet. "Will you give it to Josepha for me?"

She nods, sobered by our leaving. "Do I get to go to California, too, Auntie Estelita?"

"Of course." Your voice is sincere. "But first you get to see your papa in Miami. Won't that be nice?"

Marta says yes, she misses her papa. The boys chase each other around the ficus tree with sticks, and Mercedes orders them over. "Hug your auntie and cousin goodbye." They do as they're told, Tabo's hand reaching out from behind your skirt to slap Victor. "Got you," he says, and they're off running again.

Through all of this, Grandmother Maria stands on the porch with her suitcase clutched in one hand, guarded and unapproachable. From the car, Robert Stikes says, "We'd better get a move on. Rain's made the direct route impassable, so we have to go the long way around." It's surprising how noticeably American he is, his accent and abrupt mannerisms. It makes me feel as if I've been gone a very long time.

Grandmother Maria comes off the porch, stepping around a mud puddle to press her lips first to Mercedes's cheek and then Oneila's, her eldest daughter sliding her hand into her mother's for a brief moment before letting go. The rest of her grandchildren give her quick hugs before she steps up to Robert Stikes, who takes her suitcase and opens the passenger door for her.

You and I climb into the back. I twist around as we pull away, willing Josepha to rush out the front door. This can't be the end. I want something scripted, for one of us to shout for the car to stop, for us to embrace and fall on our knees in apology. Forgiveness all around. Tears and hugs and promises of seeing each other soon.

Our slow crawl away is torture. You sit with a helpless expression as your childhood home disappears down the washed-out road, my grandmother a stoic pillar in the front seat. Greenery whirs past as Mr. Stikes steps on the gas, swerving expertly around ruts deep enough for bodies to hide in. I don't believe what you said about California. They will never come visit us. I will never see any of them again.

But I am wrong. It is you who never sees them again. They come to California. All of them. Seven years later, out of guilt or love or sorrow, everyone we left behind that day in Cuba will gather at the San Fernando Mission Catholic Cemetery for your funeral.

All but Josepha, but by then it doesn't matter. By then my fury is so blinding I wouldn't have seen her, anyway.

Chapter Twenty-Six

Onward and Upward

Daughter,

My sister's pain is too big, her daughter's even bigger. No words of apology from me will make any difference. What they need is someone to blame. My sisters have always needed someone to blame. They have each other and their anger and do not need me.

I separated myself long ago. I can do it again.

Home greets us with the rot of garbage under the sink, a dark living room snaked with street light, a coat fallen off its hook onto the floor. It's freezing cold. Mamá flicks on the light, simultaneously picking up the coat and ordering you to take her bag to her room.

We move forward through our days, reorienting ourselves. We do not speak of what happened in Cuba. My own mother's ability to avoid the most tragic events for our family is impressive. I haven't spoken of it to you, either; but then, you are only twelve. I can't imagine you understand what sex is, much less rape.

The only thing to do is jump back into life, I tell myself, pull ourselves up by the bootstraps, as Uncle Duke would say. Onward and upward.

You return to boarding school, and I return to work. Shooting for *Rio Bravo* has been pushed to summer, but there are costume screen tests and television auditions and music gigs. Ed tells me they were going to recast the role of Consuela, but Duke promised I'd be here.

"She's a gal you can count on," he'd said.

No one asks about Cuba. The brief, sensational news story of kidnapping you out of Mexico City overshadows any questions about a revolution in a country they don't understand. At dinner parties, I retell how I dressed up as an old woman and stole you away in a cab. It gets a good laugh. Rebel soldiers attacking and violating my sisters and niece doesn't go well with duck and red wine.

But it lives in us. Mamá distances herself from my career. Instead of needling Ed about what scripts have come through his office and insisting we get another studio contract now that Republic Pictures has gone under, she joins a bridge club and volunteers at a children's home in Pasadena. Her contact with my siblings is spotty, but she spoke to Oneila and reported they all made it to Miami except for Danita and Josepha, who have gone to New York City with Bebo and his wife.

"How is Josepha?" I ask.

Mamá is at the front door putting on her hat. It is April, three months since we returned from Cuba, and the weather is pleasantly warm. Mamá fiddles with her hat in front of the mirror and doesn't look at me. "According to Oneila, Josepha doesn't speak. Do you know, Oneila told me it was my fault? Said it in just those words over the wire. 'It's your fault, Mamá. You should have stayed out of it. He wasn't really going to do anything to Nina. He was just scaring her.' My fault? In that case you could say it was my fault for marrying your father who worked for Batista who brought the rebels to our house in the first place." Done with her hat, she secures her purse over her arm and opens the front door. "My heart breaks for my granddaughter. If Danita would let me help, I would, but I am wise enough to know that it was no one's fault. Not yours or Nina's or mine. Someone was getting hurt that day. Che was out for a kill. I saw it in his eyes when he walked up the porch steps. If it wasn't Josepha, it would have been Nina, or you. How were any of us to know?" She says this with her back to me, walking out and shutting the door behind her.

This is the last time either of us ever speak of it.

The nuns tell me you have settled back into school without a fuss, resuming your B-student status and unmotivated attitude toward extracurriculars. I picture you in your dorm room with your roommate, back-to-back at your desks, warm lamplight and turned-down beds. This is exactly what you need, a controlled, orderly environment. You are better off without me and my dizzying LA lifestyle.

When you come home for spring break, I am in Las Vegas headlining a show. By the time summer arrives, I am shooting *Rio Bravo* in Arizona and miss your thirteenth birthday. I am in the dressing room with Angie Dickinson wriggling out of my long skirt when I realize what day it is. Slapping a palm to my head I cry, "Oh, I am so sorry, Angie. I can't go out for drinks with you tonight. It's my daughter's birthday."

"Your daughter?" Angie rubs the thick lipstick off her mouth with a cotton swab dipped in Vaseline. "You didn't tell me you had a daughter."

"No? I must have." I prop my hands on my hips, still a little in character. Directors always want me to thicken my accent and lay on the humor. I am about to make a sarcastic joke at your expense, Nina, but I stop myself.

"What?" Angie wipes a fresh cotton swab over her darkened brows, leaning into the mirror. The glowing light bulbs circle her face like crowned beads. "You didn't." She winks at me. "But I try not to talk about my husband around here, either. They don't like us to be too domestic. You sure you aren't up for drinks? Dean is buying. You can call your daughter from the restaurant."

I throw up my hands revealing two, large sweat marks under the sleeves of my white blouse. "That's an idea. Will a cold drink stop this? Between the desert heat and those camera lights, it's a miracle I don't melt into a puddle."

"I hear you." Angie has already discarded her costume and sits in her bra and underwear. "You just have to wear something skimpy."

"How skimpy?" I strip off my blouse and let it fall to the floor.

"Skimpy as you want." Angie stretches out her smooth, bare arms. "I'm going sleeveless and short."

I put on a cocktail dress, pull my hair into a ponytail and dab lipstick on my mouth, but when I make it upstairs to the studio bar, I am in no mood for a drink. Making the rounds, I kiss Duke's cheek and wave at Dean and Angie, who stand suspiciously close together, then I excuse myself and head back to the hotel.

In the past, when I have missed your birthday, our phone calls consist of you crying and telling me you refuse to celebrate it if I'm not there, while I say I'm sorrier than anything, but it can't be helped, and I promise to make it up to you. "We'll spend a whole week together, just the two of us," I always say. "We'll sleep in late, eat breakfast in bed and go out to dinner every night."

But the night you become a teenager, I sit on my bed in a hotel room in Tucson and listen to you tell me you had a nice birthday. "Sandy Plummer gave me a charm bracelet and came over for cake and ice cream, and we listened to *Gunsmoke* on the radio."

I twist the phone cord around my finger and ask if you and Sandy are friends now.

"Best friends."

"I'm glad to hear it. Her mom is a dear. We'll have the Plummers over for dinner when I come home."

"Sure." You sound bored.

"Tell your grandmother I said you could pick out whatever you like from the Sears catalog for your birthday."

"She already took me shopping. I got a rain slicker. It's really nice. It has a fur collar."

"Well, then, we'll do dinner to celebrate when I come home."

"Sure. I'm going to go to bed now," you say and hang up without even asking when I am coming home.

I drop the receiver in its cradle. On the opposite wall from the bed is a painting of a single cactus against a backdrop of burned desert. It feels depressingly symbolic. I get up to turn on the television, but it's coin-operated, and I don't have change. Working hard to ignore the overwhelming loneliness consuming me, I pick up my script on the bed and go over my lines for the next day. It doesn't help. I consider ringing Alfonso. The divorce papers went through last month, but I know he'd answer my call. He might even come stay for a week.

Disgusted with myself, I dismiss the idea. I don't need a man. I am happy enough.

I abandon the script and search the bottom of my purse for change but only come up with a button, a crumpled twenty-dollar bill and a book of matches. The room doesn't have a radio, and it is unnervingly quiet.

Stepping out the hotel front door doesn't help much, either. My hotel is outside the city, down the road from the Old Tucson Studios where we're shooting, and it feels like the middle of nowhere. The parking lot is empty save for a few cars, and the yellow light eking out from curtained windows makes me feel even more isolated. I am rarely lonely, I realize with a stab of self-pity. At home there is always Mamá or you, and for great chunks of time, husbands. In Las Vegas my hotel room fills with people drinking after hours or else I'm at cocktail or dinner parties that leave just enough time for me to tumble into bed afterward. I should have stayed out and had a drink with Angie, I think.

I walk around the parked cars to the edge of shrubbery bordering the pavement. Nothing but desert stretches before me, black space, the tops of the distant hills like pencil marks drawn against the night sky. It reminds me of Mexico. The air blows cool against my arms, the moonless sky filled with stars. The silence is astounding. Not a cricket chirps or a mosquito buzzes or a lizard slithers. There is not a rustle of a leaf or the beat of a bird's wing. I wonder if this is what death is like, terrifying in its immense beauty and peace and silence.

From somewhere deep inside me, a song unwinds into the night, a lullaby Farah used to sing. I am astounded I still remember it. I never sang it to you. I haven't heard it since I was five years old, and yet it returns as if my soft-footed, hip-swinging nanny is standing in the desert silence, guiding the words to me.

For just this one night, I let in the dizzying loss of my home in Cuba and my sisters and all I thought we would have again. The sadness feels indulgent, gratifying, like leaning into an ache I know will never heal. I am not a person who dwells in the past but anticipates the future. And yet I feel the profound realization in this moment that there is only here and now. This night. This dark. This silence. This unimaginable sorrow. This beauty.

I want to share it with you, my one and only, precious daughter, but I know I never will. From the same source where the song came forth, I understand that there will be many things we won't share together and that moments like these are mine alone.

Chapter Twenty-Seven

Psych Ward

Mother,

I don't blame you for Cuba. Our time there stays hot in my memory, the sweet sucking of sugarcane, saliva and spit and stringy fibers held behind puckered lips. The smell of humid earth after the rain. Mud, leaves and sticks pooling in the yard under brilliant sunshine. The sound of the wind through the palm fronds, their sharp edges clacking together, the rustle of the heavy leaves so loud it sounded like entire roofs were caving in. And then there was the laughter of so many sisters gathered together, a mother and her daughters, their children, cousins and aunts, the house as rich in family as the land was in sugarcane.

And you gave me Josepha.

When we arrived home from Cuba, you came into my room holding a gold-leaf barrette in your hand with a perplexed look on your face. "Is this yours? It was in the bottom of my purse, but I've never seen it before."

I took it from you and laid it in the palm of my hand. It was a small, fern-shaped leaf with a little clasp on the back, flat and cool and perfectly formed. "Josepha gave it to me," I said, quietly.

"Oh?" You sounded unsure but didn't push for an explanation.

When you left I climbed onto my bed and traced my fingers over the bumped edges of the gold wondering when she could have put it in your purse. We left too quickly for her to do it that last day. She must have put it there after I gave her my spoon. An apology for an apology.

Now, I keep the barrette propped against the lamp on my nightstand. It is the first thing I see when I wake up and the last thing I see when I go to sleep. Even with the guilt of what I did, after the blood and screams and silence, seeing that small gold apology allows me to hold on to a version of Josepha where she smiles and wraps her fingers around mine and whispers secrets to me in the dark.

A darkness I am trying not to fall into.

On my thirteenth birthday, when I pick up the phone and hear your voice, I want to cry. Only, the anger I feel chokes it down. All of your promises of being together I now know are lies. So I lie about the charm bracelet. Sandy didn't get me anything, and she's not my best friend, just someone I occasionally spend time with. She's better than nobody.

When we ride bikes together and I can't see her face, or we sit in the grass back-to-back eating ice cream cones, I pretend she is Josepha. I'll think it so hard that when I turn around and see her dull blue eyes looking at me, I am startled and then mad. It's not Sandy's fault, but I blame her for not being Josepha.

Sometimes, this makes me mean.

After you and I hang up, I feel badly that I hurt you, and I wish we'd talked about all the things we'd do together for my birthday when you get back from shooting *Rio Bravo*. But I wanted to hurt you. I want you to think I don't care. I'm still mad at you for making me finish up the school year at Villa Cabrini Academy.

Some things did change when we got back home. For one, Alfonso was gone. I took that in as soon as we stepped through the front door—there was no smell or sound of him, just an empty house. I thought what happened would bring us together, all of us, Grandmother, you and me. You would see that what we needed was to be a family, like your sisters, that what we had been missing all along was this unity.

You do not see this. Instead, you and Grandmother ignored what happened as if shuttering windows to a storm. You both act as if we were all just temporarily derailed, stepping right back into old LA without missing a beat. Which means I get to spend the last three months of seventh grade being teased by girls who have a million versions of my story to tell, none of which are true. They can't imagine the truth, and I'd never betray my family or you or Josepha by confessing it to them. Silence, you are teaching me, is the best way forward. So silent I am. The nuns, who can guess at a more brutal truth than my pampered Hollywood classmates, let me have my solitude. But teenage girls don't like to be ignored by their own, so by the time I leave on the first of June, they openly call me *freak*.

I don't want to be a freak. I want to be normal.

Normal is charm bracelets and birthday cakes and best friends.

Therefore, on my thirteenth birthday I eat a pink-frosted cake and strawberry ice cream with Sandy and Grandmother Maria. This, after Sandy and I smoke our first joint with Johnny Freeman in his parents' toolshed. I can barely pull the smoke into my lungs and cough so hard my eyes water, but by the time I am eating cake, I feel smoothed out and light as air. You don't know the Freemans because you haven't been around long enough to meet our new neighbors. They moved into the house across the street where old Mrs. Fitzpatrick used to live. Johnny is the youngest of three brothers, has black hair and can already grow a beard even though he's only thirteen. When he kisses me, he tastes like mint mouthwash. Sandy says her older sister told her that falling in love feels hot and tingly and that your mind goes wild with it and you can't think of anything else. I feel none of this. When Johnny comes near me, my stomach churns, and I think I might throw up. I kiss him back only because I am hoping that this will make me normal, too.

It is not until the next summer, at fourteen, when I have sex with him. This is the summer I come home from school to find that Grandmother Maria has moved out and a man named Ricardo Pego has moved in. He is handsome, in that older-man way. A doctor, you tell me proudly.

All I want to know is why Grandmother Maria moved out, sadness bubbling up as I stand at the kitchen counter. It could have just been the two of us with her gone. Why do you never want it to be just the two of us?

"Your *abuela* thought her own place would be a good idea." You stand in the morning sun, shadowed and backlit, your face tired. "She's only a ten-minute drive away."

"Okay." I shrug, confused that after all these years of wishing my grandmother would move out, I feel sorry not to hear her pattering feet coming from the bedroom. I miss her brisk morning hug and the smell of the verbena oil she rubs on the ends of her hair.

This missing does not last long. Within an hour she has arrived to envelop me, kissing each cheek, smelling familiar and spicy and insisting that we have Sunday dinners all together and that I come to her place at least three times a week for lunch.

I do, reluctantly. She lives in a small one-story with a postage-stamp front yard. The living room is decorated with large-flowered furniture and pink curtains. The kitchen has bright blue countertops and the bathroom sea-green tiles. I have nothing more to talk about with my grandmother than I ever did, so I eat quickly and hurry off to meet Johnny and Sandy at Sandy's boyfriend's house. His name is Casper, and he has a swimming pool and a liquor cabinet and absent parents.

It is in Casper's room on a blue-striped bedcover, surrounded by blue-striped wallpaper, that Johnny and I have sex for the first time. I am slightly drunk on gin and tonic, and it feels good when Johnny slides his tongue over my nipples, but when his penis touches the inside of my thigh, cool and wet, I feel Alfonso's hand. And when I look into Johnny's eyes, the empty black holes of Che's stare back at me, and I feel as if my head has just smacked the floor. I do not expect these men to show up here. I have spent the last year and a half erasing their faces, their names, their very existence. It is startling to have this one natural act bring them back so vividly; even Johnny's mint-flavored mouth turns to whiskey and cigar smoke.

"Are you okay?" he whispers, still Johnny's voice, at least. I look at his pink mouth and scrunched up eyes and try to reorient myself, but my boyfriend's face has twisted into an expression I don't understand: concern and pleasure and confusion. For the moment, I am as confused as he is.

"I'm okay." I squeeze my eyes shut, fighting the pain and throbbing and tears as I force myself into a place of cool numbness.

It is over quickly, and when Johnny rolls off and kisses my

shoulder and the air is warm against my skin again, I think maybe sex is not so bad. I will just have to remember to keep my eyes closed.

I want to tell you about it, but we have never spoken of sex, and I think you will be angry or disappointed, maybe even repulsed. When you talk of Ricardo, your face glows with a brightness I recognize as love, but I feel none of this in myself. My mind does not go wild with it, and I do not feel hot or tingly.

For me, love feels the same as fear.

You would never understand this. The summer you fall in love with Ricardo, you are rippling with delight. It is the newness, the possibility. For you, a man means a shining future. It always will, I think, no matter how many times it goes wrong.

Looking back, I should have hated Ricardo. But honestly, I never thought he was that bad. Humorless and dull as a board, but harmless. He was a doctor, after all. I forgot that most dangerous men look innocent, at first.

It isn't hard to get drugs at Villa Cabrini Academy, so my school years pass in a blur, marked only by summer.

The next summer, you will be married to Ricardo, and Johnny will have moved away. I will try my first tab of acid with Sandy and become purple dust. For the first time since Cuba, I will feel light and free and beautiful. It will intoxicate me, and I will want to be purple dust forever.

Every summer until we are nineteen years old, Sandy and I will swear a forever friendship in the whispered dark of drunken sleepovers, promising to write all year long and then forgetting.

She and I will last longer than our many boyfriends, but our friendship won't last forever.

★ ★ ★

It is Sandy who calls you when I am curled on the living room rug tripping on LSD. It is August 1965, one year after I graduate from high school. The same year Sandy spent studying biochemistry at UC Santa Barbara while I waitressed at the Pancho Villa Inn. A year in which the US sent 125,000 soldiers to Vietnam and Malcolm X was shot, and all I paid attention to was Sonny and Cher on *American Bandstand* and *The Ed Sullivan Show*. I watched a lot of TV, while avoiding news if I could. I did see the Watts riots while snorting cocaine at Tuesday Weld's pool party, but that's only because everyone was watching. Sitting on the floor in her living room wearing a bikini, the rug itching the underside of my bare legs, I stared at her TV screen, encased in shiny mahogany. We watched Molotov cocktails being thrown by angry white policeman into crowds of angry Black men who were setting buildings on fire. I didn't believe it was really happening in Los Angeles. From where I sat, the sky out the window was blue and clear of smoke, and all I cared about was if Tommy Kirk had any more marijuana. He's a movie actor, five years older than me. Disney fired him for being gay, but he can sure score good dope.

That Thursday morning in August, when I drop a tab of acid, the sun is not shining. Dark clouds have swept in threatening to rain, even though it never rains in August. I ask Sandy if she wants a tab, and she says no. She's dating a guy at college named Barry, who doesn't do that sort of thing.

"Well, good for Barry," I say, tossing my cigarette butt out the sliding glass door onto the patio before placing the tab on my tongue.

When you come home, I am lying on the floor. It seems as if I have been here for hours watching Sandy's toes—sticking out from her sandals like tiny pigs' noses—marching back and forth in front of me. Eventually, they are joined by another set of feet, thick ankles and short heels. Grandmother Maria's shoes alongside your tiny tennis shoes. Did you run here? I wonder. Your voices roll over me hushed and urgent and worried. Then I drop onto my back and smile up at your floating heads. *Don't worry*, I want to say. *Can't you see how I sparkle? I am as beautiful as you now, Mom.* But then you try and lift me, and I worry that I will fall through your fingers. *You can't lift dust*, I want to say. *You won't be able to hold on. You will lose me.*

You do lose me—to the psychiatric ward of The Good Hope Medical Foundation. Or rather, you stick me in here. You say it's for my own good, which of course I don't believe, at least not in the beginning.

But after three months in the psych ward, I begin to feel safe for the first time in years.

The week I am due to get out, I stand in the doorway of the hospital room, which I share with my roommate Delia Pereira, waiting for your phone call. If I scoot with my toes over the line of green tile that separates my room from the hallway, I can see the phone propped on the nurse's desk like a black cat I'm waiting to spring to life. *Call*, I think. You were supposed to call at 4:30 p.m. A large clock on the wall behind the desk says 4:53. Every day since you first brought me here, we've spoken at precisely 4:30. No matter how furious I was with you at the beginning, you've never missed a single one of our calls.

Nurse Doris, a bottle blonde with rouged cheeks and a stern, pink mouth, sits at the desk filing her nails. She looks like someone from Ohio who arrived fresh out of high school and dreamed of making it in the pictures, then found out she wasn't so pretty after all. Now she spends her days pinning girls' arms behind their backs and wiping shit off the walls from the crazy girl down the hall. Technically, we're all crazy in here, but there's really only the one, Samantha Padovano, sallow-cheeked with patches of hair missing where she rips it out. The rest of us were just caught with too much time on our hands.

Delia's father is an attorney who travels and sleeps with other women, and her mother is a drunk who tries to take her own life once a year. Delia is in here because she had a breakdown and smashed every dish in the house. Her little sister stepped on a piece of glass and cut her foot, and her mom said Delia had gone crazy and was a danger to them all.

Delia makes living here almost enjoyable. She doesn't expect anything of me as a friend. When I don't want to talk, she doesn't make me, and when I'm mean, she says, "You go on and freak out, girl. I've taken worse," which usually makes me feel bad and apologize.

Life in a psych ward is life with a routine. I get my blood drawn each morning, eat three meals a day, always at the same time, and see a psychiatrist named Dr. Gataki who asks how I am feeling. "Fine," I say, always fine. He is long-limbed, dark-haired and skinny, not old or young, married (there's a ring), and frustratingly calm, even when I swear at him. As long as I stay sober and act respectably sane, everyone is happy. He has gotten me to talk about the past, which I did in a defiant way at first. A *Fuck you. You want it? Here you go*, but then it started to feel good having someone listen. It was easier to talk about it all with someone who means nothing to me. I admitted to him that I don't miss the drugs, and that maybe I only did them because I was bored.

"And to numb out the past," he suggests.

I shrug. "Maybe."

They've given us a small radio in our room, and Delia's introduced me to a band called The Who. She says when she gets out she's moving to London because that's where all the cool bands are. She says I should go with her.

"That sounds fun," I say, thinking of you. Even at nineteen, I can't imagine living a continent away. I've never had the desire to travel abroad like everyone else my age. Cuba was enough for me. "I'm thinking of going to college," I say because this is more realistic.

The telephone rings, and I lean anxiously out my door making sure my feet don't cross the line of tile into the hallway. We're not allowed out of our rooms during quiet hours unless we have a prearranged phone call which Nurse Doris, and only Nurse Doris, has the power to grant. If I piss her off by stepping over the line unbidden, she might not let me out at all.

She lets the phone ring four times before lifting the receiver, propping it between her ear and shoulder so there's no pause in her nail filing. "Good Hope psychiatric clinic. Yes, ma'am. She's right here." She motions from the desk with a flap of her manicured hand.

My stockinged feet slap across the tile as I snatch the phone out of her hand. "Mom?"

"Nina," your voice sounds funny.

"What's wrong?"

"Oh," you say with a breathy laugh, "so much and so little."

"What do you mean? Why didn't you call at 4:30?"

"I got tied up, but don't worry, I promise to call on time tomorrow. Now, tell me about you. How are they treating you?"

"Fine."

"What did you eat for breakfast?"

"Bacon and eggs."

"You hate eggs."

"I know, but I ate them, anyway. If you don't eat, they assume something's wrong with you."

"Well, eggs won't kill you."

"No."

There's a beat of silence, and then you whisper, "Nina, I'm leaving Ricardo," as if he's standing near you, listening.

"Why?" I ask, oblivious to all I missed this past year living under the same roof as the two of you.

I hardly ever saw Ricardo. He got up early, and I sleep in. Neither of you were home often: usually out at restaurants or parties or working late. When our paths did cross, Ricardo would be coming home late at night from the hospital, while I'd be up watching TV. We kept our interactions single-syllabled.

I thought very little of him, but now, your silence on the other end of the phone worries me. "What did he do? Are you okay?"

"Nothing. I don't know." Your voice is thin.

"What's going on? What's wrong?" I'm imagining an affair, a pink-lipped, dully attractive nurse like Doris saddling Ricardo in his office chair. Maybe you walked in on them. "Mom?"

"You get out next week." Your voice lifts, semicheerful but not convincing.

"I know."

I'm not sure I want to get out. I've only recently come to realize how terrified I am of the world. Dr. Gataki says it's because of my past, because of Alfonso, and then my father who I couldn't trust and didn't know what he'd do next. Then there was the border police and the rebel soldiers and finally Che who was the most terrifying of all. Dr. Gataki told me the drugs weren't just to numb out the memories but also a way I'd learned to terrify myself.

"Sunday, 9:00 a.m. I'll pick you up," you are saying.

"But you'll call tomorrow?"

"4:30 precisely, I promise."

"Okay. I love you."

"I love you, too."

I hang up the phone. Doris has opened a bottle of white nail polish and is carefully painting her thumbnail. The smell is worse than the antiseptic hospital scent that lingers on everything. "Back to your room, missy," she says without looking up.

I sit on my bed and watch Delia take her afternoon nap. The winter sunlight filters through the narrow windows but fails to warm the hospital chill that blankets everything. On the nightstand is Josepha's gold barrette. It's the only thing I brought with me besides clothes. Delia asked about it, and I told her the whole truth.

"Wow, man, that's intense shit," she'd said, listening with somber respect.

I take the barrette in my hand and lie down, rolling up in my covers, the white ceiling panels overhead like neatly arranged sugar cubes. I find it impossible to sleep in the middle of the afternoon. Usually, I watch the traffic out the window or reread my father's letters. After Mexico, Chu Chu still visited once a year, but I was only allowed to see him accompanied by a chaperone courtesy of Edward Adelman's lawyer. My father loves me, I've decided. His letters don't state it directly, but he always says he wishes you had left me in Mexico with him, and on most days, I wish you had too.

I'm jealous of Delia's ability to sleep. At night, she's snoring almost the instant her head hits the pillow. I don't know how she does it. It takes me hours to fall asleep, and when I do, my dreams are colored with violence.

I am worried about you.

Delia says my attachment to you is unnatural. Mothers aren't supposed to be our best friends. "Take mine," she says, sitting cross-legged on her chair in the dining hall that first week we met. She takes a bite out of her doughnut, flips her straight hair. "I loathe her. My mom criticizes the music I listen to, my jeans, my hair." Her self-righteous voice is edgy. "She still thinks I'm a virgin. I swear to God." She leans toward me. "Can you believe she thinks being a housewife is some kind of honorable profession for a woman?"

I tell her that you are not a housewife. You're a working mom who buys me jeans, helps me iron my hair and tells me I can be whatever I want. Eating my own doughnut, sugar crumbling into my lap, I tell Delia about the time you took me on a double date with Desi Arnaz and Dean Martin, how you let me pick out a dress that made me feel pretty for the first time in my life.

"You are pretty," Delia says matter-of-factly, and I think of Josepha saying how ugly we were and wonder if she grew up pretty, too. Delia finishes her doughnut and licks the powdered sugar from her fingers. "I suppose your mother put you in here for your own good, too, and not to get you out of her hair?" she says, and I say, yes, that's exactly what you did. Delia is not convinced. "If your mom is so goddamn perfect, why are you so fucked up? Why drugs? And why don't you talk about anyone in your family besides your mom?"

I shrug and finish my doughnut. I don't tell her how, after Cuba, Josepha's bloody face was all I saw when I closed my eyes. How the sound of my skull hitting the floor ricocheted inexhaustibly in my head. Even now, as I lie rolled like a sausage in a hospital bed—a fully grown woman with years since the child who was snatched and then rescued and then dropped into a war zone—the word *family* still makes me hear the screams of my grandmother while Che's hot, fumbling fingers pulled up my skirt.

There are things families don't talk about.

That's what Dr. Gataki is for. I pull the covers up over my head and breathe into my hands to warm them. I am afraid if I leave that the silence between you and me, Mom, will be easy again, that I'll even find comfort in it, like slipping my head under warm bathwater. I'm afraid I won't be able to come up for air.

The next day I tell Dr. Gataki, "I am afraid when I leave I'll turn to drugs again, that drowning in them will be easier than living with the memories."

"Can you live with them in here?" he asks.

"Yes, but it's safe in here."

"It's safe out there, too," he says.

Only for some of us, I will later think.

Chapter Twenty-Eight

Shame

Daughter,

During our phone call, Nina, I sit on the kitchen floor in a puddle of water, your voice calming me. I want to tell you the truth, but I cannot. The air smells of burned toast. From where I sit, I can see the perfectly charred black tops poking up out of the toaster.

After we hang up, I drop the receiver and leave it dangling by its twisted cord against the kitchen wall as I turn toward the bedroom. Leaning against the back of my vanity chair, I pull off my sopping skirt and peel my wet underwear down over my scraped knees. I haven't had scraped knees since I was a child. It's a funny thing to see on a grown woman. Funny in a disturbing way.

Earlier, I was out by the pool folding laundry and remembering the times in our old house in Sherman Oaks when Mamá hung the laundry to dry on the line and we'd fold it together on the lounge chairs. I machine-dry now, but sometimes I still like to fold the wash outside in the sunshine.

The slider to the living room is open, and deep inside the

house I hear the front door slam. Ricardo is never home this early.

"Hello?" I drop a folded towel into the basket and walk toward the glass doors. Sunlight reflects off them, and all I see is my own image before Ricardo steps out so abruptly I let out a small scream, followed by a nervous laugh. "You scared the bejesus out of me."

He stands with one hand on the doorjamb, the other at his side. His white doctor's coat hangs open above his knees, and beneath it his shirt looks soaked with sweat. He's pushed his hair up off his forehead, and his face is flushed, his eyes narrow slits against the sun.

"What's wrong?" I take a step back, my hand already raised in self-defense, a weak, instinctual gesture that never does any good.

"The house is full of smoke." There is bewildered alarm in his voice, as if I've burned the house down.

"Oh, goodness." My voice shakes. "I must have forgotten about my toast. I'll air it out."

It doesn't matter what I say, the damage is done. He lunges at me, grabs the back of my head and forces me to my knees. I know, burned toast sounds ridiculous, but he has hit me for less.

"I'm sorry," I cry, another pathetic, instinctual impulse. Did any amount of pleading ever stop an abusive man? I might as well have asked how he was feeling and if there was anything I could do to help.

With a fist around my hair, he drags me across the cement decking. I crawl and slide, unable to get up, my skirt tearing under me, the skin on my knees splitting open. At the edge of the pool, the water is crystal clear and still as glass. He releases my hair long enough for me to hope that dragging me is all he intends to do. And then his small, iron fingers grip the back of my neck. It's surprising how strong his hands are. On our first date, when he helped me off with my coat, I noticed how thin and delicate his fingers were. I like a man with broad hands, the wide space at the base of a man's thumb my favorite part. As Ricardo's hand circles my neck from behind, I think I may never like any part of a man's hand again. My body is thrust forward, my chest pinned against the edge of the pool. Ricardo's fingers pinch the top of my spine, and my head plunges into the pool. Water splashes as my arms flail. I try and reach backward, grab his arm or claw his eyes. Anything. The instinct to survive is impressive, how we fight to the end. My eyes are wide-open, stinging from chlorine, my world turned a soft, blurry blue.

There is a dream I've had my whole life, or at least for as long as I can remember. I am in a room full of people I don't recognize, and everyone keeps asking me if I'm all right. I think there must be something wrong with the way I look—my hair isn't done right or I'm wearing the wrong clothes. I find a long hall with a mirror at the end, and as I move close enough to see myself, I suddenly can't breathe. It is as if the air has gone out of the room. It is not a slow loss of breath but an instant, unimaginable suffocation.

And then everything goes black.

I wake up alone. The edge of the pool shifts in and out of focus, the water rippling outward unevenly. There's not a breeze, which makes me think that not much time has passed. I am the one who has stirred up the water and now I lie immobile, heavy as brick in a cold puddle with my cheek pressed into gritty cement. My knees sting. Ricardo meant to kill me, I think. Maybe he believed he had.

I hear the sound of distant cars and the rhythmic thud of a baseball being thrown from glove to glove by the boys next door. Tommy and Alexander. Nice boys. Ten and twelve. I might have stayed there all night if I wasn't worried the ball was going to go over the fence and one of them might come looking for it.

No need to alarm the neighbors.

Shakily, I push myself up to my feet. The pool is glaringly bright, and little black threads float in front of my eyes as I make my way into the house. "Ricardo?" I call softly, looking around as if he might jump out from behind a door or the sofa. I can feel the pulse of my heart in my throat. A shadow of smoke drifts out of the kitchen toward the ceiling, thin as mist, almost undetectable. The house is quiet, other than the tick of the clock. The time. I suddenly remember our call. It is 5:03. The psychiatrist told me I wasn't to miss a single phone call with you.

"She needs consistency," he'd said. These calls were an important step in establishing trust, he told me. Missing them would be a setback.

I hurry to the kitchen, dizzy, my vision slightly blurred as I look out the window above the sink making sure Ricardo's car is not in the driveway before calling Good Hope. When you answer, I slide to the floor and rest my back against the wall wishing you were here with me. I want to tell you everything, but I don't want to upset you. The doctors say you are doing well. You will be home in a week. We are to keep things calm and normal.

Calm and normal? I don't even know what that means anymore.

When we hang up, I go to the bedroom and change into slacks to hide my knees and a T-shirt so I look casual. I secure my wet hair back with a scarf, pack a suitcase and call Virginia. You haven't met Virginia yet. She's Ricardo's colleague, the sole female doctor on staff. She told me that remaining single, childless and wearing pants suits is the only way to make it as a female in the medical profession, which made me laugh. Virginia always makes me laugh.

We met at a party three months ago. I spotted her across the room, a ball glass of bourbon in her hand, her dress slacks and jacket fitted and flattering. It was a gathering of doctors and UCLA medical school professors. I was trying to imagine what it would be like to be the only female in a male profession, say a producer or director, when she suddenly strode over and stuck out her hand. "Dr. Virginia Poleo."

I shook it. She was a foot taller than me, full-figured with a wide jaw and dark, straight hair cut into a bob. Without hesitating she asked about the bruise on my arm, what had happened. Instinctively, I drew my hand over it, but there was a sincerity in her steady, no-nonsense gaze that stopped me from lying. I didn't confess, I just kept my mouth shut, and she handed me her drink. "I've worked with Ricardo for seven years and have never seen him lose his temper until a month ago. Does he lose it at home now, too?"

"Sometimes." I took a sip of her bourbon and handed it back.

The first time Ricardo hit me was three weeks before your graduation from Villa Cabrini Academy. I remember because I was worried the bruise wouldn't be gone in time, and I'd have to explain it to you.

I'd come home late from a show in Palm Springs. I'd gotten off stage and driven straight back to LA knowing Ricardo wanted to spend the weekend together and because he'd accused me of sleeping with other men in my hotel room, which was ludicrous.

When I arrived home at one o'clock in the morning, I found him out on the deck staring into a dark firepit. I asked, laughingly, if he was waiting for it to light itself, and without a word he grabbed my arm and dragged me into the living room. The house was ablaze, as if he'd gone through every room turning on the lights. He was barefoot, his shirt unbuttoned.

I pulled my arm away, indignant. "Don't touch me like that. What has gotten into you?"

"It's one o'clock in the morning, Estelita." He had an overblown, harangued tone to his voice and outrage in his eye.

I was about to explain when his fist caught me in the chin, and I flew backward into the couch. I remember crying out in shock, pulling myself up and stumbling toward him instead of away.

He had seemed a good choice for a husband, a doctor who specializes in bones, a man who doesn't sing or act or juggle for a living. When we first met, I found him dashing in his pinstriped suits and waxed mustache, and I liked the way he talked so sincerely about his patients. He didn't try and win me with any display of romance. He was thoughtful in the way he asked where I'd like to eat and if I preferred red or white wine. I was used to men who made decisions for me, as if it was expected that their decisions were what I wanted. Ricardo would ask, solicitously, if there was anything I needed. So simple, really. I don't remember any of my other husbands asking if I needed anything. None of them waited at night for me to undress before getting into bed or left notes by the coffeepot in the morning with our names drawn in a heart.

What Ricardo didn't like was being married to an actress. He wasn't prepared for it. When we were dating, he found my short skirts and tight sweaters attractive; after marriage they were revealing and inappropriate. It angered him that I kissed other men on-screen or looked seductively into the audience at my concerts. A year after we married, he told me he didn't want me going out for auditions anymore or performing.

"You're too old, anyway," he'd say.

I was thirty-two.

It was our first real argument. He was sitting up in bed, looking at me over the top of his book as if he'd just asked what time it was. I was standing with the sheet pulled back about to climb in, and in an instant, I saw our marriage for what it was, a masquerade, a shameful display of false intimacy, false impartiality. After all this careful attention he'd given me, I was now expected to do what he said. I threw the sheet down and told him that Chu Chu had tried to keep me at home and I'd left him within the year. "I've sacrificed everything for my career. Motherhood, my family. Don't you dare think you'll be any different."

I stormed out and slept in the guest room that night, and he never brought up the subject again, but he deliberately undermines me, making aggressive remarks about how fat my thighs are getting or how I should do something about the bags under my eyes. He tells me I need to start dressing my age and buys me checkered pants and high-collared blouses for my luncheons at the Beverly Hills Badminton Club with his colleagues' wives.

I've tried to talk to Mamá about the violence, but she never liked Ricardo to begin with, and it angers her that I've only done a few television shows since my marriage. "After all this time, you're letting a man ruin your career," she tells me, no matter how many times I remind her I'm singing more than ever and getting top billing in Las Vegas. "You could have sung in Havana" is her endless retort. "You came here to be in the movies." In her mind, this is the only real success.

Just a week ago, Mamá and I argued over lunch at La Paloma's. She told me Ricardo is making me lose my confidence. "The way he insults you, it's disgusting that you allow it."

"I don't take him seriously," I say, a feeble argument. My transfer of power already so obvious.

"Oh, no? Why aren't you working, then?"

"We've had this conversation, Mamá. I am working."

"Not acting."

"I'm not acting because Republic Pictures sold the studio."

"So go out and get a contract with another studio."

"Ed says the other studios aren't contracting anymore. 'Picture by picture,' he says. Actors are free agents now. I have to go on auditions like everyone else."

"Hogwash." She stabs her steak with her knife and begins sawing away at it. "You could get a new contract if you wanted one."

There is no arguing with your grandmother, as you know, Nina.

Truth is, I am worried she is right, that Ricardo has worn away my confidence. I am getting older, and the only place I feel like I can be myself anymore is on stage. I am not used to auditioning in a small room with casting directors a foot away, staring at me. I get nervous and fumble my lines and have to take the scene from the top. They're always very nice about it, but I leave humiliated.

Singing is so much easier, and gratifying, but I am afraid Ricardo will take that away from me, too.

After he hit me that first time, he fell on his knees in apology, weeping as if he was the one with a bruised jaw. I ended up comforting him. He'd never hit me before, but he'd also never wept in front of me before. He swore it wouldn't happen again, and I believed him.

I thought I knew violent men, but this is different. Ricardo's anger comes out of nowhere. It is irrational and sporadic, and he is always sorry. He says he doesn't know what comes over him, he loves me, it won't happen again, and until today, before he held my head underwater, I kept believing him.

Virginia claims this is what every abusive husband says, but it's not what my father said to my mother after he hit her. He never apologized. He was correcting her, and I wonder, as I stand at the bedroom window watching for Virginia's car, if I've taken the abuse because in some dark place I believe I needed correcting, too.

The back of my neck hurts. I untie my scarf and shake my hair out to hide what I imagine are fingerprint bruises curled below my scalp. I glance at the clock. 6:15 p.m. I have been waiting for an hour. I didn't tell Virginia what happened. I didn't need to.

"I've been waiting for you to come to your senses," she said over the telephone. "No need for details, if you don't want. I'll be there as soon as I can."

I am grateful she doesn't ask me to explain.

In Cuba, after Josepha was raped, I went into the kitchen and took a knife from the drawer and hid it in the waistband of my underwear. Over there, I somehow made sense of the violence and sex because it was war, generations of hatred and loss and suffering. Men who believed women deserved to be abused for what our fathers and grandfathers had done. With Che, my reaction was pure hate, and I would have slit his throat if he'd come near you or me again.

Here, it is my husband. There is no war other than the one going on in our house. There is no history, no generational excuse. My husband says he loves me. So it is love and violence, and I do not know how to defend myself against such a perverse reality.

Light fades from the window. Having made the decision to leave, I am terrified. If Ricardo comes home before Virginia gets here, I don't know what I'll do.

Chapter Twenty-Nine

Who is Lupe Velez?

Mother,

I am not convinced that you have actually left Ricardo until we are driving to Virginia's from Good Hope. With both hands on the steering wheel, your cat-eye sunglasses pulled over your eyes, you tell me he hit you. You were always a nervous driver, but you are especially jumpy, swerving in and out of traffic, as you recall how Ricardo almost drowned you in the pool. It's shocking to know he hit you while I was living at home with you and I knew nothing about it, but you tell me it didn't happen often and never when I was in the house.

"Have you told Grandmother Maria?"

"No, and you're not to tell her, either."

"You tell Grandmother Maria everything."

"I tell you everything." You peel one hand from the wheel and give my knee a quick pat before gripping it again. "I don't want any secrets between us."

"But you want secrets between you and Grandmother Maria?"

"No, silly. It would upset her. It's done with. We can all

move on. We don't need to talk about it. I've brought the rest of your clothes to Virginia's, and she said we can stay as long as we like."

"Why aren't we staying with Grandmother Maria?" Dr. Gataki said I was to keep things as simple as possible, for a while. None of this feels simple.

"She has a single bedroom. We'd have to sleep on the living room floor."

"Does she know you've moved out?"

"Yes. I told her what she wanted to hear—that Ricardo was holding me back from my acting career."

It occurs to me you haven't done a movie since *Rio Bravo*, but there's been plenty of television and music venues. "Was he?"

You slam to a stop at a red light and glance at me, your expression unreadable behind your lenses. "A bit, I guess. But I have a show every weekend this month in Las Vegas, and I have a film audition next week."

"How long are we going to stay with your doctor friend?"

"Not long." You slide your sunglasses to the top of your head and look directly at me. "We're going to get our own place soon. Just the two of us. Won't that be fun? We'll have girls' night whenever we want without a man sticking his nose into things."

The place in my heart that has longed for this my whole life swells. "I'd love that, Mom."

"We need to find an apartment first. Just a rental, for now. I'll need to file for divorce." The light turns green, and you step on the gas, eyes back on the road.

"Has Ricardo tried to contact you?" I ask, the safety I felt at Good Hope vanishing in the time it took to drive away.

"He came over the day after I left to apologize and beg me to come home. I asked what he was thinking, almost killing me, which he denied. To his credit, he walked away. He seemed genuinely sorry. Sad, not angry, which has always confused me about him. I feel sorry for him more than anything."

This is so like you, always giving men the benefit of the doubt. "That's twisted, Mom. You should hate him."

You disregard this and say, "Do you remember what I used to tell you whenever you broke up with a boyfriend?"

I've had four official breakups, the last one with Josh Parker being the most serious. We only dated for three months, but he had wavy blond hair and dreamy blue eyes, and I was sure I was in love with him. "I remember," I say, then mimic your voice, throwing in the thick Spanish accent you use in your movies: "'Nina, I want you to picture Josh right now sitting on the toilet with his socks on and his underwear around his ankles. Do you see it? I want you to just think about him sitting there.'"

"That's right." You laugh. "It worked, didn't it?"

"I am totally over him. Are you picturing Ricardo?"

"This very minute. He has the hairiest legs." You start laughing so hard tears come out of your eyes, and I tell you to focus on the road before you crack up the car.

Virginia lives in a small bungalow with lots of windows in Van Nuys. There's a garden in the back with a magnolia tree and a Japanese-style fountain. She has immaculate white rugs and Asian vases the size of small children by the door. You and I sleep in the guest room where the twin beds have matching white coverlets and gold-trimmed, white nightstands that stand on either side. At the end of the hall, Virginia's room has a king-size bed covered in a dark gray Japanese silk and sliding glass doors that open onto the back patio.

It's nice to be away from the bare walls of the hospital, but I don't like being in a stranger's house. I miss Delia and feel nervous about the uncertainty of things. At least in the hospital, I didn't have to make any decisions.

After poking around the entire place, I drag my bag to the guest room and head to the kitchen. You are fumbling around in a ruffled apron that makes you look ridiculous, attempting a Betty Crocker pot roast from a cookbook you said you bought just for this dinner together.

"Are we celebrating the fact that I am no longer mentally insane?" I jump up on the counter and take an orange from the fruit bowl, trying to feel like I'm at home. "Can I eat this?"

"You can eat anything you like. You are to treat this house as your own. Virginia would want it that way." You swat my leg. "And I never said you were mentally insane."

Some juice squirts into my face as I dig my nails into the peel. "No? Just a druggie, then."

"Don't talk like that. You are an intelligent young woman who needs a little direction is all. When I was your age I had a singing career, was already married, had a baby and was about to make my first movie."

"Jesus, Mom."

"Don't swear. Hand me that measuring spoon."

I turn to where you're pointing, pick up the spoon and hand it to you. "Do you have any idea what you're doing in the kitchen?"

"None whatsoever." You push hair out of your eyes with the back of your arm and scrunch up your face as you read the recipe, mouthing the directions and carefully measuring and pouring. Watching you in the kitchen makes me think there's hope our lives can be simple and normal and easy.

When Virginia comes home, the first thing she does is take me through the house and tell me exactly what I am not to do. Do not leave the toothpaste top off. Wipe the bathroom sink down after every use. When you leave the bathroom, make sure the toilet-seat cover is down. Do not touch the thermostat, and do not leave glasses in the kitchen sink. Behind her back, you roll your eyes, making a funny face at me as you take the pot roast from the oven.

"Now that, my dears," you cry, delighted, "is a masterpiece." You look like an advertisement in your starched apron with your hands slid into potholders, your hair fluffed and your face glowing from the heat of the stove.

"It's just pot roast, Mom."

"It's my first pot roast, and I am very proud of it."

Virginia moves to your side. She is pencil-thin, pretty but severe. She wears red diamond-shaped clip-on earrings that match her lipstick, a silk blouse tucked into pleated pants and an outdated hairdo—a bob with the ends flipping up around her chin. She slides her arm around your waist and says, "It smells amazing," with a look that makes me think she would have complimented you if you'd pulled a small elephant from the oven.

During dinner, Virginia keeps touching your arm and laughing at everything you say. You are hysterical, as usual, mimicking the doctors' wives you've been forced to socialize with, declaring that if Ricardo hadn't tried to drown you, you would have drowned yourself.

"Oh, those luncheons! Talk about boring someone to death, and I hate badminton. I'm terrible at it!" You cut a second slice of pot roast and put it on Virginia's plate. It is surprisingly good. You even made a ketchup sauce to go with it.

"I'll take you to lunch at the Beverly Hills Badminton Club, and we'll show them how it's done," Virginia says. There is a lively intimacy between you two and adoration in Virginia's smile. My vision of you and me together shrivels, the swell in my heart deflating. You will always need someone else.

I eat in silence, missing Delia's company as neither of you ask me a single question.

Over the next two weeks, I watch with strained tolerance, and slight curiosity, as Virginia tries everything she can to seduce you. I have never seen a woman in love with another woman. It's astounding how quickly a gesture of friendship slips to seduction. It is also astounding how oblivious you are, and I realize you've never had a best girlfriend and must have no idea what that looks like. The fact that you don't return her advances is hopeful.

Dr. Gataki told me it was important to keep busy, so I do what I can to find a job and contemplate enrolling in city college.

On a Friday, three weeks after I get out of the hospital, I have a promising interview I am excited to tell you about. But you come home with your own good news, bursting through the door with a whoop and a squeal, attacking me on the couch where I am reading *Revolutionary Road*. You wear a short boxy red dress and little white gloves.

"I got the part! I got the part!"

"What part?"

You yank the book from my hand and fling it to the coffee table, standing and bouncing on the cushion like a child.

"Virginia won't like that."

"Virginia won't know."

"What part?"

Late afternoon sunlight warms the room. Out the window, the magnolia is in full bloom. I love the decadence of a magnolia tree, how brazenly it thrusts its huge blossoms into the air, every branch pretentious and over the top.

You throw your arms into the air, displaying your own magnificence. "You are looking at the next Lupe Velez." You take a deep bow, lose your balance on the couch and land on your feet like a cat. Giddy with excitement, you drop down next to me and swing one thigh-high white boot over my knees. "Be a dear and help me pull these ridiculous things off. I think someone put cement in my boots."

I stand, tugging at the sides of the slippery leather. "Who is Lupe Velez?"

"*Who is Lupe Velez?* Have I taught you nothing? She was a scandalously wild and promiscuous and fantastic Mexican actress."

"Sounds perfect for you," I tease, tugging harder, but the boot won't budge.

"I've never had a juicier role. Four months pregnant, and she commits suicide. I get to do a dying scene."

"I can't get it off." I drop your foot, and you flip over and hold the back of the couch with both hands. "Pull with all your might."

Practically lifting you in the air, I yank the boot so hard it slides off in a single motion, and I tumble backward, catching myself before I fall into the coffee table. I set the boot down and yank off the other. You moan with pleasure, stand up and grab my hands, dancing me around the room.

"I went for a job interview today," I say, trying to follow your lead.

"You did? For what?"

"It's just a hostess job, but it's at the Chateau Marmont."

"Ooh la la! Fancy. We need some music." You drop my arms, humming and swinging your way over to the record player. "How about a little Everly Brothers." You slide the record from its case, drop it down on the player, and there's a crackle from the needle before "Wake Up Little Susie" blares into the room.

At that moment Virginia steps in from the front hallway, and from the look on her face I think she's going to be angry, but then she smiles, kicks off her shoes and drops her bag to join us. We take turns dancing in pairs, the solo dancer moving off on their own then coming back in and switching partners. I think of us dancing in Cuba with your sisters and my cousins, the movement of the body a celebration. When the album ends, we drop breathless to the couch, and Virginia says she's starving and we should order in.

Later that night, when you and I are getting ready for bed, you tell me we're moving out.

"Are we?" I sit half-naked, pulling my pajama bottoms on, skeptical.

At the mirror, you carefully roll your hair in curlers. Blobs of cold cream are smeared under your eyes like war paint, and you wear the same silk negligee you've worn since you were married to Grant, lavender silk with lace flowers around the sleeves and neckline.

"You don't believe me?"

"Not particularly."

"Well, I'm going to start looking for a place tomorrow and prove you wrong." Your voice is lighthearted, buoyed by success and affirmation. "This movie will mean more money coming in, and I have a six-month contract in Palm Springs at the Starlite Room, which won't interfere with shooting because the picture is not slated to start until September."

"If I get that job, I can help with rent," I say, picturing our place, small but quaint, with a view of the city.

Buttoning up my pajama shirt, I climb into bed and watch you wipe the cream away from your eyes, poking the soft skin and angling your face to inspect your profile. "I used to practice my smile as a little girl in Cuba. After my first performance, Mamá gave me a mirror and told me a woman's smile is the best weapon she has. The perfect smile, she said, is a mix of seduction and secrecy and power."

"Grandmother Maria's smile is all power," I say. "Her smile is the final say. End of story. No arguing."

You laugh and snap off the vanity light. "When you have that much power, you don't need seduction. I miss your grandmother."

"You just had dinner with her."

"I know, but I miss living with her." Instead of climbing into your twin bed, you climb into mine and lay your head on my shoulder.

"How are you going to tell Virginia we're leaving?" I ask.

"What do you mean how?" You fold the coverlet over your lap. "I'll just tell her. I'm sure she'll be happy to have her house to herself again."

"Mom."

"What?"

"Virginia is madly in love with you."

You pull away, incredulity then hilarity crossing your face. "What a preposterous thing to say, Nina."

"Women fall in love with each other, you know."

"I know." You are defensive, befuddled. You really didn't have any idea what was going on. "But it's not a normal thing, good lord, and it's indecent. I am sure that's not what's happening here. A woman can offer her friendship, can't she?"

"Sure, but this one has fallen in love with you. Anyone with eyes in their head can see that."

You climb out of my bed and into yours, fussing with your pillow and making disapproving clicks of your tongue. "Well, that's nonsense. I'll tell her in the morning over breakfast, and

I'm sure she'll be nothing but grateful to have us out of her hair." You snap off your light and slide into bed.

I am sure she'll be more than that, but I keep this to myself.

Chapter Thirty

One Last Day

Daughter,

The next morning, I get up early so I can catch Virginia before she leaves for work. I intend to go apartment-hunting right away, and it seems disrespectful not to tell Virginia.

I put out of my head what you said last night. Preposterous.

The sun has barely risen. In the kitchen, pale strands of light slant across the peppermint-green countertops and fall across the floor. The cleaning lady was here yesterday, so the floors are waxed and slippery under my bare feet. In the magnolia tree, a flock of birds are making a racket. Over them, I can hear the hum of Virginia's hair dryer coming from the bathroom. Taking Folgers Crystals from the cupboard, I measure a tablespoon of coffee into a cup, pour hot tap water over and stir it into a weak, watery substitute. I swore I'd never drink the stuff again, but Cuban coffee is not easy to come by in LA.

I think of my father roasting his own beans, rich and pungent. After the servants revolted, Papa took over coffee-making. I'd watch him from my stool at the counter as he cranked the silver handle on the grinder, boiled water and poured it over the coffee grinds. He'd watch the seconds on the clock, strain it at just the right moment, then add sugar and whip it until a thin frothy layer was on top. Before he took his first sip, he'd hold his mug up to his nose and inhale. It was the only time I remember him looking truly satisfied with something.

I'm dissolving a second scoop of crystals under the hot tap water when I hear the thud of Virginia's heels down the hallway. She walks into the kitchen wearing slacks with a soft buttery blouse, her hair curled and pinned at the sides.

She smiles, surprised to see me, and takes the coffee I offer her. "What's going on?" she says, humorously suspicious as she glances at my bathrobe.

"It's too early to get dressed." I tighten the belt around my robe and pick up my own cup of coffee loaded with milk and sugar.

"Why are you up so early?"

"I needed to tell you something."

Virginia glances at the clock. "I have five minutes. What's up?" She pulls out a kitchen chair and sits sideways on it, her coffee perched on one knee.

"I'm going apartment-hunting today."

"Oh?" Virginia doesn't smile.

I rest a hand on her arm. "I owe you my life. And to welcome Nina and me into your home, I couldn't ask for a better friend, but I imagine it'll be a relief to have us out of your hair."

"It won't be." Virginia places her hand on top of mine. "You don't need to go, Estelita. I don't want you to, actually."

This is not what I expected, and it flusters me. "You don't really want us living here, do you?"

"Stay," she says firmly. "You and Nina both, for now. Nina

will find her own way soon enough. She's the age for it. You and I make a good pair, don't you think?"

The tips of her fingers stroke the top of my hand, and I realize you were right, Nina: it is seductive and faintly arousing. I jerk away and move to the refrigerator, open it and practically bury my head inside. "Are you hungry? Do you eat breakfast before work?" I pull out the egg carton and set it on the counter keeping my back to her.

"I generally grab a piece of fruit on my way out."

"I'll make eggs for myself, then."

I take a bowl from the cupboard, crack an egg into it and begin whisking it with a fork when I feel Virginia's arms around my waist. "Do you eat breakfast?" she whispers in my ear, and I feel a swell of arousal and indignation. This is not supposed to be happening.

I pull away, turning with the fork held out like a weapon, egg dripping onto the floor. Outside the birds have stopped singing.

"You're making a mess." Virginia smiles. "And I don't even care. You can get egg all over my perfectly clean floor anytime you like." Reaching out, she slides the fork from my hand, stepping closer to drop it in the bowl, her body right up against mine. I push her back, and she retreats with her hands lifted in surrender. I think of Ricardo coming at me by the pool, how I'd raised my hand at him, how little that had done.

"This is perfectly normal, you know," she says, placating, as if I am a child who needs to be shown the way. "I think I fell in love with you the moment I saw you at that boring cocktail party. You're so beautiful and funny. You're everything, Este. I imagine every woman or man who crosses paths with you falls in love. How could they not?"

This is an absurd thing to say, and I hate that she uses my nickname. Only Danita calls me that. "I don't—" I flap a hand in the air at her. "This, whatever this is. I don't do this sort of thing."

"What? Love another human being?"

"You know."

She looks hurt, and I am sorry for that, but I never meant for this to happen. Virginia takes my hand, pushy as any man. "You haven't tried it." Her touch is tender, but it bruises me. It's like every other lover who's tried to control me. I yank my hand back. "I do not want anything to do with this. I am not that sort of woman. It is disgusting."

Virginia recoils, dropping her arms, her softness turned hard. "That's ungrateful of you. I'm the reason you left Ricardo. If I wasn't here, what would you have done? At least don't move out, not yet, please?"

It's too much. I don't want her love, and I don't want to owe anyone anything anymore.

"Do not touch me ever again," I say and shove past her out of the kitchen, through the living room and down the hall to the bedroom, stopping myself from slamming the door. You are still asleep, and the last thing I want is for you to wake up to this. I shut the door softly and sit on the edge of your bed. My hands are trembling. You were right, Nina. I have been wrong about everything. How am I so out of touch at thirty-seven years old, and how do you know so much? Softly, so as not to wake you, I place a hand on your head, feel the heat under my palm and remember holding your soft baby head once long ago. You are so grown-up and beautiful in your own, simple way. You are almost twenty years old, and I have missed your teen years. They went so fast. Things will be different, I tell myself. I will pay attention. I will be a better mother.

I wait to hear the sound of the front door opening, shutting, and wait for Virginia's car to start up, then pull out of the driveway before I get up and go to the closet. The kitchen drama has sparked a determination in me that I haven't felt since Cuba and an independence that feels necessary. After the Castro revolution, I no longer trusted feeling that great things were waiting ahead of me because I no longer believed I deserved them. Now, I've booked a role in a major film, and Mamá had nothing to do with it. I left Ricardo. I am leaving Virginia. My daughter is home. And this time, we will find our way together.

I choose a straight knee-length dress of white polyester with a fat black stripe down the side and one straight across my chest. Bold stripes, I think. Confident. I would have hated something like this ten years ago. I pull on a pair of white stockings and choose black pumps instead of my intolerable, knee-high boots.

In the kitchen, I reheat my coffee and worry that I overreacted. I was too harsh with Virginia. I should have let her down gently or led her on a bit to placate her desire. I'd have done as much with a man. But it's precisely because she isn't a man that I'm so angry. Of all people, she should know better. Women stick together. Sisters stick together, or so I thought. I dump my coffee down the sink and leave you a note on the table saying I will be gone all day. *There's a frozen dinner in the freezer,* I write. *I'll be back later from rehearsal. Love you, Mom.*

It's strange to think that I had no idea this would be my last day on earth. Everything I did was normal. If I had known, would I have done anything differently? I might have chosen the green dress with three-quarter sleeves or gone for a stroll along the ocean, breathing in the salt air and listening to seagulls squawk. At the very least, I would have spent a girlfriend day with you, doing whatever we pleased.

Instead, I go to Ricardo's office at the hospital.

The bright white hospital hallways smell of antiseptic. Vir-

ginia's office door is closed, thank goodness, and I hurry past it
to Ricardo's, barging past his secretary into his dark-paneled,
windowless office, all of his furniture still smelling of new
leather. Ricardo looks small and angry sitting behind his
desk. Here, I am not afraid of him. He wouldn't dare hit me
in front of his secretary, and I strategically left the door open.

"I'm filing for a divorce," I say, white-knuckling my purse,
my chest tight.

He caps his pen and sets it down, controlled. "You are
making a mistake."

"Well, it's mine to make."

"That's not true, now, is it, Estelita?" His voice is soothing, coy. He stands, moves around the desk and tries to take
me in his arms. I shove him away, and just like with Virginia,
my rejection sparks anger, and his tone pitches into aggres-
sion. "We can work it out."

"Is that so? Your tone of voice says otherwise."

"Estelita, you cannot leave me."

"I can."

"I won't let you."

"You don't have a choice," I say and walk out of his office,
my neck hot. I can feel where his fingers drove my head underwater, and it makes my skull tingle. His secretary gives
me a weak smile, and I don't smile back. I don't always have
to smile, I think.

In the hallway, the air is cool, and no one follows me. I
can do this, I tell myself, fear and joy bubbling side by side.
I can walk away from men like Ricardo.

Propelled by my newfound independence, I go to a Realtor's and spend the day looking at apartments. There's one
in Sherman Oaks that looks promising, with a deck and a
swimming pool. I tell the Realtor I'll come back tomorrow
to look at it with my daughter.

Before my rehearsal, I eat in a small Italian restaurant on Sepulveda, linguini and clams and a glass of white wine. The studio is only five blocks from the restaurant, so I leave my car parked on the street and walk. The sky is clear, and a few stars sparkle past the glare of streetlights.

I am rehearsing for next weekend's performance at the Chi Chi in Palm Springs. Ed shows up at the studio and sits in the back as I go through my number. When I leave, he holds the door open for me as he tells me that my voice is as spectacular as ever.

"You flatter me." I step into the street and slide my arm under his.

"I flatter no one. It's the truth, and if you weren't the best, you wouldn't be mine so you'd better stay that way."

"Yes, sir."

The night has grown chilly, and I have forgotten a coat. Ed slides his off and wraps it over my shoulders.

"Such a gentleman." I kiss his cheek, and he gives an abashed smile. "There's no need to walk me all the way to my car. I parked three blocks away."

"I'm not letting you walk alone at night on these streets. This isn't the best neighborhood."

"I'm sure I'll be fine."

"Still not leaving you. Besides, I haven't officially congratulated you on getting the role of Lupe Velez."

"You're the one who told me I got the part."

"Yes, but I didn't say *congratulations*."

"No, I suppose you didn't."

"Too much flattery's not good for a gal. But this is a big one. It's going to be your comeback, little lady."

I wrap an arm around his plump waist. "Or my beginning. I've never booked a role this substantial."

"You're going to have to get serious."

"I'm always serious." I pinch him, and he grimaces. We walk in silence for a few blocks before I say, "I'm getting a divorce."

"Sorry to hear that."

"No, it's good. Nina and I are going to get our own place."

"How is Nina?"

We've reached my car, and I pull out my keys, jiggling them in my hand. "She's good, I think. The hospital seems to have settled her, for now."

"She's young. Kids experiment."

"Right." I kiss his cheek and go to remove his coat, but he says, "No, keep it. You can bring it to me next week at your table read. I'll be eavesdropping outside the studio door. This is going to be one crackerjack of a picture."

"I don't know what I'd do without you." I kiss his cheek again, and he gives me an army salute as I get into my car.

Through the rearview mirror, I watch him standing on the sidewalk as I pull away, his combed-over hair shining silver in the streetlight. Ed is not in love with me, I think, wishing Virginia were here so I could say as much to her. He's what a true friend looks like.

Rehearsal has energized me, and I feel restless and wide-awake. I turn on the radio and sing along to The Temptations thinking about driving to Mamá's to tell her about the movie role. I want it to be the perfect moment, which tonight probably isn't. It's past ten, and she's most likely in bed. I'll tell her tomorrow, I decide, heading back to Virginia's, hoping you are awake and I can tell you about the apartment I found today.

The house is dark when I pull in, and Virginia's car is not in the driveway. It is a Saturday night, and I wonder if she's gone out. She rarely goes anywhere besides a required doctors' function. When I turn my key in the front door, I discover it's already unlocked, which is annoying, but not alarming. You often forget to lock the door.

I flick on the hall light and call your name. There's no answer. I don't like it when you're out late. Late nights mean partying, and you've been on the straight and narrow since you were released. I leave Ed's coat hanging in the hall and head to the kitchen where I see a note on the table. *Gone out with Delia. She came home from the hospital today. Don't worry, we're just going to a movie. I should be home by 11pm. Nina.* Relieved, I make myself a gin and tonic and go into the living room to catch the end of *Doctor Zhivago* on NBC's Saturday Night at the Movies. When Virginia comes home, I plan to tell her I am sorry I was rude this morning, but I don't share her feelings. She must understand. It's not exactly your average declaration of love, if that's even what it was.

At eleven o'clock the movie ends, and neither of you are home yet. I click off the television and look out the window. A sliver of a moon sits low in the sky, and the street is empty. I wonder if Delia is bringing you home. I should meet this Delia, I think, heading to the bathroom.

The walls of Virginia's bathroom are covered in pink-and-black tile, and she has a matching pink-and-black soap dish and toothbrush holder. I undress, thinking about what I'll buy to decorate our new apartment. I put on my nightgown, wipe the makeup off my face with cold cream and brush my teeth. In the medicine cabinet is my bottle of Valium. Ricardo first prescribed these to me a year ago when I was having trouble sleeping. They do wonders. Twisting off the cap, I drop the last two pills into my hand surprised that's all I have left. I was certain I had more. I head to the kitchen for water wondering if Virginia will write me a new prescription.

In the blue glow of our streetlight, I fill a glass of tap water. I am about to pop the pills into my mouth when I pause and notice that I hold two smooth white tablets in my palm. Usually, they are a pale yellow with a *V* stamped in the middle. A fleeting thought passes across my mind that something is not quite right. Are these my pills? The light is not good, I tell myself, and I can't see all that well. I toss the two pills into my mouth and wash them down with water, which is so cold it gives me an instant headache.

Or maybe it's not from the water. Moments pass, how long I don't know. A gust of wind rattles the windowpanes above the kitchen sink, and I watch the branches of the cyprus tree lift and sway outside the windows and worry about my sisters. A storm is coming. Where are you, Nina? With Josepha? I must make sure you are not under the ficus tree. You don't know Cuban storms. The branches could come down on you. But when I turn to look for you, the kitchen confuses me. Where is Mamá? This is not our kitchen. Dizzy, I collapse on my knees and find that I have vomited all over the floor, gin and linguini and clams splashed over shiny, peppermint-green tiles. I think *Oh, yes, this is Virginia's kitchen, and she doesn't mind if I spill eggs on her floor because she is in love with me.*

I crouch on all fours. Breathing is painful, nearly impossible. The pills, I think, those were not my pills. My heart races faster, and my chest squeezes. I crawl down the hall toward the bathroom, my stomach convulsing. Hot pain. Sweat. Everything seizing. My gut lurches, and for a horrifying moment I wonder if I am going to soil myself, and then I think I might vomit again. Only nothing comes. When I make it through the door, I collapse on my side on the bumpy, pink bath mat. My eyes blink rapidly, and I try to focus on where the edge of pink tile meets the foot of the sink. The line ripples and blurs. I can see my hand lying near my face, my fingers curled slightly over my palm, my thumbnail painted red. I try and hold on, but I'm plunging underwater. The air has gone out of the room, the oxygen sucked from my lungs. *Where are you, Nina?* I do not want to die alone.

Chapter Thirty-One

Shells

Mother,

The smell hits me when I step into the kitchen: sour and noxious, a smell that will haunt me after tonight. It is when I flick on the light that I see the vomit on the floor.

"Mom?" I call and hear a moan from the bathroom.

You have collapsed on your side with hair plastered against your cheekbones. A chill goes down my spine, and I stifle a cry, dropping to my knees on the pink throw rug and pulling your head into my lap. It flops against my arm as if you've lost all control of your neck. "What's wrong? Are you sick? Mom, can you hear me?"

Your eyes flutter open, and there is a look of terror in them that scares me as much as the odd angle of your body and the vomit in the kitchen. Your voice is sharp and ragged and barely above a whisper. "*El me dio algo. El me dio algo*, Nina."

"What? What were you given, Mom?" Your eyes drop shut, and I shake you, hard, but they don't open. "Mom! Mom! Wake up. What were you given? Who gave you something?"

Your eyes stay closed, breathy words crawling from your

lips, each an immense effort. "Ambulance...call...not Mamá... she worries...not Mamá."

Your head drops forward, rolling from my arm to my knee. I ease you to the floor and run to the kitchen, digging the phone book from the drawer. The emergency numbers are on the first page, and I grab the phone, shaking all over as I dial the hospital.

A woman answers, and I blurt out, "I need an ambulance, quickly. My mother is sick."

"How sick?"

"Very."

"What are her symptoms, dear?" The woman is infuriatingly calm.

"Throwing up, and she can't stand."

"Can you put her on?"

"No." I am getting angry. Why is she asking me all of this? "I said she can't stand. She needs an ambulance."

"Don't worry, dear, I'll send one right now. What's your address?"

I give her our address, hang up and rush back. You haven't moved. You look small as a child, your silk nightdress shell-smooth over the still form of your curved back. "Mom?" I crouch down and pull the sticky hair from your cheeks. I am scared. Your face is an unnatural red, your forehead sweats, your smooth, white eyelids shielding your eyes don't flutter or shift. I am shaking so hard I can barely put my hand to your mouth.

Your breath is faint and soft on my palm, so I go back to the kitchen and dial Grandmother Maria. I don't care what you say. I need her.

It takes seven rings before she answers, her voice groggy. "Hello?"

"Grandmother? It's Nina. Mom is sick. Very sick. I called an ambulance. You need to come right now."

"Is Virginia there?"

"No." Where is Virginia? If there was ever a time I'd want her around, it would be right now.

"I'm coming, Nina. I'm coming." The line goes dead. I hang up and return to you.

Awkwardly, I lift you from the floor, supporting your neck under one arm and your knees under the other. You are small and light, but I am not strong, and I have a hard time getting you out without hitting your dangling legs against the bathroom doorframe. I manage to make it down the hall and into your room, dropping you on the bed harder than I intend. You moan, and a frothy string of vomit dribbles out the side of your mouth.

"I'm sorry, I'm so sorry." I smooth your hair and press my palm to your clammy forehead. The color has slid from your cheeks, and your skin is cool to the touch. I arrange your nightgown over your knees and crawl over you, half sitting up as I move your body so that you are leaning against me. We haven't curled together like this since we lay on the church floor in Mexico. "What do I do, Mom?" I whisper. "Tell me what to do." It's my turn to rescue you, and I don't know how.

Your face contorts, and your body writhes as if something is tearing you up inside. It makes me hurt all over, watching your brow furrow and your jaw clench, your back growing stiff against me. It feels like an eternity passes, one in which I watch your muscles slowly relax, your face pale and your breath grow quick and shallow.

In reality, it is less than ten minutes before Grandmother Maria explodes through the bedroom door in her nightgown and bedroom slippers. She has beaten the ambulance, driven through the Los Angeles streets at seventy miles an hour in her nightclothes.

But she has not driven fast enough.

When her eyes fall on you, her cry shreds the air. She falls where she stands, crawling to you on hands and knees, her face twisted and tortured, and I am reminded of her crawl toward Josepha and Che, how little it did then and how little it does now. *"No mi Estelita, no mi niña, no mi niña."* And yet, not even in Cuba when she lost her husband and was witness to her granddaughter's rape was she this undone. Every line in her face, the gape of her mouth and the sheen in her eyes holds a suffering so huge I can't look at her. It is all of her pain rolled into one, her husband and children and grandchildren. She lived her life for you. Without you, there is nothing.

The body that leans against me now feels heavier than the one I lifted from the bathroom floor, as if your lightness came from the lightness of your soul. Nothing here but an empty shell anchored to the bed, filled with the weight of sand. I feel it under my fingernails, grit and salt. I hear the thunder of waves crashing against rock, and then your bedroom ceiling opens to the night, and I see your beautiful, colorless face etched in the sky, your dark brows arched, your full lips pale. My throat seizes. How is it that you will never reach out to me again? Never speak to me or look at me again? My mind collapses under the finality, the incomprehension: How are you here and not here? Where have you gone?

Chapter Thirty-Two

Death

Daughter,

I have gone nowhere and everywhere, Nina. It is dark and light and terrifying and beautiful.

You were with me and are with me still. There is grit and sand under my nails, too, but we are not hollowed shells, we are songs set free.

And there is so much more for you to sing, so many stories to tell, so much life for you yet to live, Nina the Memory Keeper.

Thirty-Three

March 13, 1966

Crazy Nina

Mother,

The morning after your death everything hurts. It is as if my skin has been peeled away from my body. The sheets hurt my limbs, the light my eyes, the lawn mower grinding outside the window hurts my head. How can someone be mowing the lawn when you are dead? How can anyone be doing anything? I want to bury myself with you, but instead I am forced to wake up and continue to live in this ugly, terrifying world.

Without you nothing is beautiful.

I get up, dress in bell-bottom jeans and a ratty T-shirt and go to the kitchen where my grandmother and Virginia sit at the table drinking coffee. I hate them for drinking coffee, for waking and dressing and moving forward. Virginia rises and folds me into her arms. I let her hug me, my body stiff and unresponsive. When she pulls away, I see her eyes are red from crying.

"My God. Oh, dear God, I'm so sorry," she whispers.

"Where were you last night?" This morning, I am dry-eyed and angry.

"I was having a drink with a colleague. I wish I'd been home. I had no idea she was sick."

"She wasn't sick." I fill a glass of water and drink it down in one breath. Grandmother Maria is watching me, her resilience restored.

"I made you breakfast. You need to eat." She points to a plate of eggs and toast.

I set my glass on the counter with a sharp clink. "I'm not hungry."

"Don't make her eat if she doesn't want to." Virginia sits back down. She is dressed in her Saturday casuals: capri pants and a white button-down shirt, her hair messy from sleep, her face pale and puffy.

Grandmother Maria snaps her head in Virginia's direction. "*Mi hermosa nieta* will do whatever I think is best for her. Eat," she orders me.

I sit down and shove a forkful of eggs into my mouth. You, Mom, know I hate eggs. How does no one else know this about me? Grandmother just doesn't care, I think, scraping every last bit of yoke into my mouth to prove a point.

"There. Happy?" I stand up and dump the empty plate in the sink. Grandmother rises and unhooks her purse from the back of her chair.

"Come," she says. "Last night I told the police I would bring you over this morning."

"To tell them what happened?"

"Yes."

Virginia twirls her empty coffee cup on the table. "Are they doing an autopsy?"

Grandmother turns her back to Virginia. She doesn't like this woman. "I don't know. I have no authority. I am just her *madre*. Come, Nina."

I follow my grandmother outside where the world feels

stretched thin: the roads, the buildings and sky. The brick police station and the large men in padded uniforms inside, they all look unreal, like actors. The officer sitting in the chair across from me is young, with a soft pink face, freckles and curly hair that's been cut short on the sides with tight curls springing up on top. Pinned to his jacket is a badge with *Officer Brown* on it. They took Grandmother Maria to a room where I can see her through a large, glass window. She sits—back erect, purse clutched in her lap—on the edge of her chair.

I look back at Officer Brown, who moves his knee rapidly up and down, his eyes shifting from the wall behind me to his notes. He is uncomfortable. "I know this is hard, but I need you to tell me exactly what happened last night when you found your mother."

My words rush out, fast and urgent. I tell him everything, from the vomit in the kitchen to finding you on the bathroom floor to calling the ambulance to Grandmother Maria arriving. When I come to the end I say, "Ricardo killed her. Dr. Ricardo Pego. He gave her something. She said so."

The officer looks confused. "Her husband?"

"They were getting a divorce."

"I see. That was a reason to kill her?"

The sarcasm in his voice makes me boil. I want to rip the paperwork he keeps fiddling with out of his hands.

I squeeze the tops of my knees. "She was filing for a divorce. He'd tried to kill her before."

"Did he? How, exactly?" His tone holds a hint of humor, as if we're having a bit of fun.

"He tried to drown her in a pool."

"Were you a witness to this?"

"No."

"Did she report it to the police?"

"I don't know."

"Has she ever reported her husband to the police?"

"I don't know."

"The night she died, what were her exact words?"

"'*El me dio algo.*' It means 'I was given something.'"

"Did she say *who* gave her something?"

"No."

"So it could be anyone?"

"Ricardo is a doctor. He has access to medicine. He tried to kill her before. He gave her something!" I shout, my cheeks red hot.

The officer scoots forward in his chair. "Calm down, missy. I'm not saying you're wrong, it's just…" He glances at his papers again. "This is not a murder investigation. It's just a routine questioning."

"What did she die of then?"

"It says cause of death unknown."

"Well, there you go."

"Which could easily mean natural causes. Influenza. Infection."

"That's impossible. She wasn't sick. She was at rehearsal right before she came home. Ask her manager or whoever was at the studio. They'll all tell you…she…was…*not…sick*!"

Officer Brown sighs heavily, his lips blowing out as he picks up a pencil and begins tapping it on his thigh. "I'll be right back." He stands, and I watch him swagger to a desk where a heavyset officer is on the telephone. The officer raises his hand to indicate he is not to be interrupted, and Officer Brown leans on his desk, waiting. When the officer hangs up, the two men begin talking and nodding, glancing at me, but I can't hear a thing over the ringing telephones and clanking typewriters. After a few minutes, Officer Brown returns, sits down heavily and begins jiggling his knee again.

"Officer Renaldo tells me you were released from the psychiatric ward of Good Hope not too long ago."

"So?" I don't like the way he's looking at me.

"Did you like your stepfather?"

"What does that have to do with anything? Or my being in a psych ward?"

Officer Brown gathers his papers and taps them on the desk as if the interview is done. "It discredits your word, for one thing."

His dismissal sets my throat on fire. I stand up. "I'm not insane! I did a few drugs. None of that should have anything to do with my mother. Have you questioned Ricardo?"

"Yes." Officer Brown stands. "He was at home watching television and then went to bed."

"That's not a very good alibi."

"Since this is not a murder case, we don't need an alibi. It seems to me you've watched too much *Perry Mason*."

I want to hit him. Instead I start screaming. "You're wrong! She was poisoned. They'll do an autopsy and find out exactly what killed her, and you'll be fired for not doing your goddamn job!"

The officer takes hold of my arm. "I think we both know it's not in your best interest to talk to a police officer like that." Officer Renaldo has risen and gone into the room where Grandmother Maria sits. He points to me through the window, and she stands and follows him out, shaking her head at me and apologizing to the policeman as she drags me from the building into blinding sunlight.

"Nina, what has gotten into you? You don't scream at a policeman like that. They'll think you're crazier than they already do."

"I don't care." I yank my arm out of her hand. "Someone killed her! She said so. I was there."

Grandmother keeps walking, her stride purposeful. When we get to the car, she opens her door, gets in and reaches over to unlock mine. We drive in silence back to her house where she pulls into the driveway, turns off the engine and gets out without looking at me.

I follow her inside. The house smells faintly of cooked onions.

"You will sleep on the couch," she says, pulling sheets and a blanket from the hall closet.

"It's eleven o'clock in the morning." I slump against the wall and cross my arms over my chest. I don't want to be here. I don't want to be anywhere. "When are they doing the autopsy?"

"I have no idea."

"What happens now?"

"A funeral."

"Are you arranging it?"

"Ricardo."

"How can you let him do that?"

"He is her husband."

"He killed her!"

"Nina." Grandmother Maria dumps the sheets on the couch and comes over, placing her hands on my shoulders. "This is not going to help."

"Don't you want to know how she died?"

"The doctors at the hospital know what they are doing. If there was something suspicious about her death, they'd know."

"You weren't with her. You didn't see her. She wasn't sick. She said someone gave her something."

"We will wait for the autopsy. Until then, stop this. I don't want to hear any more about it. You are making it worse." She walks into the kitchen, her robust hips swinging, her silver hair curled on her head.

For all her strength, I think, she is too weak to face the truth, because the truth is that we are all to blame for Ricardo's killing you. He was violent and dangerous. You told me so yourself, and even if you never told Grandmother, she knew it, too. Virginia knew it. We all knew it, and no one did anything to protect you.

My grandmother and I spend the day in front of the television eating peanuts from a tin can and watching *Supermarket Sweep*, *The Dating Game* and *The Donna Reed Show*. It is almost five o'clock when the telephone rings, startling Grandmother Maria from her sleep in the chair, her head rolled to one side. She jumps up, clicks off the television and snatches up the phone.

"Hello?... Yes, this is she." She nods and blinks, saying *yes* and *I see*, and finally *thank you* before hanging up and sitting back down. Outside the sky is darkening. Without the glow of the television, the room feels ominous.

"That was the hospital." Grandmother sounds resolved. "Ricardo told them not to do an autopsy."

"Can he do that?"

"He is her husband. He can do whatever he likes."

I say nothing. Even in death I cannot save you. I think of Che and Josepha, of violent men and helpless women. I think of Virginia. She's not a helpless woman. She is a doctor, too. Maybe she killed you because she didn't want you to leave her. Ricardo didn't want you to leave him. No one wanted you to leave them. And now you have gone and left us all.

The silence and darkness in the room bear down on me. I close my eyes and recreate the sensation of your breath on the palm of my hand, the sweetness of your perfume. I feel the impression of your body against mine growing heavier and heavier until I am pinned under the weight of your death. A death I cannot avenge or make sense of.

* * *

Your funeral is not beautiful. It is not a celebration of life but a trick to make us all face your death in somber black clothing. You hated black. Why is your coffin not painted bright green and pink and yellow? Those were your colors. You told me that, when you were sad, all you had to do was close your eyes and see the buildings in Cuba lined up in their bright, laughing colors and listen for the music playing in the streets of your hometown, Guanajay, and nothing could keep you down.

"Music is color," you told me, "and there was always music in Cuba. On every street corner, in every house, through every celebration and every tragedy, we always had music and color. Close your eyes, Nina. Go on, try it. I will sing to you, and you will see the colors and feel laughter bubble in your belly."

Your song rose and fell, and I could see the Cuban blue of the ocean, and the bright red blooms of flamboyant trees and the laughing, yellow buildings.

No one sings at your funeral. The minister, a tiny man with white hair, reads verses that I can't follow, even with my Catholic education. There are no maracas or drums, and no one wears pink. Not even Danita, your look-alike sister. When I first see her, I want to rush into her arms and smell her and hold her and pretend she is you. But when she looks at me, there is so much sadness and confusion between us, I just shake her hand and try not to look her in the eye. Mercedes and Oneila are here, carrying the weight of age and grief, holding each other as they did in Cuba. Mercedes hugs me and Oneila pats my shoulder. Grandmother Maria stands beside them. It is strange to see them all here in Los Angeles, but then, everything is strange. I look for Josepha, wondering if she has grown into a woman I can't recognize, but none of my cousins have come. Why would they, I think, grateful that at least your sisters came back for you.

As we gather to mourn, my eyes fall on Ricardo across the opening of your grave. He is meticulously dressed in a fitted wool suit, the respectful, upstanding doctor with a subtle glow to his clean-shaven, deeply lined cheeks. The sight of him turns me inside out, and I look away, trying to regain a different point of focus. Faces, familiar and unfamiliar, huddle row upon row like black crows perched under the clear blue sky. There is Virginia, weeping, and Uncle Duke, and Pilar, and Ed Adelman, actors and musicians I recognize from dinner parties, and ones I recognize from movies or television and people I don't recognize at all.

The minister pauses as the chatter of birds in the tree overhead grows louder. I like their disregard for the human drama taking place below them. Reaching for a wreath of red roses that hangs on a chair near the coffin, the minister clears his throat and says, "In honor of his late wife, Estelita Rodriguez, Dr. Ricardo Pego will lay this wreath on her coffin."

The outrage and grief brewing in my gut boils over. There is no point of focus, no distractions. I scream and lunge forward, deranged, uncontrollable. "Get away from her! You killed her! You killed my mother!" He will not touch her ever again. I will stop him.

People turn, gasping and whispering as they shuffle out of my way. The minister and Ricardo stare at me, the wreath frozen between them. "You killed my mother!" I scream, stumbling as a pair of firm hands gently take hold of my shoulders and ease me backward, a soothing voice saying, "It's all right, now. It's all right. Come on, we're going to go have a little breather now. You just hang on, sweetheart. Everything is going to be all right."

A small, lithe man holds my arm and leads me to a car

parked on the narrow graveyard road. His driver opens the door, and I slide onto a shiny leather back seat. The man slides in next to me. He wears a dark blue suit jacket over a white shirt with a wide, pointy collar. I recognize Sammy Davis Jr. from *The Ed Sullivan Show.* I didn't know, Mom, that you knew him. He smiles easily at me, unconcerned, as if he pulls screaming young women away from funerals every day.

Patting my hand he says, "You all right?" Hysterical sobs escape me, and he nods respectfully. "Yeah, I thought as much. It's no easy thing losing a parent. Your mama was a beautiful woman. Could make a fellow laugh like no one I knew. And those hips!" He whistles, shaking his head like you are walking by him at that minute. "Those hips…" He breathes out, leaning back and grinning. "I loved watching her on stage. She was nice on-screen, too, but on stage, well, on stage she'd shine like the sun. She was a breath of life so large she filled all of us. We're going to miss that."

He falls silent, smoothing his palms over his knees while I cry. When Grandmother Maria comes for me, I am slumped in a heap on the seat. "I'll follow you back home. Best not to move her into another car. She doesn't need to see that crowd again." Sammy Davis Jr. pats my back. "I know all these people act like they knew your mama, but no one knew her like you did."

I want to tell him he is wrong. The people who loved you up on stage knew you just as well as I did. You gave your true self to everyone.

At home, I'm given a sedative and put to bed. Crazy Nina. I haven't done any drugs since getting out of Good Hope, and now they are freely given to me. I don't mind. I like painkillers. I melt and slip under and hold my breath.

In my drugged stupor, all I think about is you and that I will carry the truth of your story into old age and that no one will ever believe me.

Thirty-Four

August, 1966

My Julian

Mother,

I am cold and wet, and my face hurts as I stand looking into the black hole of your grave. Only there is no coffin, just empty space. And then I see that you are standing across from me, right on the edge. You wear your green silk evening gown and your hair in pin curls. Your brows are painted black, your lips red. You are not looking at me but into the grave, and I wonder why, because if you are not in that hole, then who is? And then there is a man behind you, and I think it is Ricardo, but he's too young, and he pushes you so suddenly I don't even see you fall. I scream and leap after you, expecting free fall, silence, stillness, but the air is sharp and compact and splintered with glass.

I don't want to die, I think, even if I find you on the bottom.

"Mom?" I scream. "Where are you?"

"I am right here, Nina. I have not gone anywhere," you say and laugh that singsongy sound, the kind that rolls up from your belly like a drumbeat. I feel your arms then, tight around me, easing me to the ground. I think of my arms around you when you were dying, how you were always better at saving me than I was at saving you.

There is the sound of surf pounding, and when I open my eyes, I glimpse flashes of moonlight spliced through black night and see your beautiful, colorless face in the sky, just as I saw it the night you died. Your dark arched brows and full, pale lips. There is sand under my fingernails, grit and salt, and I hear the thunder of waves against rock. I am not dust, I think. I have not fallen through your fingers. I am solid and whole, and you have been carrying me all along.

I push myself into a sitting position and the world wavers. My face hurts, and when I touch my cheeks, they are sticky, and the tips of my fingers come away dark with blood. A full, fat moon hangs like a balloon let loose over a black sea that throws waves at my feet, my sneakers licked with foam.

A Big Sur moon, I remember, a Big Sur sea.

Next to me Bret sits cross-legged chanting. The fucker is chanting while I lie here dripping blood. His hands rest palm up on his knees, thumb and ring finger touching, his eyes closed. I don't know what he's chanting, some Indian-guru chant he tried to teach me. I could never remember it and always resorted to *om* instead. *Om* is not going to help us now.

The car is farther up the beach tilted on its side, half on the hillside, half on sand, smoke hissing from the engine. Its underside looks like the dark belly of a beetle, the two wheels up in the air like flailing legs. On the sand, glass from the shattered windows sparkle in the moonlight, and I worry that people—children and parents and lovers—will cut their feet when they walk by. How did I get next to the water? Maybe Bret had the decency to pull me from the car. Probably not. More likely I crawled out or was thrown. Sand is a soft landing. Nothing feels broken, but my face stings, and I am cold and shaking.

I am weak and tired, and all I can think about is lying down, but as I sink back onto the sand, I see a dark shape in the water. At first I think it is you, emerging not from the sky but from the sea. Then I wonder if it is a porpoise or a dolphin, the shape rising slowly from the waves and coming toward me, seal-skinned, like a science fiction novel coming to life. It crouches beside me and pulls a snorkel from its mouth and the mask from its eyes. Drops of cold water drip from the man's wetsuit onto my bare legs.

"My God, are you all right?" The man touches my shoulder, gently, raccoon circles from his mask pressed into the skin around his bright eyes.

"No." I shake my head.

"No, no, you don't look all right. Is he okay?" He gestures to Bret, and I say, "No, but he never was to begin with."

The man chuckles and shakes his head. "At least you have your wits about you. We're going to get you help. I have flares with me. Just give me a minute to set them off, and I'll be right back, okay?"

I nod. Flares. Help. Police. "Where's my doll?" I cry, stricken with reality.

"Your doll?"

Now he won't think I have my wits about me. "Find my doll. I need my doll."

He pats the air as if calming a small child. A doll seems to imply that. "I'll find it. Just let me get those flares lit first, and I'll see if it's near the car, okay?"

My hero from the sea, I think. My Neptune. When I was three, you read me a story about Neptune, and because you and Grandmother Maria were the only grown-ups I knew, for a short while I thought all men were gods. Maybe, finally, this one really is. Maybe you sent him from the sea to fall in love with me.

I sink onto my side. There is sand in my hair, in my cut skin, in my shoes and underwear. I remember when I was little and I hated wearing underwear, and you told me I had to.

"Why?" I insisted, stomping my foot.

"What if you're in a car accident and you don't have underwear on?" you said, utterly serious. "You don't want that to happen."

I smile into the night. *See, Mom? I did as I was told.*

Uncontrollably, my eyes drop shut, and I hear a crackle and burst. When I open them again, I see a streak of red shooting into the sky like a glorious celebration. My ears ring, and smoke fills the sky and swallows the moon.

When I wake again, the dark sea still pounds beside me, except this time someone is holding me. A warm hand rests on my shoulder, and my head is lying on a man's thick, wet thigh that smells of seaweed. My Neptune. I hear sirens—not mermaids but the screaming peals of an ambulance. I force myself up on one arm and see my ugly, hairless, naked plastic doll in the sand.

"Help has arrived." The man gestures up the hill as I scramble to my hands and knees, digging a hole as fast as I can, my whole body hurting. I shove her down, twisting her legs and arms, her head like a shiny ball bobbing to the surface. I dig deeper, cover her in sand.

The man watches. "What do you have in there?"

"Drugs."

"Ah."

I sit back, and he puts out an arm for me to lean against. "Thank you."

"You're welcome."

Blue lights flash above me on Bixby Bridge. The sirens quiet, and I hear doors slamming and voices.

"Who are you?" I ask, wishing I could rest against this man's arm all night. "Why did you come from the sea?"

"I'm a marine biologist," he says. "Sam."

So, not a god, just Sam the Scientist. Maybe he will still love me, I think. I need someone to love me.

But Sam is gone, and I'm laid out on a stretcher. This makes me laugh out loud. How many stretchers have there been in our lives? How stupid of us all to need them. Suicide. Murder. Accident. And what about Josepha? I see her split-open face, her split-open legs. She never had the luxury of a stretcher, but rape doesn't count as a death.

It should. Women die countless deaths at the hands of abusive men. Parts of you die off. That counts. How many deaths did you die, Mom?

Thick straps hold down my chest and legs. My neck is held by a brace as the men on either end jostle and tilt and carry me up the hill.

I am so tired, but it's too bright inside the ambulance to sleep. Besides, the EMT's hands are touching my face, which stings.

"Ow," I cry and blink up at a man with toffee-colored skin and light brown eyes flecked with specks of gold. Turns out I'm no longer in the ambulance but on a hard bed in a bright hospital room.

"Sorry." He pulls his hand away, pinching a small shard of glass between silver tipped tweezers. "We have to get this glass out of your face. Do you need another painkiller?"

"How about the whole bottle?" I say, and he smiles. It's the sweetest, softest smile I have ever seen.

"Well, then, we'd have to pump your stomach, and that's a messy business. Let's stick to getting this glass out. I'm Julian."

"Nina."

"Nice to meet you, Nina. I'll do this carefully so there won't be any scars."

He puts a hand under my chin and lifts my face to the light. I close my eyes, seeing Julian's smile behind my lids while his fingertips, soft and light as cotton balls, rest against my chin as he delicately removes each tiny piece of glass from my face.

He is my real hero, only I don't know this yet.

After the hospital, I have nowhere to go but back to my redwood tree where my Labrador puppy, Bilbo, waits for me. I have never had a pet before. He showed up the first night Delia and I slept in this tree three months ago, and he's been here ever since. When he sees me, he licks my face and whines, and I give him the package of ham I bought at the only grocery store in Ventana.

I wanted to return to work at Nepenthe once I was released from the Carmel Hospital, but my manager took one look at the cuts all over my face and told me to stay home until I had healed. He'd heard about the accident, everyone in Big Sur had. No one could believe all I'd sustained were cuts and bruises or that Bret left the hospital to hitchhike up to San Francisco.

"Your job's not going anywhere," my manager reassured me, his thin, muscular arm around my shoulder. "Have that mother of yours look after you until you're healed up, okay?" When I applied for the job, I lied and said I lived with my mother on Partington Ridge.

Now, three days later, I sit on my bunched-up sleeping bag with Bilbo asleep at my feet. I lean back against the smooth tree trunk reading *The Lord of the Rings* by the light streaming through an opening in the trunk that is large enough to walk through.

A knock against the trunk startles me, and a man sticks his head in. "Nina Martinez?" His face is in shadow, and I can't make it out. "It's Julian, from the hospital."

"Oh." I lower my book. Bilbo raises his head, looks at him and settles his head back on his paws.

"Not a very good watchdog."

"He's a stray who love strangers because they feed him."

"May I come in?"

"It's a five-dollar entry fee. I like to think of my tree as a tourist attraction."

"How about homemade empanadas instead?" He ducks inside, then straightens to survey the redwood walls encircling him, the trunk wrinkled with age. He runs his hand along it. "This is far out. It's so big." He whistles and drops in front of me to sit on his knees in the dirt, patting Bilbo on the head. "You don't have a roommate?"

He's joking, but I say, "I did, actually. She went back to LA a few weeks ago. This is her summer home."

Julian laughs, his whole face angled so it's lit with the light streaming into the tree. He untangles his arm from the backpack that's been hanging over one shoulder and takes out a paper plate wrapped in a linen dishcloth. Inside are a pile of golden fried empanadas.

"My mother's," he says proudly. "I told her about you, and she asked me where you lived, and I said I didn't know. Then she asked who picked you up from the hospital, and I said you left on foot. Then she told me I was a fool to let you go with no one to take care of you. That I was to find you and feed you."

"So you're here because of your mother?" I tease.

Julian smiles, and it's the same soft smile he gave me while picking glass from my face. "My mother likes to say that she is only helping along a thing already set in motion. Good or bad, so no blame either way. She plays it safe."

"Is this good or bad?" I take the plate he's holding out to me.

"Good." Julian nods, confident. "It was bad," he looks pointedly at my face, "but already you are healing. So now—" he gestures at our surroundings "—it is good."

"How did you know where to find me?"

"Big Sur is small. Not too hard to find a girl living alone in a redwood tree."

I pick up a still–slightly warm empanada. "These look amazing. Thank you. I've been living on saltines and peanut butter."

"I dig peanut butter."

"Me, too. Where do you live?" I take a bite, and the crust flakes away to a center stuffed with spiced beef, paprika and cumin so strong the scent fills my earthy room.

"At Packard Ranch."

"Packard…as in Hewlett-Packard?"

"My father is a caretaker for the ranch. Mr. Packard built a home for us when we moved from Krenkel Corner. I live there with my older sister Rosita, my older brother Miguel and my twin brother Juan."

"Twins?"

"Identical, born on Halloween." Julian wiggles his eyebrows up and down. "My mother used to say the devil did it. Oh, did we raise hell growing up. The stories I could tell you." He laughs with his entire belly. "And where do you hail from, madame? You were not born in this tree, were you?"

I shake my head. "I was born in New York City to a mother who is dead and a father I see very little of."

Julian looks down at his feet, as if this truth is hard to comprehend. "Do you have any other family?"

I hesitate, thinking of how I left Grandmother Maria without telling her where I was going or saying goodbye. "A grandmother," I finally say.

"That's family." He sets the plate on the earth floor between us and takes an empanada for himself.

We eat in comfortable silence. When Julian finishes, he wipes his hands on his pants and looks at me. "When I was fifteen, I left home for two months without telling anyone. I hitchhiked up the coast and slept on the beach and ate food from tin cans. I wanted to see what it was like not to be attached to my brother, not to have to help anyone or do what anyone else told me. What I discovered was that I was lonely, and it felt good to be needed. When I returned home, my father sat me down and said that family is not a choice. They are our bones and our blood, our past and our future. 'It's not always good,' he told me, 'but it's always important. Pain and love and laughter and anger go together.'" Julian picks up a stone and jiggles it in his palm. "My father thinks he is very wise." He smiles, standing up. Bilbo stands with him, wagging his tail against Julian's pant leg.

When I see he plans to leave, there's an ache in my chest. I don't want him to go. He's right: it is lonely.

Squatting, Julian takes a pen from his backpack, tears off an edge of the paper plate and writes something down on it. When he presses the torn paper into my hand, his touch is soft and lingering, and the pressure sets my skin tingling. "If you need anything." He drops my hand with a tone so carefree and easy that I want to get up and follow him to whatever untroubled place he comes from.

Leaning out from the archway of my tree, I watch him pass more redwoods so tall and mighty that he becomes as small as an insect in the distance.

"Bye," I call out.

"Later, Nina."

I like that he says this instead of goodbye. And when I look down at the torn paper, I see his name, Julian Lopez, written above a Big Sur address.

I lie that night with the note tucked inside my pants pocket picturing Julian's clear eyes and uncomplicated smile as I snuggle up against Bilbo and wonder what it would be like to run a hand over that boy's honey-colored skin. Tonight, my hollow tree feels sad and lonely. Besides, it's damn cold in my sleeping bag. It will only get colder, I think, aware that I cannot stay here all winter. Julian's visit, his gesture of kindness, bringing me food from his mother who has never even met me, has made me feel sorry I left my grandmother all alone.

In a month, I will hitchhike back to her, back to the pleasure of a hot shower, television, sherbet ice cream and a bed with clean sheets. Grandmother Maria will place papery hands on my cheeks and kiss me, welcoming Bilbo and me into her small home with tears of gratitude.

But before that happens, I find a way to say goodbye.

After the car accident, when I saw you in the sky and felt your arms around me, when I was certain you were the one who had set me gently on the sand away from the car and I heard you say *I am right here, Nina. I have not gone anywhere*, I knew I couldn't go through the rest of my life expecting you to save me. I had to let you go.

Only, I am not ready to let go. In Big Sur, with no drugs or boyfriends, just Bilbo who asks very little of me, I am finally able to be alone with you. You sit with me on the dirt floor of my tree while I eat sliced bread from the bag, you stand in the gas-station bathroom looking bemused as I wash out my clothes, and you rest silently with me on the beach and lay your head on my shoulder and don't ask any questions. You are with me while I crush eucalyptus leaves between my fingers and press them to my nose, and there every morning as I walk to the water and watch the fog burn off to sunshine, lifting my face to it, waiting for the sand and rocks to heat up so we can lie in it together and gather its warmth. I learn to be with you without needing you, and this shakes something awake deep down inside me where I've shoved all the Incidents, your death abutting my abusive stepfather, the absence of a real one, the rape of a cousin and the drug-numbed loss of my teen years. And so, I reach for them, pull them out and lay them open on the beach.

For each Incident, for my father and Josepha and you and Alfonso and Che, I place a piece of driftwood upright in the sand. I sit wrapped in my sleeping bag on the hard-packed, stony beach; the sea smells sharp and fishy in my nose. There are mountains of cumulus clouds on the horizon. I stay for a long time watching the tide come in, the waves lapping toward my towers of wood and memory, the pieces falling and sliding toward the mouth of the sea. Some get stuck and lie helpless until the waves return to lift them away, and as the Incidents of our past grow to dark specks on the ocean's surface, doubt runs through me. I am washing away our story.

Stricken, I drop my sleeping bag and run barefoot into the waves, my jeans rolled to my knees. I want to sink into the water, to cover my eyes and weep, but I hear a voice, sharp and clear. *Nina*, it says, *you cannot grow small anymore*, and I understand that it isn't your voice I hear this time but my own. So, I widen my arms, force them out into the air, lift my full face to the sky and scream. I scream and scream until my throat is raw, my face hot and wet with spray. The sand and salt and seaweed sting my calves and ankles, and my feet are numb, but something soars out of me, and I am left weak and relieved.

Instead of flying off into the ocean, I simply give over to it.

In a way, I have been hollowed out and emptied and washed up on shore because I know that everything will be different. I can keep you inside me and let you go. My story will not be your story. I am the sole narrator now, and I do not need to follow the Brets of the world when I can seek the Julians.

I touch his note in my pocket, safe and dry and filled with possibility. I don't need center stage, or any larger-than-life moments. I can hold your memory but not be swallowed by it. My life can be simple and beautiful. It can be whatever I choose to make it.

Epilogue

When the writer comes, I am an old woman with Julian and the sea by my side.

I do not know that the girl is a writer when she steps through the door with her mother. I don't think she knows she is a writer, yet.

I am unprepared for the visit. The washing machine is broken, and the needed part won't be in until next week, which means there's laundry piled in the bathroom, and I have absolutely nothing clean to wear. Julian went to work with the same shirt on he wore yesterday.

"That's filthy," I said earlier this morning, propped on one elbow in bed watching him button his cuffs.

"I don't think the fence post I'm fixing will mind," he said, smiling at me as he tucked his shirt into his jeans and secured his belt. "What are you doing awake so early, anyway?"

I flopped back down. "The wind woke me."

"It'll blow off the fog." Julian leaned over me with both hands on the bed. "You know how I like to kiss you goodbye in your sleep."

I closed my eyes and smiled. "There. Asleep."

Julian pressed his lips to mine and whispered "Love you" before picking up his boots and slipping out of the bedroom.

Even on Saturdays, Julian is up and out first thing. He and his twin brother have taken over caretaking the Packard property for their father, and they're usually at it before the sun rises. Julian is a hard worker and loyal as the day is long. No matter how early he leaves, he never forgets to kiss me goodbye. I always pretend to be asleep, but I almost never am. A few years back I woke to a silent house and was filled with dread at the thought that he'd left without that kiss, but then I heard the toilet flush and realized I'd just slept through his morning routine.

Today, the wind howls me out of bed and into the kitchen to make a pot of coffee.

Julian and I live in the same house where he and his siblings grew up. The road to the house winds down off Route 1 and ends on a twisted cliff overlooking the sea. It's small, with dark-paneled walls and tiny windows. The older Lopez siblings live in town, but I wouldn't dream of living anywhere else. From the kitchen window I can see the ocean far below, undulating like a breathing body, the sound of the surf a constant surging in my veins. Its moods, I think, are no different than humans', placid and tranquil or mighty with rage, depending on the weather.

When the coffee is brewed, dark and sweet, I sit at the round kitchen table and watch the sky lighten to a washed-out gray. This early hour is my favorite time of day. The night requires sleep, the day action, but the crack of time separating the two requires absolutely nothing. It is a pause and an inhale, the breath between movement and stillness. It is my remembering hour. Today, my mother is more vivid in my mind than she has been in years. I see her dancing with her sister Danita in a whitewashed living room in Guanajay as the sky outside my window in Big Sur sheds its gray and burns a vibrant blue. A Cuban blue, I think. One my mother would have loved.

Later, kneeling in the hallway repotting my jade plant, my sister-in-law Rosita comes banging through the front door. "Yoo-hoo, Nina." She shifts her bag of groceries to her other hip so she can lean down and give me a one-armed hug. "I've brought muffins from Deetjen's," she says, heading to the kitchen, the smell of freshly baked pastries trailing her.

I pat down the dirt around my newly arranged plant and heave myself to my feet with some difficulty. My knees are not what they used to be, and this annoys me to no end.

In the kitchen, Rosita is arranging the muffins on a plate.

"Raisin-walnut?" I ask, washing my hands in the sink.

"And blueberry with lemon poppy seed." Rosita crumples the paper bag and tosses it into the garbage. "I hope it's all right, but an old childhood friend and her daughter are coming to visit. She lived in this house with us for a spell when we were kids and wanted to see it again."

"Of course." I dry my hands and give Rosita a proper hug. She has become a sister to me. "Hopefully she won't have to use the bathroom. There's laundry piled sky-high."

"Julian can't fix it?"

"He's waiting for a part. Oh," I cry suddenly, "I forgot to tell you, Daniel started a new band." Daniel is my son, his birth one of the most extraordinary things that has ever happened to me.

"He did? That's fantastic. What is it called?"

"Head Rush." I roll my eyes.

"Yikes," Rosita says and we both laugh.

Raising him wasn't easy, but he has become a man I am proud of, and unlike my single mother, I had Julian beside me every step of the way. The entire loud, loving Lopez family has been beside me.

And after all these years, to everyone's astonishment, I still have Grandmother Maria, who, at a hundred and one years of age—still swearing to God she's sixty—stands straight-backed and is as bossy as ever. On Sundays, when the entire family gathers at our house for dinner, Grandmother Maria is given liberty to tell each family member exactly what they should—and shouldn't—be doing with their lives. Love, work, hobbies, all of it. The Lopezes take her very seriously. Marriages have been called off, jobs changed, hobbies picked up or abandoned. They all adore her, especially Julian's father, Raphael, but that's probably because she laughs loudest at his jokes. Once she laughed so hard she cried, "Heavens to Betsy, I've peed my pants!" which only made her laugh harder.

It was precisely the sort of thing my mother would have said.

When Rosita's friend arrives, an energetic woman who gives us both hearty hugs, she and Rosita arrange themselves over muffins and coffee in the sunroom, and I find myself alone in the kitchen with the woman's daughter. She is young, maybe all of nineteen, still carrying the self-consciousness of a teenager. Out of habit, and because I don't know what else to talk about, I tell her my mother's story. The girl listens with polite, rapt interest. Little do I know that she is tucking away every detail, that she will one day return as a writer to hold the memories with me.

Later that night, pressed up against my husband, his skin smelling of sage soap and salty air, I lie awake for a long time letting the past roll over me. I think of the first time I met Julian, how tenderly he pulled each tiny piece of glass from my face, how we ate empanadas together and I had looked at him and longed for the very thing I now have. I remember the hour I held my mother dying and the moment I sailed off Bixby Bridge, certain of my own death. On nights like these, I can still feel the weight of my mother in my arms as I carried her from the bathroom and the weightlessness of mine in hers as she carried me from the car.

I still miss her, but not as much. I have been the keeper of her story, and the pain is there, the memories, but they have been smoothed out like sea glass, and there are no more sharp edges. I have made peace with them. I have made a good life. One she would be proud of.

And in the end, Julian was right: my face healed without a single scar.

★ ★ ★ ★ ★

Acknowledgments

For their continued commitment, guidance and support, I am indebted to Sanford J. Greenburger Associates; my agent and champion, Stephanie Delman; Heide Lange for first believing in me all those years ago; Stefanie Diaz for her skill with foreign rights; and everyone who manages the behind-the-scenes details that make this happen.

For her editorial insights, patience and sheer delightful personality, I am immensely grateful to my editor, Laura Brown, and to Park Row Books for the integrity and thoughtfulness with which they handle their authors. To my fabulously efficient publicist, Justine Sha, without whose management I'd be lost. Thank you to the whole team at Park Row for their expertise, creative design, marketing and promotional skills: Erika Imranyi, Randy Chan, Rachel Haller and Kathleen Oudit.

Thank you to my dear mother, Ariane Goodwin, for introducing me to Nina, for being my travel and research partner in Cuba, for patiently listening to me read unedited chapters and for being there every step of the way with the manuscript.

For those whose generosity, excitement and belief in my work has sustained me, thank you to Lilia Teal, Isaiah Weiss, Tae, Luna and Willow, Robert Burdick, Michelle King and Bonnie Miller. Thank you to Silas and Rowan for continuing to be mischievous and delightful, and to Stephen for being my anchor, my home and the love of my life.

Finally, to Nina Lopez, for honoring me with this story, for trusting and believing in me to write it and for your gracious, enthusiastic reception of this book.

And to Estelita Rodriguez, for living your life with passion, for striving for your dreams and for giving the world beauty and laughter and song. You are missed.